SUCH IS LIFE

Being Certain Extracts from the Diary of

Tom Collins

New Introduction by
David Malouf

THE HOGARTH PRESS
LONDON

Published in 1986 by
The Hogarth Press
Chatto and Windus Ltd
40 William IV Street, London WC2N 4DF

First published in Great Britain, in an abridged edition, by
Jonathan Cape Ltd 1937
Hogarth edition offset from unabridged Angus and Robertson 1944 edition
Introduction copyright © David Malouf 1986

Rupert Bunny   Australian   1864-1947
Self Portrait
Oil on Canvas   65 x 50 cm
Felton Bequest 1927
National Gallery of Victoria, Melbourne

British Library Cataloguing in Publication Data

Collins, Tom
Such is life.
Rn: Joseph Furphy   I. Title
823[F]   PR9619.2.F82

ISBN 0 7012 0694 2

Printed in Finland by
Werner Södeström Oy

THE AUTHOR

'Tom Collins' was the pseudonym for Joseph Furphy, who was
born at Port Phillip, Victoria, in 1843, two years after his
parents had emigrated from Ireland to Australia. As a boy, he
helped his father work the land, first in the Yarra Valley and
afterwards at Kyneton, where he finished his schooling. Then
he took on a gamut of jobs: he operated a steam-threshing
plant; he tried goldmining a couple of times, unsuccessfully;
he worked on a selection at Corop, near Stanhope – but poor
weather gave him bad luck there too. At last he hit upon the
profession which was to inspire his classic tale of Australia: he
became a bullock driver, setting off from his home in Hay,
New South Wales, with a wagon and four bullocks for the
Riverina, sometimes with his wife, Leonie Germaine, (they
were married in 1868) and their three children in tow.

Joseph Furphy described himself as 'half bushman and half
bookworm' and, although the drought of 1883 forced him from
the open air into his brother's famous iron foundry at Shepparton, he was able to devote time, at nights at least, to writing
what was to become *Such is Life* (published in 1903, six years
after it had been submitted to the *Bulletin*) using the name
Tom Collins, the mythical source of every tall bush story.
His other books – *Poems* (1916), *Rigby's Romance* (1921) and
The Buln Buln and the Brogla (1948) – were all published
posthumously.

In 1904 Furphy moved to Fremantle, Western Australia, to
join his children. Here he built a house and created a garden,
as he had done before at Corop, with his own hands – it still
stands as a memorial to him. He died in 1912.

INTRODUCTION

Such is Life! Most famous of all famous last words in the brief history of Australia: spoken on the scaffold of the Old Melbourne Gaol by the bushranger Ned Kelly, and accepting, with a laconic refusal of emotion, life's bitter but inescapable irony. Something in those words has appealed to Australians as a proper response to what life in Australia presents. That it appealed to Furphy is clear from the way he uses the tag as refrain throughout his book, constantly discovering new tones for it as it is applied to the unpredictability, the awful predictability, the injustice, the poetic justice, the tragedy, perversity and humour of what he calls 'that engaging problem', Life.

Here are just two examples. The first concerns the two men who have been 'dummying' in a land swindle for M'Gregor:

. . . if they had owned all the land they secured for M'Gregor, by perjury, and personation, and straightfoward dummyism, they would have been little squatters themselves. At the same time, they were true-hearted, kindly, unselfish men, according to their uncertain light; and in all probability they're gone to heaven. Such is life, boys.

That 'such', as we see, illustrates no single or simple view. The second involves the narrator's mate Rory, one of the most attractive characters in the book:

So he sorrowed his way northward, in renewed search of his brother Larry; and, as I watched his diminishing figure, I prayed that he might be enticed into the most shocking company in Echuca, and be made fightably drunk, and fall in for a remembersome hammering, and get robbed of everything, and be given in charge for making a disturbance, and wind up the adventure with a month in Her Majesty's jail. It seemed to me that no milder dispensation of

Providence would satisfy his moral requirements. Drastic, but such is life.

The play of mind these two instances offer, the delight in ninety-degree shifts, the contrariness, the quirky humour, are already prepared for in *Such is Life* before we even arrive at the opening sentence: 'Unemployed at last!' There is, in the best editions, an author's introduction. Easy to ignore as being unnecessary to the story, and therefore dispensable, it needs to be read, not as an introduction to the book but to the author. It is a warning. With an effrontery every bit as bold as Furphy's description of *Such is Life* (in a letter to A.G. Stephens of the *Bulletin*) as 'offensively Australian', it begins: 'Contrary to usage, these memoirs are published, not "in compliance with the entreaties of friends," but in direct opposition thereto.' 'Contrary to usage' here takes us a good way towards our author's characteristic turn of mind. So, as they occur later in these fourteen lines, do 'contrary direction' and 'wayward'. The whole piece is founded on the inversion of conventional notions, the rejection of respectability, 'local pre-eminence' and 'literary propriety'.

But who is the author of this compendium of Australian folk humour, this vastly erudite joke-book and hymn to the humble bullockie? And who is this 'Tom Collins' whose diary we are invited to dip into on such a delightfully random principle?

In fact, no author's name appears on the title page. We know of Joseph Furphy only from history, and it is one of nature's weird felicities – a very Furphy touch – that the name should recur in the slang of a later generation as meaning 'false report or rumour; absurd story' (a usage that derives not at all from Joseph Furphy's *Such is Life*, but from his brother John's water carts, manufactured at the family's iron foundry in Shepparton and used on nearly every Australian sheep farm; during the Great War they were shipped to Europe and trundled from trench to trench, bearing the latest gossip as well as water for the troops). Furphy, the real author, never names himself and does not appear. He remains submerged – like the plot of his book, such as it is – to be recognized only by those readers who are in the know. The named author, Tom Collins, is a furphy, Tom Collins being in Australian bush speech the generic name for a teller of tales.

Tom Collins. What is his role as a furphy? What are we to make of Joseph Furphy's game of hide and seek? For if we learn one thing about our author from a reading of *Such is Life*, it is how slippery he is, how difficult he makes it for us to catch him out or pin him down; and if we learn another, it is that he is *not* Tom Collins. Tom Collins may share the waywardness and love of contrary directions, the joy in elaborate and perverse play of his maker (one is tempted, caught up in a Furphy mood, to write *his Maker*); he is as deeply studied in the Bible and in Shakespeare; takes the same delight in violating decorum with a mixture of high and low language, and in puns, malapropisms, odd foreign and English dialects, recondite facts; is very much, that is – this Deputy-Assistant-Sub-Inspector of the New South Wales Civil Service (ninth class) – an autodidact and bush encyclopaedist: pedantic, tediously preachy, full of high allusion, deep philosophy and nonsense – but he is these things set at a distance. Much of the fun in *Such is Life* lies in what the author knows (and invites the reader to share) that Tom Collins does not – for all his self-proclaimed 'intuition that reads men like signboards'. Collins is fond of attacking what he calls 'the shallow, inattentive reader'. But he is the one who fails to recognise the (untold) story of Molly and Warrigal Alf. What sort of narrator is it, we might ask, who does not recognize the tale he is telling? Just the sort, we should answer, that Furphy *would* create and needs for his subversive purpose. For I take it that *Such is Life* is a deeply subversive work that presents itself, slyly, as an innocent one. Why subversive, and in what ways, we have still to see, but it is as well to observe who is being evoked here as the onlie begetter of the book.

'Unemployed at last!' That oddly cheerful exclamation with which *Such is Life* opens establishes idleness as the condition of the book's existence and, since it is the devil who finds work for idle hands, makes all that follows of doubtful provenance. *Such is Life* is either devil's work or it is Tom Collins's attempt to beat the devil at his own game. The tone of his flights at 'that amusingly short-sighted old Conspirator' is, we may think, that of a familiar; (and second readers of the book may even be reminded, by reflection, of the author himself – that 'short-sighted' is, as we shall see, particularly apt). 'It will only be fair to notify him,' Collins writes, 'that his age and experience, even his captivating habits and well-known hospitality, will be treated with scorn rather than respect, in the paragraphs *he virtually forces me to write*' (my italics).

The question immediately arises: how reliable is Tom Collins, not just as a narrator – he is, in this respect, archetypally *un*reliable – but in intent? To what extent is he an actor? To what extent is he a confidence man? To what extent is he a deceiver, not only of himself and of others but of the 'shallow, inattentive reader' as well? Or, to ask the question in another form, what are we to make of that quality he attributes to his merry devil but so plainly shares: short-sightedness?

In the very last pages of the book Tom Collins is faced with a pathetic figure, a swagman called Andrew, half blind with sandy blight and deeply ashamed that he has done three months in jail for arson. We recognize the man immediately. He is Andy, the deaf swagman whose progress up and down the river, looking for work, contrasted so strongly with Tom Collins's own blind wanderings in Chapter Three, a man whose provenance and eventual fate Tom Collins had spent several pages speculating upon in his most lofty and 'human-itarian' style. He fails utterly to recognize the man now; and of course the swagman, being half blind, and Tom Collins dis-guised in dark glasses, a bell topper and a long alpaca coat, has no chance of recognizing him. Collins's amused speculations at this point are reserved for someone else – the Scotsman, Tom Armstrong, Andrew's guide and companion – and the ease with which *he* accepts Collins's assurance that he is not what he seems to be; that is, the man who tricked Armstrong over the affair of Warrigal Alf's bullocks:

There were lessons to be gathered from Tom Armstrong's prompt acceptance of such *alibi* evidence, touching myself, as would have merely tended to unfathomable speculations on metempsychosis in an ether-poised Hamlet-mind. Tom, though crushing for a couple of ounces, was one of your practical, decided, cocksure men; guided by unweighed, unanalysed phenomena, and governed by conviction alone – the latter being based simply, though solidly, upon itself. These men are deaf to the symphony of the Silences; blind to the horizonless areas of the Unknown; unresponsive to the touch of the Impalpable; oblivious to the machinery of the Moral Universe . . .

and so on till he gets up to go and, in a moment of spontaneous charity or mateship, turns to the swagman:

'Here, mate,' said I, fearlessly removing my clouded glasses, and handing them, with their case, to Andrew; 'you'll find the advantage of these.'

It's good advice that; from one who knows. Tom Collins has certainly found the advantage of them, in shielding himself and others from the truth that the act of arson Andrew was jailed for was his own doing. But such is life.

This is one of the book's cruellest jokes, this little play on deafness and blindness; a kind of colonial comic *King Lear* if Tom Collins's blindness is innocent, a piece of devilish effrontery if it is not. But perhaps *Lear* is a less appropriate reference here than *Hamlet*. (The Hamlet sub-text in *Such is Life* is as rich as in *Ulysses*.) It is Tom Collins's idealism that makes him so fatal to some men in this book, his tendency to retreat into his 'Hamlet-mind' as he calls it, to blind himself with philosophy and deafen himself with high sound. But is it, I wonder, Hamlet the philosopher-prince we are meant to summon up, the idealist of fatal good intentions, or Hamlet the real (or feigned) madman? The final paragraph of the book presents Tom Collins in several roles, as actor/confidence man; but there is another word submerged in the elaborate texture of transformed misquotation:

Now I had to enact the Cynic philosopher to Moriarty and Butler, and the aristocratic man with a 'past' to Mrs Beaudesart; with the satisfaction of knowing that each of these was acting a part to me.

Such is life, my fellow-mummers – just like a poor player that bluffs and feints his hour upon the stage, and then cheapens down to mere nonentity. But let me not hear any small witticism to the further effect that its story is a tale told by a vulgarian, full of slang and blanky, signifying – nothing.

We are in another play, of course, but the word is 'idiot'; a tale told by an idiot. Are we perhaps to invert the Hamlet question and ask ourselves if Tom Collins, Deputy-Assistant-Sub-Inspector of the N.S.W. Civil Service (ninth class), is not a figment of his, our narrator's, own imagination, a man feigning sanity and doing it so well sometimes that even he is convinced? This final episode of the book looks back to Chapter Three and Tom Collins's adventures there as naked, unaccommodated man – Poor Tom, lunatic.

The crux of the book, Chapter Three, begins with an account, reasonable enough in its conclusions, from the —— Express. It concerns an escaped lunatic. Reasonable enough, Tom Collins tells us, to be entirely false; and he ought to know because, as he confesses, 'I was that homicidal lunatic'. He then proceeds to give us his own *true* account, a chain of improbably comic 'fatalities' involving a dog, a pipe, a deaf swagman, a stolen bark, involuntary loss of nethergarments, wanderings in the dark, the encounter with a young man, Jim, who turns out to be a young woman with whom Collins quickly falls in love, and the firing of a haystack – all meant to illustrate, like everything else we are told in the book, the odd and errant line between cause and effect and the problematical relationship between 'unfettered alternatives' freely chosen and 'rigorous destiny'.

Tom Collins's tone as he recounts all this is that of the aggrieved innocent. But Tom Collins's innocence, like his reliability, is to be taken with a grain of salt. The point of the episode is that it places him, most effectively, on the outer limits of society, where all things are immediately in doubt. Like Ishmael in the 'Try Works' chapter of *Moby Dick*, Tom Collins has got himself turned about on that river in the dark, and his presumed lunacy is the sign of this; he has lost all sense of orientation, moral as well as geographical, at the same time as he lost that distinguishing mark of the socialized creature, his clothes. He has to begin from scratch, and what he discovers is that to get back inside and make himself respectable he must break every social code. Once reversed (mad?), he sees everything from the opposite point of view, and from there, outside and naked in the dark, nothing civilized or Christian makes sense. He has to make his own sense – so does the reader. The result is an exploratory form of anarchy, playful on the part of the author, desperate on the part of the protagonist, in which everything gets turned on its head, and, when righted, can never be the same again.

Here is Tom Collins justifying his burning of the haystack, and innocently, reasonably, subverting all those laws of social contract and property that he might appear, in his more usual guise as moralist and spokesman for old bush values, to espouse. It is, we might note, his second bit of incendiarism. The first, confessed to only between the lines, was a youthful accident (or so he claims), though no less destructive for all that of 'half a county'. He writes on this second occasion:

Before you join the hue-and-cry against the 'barbarous incendiary' of the —— *Express*, just put yourself in my place and you won't fail to realise what a profitable transaction it was to get a *puris naturalibus* lunatic clothed and in his right mind again by the sacrifice of a mere eyesore on a farm. The old straw-stack wasn't worth eighteen pence, but I would gladly have purchased its destruction with as many pounds – to be paid, say in nine monthly instalments. To be sure, it didn't belong to me; but then, neither did the splitters' bark. So there you are.

That phrase 'So there you are', with its echo of the more common 'Such is life', is a bit of pure cheek considering the chop logic that precedes it. But the whole passage is insolent in intention, however reasonable it may be in tone. 'Profitable transaction' and the business of monthly instalments are insolence undisguised. The method is the one Melville is so fond of in *Moby Dick*, the progress to a subversive conclusion by reasonable steps, as when he proves that the only way to be a good Christian is to practise paganism. We too might see the need to reassess things, Tom Collins tells us, if we were in his place.

As a 'property', however, the haystack is not crucial to Tom Collins, since it is to be a fatal influence not, as it turns out, on his life, but on the life of the swagman Andy. On the odd line this book establishes between cause and effect, the 'unfettered alternatives' enjoyed by one man may lead, quite reasonably, to the 'rigorous destiny' of another. So much for the logic, let alone the justice of things.

The crucial 'property' in Tom Collins's case is unmentionable, appearing in the text only as a ——. It is the pair of trousers that represent a man's ticket of entry to civilized society, the real flag, as he puts it, of our humanity – more significant even than the 'British flag which covers fabulous millions of our fellow-worms', since it covers 'in a more essential manner, one half of civilized humanity'. The attempt to secure one of these tickets of re-entry to the decent company of men – to come in under the flag – leads Collins to even more radical reversals and subversions of accepted values than the haystack, since in the dark in which he finds himself he loses not only all distinction of property and propriety, but of sex as well.

His efforts to tear the trousers off various strangers in the night (a perfectly reasonable procedure as he presents it) reach their climax in the case of an androgynous creature who is, surely, that 'young Jim' who later turns out to be Miss Quarterman – the girl with whom Collins falls immediately in love. Here, after trying unsuccessfully to remove his/her 'unmentionables', he goes on:

. . . I have frequently had occasion to observe that when woman finds herself in a tight place, her first impulse is to set the wild echoes flying; whereas, man resists or submits in silence, except, perhaps, for a few bad words ground out between his teeth. Therefore, when the legal owner of the —— which I was in the act of unfastening, suddenly splintered the firmament with a double-barrelled screech, the thought flashed through my mind that he was one of those De Lacy Evanses we often read of in novels; and in two seconds I was fifty yards away, trying to choose between the opposing anomalies of the case. A little reflection showed the balance of probability strongly against a disguise which I have never met with in actual life . . .

The passage looks forward to the untold story of Nosey Alf, whose sex and history Tom Collins never recognizes; but it is part, too, of the book's odd preoccupation (or the narrator's) with ambiguous gender. When Collins does realise that 'Jim' is a woman, he describes her in terms that emphasise the monstrous in her: as 'a magnificent young *woman*, riding barebacked, *à la* clothes-peg; the fine contour of her figure displayed with an amazonian audacity which seemed to make her nearly as horrid as myself'. Almost all the women in the book, including this beauty, wear what Collins calls 'the pathetic evidence of Australian nationality on their lip' – that is, a moustache. 'Who could have deduced,' he writes, 'from certain subtly interlaced conditions of food, atmosphere, association, and what not, the development of those silky honours that grace the upper lip of the Australienne?' All very odd, we might think, this linking of nationality and the transmigration of sexual characteristics, in a writer who is sometimes seen as speaking for the central values of the old bush tradition and an unqualified nationalist. It is the tone here that makes one wonder what game Furphy is playing. It is a game that brings him closer to Sterne or to the Melville of *Moby Dick* and *The Confidance Man* than to Henry Lawson.

The likeness to Melville was first noted more than forty years ago by Hartley Grattan. It is worth pursuing. In *Moby Dick*, Melville too writes a subversive masterpiece and evokes the devil as the father of his book, setting his grand philosophical arguments (many of them parody) in a world where men are observed, with scrupulous attention to the details of tools and jargon, at a rough colonial trade. The temper of both writers is aggressively democratic. Both launch attacks on the prudery of their society, in each case with an odd mixture of schoolboy naughtiness and sly cheek. Compare the chapters called 'The Cassock' and 'A Squeeze of the Hand' in *Moby Dick* with the passage here where the virtue that is next to godliness is confessed to as if what Collins really had in mind was solitary vice. Most important of all is the transportation into the linguistic body of their work of Shakespeare and the Bible. In Melville's case a new and original language is forged out of imaginative pastiche. In Furphy's, the journalistic game of comic misquotation and misapplication is practised so thoroughly and so brilliantly as to produce what is, in effect, a new form. These writers are both very original and at the same time utterly parasitic on earlier literature. It is worth making the point that *Such is Life*, for all its Australianness, has its roots in English literature and can scarcely be read without reference to it; that is to say, it is, like *Moby Dick*, a *colonial* masterpiece – product of a society that has found its own new and unique material but not as yet a tradition, other than the one it has inherited with the language. What Melville and Furphy do is work sideways from the old one; or they turn it upside down or back to front; or they use its own words to subvert it. But there is a lack of consistency in what they do. They write books that are brilliant, wayward, astonishingly free and inventive; realistic at one moment to the point of documentary, at others utterly fantastic; sometimes serious and then merely cheeky; often very modern in the freedoms they claim for the spirit of fiction and then deeply old-fashioned – books, in the final view, that are puzzles; in one case a shoal of red herrings, in the other a great white whale.

But it would be unfair to leave Furphy there: not, that is, to take up that suggestion of the 'modern' in him and insist how clearly he recognizes in fiction, as well as in life, that 'engaging problem' which becomes the subject of his book. He is writing an early version of the anti-novel, asserting his own power and presence as maker, as magician, and his own freedom, almost on a whim, to change the ground of what he is doing whenever he wills. Asserting his freedom, as well, to disappear.

Such is Life is a key work in Australian writing and in the development of Australian notions of culture and nationhood. But that isn't its only interest. It belongs as well to the tradition

Furphy was writing out of, among the great books in the English language. A brilliant tease, it is also, in the reading, a unique and irreplaceable experience, speaking up as it does so oddly, eloquently, infuriatingly, and with so much anger at injustice and visionary optimism, for Life and for the delight of making Fiction. There is, simply, no other book like it.

David Malouf, Sydney 1985

Australia and
the South East

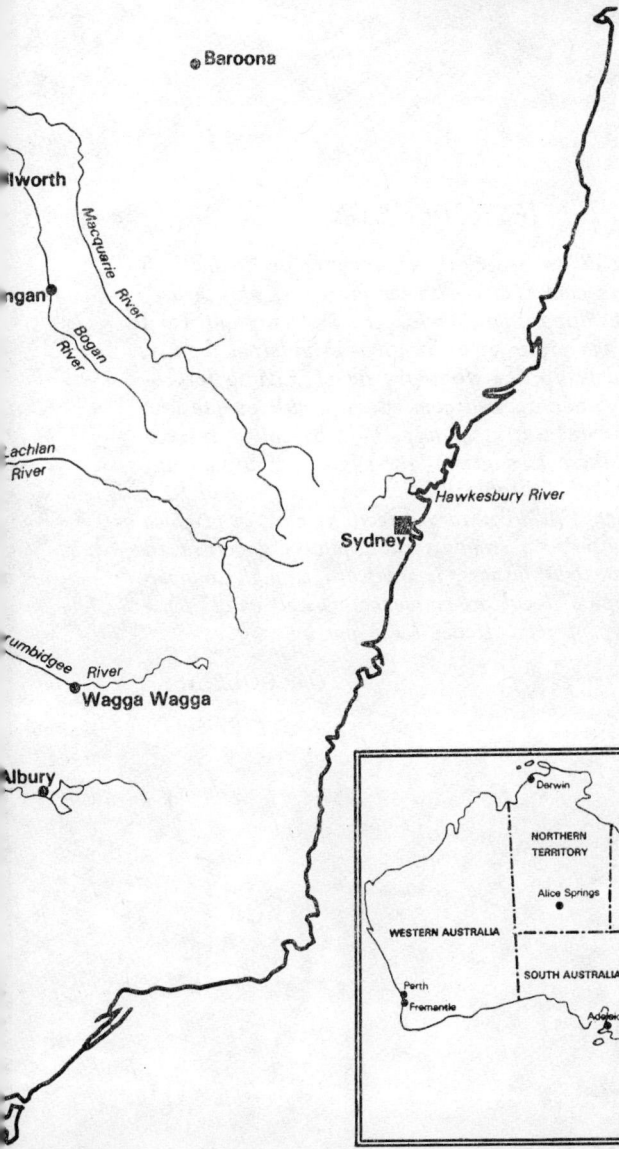

Baroona

...lworth

Macquarie River

...ngan

Bogan River

Lachlan River

Hawkesbury River

Sydney

...rumbidgee River

Wagga Wagga

Albury

Darwin

NORTHERN TERRITORY

Alice Springs

QUEENSLAND

WESTERN AUSTRALIA

SOUTH AUSTRALIA

Brisbane

NEW SOUTH WALES

Perth

Fremantle

Adelaide

RIVERINA

Sydney

Canberra

VICTORIA

Melbourne

TASMANIA

INTRODUCTION

CONTRARY to usage, these memoirs are published, not "in compliance with the entreaties of friends," but in direct opposition thereto. It has been pointed out to me that the prizes of civilisation—Municipal dignity, Churchwardenship, the Honorary Bench, and so forth— do not wait upon avowed comradeship with people who can by no management of hyperbole be called respectable. But there is a grim, fakeer-like pleasure in any renunciation of desirable things, when the line of least resistance leads in a contrary direction; and, in my own case, the impulse of reminiscence, fatally governed by an inveterate truthfulness, is wayward enough to overbear all hope of local pre-eminence, as well as all sense of literary propriety. Hence these pages.

TOM COLLINS.

CONTENTS

CHAPTER I

UNEMPLOYED at last!

.   .   .   .

Scientifically, such a contingency can never have befallen of itself. According to one theory of the Universe, the momentum of Original Impress has been tending toward this far-off, divine event ever since a scrap of fire-mist flew from the solar centre to form our planet. Not this event alone, of course; but every occurrence, past and present, from the fall of captured Troy to the fall of a captured insect. According to another theory, I hold an independent diploma as one of the architects of our Social System, with a commission to use my own judgment, and take my own risks, like any other unit of humanity. This theory, unlike the first, entails frequent hitches and cross-purposes; and to some malign operation of these I should owe my present holiday.

Orthodoxly, we are reduced to one assumption: namely, that my indomitable old Adversary has suddenly called to mind Dr. Watts's friendly hint respecting the easy enlistment of idle hands.

Good. If either of the two first hypotheses be correct, my enforced furlough tacitly conveys the responsibility of extending a ray of information, however narrow and feeble, across the path of such fellow-pilgrims as have led lives more sedentary than my own— particularly as I have enough money to frank myself in a frugal way for some weeks, as well as to purchase the few requisites of authorship.

If, on the other hand, my supposed safeguard of drudgery has been cut off at the meter by that amusingly short-sighted old Conspirator, it will be only fair to notify him that his age and experience, even his captivating habits and well-known hospitality, will be treated with scorn, rather than respect, in the paragraphs which he virtually forces me to write; and he is hereby invited to view his own feather on the fatal dart.

Whilst a peculiar defect—which I scarcely like to call an oversight in mental construction—shuts me out from the flowery path-

way of the romancer, a co-ordinate requital endows me, I trust, with
the more sterling, if less ornamental qualities of the chronicler.
This fairly equitable compensation embraces, I have been told,
three distinct attributes: an intuition which reads men like signboards; a limpid veracity; and a memory which habitually stereo-
types all impressions except those relating to personal injuries.

Submitting, then, to the constitutional interdict already glanced
at, and availing myself of the implied license to utilise that homely
talent of which I am the bailee, I purpose taking certain entries
from my diary, and amplifying these to the minutest detail of
occurrence or conversation. This will afford to the observant reader
a fair picture of Life, as that engaging problem has presented itself
to me.

Twenty-two consecutive editions of *Letts's Pocket Diary*, with one
week in each opening, lie on the table before me; all filled up, and
in a decent state of preservation. I think I shall undertake the
annotation of a week's record. A man might, if he were of a fearful
heart, stagger in this attempt; but I shut my eyes, and take up one
of the little volumes. It proves to be the edition of 1883. Again
I shut my eyes while I open the book at random. It is the week
beginning with Sunday, the 9th of September.

SUN. SEPT. 9. Thomp. Coop. &c. 10-Mile Pines. Cleo. Duff. Selec.

The fore part of the day was altogether devoid of interest or
event. Overhead, the sun blazing wastefully and thanklessly
through a rarefied atmosphere; underfoot, the hot, black clay,
thirsting for spring rain, and bare except for inedible roley-poleys,
coarse tussocks, and the woody stubble of close-eaten salt-bush;
between sky and earth, a solitary wayfarer, wisely lapt in philosophic torpor. Ten yards behind the grey saddle-horse follows a
black pack-horse, lightly loaded; and three yards behind the pack-
horse ambles listlessly a tall, slate-coloured kangaroo dog, furnished
with the usual poison muzzle—a light wire basket, worn after the
manner of a nose-bag.

Mile after mile we go at a good walk, till the dark boundary of
the scrub country disappears northward in the glassy haze, and in
front, southward, the level black-soil plains of Riverina Proper
mark a straight sky-line, broken here and there by a monumental
clump or pine-ridge. And away beyond the horizon, southward still,
the geodesic curve carries that monotony across the zone of salt-bush,
myall, and swamp box; across the Lachlan and Murrumbidgee, and
on to the Victorian border—say, two hundred and fifty miles.

Just about mid-day, the station track I was following intersected and joined the stock route; and against the background of a pine-ridge, a mile ahead, I saw some wool-teams. When I overtook them, they had stopped for dinner among the trees. One of the party was an intimate friend of mine, and three others were acquaintances; so, without any of the ceremony which prevails in more refined circles, I hooked Fancy's rein on a pine branch, pulled the pack-saddle off Bunyip, and sat down with the rest, to screen the tea through my teeth and flick the diligent little operatives out of the cold mutton with the point of my pocket-knife.

There were five bullock-teams altogether: Thompson's twenty; Cooper's eighteen; Dixon's eighteen; and Price's two teams of fourteen each. Three of the wagons, in accordance with a fashion of the day, bore names painted along the board inside the guard irons. Thompson's was the *Wanderer*; Cooper's, the *Hawkesbury*; and Dixon's, the *Wombat*. All were platform wagons, except Cooper's, which was the Sydney-side pattern.

To avoid the vulgarity of ushering this company into the presence of the punctilious reader without even the ceremony of a Bedouin introduction—(This is my friend, N or M; if he steals anything, I will be responsible for it): a form of introduction, by the way, too sweeping in its suretyship for prudent men to use in Riverina—I shall describe the group, severally, with such succinctness as may be compatible with my somewhat discursive style.

Steve Thompson was a Victorian. He was scarcely a typical bullock driver, since fifteen years of that occupation had not brutalised his temper, nor ensanguined his vocabulary, nor frayed the terminal 'g' from his participles. I knew him well, for we had been partners in dogflesh and colleagues in larceny when we were, as poets feign, nearer to heaven than in maturer life. And, wide as Riverina is, we often encountered fortuitously, and were always glad to fraternise. Physically, Thompson was tall and lazy, as bullock drivers ought to be.

Cooper was an entire stranger to me, but as he stoutly contended that Hay and Deniliquin were in Port Phillip, I inferred him to be a citizen of the mother colony. Four months before, he had happened to strike the very first consignment of goods delivered at Nyngan by rail, for the Western country. He had chanced seven tons of this, for Kenilworth; had there met Thompson, delivering salt from Hay; and now the two, freighted with Kenilworth wool, were making the trip to Hay together. Kenilworth was on the commercial divide, having a choice of two evils—the long, uninviting track southward to the Murrumbidgee, and the badly watered route eastward to the Bogan. This was Cooper's first experience of Riverina, and he swore in no apprentice style that it would be his last. A correlative proof of the honest fellow's Eastern extraction lay in the fact that he was three inches taller, three stone heavier, and thirty degrees lazier, than Thompson.

I had known Dixon for many years. He was a magnificent specimen of crude humanity; strong, lithe, graceful, and not too big— just such a man as your novelist would picture as the nurse-swapped offspring of some rotund or rickety aristocrat. But being, for my own part, as I plainly stated at the outset, incapable of such romancing, I must register Dixon as one whose ignoble blood had crept through scoundrels since the Flood. Though, when you come to look at it leisurely, this would n't interfere with aristocratic, or even regal, descent—rather the reverse.

Old Price had carted goods from Melbourne to Bendigo in '52; a hundred miles, for £100 per ton. He had had two teams at that time, and, being a man of prudence and sagacity, had two teams still, and was able to pay his way. I had known him since I was about the height of this table; he was Old Price then; he is Old Price still; and he will probably be Old Price when my head is dredged with the white flour of a blameless life, and I am pottering about with a stick, hating young fellows, and making myself generally disagreeable. Price's second team was driven by his son Mosey, a tight little fellow, whose body was about five-and-twenty, but whose head, according to the ancient adage, had worn out many a good pair of shoulders.

Willoughby, who was travelling loose with Thompson and Cooper, was a whaler. Not owing to any inherent incapacity, for he had taken his B.A. at an English university, and was, notwithstanding his rags and dirt, a remarkably fine-looking man; bearing a striking resemblance to Dixon, even in features. But as the wives of Napoleon's generals could never learn to walk on a carpet, so the aimless popinjay of adult age can never learn to take a man's place among rough-and-ready workers. Even in spite of Willoughby's personal resemblance to Dixon, there was a suggestion of latent physical force and leathery durability in the bullock driver, altogether lacking in the whaler, and equiponderated only by a certain air of refinement. How could it be otherwise? Willoughby, of course, had no horse—in fact, like Bassanio, all the wealth he had ran in his veins; he was a gentleman. Well for the world if all representatives of his Order were as harmless, as inexpensive, and as unobtrusive as this poor fellow, now situated like that most capricious poet, honest Ovid, among the Goths.

One generally feels a sort of diffidence in introducing one's self; but I may remark that I was at that time a Government official, of the ninth class; paid rather according to my grade than my merit, and not by any means in proportion to the loafing I had to do. Candidly, I was only a Deputy-Assistant-Sub-Inspector, but with the reversion of the Assistant-Sub-Inspectorship itself when it should please Atropos to snip the thread of my superior officer.

The repast being concluded, the drivers went into committee on the subject of grass—a vital question in '83, as you may remember.

"It 's this way," said Mosey imperatively, and deftly weaving into his address the thin red line of puissant adjective; "You dunno what you 're doin' when you 're foolin' with this run. She 's hair-trigger at the best o' times, an' she 's on full cock this year. Best watched station on the track. It 's risk whatever way you take it. We 're middlin' safe to be collared in the selection, an' we 're jist as safe to be collared in the ram-paddock. Choice between the divil an' the dam. An' there 's too big a township o' wagons together. Two 's enough, an' three 's a glutton, for sich a season as this."

"I think Cooper and I had better push on to the ram-paddock," suggested Thompson. "You three can work on the selection. Division of labour 's the secret of success, they say."

"Secret of England's greatness," mused Dixon. "I forgit what the (irrelevant expletive) that is."

"The true secret of England's greatness lies in her dependencies, Mr. Dixon," replied Willoughbly handsomely; and straightway the serene, appreciative expression of the bullock driver's face, rightly interpreted, showed that his mind was engaged in a Græco-Roman conflict with the polysyllable, the latter being uppermost.

"Well, no," said Mosey, replying to Thompson; "no use separatin' now; it 's on'y spreadin' the risk; we should 'a' separated yesterday. I would n't misdoubt the selection, on'y Cunningham told me the other day, Magomery's shiftin' somebody to live there. If that 's so, it 's up a tree, straight. The ram-paddick 's always a risk—too near the station."

"The hut on the selection was empty a week ago," I remarked. "I know it, for I camped there one night."

"Good grass?" inquired a chorus of voices.

"About the best I 've had this season."

"We 'll chance the selection," said Mosey decidedly. "Somebody can ride on ahead, an' see the coast clear. But they won't watch a bit of a paddick in the thick o' the shearin', when there 's nobody livin' in it."

"Squatters hed orter fine grass f'r wool teams, an' glad o' the chance," observed Price, with unprintable emphasis.

"Lot of sense in that remark," commented Mosey, with a similar potency of adjective.

"Well, this is about the last place God made," growled Cooper, the crimson thread of kinship running conspicuously through his observation, notwithstanding its narrow provinciality.

"Roll up, Port Phillipers! the Sydney man 's goin' to strike a match!" retorted Mosey. "I wonder what fetched a feller like you on-to bad startin'-ground. I swear we did n't want no lessons."

Cooper was too lazy to reply; and we smoked dreamily, while my kangaroo dog silently abstracted a boiled leg of mutton from Price's tucker-box, and carried it out of sight. By-and-by, all eyes converged on a shapeless streak which had moved into sight in the restless, glassy glitter of the plain, about a mile away.

"Warrigal Alf going out on the lower track," remarked Thompson, at length. "He was coming behind Baxter and Donovan yesterday, but he stopped opposite the station, talking to Montgomery and Martin, and the other fellows lost the run of him. I wonder where he camped last night? He ought to be able to tell us where the safest grass is, considering he 's had a load in from the station. But to tell you the truth, I 'm in favour of the ram-paddock. If we 're caught there, we 'll most likely only get insulted—and we can stand a lot of that—but if we 're caught in the selection, it 's about seven years. Then we can make the Lignum Swamp to-morrow from the ram-paddock, and we can't make it from the selection. So I think we better be moving; it 'll be dark enough before we unyoke. I 've worked on that ram-paddock so often that I seem to have a sort of title to it."

"But there 's lots o' changes since you was here last," said Mosey. "Magomery he 's beginnin' to think he 's got a sort o' title to the ram-paddick now, considerin' it 's all purchased. Tell you what I 'll do; I 'll slip over in two minits on Valiparaiser, an' consult with Alf. Me an' him 's as thick as thieves."

"I 'll go with you, Mosey," said I. "I 've got some messages for him. Keep an eye on my dog, Steve."

Mosey untied the fine upstanding grey horse from the rear of his wagon; I hitched Bunyip to a tree, and mounted Fancy, and we cantered away together across the plain; the ponderous empty wagon—Sydney-side pattern—with eight bullocks in yoke and twelve travelling loose, coming more clearly into detail through the vibrating translucence of the lower atmosphere. Alf did n't deign to stop. I noticed a sinister smile on his sad, stern face as Mosey gaily accosted him.

"An' how 's the world usin' you, Alf? Got red o' Pilot, I notice. Ever see sich a suck-in? Best at a distance, ain't he? Tell you what I come over for, Alf: They say things is middlin' hot here on Runnymede; an' we 're in a (sheol) of a (adjective) st—nk about what to do with our frames to-night. Our wagons is over there on the other track, among the pines. Where did you stop las' night? Your carrion 's as full as ticks."

"I had them in the selection; took them out this morning after they lay down."

"Good shot!"

"Why, I don't see how it concerns you."

"The selection 's reasonable safe—ain't it?"

"Please yourself about that."

"Is the ram-paddick safe?"

"No."

"Is there enough water in the tank at the selection?"

"How do I know? There was enough for me."

"I say, Alf," said I: "Styles, of Karowra, told me to let you know, if possible, that you were right about the boring rods; and he'll settle with you any time you call. Also there's a letter for you at Lochleven Station. Two items."

"I 'm very much obliged to you for your trouble, Collins," replied Alf, with a shade less of moroseness in his tone.

"Well, take care o' yourself, ole son; you ain't always got me to look after you," said Mosey pleasantly; and we turned our horses and rode away. "Evil-natured beggar, that," he continued. "He 's floggin' the cat now, 'cos he laid us on to the selection in spite of his self. If that feller don't go to the bottomless for his disagreeableness, there 's somethin' radic'ly wrong about Providence. I 'm a great believer in Providence, myself, Tom; an' what 's more, I try to live up to my (adj.) religion. I 'm sure *I* don't want to see any pore (fellow) chained up in fire an' brimstone for millions o' millions o' years, an' a worm tormentin' him besides; but I don't see what the (adj. sheol) else they can do with Alf. Awful to think of it." Mosey sighed piously, then resumed, "Grand dog you got since I seen you last. Found the (animal), I s'pose?"

"No, Mosey. Bought him fair."

"Jist so, jist so. You ought to give him to me. He 's bound to

pick up a bait with you; you 're sich a careless &c., &c." And so
the conversation ran on the subject of dogs during the return ride.

On our reaching the wagons, it was unanimously resolved that
the selection should be patronised. This being so, there was no
hurry—rather the reverse—for the selection was not to be reached
till dusk.

You will understand that the bullock drivers' choice of accommodation lay between the selection, the ram-paddock, and a perisher
on the plain. The selection was four or five miles ahead; the near
corner of the ram-paddock about two miles farther still; whilst a
perisher on the plain is seldom hard to find in a bad season, when
the country is stocked for good seasons. Runnymede home-station
—Mooney and Montgomery, owners; J. G. Montgomery, managing
partner—was a mile or so beyond the further corner of the ram-
paddock, and was the central source of danger.

Presently the tea leaves were thrown out of the billies; the
tucker-boxes were packed on the pole-fetchels; and the teams got
under way. Thompson pressed me to camp with him and Cooper
for the night, and I readily consented; thus temporarily eluding a
fatality which was in the habit of driving me from any given direction to Runnymede homestead—a fatality which, I trust, I shall
have no further occasion to notice in these pages.

We therefore tied Fancy beside Thompson's horse at the rear of
his wagon, and disposed Bunyip's pack-saddle and load on the top
of the wool; the horse, of course, following Fancy according to his
daily habit.

A quarter of a mile of stiff pulling through the sand of the pine-
ridge, and the plain opened out again. A short, dark, irregular
line, cleanly separated from the horizon by the wavy glassiness of
the lower air, indicated the clump of box on the selection, four
miles ahead; and this comprised the landscape.

Soon we became aware of two teams coming to meet us; then
three horsemen behind, emerging from the pine-ridge we had left.
As the horsemen gradually decreased their distance, the teams met
and passed us without salutation; sullenly drawing off the track, in
the deference always conceded to wool. Victorian poverty spoke in
every detail of the working plant; Victorian energy and greed in
the unmerciful loads of salt and wire, for the scrub country out
back. The Victorian carrier, formidable by his lack of professional
etiquette and his extreme thrift, is neither admired nor caressed by
the somewhat select practitioners of Riverina.

Then the three horsemen overtook Cooper, pausing a little, after the custom of the country, to gossip with him as they passed. According to another custom of the country, Thompson, Willoughby and I began to criticise them.

"I know the bloke with the linen coat," remarked Thompson. "His name 's M'Nab; he 's a contractor. That half-caste has been with him for years, tailing horses and so forth, for his tucker and rags. Mac 's no great chop."

"He lets his man Friday have the best horse, at all events," said I. "Grand-looking beast, that black one the half-caste is riding."

"By Jove, yes," replied Willoughby. "Now, Thompson—referring to the discussion we had this morning—that is the class of horse we mount in our light cavalry."

"And that strapping red-headed galoot, riding the bag of bones beside him, is what you would call excellent war-material?" I suggested.

"Precisely, Mr. Collins," replied the whaler. "Nature produces such men expressly for rank and file; and I should imagine that their existence furnishes sufficient rejoinder to the levelling theory."

"Quite possible the chap 's as good as either of you," remarked Thompson, seizing the opportunity for reproof. "Do you know anything against him?"

"Well, to quote Madame de Staël," replied Willoughby; "he abuses a man's privilege of being ugly."

"Moreover, he has left undone a thing that he ought to have done," I rejoined. "He ought to be taking a spell of carrying that mare. And pat he comes, like the catastrophe of the old comedy". . .

" 'Day, chaps," said Rufus, as he joined us. "Keep on your pins, you beggar"—and he drove both spurs into his mare's shrinking flanks. "Grey mare belongs to you, boss—don't she?—an' the black moke with the Roman nose follerin'? I was thinkin' we might manage to knock up some sort o' swap. Now this mare 's a Patriarch, she is; and you might n't think it. I won this here saddle with her at a bit of a meetin' las' week, an' rode her my own self—an' that's oc'lar demonster. I tell you, if this here mare had a week spell, you could n't hold her; an' she 'd go a hundred mile between sunrise an' sunset, at the same bat. Yes, boss; it 's the breed does it. I seen some good horses about the King, but swelp me Gawd I never seen a patch on this mare; an' you might n't think it to look at her jist now. Fact is, boss, she wants a week or a fortnit spell. Couldn n't we work up some sort o' swap for that ole black moke o' yours, with the big head? If I got a trifle o' cash to boot, I would n't mind slingin' in this saddle, an' takin' yours. Now, boss, don't be a (adj.) fool."

"To tell you the truth," I replied, "that black horse has carried a pack so long that he 's about cooked for saddle. But he does me right enough."

"Then I 'll tell you what I 'll do!" exclaimed Rufus impulsively. "Look here! At a word! I 'll go you an even swap for that little weed of a grey mare! At a word, mind! I 'm a reckless sort o' (person) when I take the notion! but without a word of exaggeration, I would n't do it on'y for being fixed the way I am. This here mare 's got a fortune in her for a man like you."

"Now howl' yer tongue!" interposed M'Nab, who, with the half-caste—a lithe, active lad of eighteen—had joined us. "Is it swappin' ye want wi' decent men? Sure thon poor craytur iv a baste hes n't got the sthrenth fur till kerry it own hide, let alone a great gommeril on it back. An' thon 's furnent ye! Hello, Tamson! begog A did n't know ye at wanst."

"Good day, Mr. M'Nab. Alterations since I delivered you that wire at Poondoo. Been in the wars?" For M'Nab was leaning forward and sideways in his saddle, evidently in pain.

"Yis," replied the contractor frankly. "There was some Irish rascals at the pub. thonder, where we stapped las' night; an' wan word brung on another, an' at long an' at last we fell to, so we did; an' A 'm dam but they got the bether o' me, being three agin wan. A b'lee some o' me ribs is bruk."

"I 'm sorry to hear that," said Thompson, straining a point for courtesy.

"Are you an Orangeman too, sonny?" I asked the half-caste aside; for the young fellow had a bunged eye, and a flake of skin off his cheek-bone.

"No, by Cripes!" responded my countryman emphatically. "Not me. That cove 's a (adj.) liar. He don't give a dam, s'posin' a feller's soul gits bashed out. Best sight I seen for many a day was seein' him gittin' kicked. If the mean begger'd on'y square up with me, I 'd let summedy else do his"——

"Thon 's a brave wee shilty, sur—thon grey wan o' yours," broke in the contractor, who had been conversing with Thompson, whilst looking enviously at Fancy, hitched behind the wagon. "Boys o' dear," he added reflectively, "she 's just sich another as may wee Dolly; an' A 've been luckin' fur a match fur Dolly this menny 's the day. How oul' is she, sur?"

"Six, this spring."

"Ay-that! Ye wud n't be fur partin' we her, sur? A 'm mortial covetious fur till git thon baste. Houl' an"—he pondered a moment, glancing first at the honest-looking hack he was riding, then at the magnificent animal which carried the half-caste. "Houl' an. Gimme a thrifle fur luck, an' take ether wan o' them two. A 'll thrust ye till do the leck fur me some time afther."

He had been travelling with the red-headed fellow, and the fascination of swapping was upon him, poorly backed by his suicidal candour. The utter simplicity of his bracketing his own two horses —worth, respectively, to all appearance, £8 and £30—and the frank confession of his desire to have my mare at any price, made me feel honestly compunctious.

"Now thon 's a brave loose lump iv a baste," he continued, following my eye as I glanced over the half-caste's splendid mount. "Aisy till ketch, an' as quite as ye plaze."

"How old is he, Mr. M'Nab?"

"He must be purty oul', he 's so quite and thractable. Ye kin luck at his mouth. A don't ondherstand the marks myself."

I opened the horse's mouth. He was just five. I regret to record that I shook my head gravely, and observed:

"You 've had him a long time, Mr. M'Nab?"

"Divil a long. A got him in a swap, as it might be this time yistherday. There 's the resate. An' here 's the resate the man got when he bought him out o' Hillston poun'. Ye can't go beyant a poun' resate."

"Why do you want to get rid of the horse, Mr. M'Nab?"

"Begog, A don't want till git red iv the baste, sich as he is," replied M'Nab resentfully. "But A want thon wee shilty, an' A evened a swap till ye, fur it 's a prodistaner thing nor lavin' a man on his feet, so it is."

"See anything wrong with the horse, Steve?" I asked in an undertone.

"Perfect to the eye," murmured Thompson. "Try him a mile, full tilt."

I made the proposal to M'Nab, and he eagerly agreed. At my suggestion, the half-caste unhitched and tried Fancy, while I mounted the black horse, and turned him across the plain. I tried him at all paces; but never before had I met with anything to equal that elastic step and long, easy, powerful stride. To ride that horse was to feel free, exultant, invincible. His gallop was like *Marching Through Georgia*, vigorously rendered by a good brass band. All that has been written of man's noblest friend—from the dim, uncertain time when some unknown hand, in a leisure moment, dashed off the Thirty-ninth chapter of the Book of Job, to the yesterday when Long Gordon translated into ringing verse the rhythmic clatter of the hoof-beats he loved so well—all might find fulfilment in this unvalued beast, now providentially owned by the softest of foreigners.

"Well?" interrogated M'Nab, as I rejoined him.

"Don't you think he's a bit chest-foundered?" I asked in reply.

"Divil a wan o' me knows. Mebbe he is, begog. Sure A hed n't him long enough fur till fine out."

"And how much boot are you going to give me?" I asked, with a feeling of shame which did honour to my heart.

"Och, now, lave this! Boot! is it? Sure A cud kerry thon wee shilty ondher may oxther! Ye have a right till be givin' me a thrifle fur luck. A 'll let ye aff we two notes."

But after five minutes' more palaver, M'Nab agreed to an even swap. I had pen and ink in my pocket; my note-book supplied paper; and receipts were soon exchanged. Then the saddles were shifted, and we cantered ahead till we rejoined Thompson. I tied my new acquisition behind the wagon, where, for the first five minutes, he severely tested the inch rope which secured him.

"Now, Mr. M'Nab," said I, "I 'll give you my word that the mare is just what you see. You may as well tell me what's wrong with the horse?"

"Ax Billy about thon. Mebbe he 's foun' out some thricks, or somethin'."

"Well, look here," said Billy devoutly—"I hope Gord 'll strike me stark, stiff, stone dead off o' this saddle if the horse has any tricks, or anythin' wrong with him, no more nor the man in the moon. Onna bright. There! I've swore it."

"Well, the mare is as good as gold," I reiterated. "She's one among a hundred. Call her Fancy."

"The horse's name 's Clayopathra," rejoined M'Nab; "an' by gog ye 'll fine him wan out iv a thousan'. A chris'ned him Clayopathra, fur A thought till run him."

"A very good name too," I replied affably. "I should be sorry to change it."

And I never did change it, though, often afterward, men of clerkly attainments took me aside and kindly pointed out what they conceived to be a blunder. I have dwelt, perhaps tediously, upon this swap; my excuses are—first, that, having made few such good bargains during the days of my vanity, the memory is a pleasant one; and, second, that the horse will necessarily play a certain part in these memoirs.

"Well, we 'll be pushin' an, Billy," said M'Nab; "the sun 's gittin' low. An' you need n't tail me up enny fardher," he added, turning to Rufus. "Loaf an these people the night. A man thravellin' his lone, an' nat a shillin' in his pocket!"

"O, go an' bark up a tree, you mongrel!" replied the war-material, with profusion of adjective. "Fat lot o' good tailin' you up! A man that sets down to his dinner without askin' another man whether he 's got a mouth on him or not! Polite sort o' (person) you are! Gerrout! you bin dragged up on the cheap!"

"Come! A 'll bate ye fifty poun' A 'm betther rairt nor you! Houl' an!—A 'll bate ye a hundher'—two hundher', if ye lek, an' stake the money down this minit"——

"Stiddy, now! draw it mild, you fellers there!" thundered Cooper from behind. "Must n't have no quarrellin' while I 'm knockin' round."

"Ye 'll be late gettin' to the ram-paddock, Tamson," remarked M'Nab, treating Cooper with the silent contempt usually lavished upon men of his physique. "Axpect thon 's where ye 're makin' fur?"

"I say—you better camp with us to-night," suggested Thompson, evading the implied inquiry.

Without replying, the contractor put his horse into a canter, and, accompanied by his esquire, went on his way, pausing only to speak to Mosey for a few minutes as he passed the foremost team.

"Curious sample o' (folks) you drop across on the track some-times," remarked Rufus, who remained with us.

"No end to the variety," I replied. Then lowering my voice and glancing furtively round, I asked experimentally, "Have n't I seen you before, somewhere?"

"Queensland, most likely," he conjectured, whilst finding some-thing of interest on the horizon, at the side farthest from me. "Native o' that district, I am. Jist comin' across for the fust time. What 's that bloke's name with the nex' team ahead—if it 's a fair question?"

"Bob Dixon."

"Gosh, I 'm in luck!" He spurred his mare forward, and attached himself to Dixon for the rest of the afternoon.

But time, according to its deplorable habit, had been passing, and the glitter had died off the plain as the sun went on its way to make a futile attempt at purifying the microbe-laden atmosphere of Europe.

At last we reached the spot selected as a camp. Close on our left was the clump of swamp box which covered about fifty acres of the nearer portion of the selection, leaving a few scattered trees outside the fence. On our right, the bare plain extended indefinitely.

I ought to explain that this selection was a mile-square block, which had been taken up, four years previously, by a business man of Melbourne, whose aim was to show the public how to graze scientifically on a small area. Now Runnymede owned the selection, whilst its former occupier was vending sixpenny parcels of inferior fruit on a railway platform. The fence—erected by the experimentalist—was of the best kind; two rails and four wires; sheep-proof and cattle-proof.

The wagons drew off the track, and stopped beside the fence in the deepening twilight. The bullocks were unyoked with all speed, and stood around waiting to see what provision would be made for the night.

"Look 'ere," said Mosey, taking a dead pine sapling from the stock of firewood under his wagon, and, of course, emphasising his address by an easy and not ungraceful clatter of the adjective used so largely by poets in denunciation of war—"we ain't goin' to travel these carrion a mile to the gate, an' most likely fine it locked when we git there. Hold on till I git my internal machine to work on the fence. Dad! Where 's that old more-poke? O, you 're there, are you? Fetch the jack off o' your wagon—come! fly roun'! you 're (very) slow for a young fellow. Bum," (abbreviation of "bummer," and applied to the red-headed fellow) "you surround them carrion, or we 'll be losin' the run o' them two steers."

A low groan from Bum's mare followed the heavy stroke of the ruffian's spurs. "Some o' you other (fellows) keep roun' that side," said he; "I 'll go this road. Up! you Red Roverite!"—No use . . . The mare had had enough for one day; she stumbled, and fell, rolling heavily over her rider. "What the (quadruple expletive) 's the matter with her?" he continued, extricating himself, and kicking the beast till she staggered to her feet. "Come on agen, an' don't gimme no more o' your religiousness." He remounted, and the mare, under the strong stimulus of his spurs, cantered laboriously out into the dark.

Meanwhile, Mosey had taken a hand-saw from its receptacle on his wagon, and had cut the pine spar to a length of about eighteen inches less than a panel of the fence. "Lash this 'ere saplin' hard down on the top rail," he now commanded. Price and Dixon obeyed, and Mosey laid his powerful bottle-jack on the rail, filling up the space, and began to turn it with a long bolt, by way of lever. "You see, Tom," he remarked to me; "this fixter 'll put the crooked maginnis on any fence from 'ere to 'ell. It 's got to come. No matter how tight rails is shouldered, they 'll spring some; an' if every post 'll give on'y half a inch, why then, ten posts makes five or six inches; an' that 's about all you want. Then in the morning, you can fix the fence so 's the ole-man divil his self could n't ball you out. Ah!— — —! That 's what comes o' blowin'." For the post, being wild and free in the grain, had burst along the two mortices; one half running completely off, just above the ground. "Serve people right for puttin' in rails when wire would do," he continued, removing the screw-jack. "Accidents will happen—best reg'lated famblies. 'T ain't our business, anyhow. Now, chaps, round up yer carrion, an' shove 'em in."

The four wires in the lower part of the fence rung like harp-strings as the cattle stepped into or over them, and in a few minutes the whole live stock of the caravan—eighty-four bullocks and seven horses—were in the selection, but too thirsty to feed. Then whilst Thompson, Mosey, Willoughby and I tailed them toward the tank, Dixon hurried on ahead with his five-gallon oil-drum, in order to replenish it before the water was disturbed; and Price, by Mosey's orders, accompanied him on the same business. We steadied the bullocks at the tank till all were satisfied, then headed them back to within fifty yards of the wagons, where we hobbled all the horses, except Bum's mare.

"Steve," said I to my old schoolmate: "of course, you and I are seized of the true inwardness of duffing; but to those who live cleanly, as noblemen should, this would appear a dirty trans-action."

"The world 's full of dirty transactions, Tom," replied the bullock driver wearily. "It 's a dirty transaction to round up a man's team in a ten-mile paddock, and stick a bob a head on them, but that 's a thing that I 'm very familiar with; it 's a dirty transaction to refuse water to perishing beasts, but I 've been refused times out of number, and will be to the end of the chapter; it 's a dirty transaction to persecute men for having no occupation but carting, yet that 's what nine-tenths of the squatters do, and this Montgomery is one of the nine. You 're a bit sarcastic. How long is it since you were one of the cheekiest grass-stealers on the track?"

"Never, Steve. You 've been drinking."

"Anyway, you need n't be more of a hypocrite than you can help," grumbled Thompson. "If you want a problem to work out, just consider that God constructed cattle for living on grass, and the grass for them to live on, and that, last night, and to-night, and to-morrow night, and mostly every night, we 've a choice between two dirty transactions—one is, to let the bullocks starve, and the other is to steal grass for them. For my own part, I 'm sick and tired of studying why some people should be in a position where they have to go out of their way to do wrong, and other people are cornered to that extent that they can't live without doing wrong, and can't suicide without jumping out of the frying-pan into the fire. Wonder if any allowance is made for bullock drivers?—or are they supposed to be able to make enough money to retire into some decent life before they die? Well, thank God for one good camp, at all events."

"How 's the water?" asked Cooper, meeting us at the fence.

"Enough for to-night," replied Thompson; "but very little left for posterity."

"After us, the Deluge," observed Willoughby.

"I hope so," replied Cooper devoutly. "Lord knows, it 's badly wanted; and I 'm sure we don't grudge nobody the benefit. Turnin' out nice an' cool, ain't it? The bullocks 'll be able to do their selves some sort o' justice."

It was a clear but moonless night; the dark blue canopy spangled with myriad stars—grandeur, peace, and purity above; squalor, worry, and profanity below. Fit basis for many an ancient system of Theology—unscientific, if you will, but by no means contemptible.

Price and Cooper, being cooks, had kindled an unobtrusive fire in a crab-hole, where three billies were soon boiling. And the tea, when cool enough, needed no light to escort a due proportion of simple provender into that mysterious laboratory which should never be considered too curiously.

After supper, we lay around, resting ourselves; everyone smoking tranquilly except Willoughby. Dixon and Bum were evidently old friends; they reclined with their heads together, occasionally laughing and whispering—a piece of bad manners silently but strongly resented by the rest of the company.

"I 'll jist go an' have a squint at the carrion," remarked Mosey, at length, with the inevitable adjective; and, passing through the broken fence, he disappeared in the timber and old-man salt-bush.

"Wants some o' the flashness took outen him," remarked Price, in arrogant assertion of parental authority, yet glancing apprehensively after Mosey as he spoke.

"Should 'a' thought about that before," observed Cooper gravely. "Too late now. You ain't good enough."

A few minutes silence ensued, while each member of the company thought the matter over in his own way. Then Mosey returned.

"Grass up over yer boots, an' the carrion goin' into it lemons," he remarked. "I do like to give this Runnymede the benefit o' the act. 'On't ole Martin be ropeable when he sees that fence! Magomery's as hard as nails, his own self; but he ain't the class o' feller that watches from behine a tree—keeps curs like Martin to do his dirty work. But he 'd like to nip every divil of us if he got half a slant. I notice, the more swellisher a man is, the more miserabler he is about a bite o' grass for a team, or a feed for a traveller. Magomery's got an edge on you, Thompson—you and Cunningham —for workin' on Nosey Alf's horse-paddick, an' for leavin' some gates open. Moriarty, the storekeeper, he told me about it."

"Well, we did n't work on Alf's horse-paddick, and we did n't leave any gates open," replied Thompson. "We lost the steers from the ram-paddick, here, and we found them away in the Sedan paddock. Certainly, we camped them all night in the Connelly paddock, but we never touched Alf's grass, and we left no gates open."

"Chorus, boys!" said Mosey flippantly.

"O, what a (adj.) lie!" echoed Dixon, Bum, and the precentor himself. Thompson sighed; Cooper growled; and Willoughby coughed deprecatingly.

"I don't blame ole Martin to have a bit of a nose on me," continued Mosey laughingly. "Lord! did n't I git the loan of him cheap las' summer! Me an' the old man was comin' down from Karowra with the last o' the clip; an' these paddicks was as bare as the palm o' your hand; so we goes on past here, an' camps half-ways between the fur corner o' the ram-paddick an' the station gate; an' looses out about an hour after sundown. It was sort o' cloudy moonlight that night; an' I takes the carrion straight on, an' shoves 'em in the horse-paddick, an' shuts the gate. Then I fetches 'em into a sort of a holler, where the best grass was, an' I takes the saddle an' bridle off o' the horse, an' lays down, an' watches the carrion wirin' in. Well, you know, ole Martin, the head boundary man, he 's about as nice a varmin as Warrigal Alf; an' the young fellers at the barracks they 'on't corroborate with him, no road; an' he thinks his self a cut above the hut, so he lives with Daddy Montague, in Latham's ole place, down at the fur corner o' the horse-paddick.

Well, this ole beggar he 's buckin' up to Miss King, the governess, an' Moriarty, the storekeeper, he 's buckin' up to her too"——

"Clever feller, that Moriarty," interposed Price, in pathetic syco-phancy. "Rummest young (fellow) goin', when he likes to come out. Ain't he, Mosey?" He paused and laughed heartily. "Las' time I unloaded at Runnymede—an' it was on'y one ton lebm; for we was going out emp'y for wool, on account o' them two Vic. chaps snappin' our loads. I disremember if I tole you the yarn when I pulled you at the Willandra. Anyhow it was raining like (incongruous comparison) when I drawed up at the store; an' Moriarty he fetches me inter the office, an' gives me a stiffener o' brandy. Or whisky? Now, (hair-raising imprecation) if I don't disremember which. But I think it was brandy. Yes, it was brandy."

"Well?" interrogated Mosey, after a pause.

"On'y jist showin' how one idear sort o' fetches up another," replied the old man, with simulated ease of manner.

"Well, you are a (adj.) fool. But as I was telling you chaps: About eleven o'clock, who should come dodgin' down the paddick but ole Martin. Bin pokin' roun' after Miss King, I s'pose. He walks right bang through the carrion, thinkin' they was the station bullicks; an' me layin' there, laughin' in to myself. By-'n'-by he stops an' considthers, an' then he goes roun' examinin' them, an' smellin' about, an' then he has a long squint at Valiparaiser; an' in the heel o' the hunt he rounds up the lot, an' sails off to the yard with 'em; an' me follerin' ready to collar 'em when the coast was clear. By-'n'-by I sees him leavin' the yard, an' I goes to it, an' lo an' behold you! there was a padlock on the gate as big as a sar-dine-box.

"Well, we had a bunch o' keys at the camp. I had snavelled 'em at the railway station, las' time we was at Deniliquin, thinkin' they might come in useful. So I heads for the camp at the rate o' knots. Collars the keys, an' gits a drink o' tea, an' takes a bit o' brownie in my fist, an' back I goes, doin' the trip in about an hour. Pro-vidential, one o' the keys fits the lock, so I whips out the carrion, an' shoves 'em down to where the ole sinner took 'em from. Well, there was two station teams in the paddick—I s'pose they wanted 'em very early for somethin'—so I saddles Valiparaiser an' scoots across to where I seen these bullicks when I was goin' for the keys; an' I shoves 'em into the yard; an' I rakes up a ole grey horse, lame o' four legs, an' shoves him in along o' the carrion, an' locks the gate, an' goes back to our lot, an' keeps an eye on 'em till they laid down, fit to bust. Lord! how I laughed that night! I seen Martin watchin' us nex' mornin', after we started. He 's got a set on me for that, among other things."

"Has n't Warrigal Alf got a set on you too?" asked Thompson coldly. "Strikes me, you 're not the safest man in the world to travel with."

"Yes, Alf gives me the prayers o' the Church now an' agen," replied Mosey complacently. "It was this way: The winter afore last, we got a leader in a swap at Deniliquin. Same time I made the keys. Yaller, hoop-horned bullick—I dunno if you seen him with us? Well, this Pilot, you could n't pack him"——Here Cooper slowly rose, and walked across to his wagon——"Lazy mountain o' mullick, that."

"Burden to his own self," assented Price obsequiously.

"Thick-headed galoot, appearingly," suggested Bum.

"Ought to be hunted back to the Sydney side," contributed Dixon.

——"You could n't pack him for a near side leader," resumed Mosey; "but there was nothin' for it but shepherd all night. You might bet yer soul agen five bob, Pilot was off. Whenever he seen a fence, he'd go through it, an' whenever he seen a river, he 'd swim it; an' the whole fraternity stringin' after, thinkin' he was on for somethin' worth while. Grand leader, but a beggar to clear. Well, las' year, when we went up emp'y to Bargoona—same trip the ole man got that wonderful drink off Moriarty—who should we fine there but this Alf, waitin' for wool, an' due for the fust load. No fear o' him goin' up emp'y nyther. He 'd manage to collar six ton"——

"Don't mention that name if you can help it, Mosey," interrupted Cooper, as he returned to the group, carrying a blanket and the little bag of dead grass which he used as a pillow. I 'm a good-tempered man," he continued, in sullen apology; "but it gives me the wilds and the melancholies, does that name."

"Which?—Bargoona?"

"No; the other name. You 've got Nosey Alf, an' Warrigal Alf, an' (sheol) knows how many other Alfs. I got reason to hate that name."

"Well," resumed Mosey, after a pause, "as I was tellin' you, this cove he was there; an' it so happened his near side leader had got bit with a snake, an' died; an' as luck would have it, he 'd sold the pick of his bullicks to a tank-sinker, an' bought steers in theyre place; an' he had n't another bullick fit to shove in the near side lead to tackle sich a road as he 'd got in front of him. Well, this

cove he makes fistfuls o' money, but he 's always dog-poor, so
he"——

"Which cove makes fistfuls o' money?" demanded Price, roused
from a reverie by the magic dissyllable.

"Fine out, you (adj.) ole fool. So he was flyblowed as usual in
regard o' cash; an' he was badly in want of a near side leader; an'
I kep' showin' off this Pilot, shifting wagons from the door o' the
shed, an' tinkerin' about; an' he offered us two good bullicks for
the counterfit; an' me an' the ole man we hum'd and ha'd, an' let
on we did n't want to part with him; an' me as thin as a whippin'-
post with watchin' the yaller-hided dodger every night, to keep him
from goin' overland to the bounds o' creation. Well, at long an' at
last we swapped level for Valiparaiser. I seen the workin' o' Providence in it from fust to last. The horse he 's worth twenty notes,
all out; an' Pilot he was dear at a gift. I say, Tom; that 's a grand
horse you got off o' the Far-downer. Goes like a greyhound. Gosh,
you had that bloke to rights. He 's whippin' the cat now like fury.
I was chiackin' him about the deal, when he told me you swapped
level; an' he wanted to change the subject. 'I 'm frightened you 'll
be short o' grass to-night,' says he. 'Where you goin' to camp?'
says he. The (adj.) fool!"

"What did you tell him?" asked Thompson.

"Ram-paddick, of course. You don't ketch me tellin' the truth
about where I 'm goin' to camp. But you got a rakin' horse, Tom;
an' I give you credit for gittin' at the blind side o' the turf-cutter."

"He 'll do me well enough for poking about," I replied modestly.
"But how did the other fellow get on with Pilot?"

"It was the fun o' the world," resumed Mosey. "The other feller
he left the shed three days ahead of us; an' when we drawed out,
an' camped at the Four-mile Tank, this feller's wagon was standin'
there yet; an' no sign o' him nor his carrion. I was thinkin' he 'd
have some fun with Pilot, 'specially on account of havin' to do his
bullick-huntin' on foot; for he could n't afford to git another horse
till he delivered. Well, I never seen him agen till to-day when we
stopped for dinner; but the feller at the Bilby Well he told me
about it when we was goin' back to Bargoona, nex' trip.

"Seems, the other feller he goes out in the mornin' on foot,
thinkin' to fine his carrion among that mulgar in the corner to yer
left; an' when he got to the corner, there was a hole in the fence, an'
the tracks through. Course, he runs the tracks; he runs 'em all day,
an' at night he lays down, an' I s'pose he swears his self to sleep.
Nex' mornin' off he scoots agen, an' jist before sundown he hears

the bells, an' he pipes the tail end o' the string ahead; an' the front end was jist at the Bilby Well—sixty good mile, if it 's an inch, an' scrub all the road. Pilot he had n't thought worth while to go roun' by the Boundary Tank, to git on the wool track; he jist went ahead like a surveyor, an' the fences was like spiders' webs to him. It was blazing hot weather; and the other fellow he never seen tucker nor water all the trip, for he would n't leave the track. Laugh? Lord! I thought I 'd 'a' busted when the bloke at the well told me. I noticed the other feller was a bit narked when he seen me on the horse to-day. He 's got red o' Pilot."

"Look here, Mosey," said Thompson slowly: "I 'd rather—so help me God—I 'd rather cut my own throat than do a trick like that. Are n't you frightened of bringing a curse on yourself?"

"I ain't (adj.) fool enough to believe in curses," replied Mosey —his altered tone nevertheless belying his bravado.

"Simply because you don't keep your eyes open," retorted Thompson. "Is n't it well known that a grog-seller's money never gets to his children? Is n't it well known that if you mislead a woman, a curse 'll follow you like your shadow? Is n't it well known that if you're disobedient to your parents, something 'll happen to you? Is n't it well known that Sabbath-breaking brings a curse on a man that he can't shake off till he reforms? Now you stole that horse in the dirtiest way; and stealing—well, anything except grass or water—brings as heavy a curse as anything you can do. Mark my words."

"The Jackdaw of Rheims is a case in point," remarked Willoughby aside to me.

"Well," said Price emphatically, and qualifying every word that would bear qualification, "so fur as workin' on Sundays goes, I 'm well sure I allus worked on Sundays, an' I 'm well sure I allus will; an' I 'm well sure 'ere ain't no cuss on me. Why, I dunno what the (complicated expletive) a cuss is! I 'll get a blanket fer to lay on," he added; "this ground 's sorter damp." And he went across to his wagon.

"He 's got a curse on him as big as Mount Macedon, and he does n't know it," muttered Thompson.

"Bearing out the prophecy," said I aside to Willoughby, "that the sinner, being a hundred years old, shall be accursed."

"You ought to show him a bit more respect, Mosey," remarked Cooper gravely.

"Well, to tell you the truth," replied Mosey frankly, "I got no patience with the ole bunyip. Can't suffer fools, no road."

"Well, I don't want to be shovin' in my jor, but I 'd take him to be more rogue than fool," suggested Bum.

"Time he was thinkin' about repentin', anyhow," observed Dixon.

"Now, really Thompson—do you believe in these special malisons?" asked Willoughby, as Price rejoined the company. "Are you so superstitious? I should n't have thought it."

"I 've good reason to believe in them," replied Thompson. "You asked me this morning why I did n't have two teams. Now I 'll tell you the reason. It 's because I 'm not allowed to keep two teams. I 've got a curse on me. Many a long year ago, when I finished my second season, I found myself at Moama, with a hundred and ten notes to the good, and the prospect of going straight ahead, like the cube root—or the square of the hypotenuse, is it? I forget the exact term, but no matter. Well, the curse came on me in this way: Charley Webber, the young fellow I was travelling with, got a letter from some relations in New Zealand, advising him to settle there; so he offered me his plant for two-thirds of its value—fifty notes down and fifty more when he would send for it. Sheer good-nature of him, for he knew he could have the lot if he liked. But there 's not many fellows of Charley's stamp. So I paid him the fifty notes and we parted. He was to send me his address as soon as he reached New Zealand; but he never got there. The vessel was wrecked on some place they call the North Spit; and Charley was one of the missing. Never heard of him from that day to this."

"Good (ensanguined) shot!" remarked Mosey. "I wish that same specie of a curse would come on me."

"My (ensanguined) colonial!" assented Dixon and Bum, with one accord.

"Well, nobody knows anything about the geography of New Zealand," continued Thompson, "and I purposely forgot the address of Charley's people. Any honest man would have hunted them up, but that was n't my style; I was n't a wheat-sample; I was a tare. Compromised with my conscience. Thought there was no time to lose in making an independence—making haste to be rich, and considering not that 's there 's many a slip between the cup and the lip, as Solomon puts it. I said to myself, 'That 's all right; I 'll pay it some time.' Now see the consequence——

"Just two years after I bid the poor fellow good-bye—two years to the very day, and not very lucky years, neither—I found myself in the middle of the Death Track, with flour for Wilcannia; one wagon left behind, and the bullocks dropping off like fish out of water; bullocks worth ten notes going as if they were n't worth half-a-crown. It was like the retreat from Moscow. Finally, I lost fourteen on the trip—exactly the number I had got dishonestly. As for the second wagon, I gave it to Baxter for fetching the load the last fifty mile. I thought this might clear away the curse, so I did n't fret over it. I felt as if Charley had got satisfaction. But I was n't going to get off so cheap. Two years afterward—you remember, Dixon?—I bought that thin team and the Melbourne wagon from Pribble, the contractor. Dixon, here, was driving for Pribble at that very time, and he can tell you how Dick the Devil cleaned me out of my fine old picked team and the new wagon, leaving me to begin afresh with the remains of Pribble's skeletons and my own old wagon. Then a year or two afterward, I went in debt to buy that plant of Mulligan's—him that was killed off the colt at Mossgiel—and that same winter the pleuro broke out in my lot, and they went like rotten sheep till fourteen were gone; and then, of course, the plague was stopped. Not having any use for Mulligan's wagon, I swapped her for a new thirty-by-twenty-four wool-rag, and a Wagga pot, good for eight or ten mile on a still night; and, within a month, Ramsay's punt went down with my wagon; she's in the bottom of the Murrumbidgee now, with eight ton of bricks to steady her, and the tarpaulin and bell to keep her company. She 'll be fetching the most critical planks out of a steamer some of these times, and I 'll get seven years for leaving her there. Afterward, when I was hauling logs for pontooning, on the Goulburn, I kept buying up steers and breaking them in, till I had two twelves; and one day I left sixteen of them standing in yoke while I went looking round for a good log; and suddenly I heard a crash that rattled back and forward across the river for a quarter of an hour. I had a presentiment that Providence was on the job again, and I was n't disappointed. One of the fallers had left a tree nearly through when he went to dinner; and a gust of wind sent it over, and it carried a couple of other trees before it, right on the spot where my team was folded up in the shade. Eight of them went that trip, between killed and crippled, leaving me with sixteen. My next piece of luck was to lose that new Yankee wagon in the Eight-mile Mallee, on Birrawong. Then I could see plain enough that Providence had taken up Charley's case, and was prepared to block me of keeping two teams; so I determined to have one good one. Now, I 've always stood pretty well with the agents and squatters, and I know my way round Riverina, so I can turn over as much money as any single-team man on the track, bar

Warrigal Alf (I beg your pardon, Cooper; I forgot)—but what 's the use of money to me? Only vanity and vexation of spirit, as Shakespear says. I get up to a certain point, and then I 'm knocked stiff. Mind, I 've only given you a small, insignificant sample of the misfortunes I 've had since I cheated that dead man; but if they don't prove there 's a curse on me, then there 's no such thing as proof in this world."

Price cleared his throat. "Them misforcunes was invidiously owin' to yer own (adj.) misjudgment," he said dogmatically.

"Serve you right for not havin' better luck," added Dixon.

"Learn you sense, anyhow," remarked Mosey.

"Misforcunes does some people good," hazarded Bum.

"Yes," replied Thompson gently. "I 've had my turn. I hope I take it like a man. Your turns will come sooner or later, as sure as you 've got heads on your bodies—perhaps next year; perhaps next week; perhaps to-morrow. Let 's see how you 'll take it. Mind, there 's a curse on every one of us. And look here—we had no business to travel to-day; there was a bite of feed in the Patagonia Swamp, if it came to the worst. Now we 're in for it. I 've got a presentiment that something 'll happen before to-morrow night. Just mark my words."

A constrained silence fell on the grown-up children, till Willoughby politely sought to restore ease by contributing his quota to the evening's feast of reason——

"There occurs to my mind a capital thing," he said; "a capital thing, indeed, though apropos of nothing in particular. A student, returning from a stroll, encountered a countryman, carrying a hare in his hand. 'Friend,' said the student quietly, 'is that thine own hare or a wig?' The joke, of course, lies in the play on the word 'hare'."

Willoughby's courteous effort was worse than wasted, for the general depression deepened.

"You 're right, Thompson," said Cooper, at length. "Mostly everybody 's got a curse on them. I got a curse on me. I got it through swearin' and Sabbath-breakin'. I 've tried to knock off swearin' fifty dozen times, but I might as well try to fly. Last time I tried to knock it off was when I left Nyngan for Kenilworth, four months ago; but there happened to be a two-hundredweight bag o' rice in the bottom o' the load; an' something tore her, an' she started leakin' through the cracks in the floor o' the wagon; an' I could n't git at her no road, for there was seven ton on top of her; an' the blasted stuff it kep' dribble-dribble till you could 'a' tracked

me at a gallop for over a hundred mile; an' me swearin' at it till
I was black in the face; an' it always stopped dribblin' at night,
like as if it was to aggravate a man. If it had n't been for that rice,
I 'd 'a' kep' from swearin' that trip; an' then, comin' down from
Kenilworth with Thompson, I 'd 'a' kep' from it easy; for Thomp-
son he never swears. I give him credit for that much."

"I don't claim any credit," remarked Thompson, with the unconscious spiritual swagger which so often antecedes, and possibly
generates, lapse. "I never could see that swearing did any good;
so I just say to myself, 'You 'd like to come out, would you?—
well, then, once for all, you won't.'"

"You 're a happy man, curse and all," replied the giant gloomily.
"For my own part, I was brought up careful, but I 've turned out
a (adj.) failure. Nobody would think, seeing me so brisk an' cheerful, that I got more worry nor anybody on'y myself could stand. I
got more trouble nor all you fellers put together." He paused,
evidently battling feebly with that impulse which bids us ease the
loaded breast, even when discovery 's pain. His voice was even
lower and sadder as he resumed:

"My father he was well off, with a comfortable place of his own
on the Hawkesbury; an' there was on'y me an' my sister Molly;
for my mother died of a cold she caught when I was about twelve
or fourteen, and Molly she was hardly so old. If you was to travel
the country, you would n't meet another man like my ole dad. He
was what you might call"——

"My farther he was a sojer," interposed Dixon. "He could whack
any man of his weight in the 40th. Las' word he says to me: 'Bob,'
says he; 'be a man—an' keep Injun ink off o' yer arms, for you
never know,' says he, 'what you might do.'"

"Not many men like my ole dad," pursued Cooper. "Fetch up
your youngsters in the natur' an' admiration o' the Lord, an' don't
be frightened to dress the knots off o' them. That was his idear,
an' he went through with it straight. 'William,' says he to me; 'if
I catch a oath out o' your mouth, I 'll welt the (adj.) hide off o'
you;' an' many 's the time he done it. 'Always show respect to an
ole man or an ole woman,' says he; 'an' never kick up a row with
nobody; an' when you see a row startin', you strike in an' squash it,
for blessed be the peacemakers; an' never you git drunk, nor yet
laugh at a drunk man; an' never take your Maker's name in vain,
or by (sheol) He 'll make it hot for you.' That was my father's
style with me. Same with my sister. He used to lay a bit of a
buggy-trace on the table, after supper: 'There, Molly,' says he;

'that's for girls as goes gallivantin' about after night;' an' many's the dose of it Molly got for flyin' round in the moonlight. Consequently, as you might say, she growed up to be the best girl, an' the cleverest, in the district. The other girls was weeds aside of her; she stood inches higher nor any o' them, an' she was a picter' to look at. Strong as whalebone, she was, an' not a lazy bone in her body. She was different from me in regard o' learnin', for she always liked to have her nose in a book, an' she went a lot to school. An' as for singin' or playin' anything in the shape o' music —why, there was nobody about could hold a candle to her. She was fair mad on it; an' my ole dad he sent her to Sydney for over a year o' purpose to fetch her out. Peanner, or flute, or fiddle, or the curliest instrument out of a brass band, it was all one to her; it come sort o' natural to her to fetch music out of anything. Pore Molly!" Cooper paused awhile before he resumed——

"She never took up with none o' the fellers. I knowed fellers try to kiss her; but her style was to stiffen them with a clip under the ear, an' they sort o' took the hint, an' never come back. But by-'n'-by a man from the Queensland border, he bought the place next ours but one; an' our two fam'lies got acquainted. Wonderful clever ole feller he was, in regard o' findin' out new gases, an' smells, an' cures for snake-bites, an' stuff that would go off like a cannon if you looked at it. This cove had got one son an' two daughters, an' his missis was sickly. Well, the son he was a young chap, about my own age at the time"——

"An' how old was you then?" demanded Mosey.

"About two-an'-twenty. He seemed to be a fine, off-handed, straightforrid, well-edicated young feller; an' me an' him we soon got great cronies; an' by-'n'-by I seen he was collared on Molly, an' she was collared on him. Well, thank God! he's got a curse on him that he won't get rid of in a hurry. Thank God for that much!"

"Ruined her?" queried Mosey briskly.

Cooper passed the question with unconscious dignity, and resumed. "Things went on this way for a couple o' year; an' this feller's people was agreeable; an', to make a long story short, the time was fixed for two months on ahead."

"Your father was agreeable, of course?" said Thompson.

"He was dead," replied Cooper reverently. "Gone to eternity, I hope. He deserved to go there if ever any livin' man did. He died about a year after these people come to settle near our place."

"What was the young feller's name?" queried Mosey.

"Never you mind. Well, to make a long story short, one day pore Molly wanted to go somewhere, an' she jumped on-to a horse I'd just left in the yard, an' she shoved her foot in the stirrup-leather; an' the horse he was a reg'lar devil; an' he played up with her in the yard; an' her heel went through the loop o' the leather, an' she come off an' hung by her ankle; an' the horse he was shod all round, an' he kicked her in the face"——Cooper paused.

"Killed her?" suggested Mosey.

"I caught the horse, an' got her clear, an' carried her into the house, all covered with blood, an' just like a corp; an' I left her there with the married woman we had, while I went for the doctor. Well, there she laid for weeks, half-ways between dead an' alive, an' me like a feller in a dream, thinkin' an' thinkin', an' not able to rec'lect anything but the hammerin's I used to give her, an' the things I used to take off of her, an' set her cryin'. I would n't go through that lot agen, not if I got a pension for it. Well, by-'n'-by she got her senses complete; an' this young feller he had been hangin' about the house every day, sayin' nothing to nobody; but when she begun to come round, he begun to keep away. At last she was all right in regard o' health, but she was disfigured for life; she had to wear a crape veil down to her mouth. Then the young feller he used to come sometimes an' just shake hands with her, but otherways he would n't touch her with a forty-foot pole. Then he begun to stop away altogether; an' by-'n'-by he suddenly got married to a girl out o' the lowest pub. for ten mile round; an' his father—real decent ole bloke he was—he told him never to show his face about the place agen. But there was no end o' go in him. He had an uncle in Sydney, middlin' rich, a ship-chandler, an' this"——

"What 's a ship-chandler?" demanded Mosey.

"A man that supplies candles to ships," I replied.

"This uncle he 'd had a saw-mill left on his hands, out somewhere south; an' he give the saw-mill to the young feller on sort o' time-payment; an' I believe he got on splendid for a couple or three year; an' his wife had one picaninny—so we come to hear—an' suddenly he balled her out with some other feller. I on'y got hear-say for it, mind, but I know it 's true; for it 's just what ought to happen. Anyhow, the hand of God was on him, an' he got it hot an' heavy. Accordin' to accounts, he sold out, an' give her the bulk o' the cash, an' then he travelled. Last year, out on the Namoi, a man told me he seen him bullock drivin' in the Bland country, seven year ago. It might be him, or it might n't. I don't know,

an' I don't want to know; for he 's done all the harm he could. I
got to thank him for all my troubles. On'y for him, I 'd 'a' been
livin' comfortable in the ole spot still. I don't mention these things
not once every three year on a average; but sometimes when you
think I 'm pleasant an' cheerful, I 'm fair wild with thinkin' about
that blasted cur; an' you chaps fetched him up fresh in my mind
to-night."

"And the poor girl—is she still at home?" asked Thompson.

"No," replied Cooper hoarsely; "she 's somewhere at the bottom o'
the Hawkesbury river; an' there 's no more home. About three or
four year after her accident, I was away in Sydney one time, on
some business about shares; an' when I come home, Molly was
gone. She 'd left a letter for me, sayin' she 'd nothing to live for;
an' we 'd meet on the other side o' the grave; an' I must always
think kind of her; an' to remember ole times, when there was on'y
the two of us; an' prayin' God to bless me for always bein' good
to her——Why it knocked me stiff, for I 'd always been a selfish,
unfeelin' "——He stopped abruptly; he had uttered the last sen-
tences only by a strong effort.

Presently Dixon, pitying his emotion, remarked to Thompson in
a gratuitously lively tone, and with diction too florid for exact
reproduction,

"Say—was I tellin' you I seen that white bullock you swapped
to Cartwright las' year? I think he 's gittin' a cancer; mebbe it 's
on'y blight; I would n't say. An' that lyin' (individual), Ike Cunningham, told me he busted his self with trefile jist after Cartwright
got him."

"Ah!" replied Thompson absently.

"What become o' yer place?" asked Mosey, turning to Cooper.

"I'll answer that question, but not to satisfy you," replied Cooper
coldly. "Well, chaps, when pore Molly's day was fixed, I scraped
up a hundred notes, an' borrered two hundred on the place, to give
her a start when the thing took place. My ole dad he left everything to me, with strict orders to see Molly through. He did n't
want to make her a bait for loafers. Well, when the thing was
squashed—me, like a fool, I was advised to lay the money out in
minin' shares for Molly; an' then I kep' risin' more money, an'
buyin' more shares; an' I got sort o' muddled somehow; an' to
make a long story short, the whole (adj.) thing went to (sheol).
It was goin' that road when I seen the last o' pore Molly; an' when
I lost her, I jist roused round an' got a team together, an' signed
everything the lyin', cheatin' (financiers) told me to sign; an' then

I cleared off. Must be gittin' on for—let 's see—Molly was twenty-three when she got her accident, an' it was three year after when she made away with herself. That was nine year ago, so she 'd be thirty-five if she was alive now. She need n't 'a' done it! O, she should n't 'a' done it!—for she 'd the satisfaction o' knowin' the curse that come on that blasted dog! I told her all the particulars I got, thinkin' to satisfy her; but I believe it on'y done her harm, for the end come a week or ten days after. Seems strange, lookin' back at it, to think how simple our fam'ly 's been broke up, an' my gran'father's old home gone into the hands o' strangers."

"Never got a trace of your sister?" asked Thompson.

"Not a trace. Some people would have it she was gone to America, or California, or somewhere—but why would she go? Me an' the Ryans—that was the married couple we had—we knowed most about it, an' we cared most; an' we was sure from the first, though we done everything that could be done. She went away at night, an' took nothing with her—not a single item o' clothes, but jist as she stood. Ah! I 'd give what little I got, an' walk a thousand mile on to the back of it, to see her pore bones buried safe, an' then I 'd be satisfied."

Cooper sighed deeply, and lit his pipe; then, for a time, the utter stillness of the bright starlight was broken only by the faint jingle of the horses' hobble-chains, and the sound of some of the nearer bullocks cropping the luxuriant grass.

"The ram-paddick 's a fool to this spot," remarked Mosey, at length. "Mind you, it was friendly of Number Two to lay us on. On'y decent thing I ever knowed him to do. He ain't the clean spud."

"He 's ill-natured, certainly," observed Thompson; "but I can't help taking an interest in him. As a general rule, the more uncivilised a man is, till you come right down to the level of the black-fellow, the better bushman he is; but I must say this of Thingamy-bob, that he comes as near the blackfellow"——

"Hold on," interrupted Dixon, whose private conversation with Bum had caused him to lose step in the march of conversation— "Who the (sheol) is this Thingamybob—bar sells?"

"I wish somebody would fetch me a drink of water," replied Thompson, dropping his subject in pointed rebuke of Dixon's behaviour. "I 'd rather perish than go for it myself; and I won't live two hours if I don't get it. It 's Cooper's fault. When he keeps the meat fresh, it walks away; and when he packs it in salt, and then roasts it in the pan—like this evening—you can see the salt all over it like frost. Grand remedy for scurvy, and Barcoo rot, and the hundreds of natural diseases that flesh is subject to, as the poet says."

"Lis'n that (adj.) liar," growled Cooper, with a fairly successful attempt at easy good-nature. "An' I 'm as bad off as him; an' there ain't a whimper out o' me."

"I 'll bring a drink for you both," said I, rising and taking two pannikins from the lid of the tucker-box. "I would n't do it only that I 'm famishing, myself; and I 'm tired of waiting for some one else to give in."

Then, whilst helping myself to a drink from the water-bag under the rear of Thompson's wagon, and filling the pannikins for my friends, I could n't possibly avoid overhearing the conversation which sprang into life the moment my back was turned——

"My lord Billy-be-damd," remarked Mosey. "Wonder why the (sheol) he ain't at Runnymede to-night, doin' the amiable with Mother Bodysark. Bright pair, them two."

"Would n't trust him as fur 's I could sling him," said Dixon. "Too thick with the (adj.) squatters for my fancy. A man never knows what game that bloke 's up to."

"Can't make him out no road," confessed Cooper. "Seems a decent, easy-goin', God-send-Sunday sort o' feller; but I 'll swear there 's more in his head nor a comb 'll take out."

"He calls himself a philosopher," murmured Thompson; "but his philosophy mostly consists in thinking he knows everything, and other people know nothing. That 's the principal point I 've seen in him; and we 've been acquainted since we were about that high. It was always his way."

"Who 's this Mother Bodysark—if it 's a fair question?" asked Cooper.

"Mrs. Beaudesart," corrected Thompson. "She 's a widow woman —sort of forty-second cousin to Mrs. Montgomery, and housekeeper at the station. I never heard of anybody grudging her to Collins."

"Between ourselves, Thompson," remarked Willoughby, "his conversation this afternoon rather amused me. It recalled to my mind an excellent and most characteristic pleasantry, which you may not have heard. The story goes that Coleridge once asked Lamb, 'Did you ever hear me preach?' 'Preach!' said Lamb; ' 'Gad, I never heard you do anything else!' And yet, if Mr. Collins had enjoyed the advantages accruing from even the rudiments of a liberal ed"——

"He 's got summick to do with Gub'ment lately," said Price cunningly. "My 'pinion, he 's shadderin' summedy."

"He ain't a gurl o' that sort," interposed Bum hastily. "My 'pinion, he 's a spieler. No more a detective nor I am."

I returned to the group. My friends drained their pannikins; Thompson threw his at the tucker-box, and Cooper was just aiming his, when Willoughby, who had shared the frosted mutton, interposed——

"If you please, Cooper."

"Seen better days, pore (fellow)," observed Cooper sympathetically, as the ripple of the water into the pannikin indicated that the whaler was at the tap.

"Can't see much worse," mused Thompson.

"My (adj.) oath—can't he?" chuckled Mosey. "Hold on till he gits old."

"People seem to think Gawd made these here colonies for a rubbage-heap," said Bum. "That 's the English idear of"——

"Stiddy, Charley," interrupted Dixon. "Everybody 's got a right to live, an' that pore (fellow) 's got jist as much right as me or you. A man ought to show respect to misforcune, Charley."

"Shall I bring a pannikin of water for any of you gentlemen?" asked Willoughby, without a trace of ironical emphasis on the last word.

"Fetch me one while yer hand 's in," replied Bum.

Willoughby brought the drink. I fancied even an accession to the subdued suavity of his manner as he picked up and replaced on the tucker-box the empty pannikin which Bum had thanklessly tossed on the ground at his feet. Then he resumed his place; and Thompson, palpably turning his back on Dixon and Bum, selected him as chief hearer of his recommenced discourse——

"Comes as near the blackfellow as it 's possible for a white man to get. And you could n't kill him with an axe. Then start him at any civilised work—such as splicing a loop on a wool rope, or making a yoke, or wedging a loose box in a wheel—and he has the best hands in the country. At the same time, it 's plain to be seen that he has been brought up in the class of society that sticks a napkin, in a bone ring, alongside your plate at dinner." Here Thompson paused, and the recurrence of some distressing memory elicited a half-suppressed sigh.

"There is nothing unreasonable in that phenomenon," remarked Willoughby—"rather the reverse. Probably the person you speak of is a gentleman. Now, the man who is a gentleman by birth and

culture—by which I mean a man of good family, who has not only
gone through the curriculum of a university, but has graduated, so
to speak, in society—such a one has every advantage in any conceivable situation. The records of military enterprise, exploration,
pioneering, and so forth, furnish abundant evidence of this very
obvious fact. You will find, I think, that high breeding and training are conditions of superiority in the human as well as in the
equine and canine races; pedigree being, of course, the primary
desideratum. *Non generant aquilæ columbas,* we say."

"Don't run away with the idear that nobody knows who Colum-
bus was," retorted Bum. "He discovered America—or else my
readin 's did me (adj.) little good."

"More power to yer (adj.) elbow, Bum," said Mosey approvingly. "But, gentleman or no gentleman, if a feller ain't propped
up with cash, this country 'll (adj.) quick fetch him to his proper
(adj.) level."

"Pardon me if I differ from you, Mosey," replied Willoughby
blandly. "A few months ago, I travelled the Lachlan with a man
fitted by birth and culture to be a leader of society; one whose
rightful place would be at least in the front rank of your Australian
aristocracy. How do you account for such a man being reduced to
solicit the demd pannikin of flour?"

"Easy," retorted the sansculotte: "the duke had jist settled down
to his proper (adj.) level—like the bloke you 'll see in the bottom
of a new pannikin when you 're drinkin' out of it."

"Mosey," said Cooper impressively; "if I git up off o' this
blanket, I 'll kick"—(I did n't catch the rest of the sentence).
"Give us none o' your (adj.) Port Phillip ignorance here."

"You can git a drink o' good water in ole Vic., anyhow," sneered
Mosey, with the usual flowers of speech.

"An' that 's about all you can git," muttered Cooper, faithfully
following the same ornate style of diction.

"Now, Mosey," said Willoughby, courteously but tenaciously,
"will you permit me to enumerate a few gentlemen—gentlemen,
remember—who have exhibited in a marked degree the qualities of
the pioneer. Let us begin with those men of whom you Victorians
are so justly proud,—Burke and Wills. Then you have——"

"Hold on, hold on," interrupted Mosey. "Don't go no furder,
for Gossake. Yer knockin' yerself bad, an' you don't know it. Wills
was a pore harmless weed, so he kin pass; but look 'ere—there
ain't a drover, nor yet a bullock driver, nor yet a stock-keeper, from
'ere to 'ell that could n't 'a' bossed that expegition straight through

to the Gulf, an' back agen, an' never turned a hair—with sich a season as Burke had. Don't sicken a man with yer Burke. He burked that expegition, right enough. ''Howlt! *Dis*-MOUNT!' Grand style o' man for sich a contract! I tell you, that (explorer) died for want of his sherry an' biscakes. Why, the ole man, here, seen him out beyond Menindie, with his——''

"Pardon me, Mosey—was Mr. Price connected with the expedition?"

"No (adj.) fear!" growled Price resentfully. "Jist happened to be there with the (adj.) teams. Went up with stores, an' come down with wool."

Willoughby, who probably had wept over the sufferings of Burke's party on their way to Menindie, seemed badly nonplussed. He murmured acquiescence in Price's authority; and Mosey continued,

"Well, the ole man, here, seen him camped, with his carpet, an' his bedsteed, an' (sheol) knows what paravinalia; an' a man nothin' to do but wait on him; an'—look here!—a cubbard made to fit one o' the camels, with compartments for his swell toggery, an'—as true as I 'm a livin' sinner!—one o' the compartments made distinctly o' purpose to hold his bell-topper!"

"Quite so," replied Willoughby approvingly. "We must bear in mind that Burke had a position to uphold in the party; and that, to maintain subordination, a commander must differentiate himself by"——

"It 's Gord's truth, anyhow," remarked Price, rousing his mind from a retrospect of its extensive past. And, no doubt, the old man was right; for a relic, answering to Mosey's description, was sold by auction in Melbourne, with other assets of the expedition, upon Brahe's return.

"They give him a lot o' credit for dyin' in the open," continued the practical little wretch, with masterly handling of expletive— "but I want to know what else a feller like him could do, when there was no git out? An' you 'll see in Melb'n', there, a statue of him, made o' cast steel, or concrete, or somethin', standin' as bold as brass in the middle o' the street! My word! An' all the thousands o' pore beggars that 's died o' thirst an' hardship in the back country—all o' them a dash sight better men nor Burke knowed how to be—where 's theyre statues? Don't talk rubbage to me. Why, there was no end to that feller's childishness. Before he leaves Bray at Cooper's Creek, he drors out—what do you think?— well, he drors out a plan o' forti—(adj.)—fications, like they got in

ole wore-out countries; an' Bray had to keep his fellers workin' an'
cursin' at this thing till the time come for them to clear. An' mind
you, this was among the tamest blackfellers in the world. Why,
Burke was dotin'. Wants a youngfeller, with some life in him, for
to boss a expegition; an' on top o' Burke's swellishness an' uselessness, dash me if he wasn't forty!"

"Well, no; he war n't too old, Mosey," interposed Price deprecatingly. "Wants a experienced man fer sich work. Same time,
you could n't best Burke fer a counterfit."

"Sing'lar thing, you 'll never hear one good word o' that man,"
observed Cooper. "Different from all the other explorers. Can't
account for it, no road."

"Another singular thing is that you 'll never read a word against
him," added Thompson. "In conversation, you 'll always learn that
Burke never did a thing worth doing or said a thing worth saying;
and that his management of that expedition would have disgraced
a new-chum schoolboy; and old Victorian policemen will tell you
that he left the force with the name of a bully and a snob, and a
man of the smallest brains. Wonder why these things never get
into print."

"*De mortuis nil nisi bonum* is an excellent maxim, Thompson,"
remarked Willoughby.

"It is that," retorted Mosey. "Divil a fear but they 'll nicely
bone anythin' in the shape o' credit. Toffs is no slouches at bar-
rickin' for theyre own push. An' I 'll tell you another dash good
maximum,—it 's to keep off of weltin' a dyin' man."

"Did you ever read Burke's Diary, Willoughby?" asked Thompson. "It 's just two or three pages of the foolishest trash that any
man ever lost time in writing; and I'm afraid it 's about a fair
sample of Burke. I wish you could talk to some fellows that I
know—Barefooted Bob, for instance. Now, there 's a man that was
never known to say a thing that he was n't sure of; and he 's been
all over the country that Burke was over, and heard all that is to be
known of the expedition. And Bob 's a man that goes with his eyes
open. I wish you could talk to him. Lots of information in the
back country that never gets down here into civilisation."

"There is a certain justice in Mosey's contention," I remarked,
addressing Willoughby. "He argues that, as Burke, by dying of
hardship, earned himself a statue, so Brown, Jones, and Robinson
—whose souls, we trust, are in a less torrid climate than their
unburied bones—should, in bare justice, have similar post-obituary
recognition. For Burke's sake, of course, the comparison in value

of service had better not be entered on. Mosey would have our cities resemble ancient Athens in respect of having more public statues than living citizens."

"Your allusion to Athens is singularly happy," replied the whaler; "but you will remember that the Athenians were, in many respects, as exclusive as ourselves. The impassable chasm which separates your illustrious explorer from Brown, Jones, and Robinson, existed also in Athens, though, perhaps, not so jealously guarded. But let us change the subject."

"Yes; do," said Cooper cordially. "I hate argyin'. Fust go off, it 's all friendly;—'Yes, my good man.'—'No, my dear feller.'—'Don't run away with that idear.'—'You 're puttin' the boot on the wrong foot.'—'You got the wrong pig by the tail.'—an' so on, as sweet as sugar. But by-'n'-by it 's, 'To (shoel) with you for a (adj.) fool!'—'You 're a (adj.) liar!'—'Who the (adj. sheol) do you think you 're talking to?'—an' one word fetchin' on another till it grows into a sort o' unpleasantness."

"Hear anything of Bob and Bat lately?" asked Thompson, after a pause.

"Both gone to have a confab with Burke; an' good enough for the likes o' them," replied Mosey. "Them sort o' varmin's the curse o' the country. I ain't a very honourable sort, myself, but I 'd go on one feed every two days before I 'd come as low as them. Well, couple or three year ago, you know, ole M'Gregor he sent the (adj.) skunks out with cattle to some new country, a hundred mile beyond (sheol); an' between hardship, an' bad tucker, an' bad conscience, they both pegged out. So a feller from the Diamantinar told me a fortnit ago."

"Smart fellows in their way," remarked Thompson. "I don't bear them any malice, though they rounded me up twice, and made me fork out each time."

"Boolka horse-paddick?" suggested Mosey. "They grabbed us there once, an' it was touch-an'-go another time. But the place is worth a bit o' risk."

"No; both times it was on Wo-Winya, on the Deniliquin side," replied Thompson. "First time was about nine years ago. Bob and Bat were dummying on the station at the time, and looking after the Skeleton paddock. Flash young fellers they were then. Cunningham and I worked on that paddock one night, as usual, coming up empty from the Murray. Of course, we were out in the morning at grey daylight, but it was a bit foggy, and instead of finding the bullocks, we found Bob and Bat cantering round, looking for them.

Cunningham and I separated, and so did the other two; and the four of us spent the liveliest half-hour you could wish for; chasing, and crossing, and meeting one another in all directions, and not a word spoken, and not a hoof to be seen. At last the fog lifted a bit, and Cunningham spotted cattle in a timbered swamp, but Bat was between him and them; so he circled round gently, and was edging up to get a good start, when Bat took the alarm, and saw the cattle; then it was neck-or-nothing with them for possession. Bob and I happened to be in sight, and when we saw our mates go off on the jump, we both went for the same spot. Cunningham beat Bat by a few lengths, and got possession; but when I got within a quarter of a mile, I saw there was only part of our lot there. Just then I saw Bob turn his horse, and race straight toward me; and when I looked in the direction he was going, I saw more cattle. I went for them with a clear start of a hundred yards, and would have won easy, only that I saw they were station cattle; and at the same time I caught sight of another little lot in a hollow to the left, and Bat travelling for them. I slewed round, and gave him a gallop for it, but he won by fifty yards. However, there was only five of our lot in the little mob. There was thirteen wanted still; and Bob had possession of them among the station cattle. So they got eighteen altogether, and we only got sixteen, after running the legs off our horses."

"Port Phillip," observed Cooper pointedly.

"Another time, going on for three years ago," continued Thompson, "Bob had me as cheap as dirt for the whole twenty, while Bat snapped Potter's horses the same night. That was on Wo-Winya again—shortly before M'Gregor sold the station to Stoddart, and just before the two of them were sent out to the Diamantina"——

"M'Gregor and Stoddart, of course?" I gently suggested.

"Yes, Tom; I thought I made that clear."

"So you did, Steve. I beg pardon."

"Don't mention it, Tom."

True friendship lay underneath this severity, for when Thompson got started on his reminiscences, he was apt to continue indefinitely, to the ruin of his own dignity.

"But why this solicitude and panic over being detected in trifling trespass?" asked Willoughby. "Like most things in this country, it appears to be purely a matter of £ s. d. Now, I have taken the liberty of totting up, in my own mind, some of your earnings. Will Thompson permit me to take his case as an illustration? I find, Thompson, that the tariff of your wool is exactly sevenpence halfpenny per ton per mile. You have eight tons on your wagon at the present time. This will give you five shillings for each mile you travel. You have travelled ten miles to-day"——

"Sabbath day's journey," sighed Thompson.

——"that is two pounds ten. Now,—all things considered—an occasional penalty of, say, one pound, appears to me by no means ruinous. It is not to be mentioned in comparison with other losses which you have been unfortunate enough to sustain, yet it appears to be your chief grievance."

"Yes; that 's one way of looking at it," muttered Thompson, after a pause. The other fellows were silently and futilely wrestling with the apparent anomaly. A metaphysical question keeps slipping away from the grasp of the bullock driver's mind like a wet melon-seed.

[Yet the solution is simple. The up-country man is decidedly open-handed; he will submit to crushing losses with cheerfulness, tempered, of course, by humility in those cases where he recognises the operation of an overhanging curse; he will subscribe to any good or bad cause with a liberality excelled only by the digger; he will pay gambling debts with the easy, careless grace which makes every P. of W. so popular in English sporting circles—in a word, the smallest of his many sins is parsimony. But the penal suggestiveness of trespass-penalty touches the sullen dignity of his nature; and the vague, but well-grounded fear of a law made and administered solely by his natural enemies makes him feel about as apprehensive as John Bunyan, though certainly more dangerous. Of course, Willoughby, born and bred a member of the governing class, could n't easily conceive the dismay with which these outlaws regarded legal seizure for trespass—or possibly prosecution in courts dominated by squatters.]

"I knows wun respectable man with two teams wot 's seed the time he 'd emp'y a double-barr'll gun on them two fellers jis' same 's if they was wild dogs," remarked Price ominously. "I happen ter mind me o' wun time this man hed ter fetch hees las' wool right on ter Deniliquin, f'm Hay, f'r two-five hextry, 'count o' there bein' no river that season. An' that man 'e war shaddered hevery day acrost Wo-Winyar, an' hees bullicks collared hevery night with Bob or Bat; an' them bullicks har'ly fit ter crawl with fair poverty. Dirty! W'y, Chows ain't in it with them varmin f'r dirtiness." Here followed a steady torrent of red vituperation, showing that Price took a strong personal interest in the respectable man with the two teams.

"To my (adj.) knowledge, they dummied land for ole M'Gregor, an' never got a cent for it," remarked Dixon. "Same time, I got nothin' to say agen 'em, for they never got a slant to snavel my lot. Brothers—ain't they?"

"No (adj.) fear," replied Mosey. "You never seen brothers hangin' together like them chaps. I know some drovers that 's been prayin' for theyre (adj.) souls every night for years, on account o' the way they used to rush travellin' stock across M'Gregor's runs. Whenever there was dirty work to be did, them two blokes was on hand to do it. An' I got it on good authority that they chanced three years chokey for perjury, when they was dummyin' for M'Gregor; an' all they got for it was the fright hangin' over them. A man should n't make a dog of his self without he 's well paid for it. That 's my (adj.) religion."

"So far as dummying is concerned," said I; "no one except their Maker and M'Gregor knows how the thing was worked. But if they had owned all the land they secured for M'Gregor, by perjury, and personation, and straightforward dummyism, they would have been little squatters themselves. At the same time, they were true-hearted, kindly, unselfish men, according to their uncertain light; and in all probability they 're gone to heaven. Such is life, boys."

"Anyhow, they ain't goin' to trouble us no furder," rejoined Mosey complacently. "Theyre toes is turned up. Lis'n!—that 's the sound I like to hear!" The sound was the deep, heavy sough of a contented bullock, as he lay down with a couple of days' rations in his capacious first stomach.

"Grass is generally a burning question with you teamsters," observed Willoughby.

"I never make no insinuations, myself," replied Dixon coldly.

"Good!" interjected Mosey. "If you was inclined that road, you might say the carrier 's got as much interest in the grass as a squatter. It 's the traveller as don't give a (compound expletive) if the whole country 's as black as Ole Nick's soot-brush."

"Well, I s'pose that 's about a fair thing for to-night," remarked Cooper; and he pulled off his boots, preparatory to wrapping himself in his blanket. "Time to vong tong cooshey, as the Frenchman says. Must n't oversleep in the mornin', if the place is ever so safe."

Then I disposed my possum rug and saddle, took off my boots, spread my coat for Pup to sleep on, lit my pipe, and lay down for the night. Thompson, Mosey, and Willoughby arranged themselves here and there, according to taste. Dixon and Methuselah retired to hammocks under the rear of their respective wagons. Bum simply lay where he was. I would do my companions what honour I can, but the stern code of the chronicler permits no quibbling with the fact that Mosey and Bum wound up the evening with a series of gestes and apothegms, such as must not tarnish these pages —Willoughby occasionally taking part, rather, I think, through courtesy than sympathy, and ably closing the service with a fescennine anecdote, beginning, 'It is related that, on one occasion, the late Marquis of Waterford'——

Willoughby had selected a smooth place near my own lair. Here he spent five minutes in spreading his exceptionally dirty blanket, and another five in tidily folding his ragged coat for a pillow. Then he removed his unmatched boots, and, unlapping from his feet the inexpensive substitute for socks known as 'prince-alberts,' he artistically spread the redolent swaths across his boots to receive the needed benefit of the night air; performing all these little offices with an unconscious elegance amusing to notice—an elegance which not another member of our party could have achieved, any more than Willoughby could have acquired the practical effectiveness of a good rough average vulgarian.

Poor shadow of departed exclusiveness!—lying there, with none so poor to do him reverence! He was a type—and, by reason of his happy temperament, an exceedingly favourable type—of the 'gentleman,' shifting for himself under normal conditions of back-country life. Urbane address, faultless syntax, even that good part which shall not be taken away, namely, the calm consciousness of inherent superiority, are of little use here. And yet your Australian novelist finds no inconsistency in placing the bookish student, or the city dandy, many degrees above the bushman, or the digger, or the pioneer, in vocations which have been the life-work of the latter. O, the wearisome nonsense of this kind which is remorselessly thrust upon a docile public! And what an opportunity for some novelist, in his rabid pursuit of originality, to merely reverse the incongruity—picturing a semi-barbarian, lassoed full-grown, and launched into polished society, there to excel the fastidious idlers of drawing-room and tennis-court in their own line! This miracle would be more reasonable than its antithesis. Without doubt, it is easier to acquire gentlemanly deportment than axe-man's muscle; easier to criticise an opera than to identify a beast seen casually twelve months before; easier to dress becomingly than to make a bee-line, straight as the sighting of a theodolite, across strange country in foggy weather; easier to recognise the various costly vintages than to live contentedly on the smell of an oil rag. When you take this back elevation of the question, the inconsistency becomes apparent. And the *longa* of Art, viewed in conjunction with the *brevis* of Life, makes it at least reasonable that when a man has faithfully served one exclusive apprenticeship, he will find it too late in the day to serve a second. Moreover, there are few advantages in training which do not, according to present social arrangements, involve corresponding penalties.

Human ignorance is, after all, more variable in character than in extent. Each sphere of life, each occupation, is burdened with its own special brand of this unhappy heritage. To remove one small section of inborn ignorance is a life-work for any man. 'Ignorance, madam, pure ignorance,' was what betrayed the great lexicographer into defining 'pastern' as 'a horse's knee.' And the Doctor was right (in his admission, of course, not in his definition). Ignorance, reader, pure ignorance is what debars you from conversing fluently and intelligibly in several dialects of the Chinese language. Yet a friend of mine, named Yabby Pelham, can do so, though the same person knows as little of book-lore as William Shakespear of Stratford knew. But if you had been brought up in a Chinese camp, on a worn-out goldfield, your own special acquirements, and corresponding ignorance, might run in grooves similar to Yabby's. Let each of us keep himself behind the spikes on this question of restricted capability.

And should some blue-blooded insect indignantly retort that, though his own ancestors have borne coat-armour for seventeen generations, and though he himself was brought up so utterly and aristocratically useless as to have been unable, at twenty years of age, to polish his own boots, yet he is now, mentally and physicaly, a man fit for anything—I can only reply, in the words of Portia, that I fear me my lady his mother played false with a smith. But this, again, would be claiming too much for heredity, at the expense of training. Remember, however, that our present subject is not the 'gentleman' of actual life. *He* is an unknown and elusive quantity, merging insensibly into saint or scoundrel, sage or fool, man or blackleg. He runs in all shapes, and in all degrees of definiteness. Our subject is that insult to common sense, that childish slap in the face of honest manhood, the 'gentleman' of fiction, and of Australian fiction pre-eminently.

Heaven knows I am no more inclined to decry social culture than moral principle; but I acknowledge no aristocracy except one of service and self-sacrifice, in which he that is chief shall be servant, and he that is greatest of all, servant of all. And it is surely time to notice the three-penny braggadocio of caste which makes the languid Captain Vernon de Vere (or words to that effect) an overmatch for half-a-dozen hard-muscled white savages, any one of whom would take his lordship by the ankles, and wipe the battlefield with his patrician visage; which makes the pale, elegant aristocrat punch Beelzebub out of Big Mick, the hod-man, who, in unpleasant reality, would feel the kick of a horse less than his antagonist would the wind of heaven, visiting his face too roughly; which makes the rosy-cheeked darling of the English rectory show the saddle-hardened specialists of the back country how to ride a buck-jumper; which makes a party of resourceful bushmen stand helpless in the presence of flood or fire, till marshalled by some hero of the croquet lawn; above all, which makes the isocratic and irreverent Australian fawn on the 'gentleman,' for no imaginable reason except that the latter says 'deuced' instead of 'sanguinary,' and 'by Jove' instead of 'by sheol.' Go to; I'll no more on 't; it hath made me mad.

And don't fall back upon the musty subterfuge which, by a shifting value of the term, represents 'gentleman' as simply signifying a man of honour, probity, education, and taste; for, by immemorial usage, by current application, and by every rule which gives definite meaning to words, the man with a shovel in his hand, a rule in his pocket, an axe on his shoulder, a leather apron on his abdomen, or any other badge of manual labour about him—his virtues else be they as pure as grace, as infinite as man may undergo—is carefully contradistinguished from the 'gentleman.' The 'gentleman' may be a drunkard, a gambler, a debauchee, a parasite, a helpless potterer; he may be a man of spotless life, able and honest; but he must on no account be a man with broad palms, a workman amongst workmen. The 'gentleman' is not necessarily gentle; but he is necessarily genteel. Etymology is not at fault here; gentility, and gentility alone, is the qualification of the 'gentleman.'

No doubt it is very nice to see a 'gentleman' who, when drunk, can lie in the gutter like a 'gentleman'; but will someone suggest a more pitiable sight than such a person trying to compete with an iron-sinewed miner on the goldfields, or with a hardy, nine-lifed bushman in the back country? In the back country, a penniless and friendless 'gentleman,' if sober and honest and possessed of some little ability, may aspire to the position of a station storekeeper. If destitute of these advantages—and reduced 'gentlemen' are not by any means always sober, honest, and capable—the best thing he can do, if he gets the chance, is to settle down thankfully into the innocent occupation so earnestly desired by Henry the Sixth of the play, and so thriftily pursued by the alleged father of any amateur elocutionist whose name is Norval on the Grampian Hills.

Of such reduced 'gentlemen' it is often said that their education becomes their curse. Here is another little subterfuge. This is one of those taking expressions which are repeated from parrot to magpie till they seem to acquire axiomatic force. It is such men's ignorance—their technical ignorance—that is their curse. Education of any kind never was, and never can be, a curse to its possessor; it is a curse only to the person whose interest lies in exploiting its possessor. Erudition, even in the humblest sphere of life, is the sweetest solace, the unfailing refuge, of the restless mind; but if the bearer thereof be not able to *do* something well enough to make a living by it, his education is simply outclassed, overborne, and crushed by his own superior ignorance.

To be sure, there are men of social culture who gallantly and conspicuously maintain an all-round superiority in the society to which I myself hereditarily belong, namely, the Lower Orders; but their appearances are like angels' visits—in the obvious, as well as in the conventional but remoter sense. I can count no less than three men of this stamp among my ten thousand acquaintances. When the twofold excellence of such ambidexters is not stultified by selfishness, you have in them a realised ideal upon which their Creator might pronounce the judgment that it is very good. Move heaven and earth, then, to multiply that ideal by the number of the population. The thing is, at least, theoretically possible; for it is in no way necessary that the manual worker should be rude and illiterate; shut out from his rightful heirship of all the ages. Nor is it any more necessary that the social aristocrat—ostentatiously useless, as he generally is—should hold virtual monopoly of the elegancies of life.

But the commonplace 'gentleman' of fiction, who, without extraneous advantage, and by mere virtue of caste-consciousness, and caste-eminence, and caste-exclusiveness, doth bestride this narrow world like a colossus——

"I am sorry to break in upon your meditations, Collins," said Willoughby deprecatingly, turning towards me on his elbow, "but you know, *Necessitas non habet leges*. I find myself without the requisite for my normal bedtime solace; and I am unusually wakeful. Could you spare me a pipeful of tobacco?"

"Certainly! Why did n't you mention it before? I had no idea you were a smoker. I feel really vexed at your reticence."

"Well, Mr. Thompson kindly lent me a supply this morning; but, unfortunately, I had a hole in my pocket that I was not aware of, and——Thanks. I 'll just take a pipeful"——

"No, no; shove it in your pocket. I 've got more in my swag. Been long in these colonies, Willoughby?"

"About a year. I spent two months in Melbourne, and nearly four in Sydney. For the last six months I have been—er—travelling in search of employment."

"You find the colonies pretty rough?"

"I do, Collins; to speak frankly, I do. Even in your cities I observe a feverish excitement, and a demnable race for what the Scriptures aptly call 'filthy lucre'; and the pastoral regions are—well—rough indeed. Your colonies are too young. In time to come, no doubt, the amenities of life will appear—for you have some magnificent private fortunes; but in the meantime one hears of nothing but work—business—and so forth. Cultivated leisure is a thing practically unknown. However, the country is merely passing through a necessary phase of development. In the near future, each of these shabby home-stations will be replaced by a noble mansion, with its spacious park; and these bare plains will reward the toil of an industrious and contented tenantry"——

"Like (sheol)!" sneered Mosey from his resting-place,—a little crestfallen notwithstanding.

"Irrigation, my dear Mosey, will meet the difficulty which very naturally arises in your mind. A scientific system of irrigation would increase the letting value of this land more than a hundred-fold. Now, if the State would carry out such a system—by Heaven! Collins, you would soon have a class of country magnates second to none in the world. You are a native of the colonies, I presume?"

"Yes; I come from the Cabbage Garden."

"Victoria, I know, is called the Cabbage Garden," rejoined Willoughby. "But—pardon me—if you are a native of Victoria, you can form no conception of what England is. Among the upper middle classes—to which I belonged—the money-making proclivity is held in very low esteem, I assure you. Our solicitude is to make ourselves mutually agreeable; and the natural result is a grace and refinement which"——

"But what the (adj. sheol) good does that do the likes o' us (fellows)?" demanded Mosey impertinently—or perhaps I should say, pertinently.

——"a grace and refinement which—if you will pardon me for

saying so—you can form no conception of. Inherited wealth is the secret of it."

"Beg parding," interposed Cooper apologetically—"I was goin' to say to Collins, before I forgit, that he can easy git over bein' a Port Philliper. Friend o' mine, out on the Macquarie, name o' Mick Shanahan, he 's one too; an' when anybody calls him a Port Phil-liper, or a Vic., or a 'Sucker, he comes out straight: 'You 're a (adj.) liar,' says he; 'I 'm a Cornstalk, born in New South Wales.' An' he proves it too. Born before the Separation, in the District of Port Phillip, Colony of New South Wales. That 's his argyment, an' there 's no gittin' over it. Good idear, ain't it?"

"It is a good idea," I replied. "I 'm glad you laid me on to it. But, Willoughby, I can't help thinking you must feel the change very acutely."

"I do. But what is the use of grumbling? *Ver non semper viret.* No doubt you are surprised to see me in my present position. It is owing, in the first place, to a curious combination of circum-stances, and in the second place, to some of my own little pranks. I am nephew to Sir Robert Brook, baronet, the present representa-tive of the Brooks of Brookcotes, Dorsetshire—a family, sir, dating from the fourteenth century. Possibly you have heard the name?"

"Often."

"Not the Brookes of the King's Elms, Hants, pray observe. The Brookes of the King's Elms gained their enormous wealth as army contractors, during the struggle with Napoleon, and their baronetcy, Heaven knows how! The baronetcy of the Brooks of Brookcotes dates from 1615, at which time my maternal ancestor, Sir Roger Brook, knight, procured his patent by supplying thirty infantry for three years in the subjugation of Ireland. Independently of the title, our family is many centuries older than the other. We spell our name without"——

"My (adj.) fambly come all the way down from the Hark," observed Mosey, with a rudeness which reflected little credit on his ancient lineage.

——"without the final 'e.' There is a manifest breach of trust in creation of these new baronetcies. It was more than implied— it was distinctly stipulated—at the origination of the Order, by James I, that the number of baronets should not exceed two hun-dred, and that there should be no new creations to supply the place of such titles as might lapse through extinction of families."

"And is there no remedy for this?" I asked.

"None whatever. Not that I am personally interested in the

exclusiveness of the Order, my connection with the Brooks of Brookcotes being on the distaff side. My mother was Sir Robert's only sister. My father was a military man—3rd Buffs—died when I was twelve or thirteen years of age. Sir Robert was a confirmed bachelor, and I was his only nephew. Now you see my position?"

"I think I do."

"Four years ago, demme if Sir Robert did n't marry a manufacturer's daughter—soap manufacturer—and within two years there was a lineal heir to Brookcotes!"

"You don't say so?"

"Fact, begad! Shortly afterward, I was detected—ha-ha! *Sua cuique voluptas*—in a *liaison* with a young person who resided with my uncle's wife as a companion. Whereupon my lady used her influence with the demd old dotard, and I was cut off with a shilling. However, he gave me a saloon passage to Melbourne, with an order on his agent in that city for £500. My lady's father also gave me letters of introduction to some friends in Sydney— business people. Fact was, they wanted to get rid of me."

"The £500 should have given you a fair start," I suggested.

"Pardon me—it is impossible for you to enter into the feelings of a man who has been brought up as presumptive heir to a rent-roll of £12,000. You cannot imagine how the mind of a gentleman shrinks from the petty details, the meanness, the vulgarities of trade. You are aware, I presume, that all avenues of ambition except the Church, the Army, and the Legislature, are closed to our class? You cannot imagine—pardon my repeating it—the exclusiveness, the fine sense of honour"——

"Holy sailor!" I heard Thompson whisper to himself.

——"which pervades the mind and controls the actions of a gentleman. As a casual illustration of what is amusingly, though somewhat provokingly, ignored here, you have, no doubt, observed that our gentlemen cricketers will acknowledge no fellowship with professionals, though they may belong to the same team, and be paid from the same funds. However, to proceed with a story which is, perhaps, not without interest. I left Melbourne before my pittance was exhausted, and presented my credentials in Sydney. Mr. Wilcox, a relation of my lady's father, and a person of some local importance, treated me at first with consideration—in fact, there was always a knife and fork for me at his table—but I noticed, as time went on, a growing coolness on his part. I ought to mention that his sister, Mrs. Bradshaw—a widow, fat, fair, and forty— had considerable capital invested in his business; and I was paying my addresses to her, deeming my birth and education a sufficient counterpoise to her wealth. I 'd have married her too, begad I would! At this time, Wilcox was establishing gelatine works; and he had the demd effron"——

"What 's gelatine?" demanded Mosey. "I 've of'en heard o' the (adj.) stuff. What the (sheol) is it used in?"

"In commerce, principally, Mosey," I replied.

"Neat, begad! As I was saying, Wilcox had the demd assurance to offer me a clerkship in his new establishment. We had a few words in consequence; and shortly afterward I left Sydney, and found my way here. Have you any acquaintance in Sydney—may I ask?"

[A word of explanation. Being only an official of the ninth class, I received my appointment in Hay. On that occasion, I asked the magistrate who received my securities and otherwise attended to the matter—I naturally asked him what chance I had for promotion. He told me that it would go strictly by seniority, but, as my immediate superior, the Assistant-Sub-Inspector, was not eligible for any higher grade—never having passed any examination whatever—and as I could not be advanced over his head, my only chance was to step into his place when he vacated it. Now, I knew he was not likely to resign, for he had a good salary all to himself, and nothing to do but refer me to the Central Office for orders. I knew in fact, that there was only one way in which he was likely to quit his niche in the edifice of the State. So I replied to Willoughby's question]

"Well, I may say I have; and yet I 'm not aware of anyone in Sydney that I would know by sight. My superior officer lives there. Remotely possible you may know him—Rudolph Winterbottom, esquire."

"Rudolph Winterbottom—did you say? Yes, by Jove! rather a happy coincidence. I remember him well. I was introduced to him on a reception day at Government House, and met him frequently afterward; dined in his company, I think, on two occasions."

"Is he a very old man?"

"No; the old gentleman is his father—Thomas Winterbottom—hale, sturdy old boy, overflowing with vitality—came out, he told me, in the time of Sir Richard Bourke. But I scarcely think Mr. Rudolph Winterbottom holds any Government situation. His private fortune is fully sufficient for all demands of even good society. Ah! now I have it! His son Rudy—his third or fourth son—holds some appointment. That will be your man."

"Very likely. An invalid—is he not? Something wrong with his lungs?"

"So I should imagine, now that you mention it. He was away on an excursion to the mountains when his father spoke of him to me."

"Git to sleep, chaps, for Gossake," murmured Cooper. "Guarantee there 'll be none o' this liveliness in the mornin', when you got to turn out."

Thus sensibly admonished, we committed ourselves to what Macbeth calls 'sore labour's bath'—the only kind of bath we were likely to have for some time.

Among the thousand natural ills, there are two to which I never have been, and probably never shall be, subject—namely, gout and insomnia. My immunity from the former might be difficult to account for, but my exemption from the latter may, I think, be attributed to the operation of a mind at peace with all below. Nevertheless, it used to be my habit to wake punctually at 2 a.m., for the purpose of remembering whether I had to listen for bells or not, and determining how long I could afford to sleep. So, at that exact hour, I opened my eyes to see the calm, splendid stars above, whilst merciful darkness half-veiled the sordid accessories of daily life below. Yet I noticed that the hammock under the rear of Dixon's wagon was empty. All the other fellows were sleeping, except Bum, who seemed to have disappeared altogether. The two were probably up to something. No business of mine. And I dropped to sleep again.

I had set myself to wake at full daylight. Just as I woke, I heard the distant patter of a galloping horse. Such a sound at such a time is ominous to duffing bullock drivers; so, as I sprang to my feet, you may be sure my companions were not much behind me. Along the track, a mile in advance of the wagons, we saw an approaching horseman. And as if this was n't enough, we heard the sound of an axe in the selection.

"Holy glory! there 's somebody livin' in the hut, after all!" ejaculated Mosey.

The house stood on a very slight rise, where the clump of swamp box terminated, a quarter of a mile away; and, sure enough, we could see, through a gap in the undergrowth of old-man salt-bush, a man chopping wood at the edge of the clump. But he seemed quite unconscious of the multitude of bullocks that, scattered all over the paddock, were laying in a fresh supply of grass.

"It 's Moriarty," sighed Thompson, gazing at the horseman. "He 's been sent to catch us. It 's all up."

Then, like the sound of many waters, rose the mingled sentiments of the company, as each man dragged on his boots with a celerity beyond description.

"You keep him on a string, Collins, while we coller as many of the carrion as we"——

"What use? It 's a summonsing match already. Look at the fence! And Martin lives in the hut, after all. He 's between us and the bullocks now—laughing at us. What business had we to travel on"——

"Demmit, suggest something. Make use of me in this emergency, I beg of you. Shall I"——

"Port Phillip, all over. Jist let me deliver this (adj.) load. That 's all I"——

"Comes o' young pups knowin' heverythink. I kep' misdoubtin' all the (adj.) time"——

"Are you fellows mad?" shouted the young storekeeper, as he dashed past the group, and pulled his blown horse round in a circle. "Out with those bullocks as quick as the devil 'll let you! Martin 's on top of you! I 've just given him the slip! We were sent from the station expressly to nip you. Fly round! blast you, fly round!"

At the word, Cooper and Thompson snatched up their bridles and darted off, followed by Price and Willoughby. Dixon and Bum were not in the crowd, but no one had leisure just then to notice their absence.

"Len 's yer horse, like a good feller," said Mosey hastily.

"To (sheol) with your cheek!" snapped Moriarty. "What next, I wonder?" Mosey snatched up his bridle, and went off at a run. "Hello, Collins! I did n't notice you in the hurry. Bright cards, ain't they? Nothing short of seven years 'll satisfy them. You 've been travelling all night?"

"No; I camped here with the teams."

"I thought, when I saw the saddled horse, that you had just turned him in to get a bite."

"He 's not saddled. There 's my saddle."

"I thought that was your horse—that black one with the new saddle on." (I should explain that Moriarty, being mounted, could see across the old-man salt-bush, which I could not.) "But, I say," he continued; "what do you mean by stopping here instead of making for the station? I 've a dash good mind to tell Mrs. Beaudesart. Why, it 's two months since you parted from her."

"Where 's Martin?" I asked.

"I left him at the ram-paddock, trying to track his horse. I suppose you have n't heard that he lives here now?"

"Well, we heard that some one was being sent to live here. By the way, Moriarty, you better keep out of sight of that fellow at the hut."

"No odds. It 's only Daddy Montague; he can't see twenty yards. But I say—Mrs. Beaudesart is sorting out her own old wedding toggery; she knows you 'll never have money enough to"——

"How does Martin come to be at the ram-paddock, if he lives here?" I interrupted.

"I 'll tell you the whole rigmarole," replied the genial ass. "Martin was at the station yesterday, crawling after Miss King, when up comes a sandy-whiskered hound of a contractor, name of M'Nab, to see about the specifications of the new fence between us and Nalrooka; and this (fellow)'s idea of getting on the soft side of Montgomery, about the fence, was to nearly break his neck running to tell him that Price, and Thompson, and a whole swag of other fellows, intended to work on the ram-paddock that night. That would be last night, of course. Now, Montgomery does n't bark about a night's grass out of the ram-paddock at this time of year, in case of emergency; but he does n't believe in people driving expressly for it; and besides, he badly wants to catch Price and Thompson, and make an example of them. Well, it happened that he had thought out early jobs for all the rest of the fellows, so what does he do—Sunday and all—but he rouses out Martin and me, and tells us to go to the ram-paddock, and quietly round up all the bullocks, and bring them to the station. No hurry, of course, so I got playing cards with some of the shearers, and Martin got yarning with the old wool-classer; and we timed ourselves to be at the ram-paddock just before daylight. Of course, the right plan would have been to go through the ration-paddock, and in by the Quondong gate; and that was what I wanted to do. Then we could have made a circuit of the ram-paddock, inside the fence, and given it a good rough overhaul. But because I proposed this, Martin insisted on going by the main road, for better riding, and to see if we could find the wagons, as a sort of guide. Sensible to the last. Well, he would have it his own way, and I did n't give a curse, so on we went; and just as we were crossing the sort of hollow at this near corner of the ram-paddock, the God-forsaken old fool thought he heard cattle in the timber. So we tied our horses at the fence, and walked across to see. Nothing there, of course, only imagination and kangaroo. We stayed about ten minutes—me moralising about fools, and him sulking—and when we came back to where we had left our horses, mine was there by himself. Martin was dancing mad, for his horse was never known to break a bridle, and he did n't know who to blame for making away with him. However, I was n't any way interested in mustering the ram-paddock, and Martin wanted his horse, so we hunted round and round, but devil a smell of horse or saddle or bridle could we find in the dark. After a while, daylight came, and I caught sight of the wool, and tumbled to the little game. Of course, I ripped across to give the fellows the office, praying and cursing fit to break my neck. What the dickens induced them to run the risk of duffing here? Maddest thing I ever knew. Martin has been living here since this day week; and his greatest pleasure in life is prowling round when he ought to be asleep."

"Warrigal Alf laid Mosey on," I replied. "At least, he said he had stayed here the night before last, and had taken his bullocks out after they lay down."

"Ah! the treacherous beggar! I 'll tell you how that came. Day before yesterday—let 's see—that was Saturday—Montgomery and Martin met Alf just at the station, coming along behind some other teams. Montgomery was sorry in his own mind for a blaggarding he gave Alf last winter, for letting his bullocks get into our horse-paddock. Seems they got adrift from Bottara, while Alf was unloading, and had gone the thirty miles, right across country, with him after them full chase. Alf was too ill-natured to explain things at the time: and he never mentioned it when he loaded our first wool, a month ago. Montgomery heard the truth of it only the other day; so when he met Alf, he stopped him, and mentioned it, and told him to shove his bullocks in Martin's paddock for that night, as grass was so scarce. It must have cut Martin to the bone to see a kindly thing done, but he had to grin and bear it—treasuring up wrath against the day of wrath, as Shakespear says."

"Then Martin may be here any minute?"

"Well, I left him a little better than two mile away, trying to track his horse, and he can't track worth a dash. Certainly, he was headed toward the station the last I saw of him. But if he 's got a spare saddle at home here, he 's pretty certain to come for a fresh horse, to hunt up the other. I 'd give five notes, if I had it, to see these (fellows) yoked up and off; for if Martin catches them, there 'll be (sheol) to pay, and no pitch hot; and, by George! there 's not half a second to lose. Just look at that fence! Ah!

here they come! Good lads! Well, take care of yourself, Tom, and give us a call at the station as soon as you can. I 'll keep out of sight till these chaps are started; then I 'll have a bit of break-fast with Daddy Montague, and invent a good watertight lie, and do a skulk for an hour or two, and then dodge on to the station as slowly as possible. I want something to go wrong in the store while Montgomery has charge himself; it 'll learn him to appre-ciate me better. I 'll have to ram it down his throat that the fellows had their bullocks out before I got here."

"Wait, Moriarty—what 's Martin's horse like? I might see him."

"Liver-colour; star and snip; white hind feet; bang tail. One of the best mokes on the station. Belongs to Martin himself. I hope he 'll scratch the bridle off, and roll on the saddle till it 's not worth a cuss. I say—if Martin should find his way here before the fellows get clear, will you just tell him I fancied I saw his horse going for the Connelly paddock, and I shot after him hell-for-leather. No message for Mrs. Beaudesart? Well, so long." And the good and faithful young servant cantered away toward an adjacent cane-grass swamp.

I was picking up my possum rug and saddle, when I heard Dixon's voice, in earnest entreaty. Looking round, I saw him sit-ting on the edge of his hammock.

"Say, Collins—will you fetch my (adj.) bullocks, while yer hand 's in? I can't har'ly move this mornin'."

"Yes, Dixon; I won't see you beat, if I can help it. What 's the matter?"

"Well, I was on top o' my load las' night, gittin'—gittin' some tobacker an' matches; an' I come a buster on top o' one o' the yokes here. It 's put a (adj.) set on me, any road."

With a few words of condolence, I entered the paddock, carrying my saddle and bridle. As I came in sight of Cleopatra, I was con-strained to pause and reflect. The horse was feeding composedly, saddled and bridled; a pair of hobbles hanging to the saddle. The bridle was a cheap affair, but the saddle was as good as they make them in Wagga, and quite new. During the previous afternoon, I had marked something incongruous in Bum's ownership of such a piece of furniture. But being always, I trust, superior to anything like surprise, I saddled and mounted Bunyip, took Cleopatra by the rein, and joined the Ishmaelites, who, on their bare-backed horses, were hurrying contingents of cattle from different directions toward the gap of the fence, whilst the fascination of overhanging danger bore so heavily on their personal and professional dignity that every eye kept an anxious look-out toward the ram-paddock. In a few minutes more, we were all outside the fence; and the drivers immediately began yoking. I hooked Cleopatra's rein on a wool-lever, and, still riding Bunyip, kept Thompson's and Cooper's bullocks together. Mosey's dog was performing the same office for him and Price. Willoughby had n't returned with the muster; and Bum was still absent.

"Did you count my (bullocks)?" demanded Dixon, limping slowly and painfully toward his big roan horse.

"O you sweet speciment!" retorted Mosey, as he picked up his second yoke. "Why the (compound expletive) don't you rouse roun'?"

"How the (same expression) ken I rouse roun'? I got the screwmatics in my (adj.) hip."

"Somethin' like you—Stan' over, Rodney, or I 'll twist the tail off o' you—You don't ketch me havin' nothin' wrong o' me when things is"——

"No, begad! no you don't!—take that! ah! would you indeed!— on you go, dem you! s-s-s-s-s! get up there!" It was Willoughby's voice among the salt-bush; and, the next moment, half-a-dozen beasts leaped the wires and darted, capering and shying, past the wagons. *"Quod petis hic est!"* panted their pursuer triumphantly. "The mouse may help the lion, remember, according to the old"——

Then such a cataract of obscenity and invective from Price and Mosey, while Cooper remarked gravely:

"Them ain't our bullocks, Willerby; them 's station cattle— shoved in that paddick for something partic'lar. Now they 're off to (sheol); an' it 's three good hours' work with a horse an' stock-whip, to git 'em in here agen. An' that kangaroo dog ain't makin' matters much better. Lord stan' by us now! for we 'll git (adv.) near hung if we 're caught."

And, to be sure, there was Pup looping himself along the plain in hot pursuit. It was no use attempting to call him off, for Nature has not endowed the kangaroo dog with sufficient instinct to bring him in touch with his master, except when the latter offers him food. But there is always some penalty attached to the possession of anything really valuable. So, though I was n't interested in the cattle, I was bound to follow them till I recovered my dog. Thompson's unpretentious stockwhip was in my hand at the time; and, judging it unlikely that Cleopatra had been broken in to the use of that disquieting implement, I was just turning Bunyip round, when Willoughby stepped forward——

"Permit me to redeem my unfortunate mistake by assisting you!" he exclaimed. "I have ridden to hounds in England. May I take this horse? Thanks. Pray remember that I shall be under your orders, Collins."

"Take care might he buck-lep," I remarked casually, as the whaler gathered Cleopatra's reins, and threw himself into the deep seat of the new saddle.

And, to my genuine astonishment, he did buck-lep. But he took no mean advantage of his rider; he allowed him time to find the off stirrup, and then led off with a forward spring about five feet high. Willoughby—small blame to him—was jerked clean out of the saddle, and lit fair across the horse's loins; in the impulse of self-preservation grasping the cantle with both hands. The small thigh-pads afforded a good rough hold, and the next buck jammed the poor fellow well under the seat of the saddle. The position was neither pleasant nor dignified, though certainly more secure for an amateur than the conventional style; particularly after the horse's tremendous plunges had raised the back of the saddle a foot or more by dint of fair wedging.

Price, Mosey, Thompson, and Cooper forgot the dangers of the time, and discontinued their work, drawing near the spot with a carefully preserved air of indifference and pre-occupation. Even Dixon ignored his screwmatics, and composed his demeanour to something like apathy.

Owing to the leverage of the saddle, the girth was gripping Cleopatra in a ticklish place, and the bow of the saddle was dipping into another ticklish place, whilst Willoughby's swinging feet provided for the ticklish places on the horse's thighs and flanks. Cleopatra mistook all this for deliberate provocation, and responded to the very best of his splendid ability. Early in the entertainment, Willoughby's hat was bucked off his head; presently the wellington boot was bucked off one foot, and the blucher off the other, the prince-alberts following in due course. Then the portion of attire known to one section of society as 'linen', and to another as the 'beef-bag', was bucked out of that necessary garment which we shrink from naming. The ground was cut up as if rooted by pigs; yet Cleopatra was only just warming to his work; and the whaler was still clinging to the saddle like a native bear to a branch.

"God help thee, Jack," I remarked listlessly; "thou hast a bitter breakfast on 't."

"He 'll tire the horse out yet," said Thompson, with an artificial yawn. "Good lad, Willoughby! stick to him a bit longer."

"Got no holt," observed Dixon. "Gone goose, any time."

"He don't want no pipeclay, anyhow," said Mosey, with childish levity. "Dark-complexion people ought to steer clear o' playful horses."

All eyes were turned on the young fellow's face in surprise and reprehension; and he uneasily attempted to carry off his inadvertent solecism with a sort of swagger.

"The horse can't hold out much longer at that rate," repeated Thompson, stooping to lace his boots.

"Can't he?" drawled Cooper, poking out the stem of his pipe with a stalk of grass. "He can hold out till something gives way. That 's what he 's in the habit o' doin', I 'm thinkin'; an' he ain't goin' to break his rule this time."

"The Far-downer got at you that trip, Collins," remarked Mosey, seeking to retrieve his dignity by turning his back on the performance. "He seen you comin'. Say, ole son—how'd you like to swap back?"

"I kep' misdoubtin' that hoss all the (adj.) time," observed Nestor wisely. "I felt sort o' jubious, on'y I did n't wanter say nothink."

"There goes the pore (fellow) at last; I knowed the horse would do it," said Cooper, as the stern captive spurn'd his weary load, and asked the image back that heaven bestowed.

"Collar the horse quick!" suggested Dixon. "Nail him now, or you 'll never ketch him."

"No great hurry," I muttered, dismounting. "However, I think I 'd better have it out with him while he 's warm. Or perhaps one of you fellows would like a try, while I do his yoking—just for a change?"

Cleopatra, now nibbling the scanty grass, glanced from time to time with grave sympathy at his late rider, who was occupying himself with his toilet.

"Ketch the (horse) quick!" reiterated Dixon.

"I would n't mind if I had my mare back again," I remarked, as I approached Cleopatra's head. "By Jacob's staff I swear I have no mind of trying conclusions with this fellow for a dull, sickening"——

The adjectives were shorn of their noun, for Cleopatra, accurately gauging his distance, suddenly sprung round and lashed out with both hind feet. You could have struck a match on the smoothest part of my earthly tabernacle as I dodged him by about half an inch. Then he went on cropping the grass as before, while I looked round and inquired with sickly bravado, "What noble Lucumo comes next, to taste our Roman cheer?"

But the bullock drivers silently repudiated the grim invitation, and hurried back to their work, which they now pursued with redoubled vigour and anxiety. I remounted Bunyip, and caught Cleopatra from his back. Then dismounting, I arranged the new saddle with ostentatious offhandedness, though in a prayerful frame of mind, and presently climbed on as if nothing was the matter. I certainly anticipated Westminster Abbey rather than a peerage; but the horse, with a nonchalance greater than my own, inasmuch as it was genuine, turned quietly round as I pressed the rein against his neck, and sailed away across the plain at his own inimitable canter. Then I looked back to see the bullock drivers disgustedly resume the work they had again suspended.

By this time the cattle had crossed a cane-grass swamp, and were out of sight; but before I had gone a quarter of a mile I saw Pup coming to meet me, limping and crestfallen. He had probably been kicked by one of the absconders; and as he could see no sign of civilisation except our camp, his sagacity had drawn him back. Well pleased, therefore, I returned to the wagons after a few minutes' absence.

"The cattle are out of sight, Steve," said I, as I rounded up the scattering bullocks. "Not worth while to go after them now."

"Let them go, by all means," replied Thompson, with a ghastly simulation of cheerfulness. "We 'll gladly stand the loss of them, and make the station a present of Bum's mare besides, if we once get out of sight of this infernal camp—Stand up, Magpie—Just let us yoke up as quickly as if our lives depended on it—which, to tell the truth, is not much of an exag——Hello! where's Damper?"

"Stuck in a gluepot, jist in front o' the (adj.) hut," replied Mosey, without pausing in his work. "I seen him there—Back, Snailey, or I 'll knock the (adj.) horn off o' you—but I thought it was one o' them station cattle till you minded me. Why the (sheol) did n't you count yer lot properly?"

A deep oath broke from the lips of the man who never swore. But he controlled himself by a strong effort.

"How much of him's above ground?" he asked.

"(Adv.) little on'y his horns; or else I 'd 'a' knowed him—Wub-back, Major," replied Mosey reluctantly, as he chained his last pair.

Then, I grieve to say, Thompson let himself out. No puerile repetition; no slovenly, slipshod work there. It was the perform-ance of a born orator and poet, and one who, like Timothy, had

known the Scriptures from a child—a long, involved litany of
seething malediction, delivered, moreover, with a measured and
effortless eloquence and a grammatical exactitude which left St.
Ernulphus a bad second. The other fellows pursued their work in
awe-stricken silence, till at length Cooper, glancing toward the
ram-paddock, said deprecatingly:

"— — it, man, don't swear; not now, anyway. I'll fetch these
ten across, an' they 'll (adv.) soon snake him out. Git that spare
rope off o' my wagon, an' foller me quick."

He brought his yoked bullocks through the gap, and drove them
rapidly to the spot indicated by Mosey. Thompson mounted his
horse and cantered after, with the heavy coil of rope across the
front of his saddle. I accompanied him. At the very extremity of
the clump, and not fifty yards from the house, was one of those
bottomless quagmires too common in Riverina. It was about twenty
yards across; and, in the very centre, Damper's head and the line
of his back appeared above the surface; the straight furrow behind
him showing that he had been bogged at the edge, but being unable
to turn, and being exceedingly strong and sound, had worked himself along to the middle, where he was slowly settling down.

In a couple of minutes, one end of the wool-rope—sixty feet long
and an inch and a-half in diameter—was looped round the roots of
the bullock's horns, and the team was attached to the fall. Then
a slow, steady strain drove Damper's nose into the ground, and
gently shifted him, first forward, then upward, then on to the surface, where he slid smoothly to the solid ground. We released him
there, and he staggered to his feet, shook himself thoroughly, and
followed the team to the camp, ravenously snatching mouthfuls of
grass as he went along.

Price and Mosey had just got under way. Willoughby was trying to yoke Dixon's leaders, while Dixon, owing to his screwmatics,
could do nothing but sit on his horse, cursing with wearisome taut-
ology, and casting glances of frantic apprehension toward the ram-
paddock. His anxiety was not unreasonable, for there had just
come into sight an upright speck, too small to be a horseman; and
it was easy to guess who was the likeliest person to be coming on
foot from that direction. There is a limit to the dignified sufficiency
even of a bullock driver; and the unhappy conjecture of circumstances had driven Dixon past this point.

"Stiddy, now; go stiddy, an' keep yer (adj.) mouth shut. Now
lay right (adv.) bang up to him; jam him agen the off-sider, so 's

he can 't shift. There! block him! (Sheol)! Let him rip now. O may the" &c., &c.

"Dixon! Dixon! I must protest"——

"Purtest be (verbed). Fetch 'em up agen. Don't be frightened; they 'on't bite. Yoke on yer other (adj.) shoulder. Right. Git well up agen him this time. Lay yer whole (adj.) weight on-to him, an' jam him, so 's he can't budge if it was to save his (adj.) life."

Willoughby, with the yoke on his shoulder, and the off-side bow in his hand, gingerly approached the excited bullocks, essaying a light touch on the near-sider's shrinking shoulder. The next moment, he was reeling backward, and both bullocks were gone. Eve's curse on Cain, in Byron's fine drama, is mere balderdash to what followed on Dixon's part.

"Dem your soul, you uncultivated savage! you force me to inform you that your helpless condition was my incentive to these well-meant efforts on your behalf—as, begad! it is now the only consideration which restrains"——

"O, go to (sheol). You 're no (adj.) good. You ain't fit to (purvey offal to Bruin). An' here 's them (adj.) sneaks gone; an' Martin he 'll be on top o' me in about two (adj.) twos; an' me left by my own (adj.) self, like a (adj.) natey cat in a (adj.) trap. May the holy" &c., &c. "If I 'd that horse," he continued, glancing furiously at Cleopatra, "I 'd make him smell (adj. sheol)."

"Nonsense, Dixon," said I pleasantly; "the horse is not annoying you. Ah! Willoughby; *Ne ultra*—no, let 's see—*Ne sutor ultra crepidam*. Let me try my hand there. I took my degree of B.D.—which does n't always signify Bachelor of Divinity—before you took your B.A. Will you just bring up the unspeakables as Dixon points them out."

"*Palmam qui meruit ferat*," responded Willoughby, instantly recovering his temper. "Smoker—Nelson—dem your skins, come up once more!"

Dixon's bullocks were exceptionally docile, for that uncultivated animal was one of the most humane and skilful drivers in Riverina; therefore, about twenty-five minutes sufficed to place his team in readiness for a start.

"You might as well come along o' me for a change," said he to Willoughby. "We 'll git on grand together. I 'm a quiet, agreeable sort o' (person), though I say it myself; an' I would n't wish for better (adj.) company nor you. Come on; you won't be sorry after."

"Quocunque trahunt fata sequamur," rejoined Willoughby, bowing gaily to me. Then taking up the whip—Dixon was a virtuoso in whips, and always carried one with six feet of handle, and twelve feet of lash—he aimed at the team, collectively, a clip which, in the most literal sense, recoiled on himself. And so the officer's son and the sojer's son took their way together; to become, as I afterward learned, the most attached and mutually considerate friends on the track. Such is life.

Thompson and Cooper, now ready for the road, were repairing the fence as well as they could. This being done, and the relics of the fire kicked about, they put their teams in motion, leaving little trace of the camp, except Bum's mare, standing asleep outside the fence. The ominous speck on the plain had approached much nearer, but had taken definite form as an emu; and now the negative blessing of escape seemed like a positive benefaction. "If," says Carlyle, "thou wert condemned to be hanged—which is probably less than thou deservest—thou wouldest esteem it happiness to be shot."

Serene gratitude therefore shone in the frank faces of the outlaws; tempered, however, in Thompson's case, by salutary remorse, for his companion had reproachfully asked him what the (adj. sheol) good his swearing had done.

We could see Price's teams stopped, half a mile away; one of the loads appearing low, and canted over to the off side; bogged, evidently. Dixon's wagon was close in front of us; Willoughby was zealously flogging himself, and occasionally we could hear Dixon's voice in encouragement and counsel.

The place where Price's wagon was stuck was not a creek, but merely a narrow belt of treacherous ground. Mosey had n't gone down six inches, but Price had happened on a bad place, and his wagon had found the bottom. All Mosey's team, except the polers, had been hooked on, but with no result beyond the breaking of a well-worn chain.

"Ain't got puddin' enough, Thompson," said Mosey, as my companions stopped their teams and went on to survey the place. "The (adv.) thunderin' ole morepoke he goes crawlin' into the rottenest place he could fine. You shove your team in nex' the polers, an' I 'll hook our lot on in front. Your chains 'll stan' to fetch (sheol) out by the (adj.) roots. Please the pigs, we 'll git out o' sight afore that ole (overseer) comes."

Thompson did as desired; and the first pull brought the wagon on to solid ground. Meanwhile Dixon and Willoughby had taken their team through, and were hurrying along. Cooper, growling maledictions on everything connected with Port Phillip—roads in particular—had selected his route, and started his team. Thompson hooked on to his own wagon, and crossed safely, but with very little to spare.

"Touch-and-go," he remarked to me; "another bale would have anchored her. Ah! Cooper 's in it, with all his cleverness."

Cooper was in it. The two-ton *Hawkesbury,* with seven-and-a-half tons of load, was down to the axle-beds; and the Cornstalk was endeavouring, by means of extracts from the sermons of Knox's soundest followers, to do something like justice to the contingency. Thompson sighed, glanced toward the ram-paddock, and hooked his team in front of Cooper's. Mosey, who had been mending his broken chain with wire, now came over with Price.

"We 'll give you a lend of our whips," said he with cheap complaisance. "Take the leaders yerself, Thompson. Stiddy now, till I give the word, or we 'll be fetching the (adj.) handle out of her. Now—pop it on-to 'em!"

Then thirty-six picked bullocks planted their feet and prised, and a hundred and seventy feet of bar chain stretched tense and rigid from the leaders' yoke to the pole-cap. The wagon crept forward. A low grumble, more a growl than a bellow, passed from beast to beast along the team—sure indication that the wagon would n't stop again if it could be taken through. The off front wheel rose slowly on harder ground; the off hind wheel rose in its turn; both near wheels ploughed deeper beneath the top-heavy weight of thirty-eight bales——

"She 's over!" thundered Cooper. "Keep her goin'—it 's her on'y chance!"

Then the heavy pine whipsticks bent like bulrushes in the drivers' skilful hands, while a spray of dissevered hair, and sometimes a line of springing blood, followed each detonation—the libretto being in keeping. A few yards forward still, while both off wheels rose to the surface, and both near wheels sank till the naves burrowed in the ground; then the wagon swung heavily over on its near side.

"Good-bye, John," said Cooper, with fine immobility. "Three-man job, by rights. Will you give us a hand, Collins?" For Price and Mosey were silently returning to their teams.

"Certainly, I will."

"Well, it 's a half-day's contract. I 'll git some breakfast ready, while you (fellows) unloosens the ropes."

Thompson and I released the bullocks from the pole, unfastened the ropes, and brought the wagon down to its wheels again. Then Cooper summoned us to breakfast.

"You 'll jist take sort o' pot-luck, Collins," he remarked. "I should 'a' baked some soda bread an' boiled some meat last night, on'y for bein' too busy doin' nothing. Laziness is catchin'. That 's why I hate a lot o' fellers campin' together; it 's nothing but yarn, yarn; an' your wagon ain't greazed, an' your tarpolin ain't looked to; an' nothin' done but yarn, yarn; an' you floggin' in your own mind at not gittin' ahead o' your work. That 's where women 's got the purchase on us (fellows). When a lot o' women gits together, one o' them reads out something religious, an' the rest all wires in at sewin', or knittin', or some (adj.) thing. They can't suffer to be idle, nor to see anybody else idle—women can't." Cooper was an observer. It was pleasant to hear him philosophise.

The work of reloading was made severe and tedious by the lack of any better skids than the poles of the two wagons—was, indeed, made impossible under the circumstances, but for Cooper's enormous and well-saved strength. Our toil was enlivened, however, by an argument as to the esoteric cause of the capsize. Cooper maintained that nothing better could have been hoped for, after leaving Kenilworth shed on a Friday; Thompson, untrammelled by such superstition, contended that the misadventure was solely due to travelling on Sunday; whilst I held it to be merely a proof that Cooper, in spite of his sins, was n't deserted yet. Each of us supported his argument by a wealth of illustrative cases, and thus fortified his own stubborn opinion to his own perfect satisfaction. Then, descending to more tangible things, we discussed Cleopatra. Here we were unanimous in deciding that the horse had, as yet, disclosed only two faults, and these not the faults of the Irishman's horse in the weary yarn. One of them, we concluded, was to buck like a demon on being first mounted, and the other was to grope backward for the person who went to catch him after delivery of loading.

In the meantime, four horsemen, with three pack-horses, went by; then two horse teams, loaded outward; then Stewart, of Kooltopa, paused to give a few words of sympathy as he drove past; then far ahead, we saw two wool teams, evidently from Boolka, converging slowly toward the main track; then more wool came in sight from the pine-ridge, five or six miles behind. By this time, it was after mid-day; and Cooper, having tied the last levers, looked round before descending from the load.

"Somebody on a grey horse comin' along the track from the ram-paddick, an' another (fellow) on a brown horse comin' across the plain," he remarked. "Wonder if one o' them 's Martin—an' he 's rose a horse at the station?"

"I was thinking about to-night," replied Thompson. "I' d forgot Martin. Duffing soon comes under the what-you-may-call-him."

"Statute of Limitations?" I suggested.

"Yes. Come and have a drink of tea, and a bit of Cooper's pastry. His cookery does n't fatten, but it fills up."

"O you (adj.) liar," gently protested the Cornstalk, as he seated himself on the ground beside the tucker-box. "Is this Martin?"— for the man on the grey horse was approaching at a canter.

"No," I replied; "he 's a stranger to me."

"But that 's Martin on the brown horse," said Thompson, with rising vexation. "Keep him on a string, Tom, if you can. Don't let him drive us into a lie about last night, for, after all, I 'll be hanged if I 'm man enough to tell him the truth, nor won't be for the next fortnight or three weeks."

By this time, the man on the grey horse was passing us. In response to Thompson's invitation, he stopped and dismounted.

"Jist help yourself, an' your friends 'll like you the better, as the sayin' is," said Cooper, handing him a pannikin.

"Thanks. I 'll do so; I did n't have any breakfast this morning," replied the stranger, picking up a johnny-cake (which liberal shepherds give a grosser name), and eating it with relish, while the interior lamina of dough spued out from between the charred crusts under the pressure of his strong teeth. "Been having a little mishap?"

"Yes; nothing broke, though."

"How long since my lads passed? I see their tracks on the road."

"About three hours," replied Thompson. "Did you meet an old man and a young fellow, with wool—grey horse behind one of the wagons? Good day, Mr. Martin. Have a drink of tea?"

"Yes, I met them," replied the stranger. "Old Price's teams, I think—Good day, Martin—six or seven miles from here; Dixon travelling behind, with another fellow driving his team—long-lost brother, apparently."

"Where did you fellows have your bullocks last night?" demanded Martin, his eye resting on the sun-cracked stucco which covered three-fourths of Damper's colossal personality.

"And did you see a dark chestnut horse; bang tail; star and snip; white hind feet; saddle and bridle on?" I asked. "I ran across Moriarty this morning," I continued, turning politely to Martin; "and he told me he was after a horse of that description; but he was in a hurry"——

"Dark chestnut horse; bang tail; star and snip; white hind feet; JR near shoulder; like 2 in circle off thigh," said the stranger reflectively. "Yes; I saw the horse this morning, but the owner has got him again—red-headed young fellow; tweed pants, strapped with moleskin. I met him at the Nalrooka boundary shortly after sunrise—thirty miles from here, I should say. I was speaking to him. He told me the horse had slung him and got away last night, and he had found him by good luck before daylight this morning. He came down on his hand, poor beggar; it 's swelled like a boxing-glove. But he 's taking it out of the horse."

Now, in the Riverina of that period, it was considered much more disgraceful to be had by a scoundrel than to commit a felony yourself; therefore Martin, partly grasping the situation, assumed an oblivious, and even drowsy, air.

"Did the young fellow say where he was going?" I asked, pitying Martin's dilemma, and admiring his greatness of soul, for I had more than once been there myself.

"No; he only wanted to borrow a pipe of tobacco; but after we parted I saw him strike out across the plain to the right."

Martin yawned, turned his horse, and rode slowly toward the selection. Very slowly, so that the stranger might overtake him soon. Come weal, come woe, he would n't trail his honour in the dust before three cynical onlookers.

"Well, I 'll push on," said the stranger, setting down his pannikin. "I want to pull my chaps, and I 'm thinking about my horse. I say"—glancing after Martin, and lowering his voice—"you fellows have a devil of a bad show for to-night."

"You 're right," replied Thompson.

"Tell you what you 'll do: Camp at the balahs, and they 'll think you 're on for the ration-paddock; then, between the two lights, just scoot for the Dead Horse Swamp."

"Never any grass there," said Thompson.

"That 's the beauty of it," replied the stranger. "They 've been putting down a tank in the middle of the swamp this winter; and the contractor had about a dozen young fellows, every one of them with a horse and a dog, kicking up (sheol) 's delight. There has n't been a smell of a sheep within coo-ee of the swamp for the last three months; and the paddock was mustered for shearing just

before the contractor left. It 's into your hand for to-night. Well,
I must"——

"I beg your pardon," said Thompson hesitatingly—"Are you
coming direct from Hay?"

"Well, I left on Saturday morning."

"The mailman was telling me," continued Thompson wistfully,
"that Permewan and Wright had three ton of dynamite for Broken
Hill. Do you know is it gone yet?"

"Not when I left," replied the Encyclopedia Australiensis.
"They 're offering eighty, and I 've no doubt they 'll spring to a
hundred. Extra-hazardous tack; and there 's not a blade of grass
once you pass the Merowie. Good day, boys." And, nodding to
us collectively, he departed.

"Steve," said I; "are you a man to go fooling with high ex-
plosives,—considering the thing that 's on you?"

"Well," replied Thompson doggedly, "it 's come to this with me,
that I must make a spoon or spoil a horn; and if that infernal thing
would only keep off till I got the stuff delivered, I 'd be right. My
bullocks are fit for any track in Australia."

"Let 's git down to Hay fust," interposed Cooper; "then you can
do as you like; but I 'll be wantin' a way-bill that 'll take me safe
out o' Port Phillip. Say, Collins; I 'll buy that new saddle off o'
you. Mine 's all in splinters, for my horse he 's a beggar to roll."

"I 'd hardly feel justified in selling it," I replied. "But I 'll tell
you what I 'll do: I 'll sell you my own saddle cheap—say, three
notes—and give you Bum's bridle in."

Cooper agreed to the proposal. Then, as Pup had been eating
about ten pounds of salt mutton, stolen from the bullock drivers'
stores, I enticed him to take a good drink of water, knowing he
would need it before the day was over. It was absolutely imperative that I should go thirty miles, and then, if possible, camp alone.
So I shook hands with the outlaws, and started; leading Bunyip
till he should become accustomed to his new companion.

If the unmannerly reader wishes to know why I was bound to a
stage of exactly thirty miles, I have no objection to state that, knowing the geography of Riverina as well as if I had laid out the whole
territory myself, I was aware of a sand-hill composed of material
unstable as water; an unfavourable place for a bucking horse, and
a favourable place for a man to dismount head foremost, if the
worst came; and that sand-hill was my destination.

CHAPTER II

WHEN I undertook the pleasant task of writing out these reminiscences, I engaged, you will remember, to amplify the record of
one week; judging that a rigidly faithful analysis of that sample
would disclose the approximate percentage of happiness, virtue,
&c., in Life. But whilst writing the annotations on Sept. 9th (which,
by the way, gratuitously overlap on the following day), I saw an
alpine difficulty looming ahead. At the Blowhard Sand-hill, on the
night of the 10th, I camped with a party of six sons of Belial,
bound for Deniliquin, with 3,000 Boolka wethers off the shears.
Now, anyone who has listened for four hours to the conversation
of a group of sheep drovers, named, respectively, Splodger, Rabbit,
Parson, Bottler, Dingo, and Hairy-toothed Ike, will agree with me
as to the impossibility of getting the dialogue of such *dramatis
personæ* into anything like printable form. The bullock drivers
were bad enough, but these fellows are out of the question.

Then it occurred to me that a wider scope of observation might
give, in perhaps fewer pages, a fairer estimate of that ageless
enigma, the true solution of which forms our all-embracing and
only responsibility. I therefore concluded to skip one calendar
month, dipping again into my old diary at Oct. 9th in the same
year, namely, '83.

After this, I shall pick out of each consecutive month the 9th
day for amplification and comment, keeping not too long in one
tune, but a snip and away. This will prospect the gutter of Life
(gutter is good) at different points; in other words, it will give us
a range of seven months instead of seven days.

The thread of narrative being thus purposely broken, no one of
these short and simple analyses can have any connection with
another—a point on which I congratulate the judicious reader and
the no less judicious writer; for the former is thereby tacitly
warned against any expectation of plot or denouement, and so
secured against disappointment, whilst the latter is relieved from

the (to him) impossible task of investing prosaic people with romance, and a generally hap-hazard economy with poetical justice. Go to, then.

TUES. OCT. 9. Goolumbulla. To Rory's.

This record transports you (saving reverence of our 'birth stain') something more than a hundred miles northward from the scene sketched in Chap. I, thus unveiling a territory blank on the map, and similarly qualified in the ordinary conversation of its inhabitants.

The Willandra Billabong, which in moderately wet seasons relieves the Middle Lachlan of some superfluous water, and in epoch-marking flood-times reluctantly debouches into the Lower Darling, divides the country between those rivers into two unequal parts. Roughly speaking—the black-soil plains (which are chiefly light red) lie to the south of this almost imperceptible depression, whilst on the north—sometimes close by, sometimes out of sight, and sometimes thirty miles away—the irregular scrub-frontier denotes an abrupt change of soil, though the uniform level is maintained.

Here you enter upon a region presenting to the rarely clouded sky an unbroken foliage-surface, with isothermal zones rigidly marked by their indigenous growths. A tract of country until yesterday bare of surface water for lack of occupation, and lacking occupation for dearth of surface water. Which goes to show that regularity of rainfall is not ensured by copious growth of timber.

However, a hundred miles back in that leafy solitude,—just where the line of water conservation, creeping northward from the Lachlan, here and there touched the line creeping southward from the Darling,—I was standing in the veranda of the barracks, on Goolumbulla station, when the narangies' pagan henchman announced, "Blikfit leddy, all li."

During the meal, Jack Ward, the senior narangy, made some remark implying that certain cattle, on a certain occasion, had scented water from a fabulous distance. Whereupon Andrews, the storekeeper, interrogated deponent with some severity, driving him down, down, to three hundred yards' range, where he made a final stand. But the two junior narangies supported Ward in the endowment of cattle with the faculty in question; and, as a matter of course, each young fellow supplemented his limited experience by a number of instances, all alike distinguished by that want of proper hang which makes the judicious grieve.

A practical knowledge of the subject, founded on irrefragable proofs, led me to side with Andrews; and it was thus that I came to quote a case in point, with all the advantage of local reference. It will be necessary to lay the facts before you:—

In Feb., '81—two years and eight months before the date of this record—I had drawn up to Goolumbulla homestead with six tons of wire. The manager, Mr. Spanker, in his fine, off-hand way, asked me to just dump it down carelessly in five or six places over the run, as the contractor would be using it at once. He would pay me for the extra mileage; and Dan O'Connell would show me where to sling it off. I objected to the mileage arrangement, inasmuch as carting over raw ground was a very different thing from travelling on a track. I wanted £1 a day for the extra time—a fair current rate, and easily counted. Mr Spanker, in reply, had no objection to paying by the day; but, as my account came to £42, and as it had taken me twelve weeks to do the two hundred and thirty miles from Hay, and as the contractor had been cursing me steadily for the last four weeks—well, if I asked him anything about it, he thought that ten shillings came nearer the mark, and was almost as easily counted. Finally, with that pliancy of temper which keeps me down in the world, I assented to these terms; whereupon Spanker, with characteristic perversity, called it fifteen.

Next day, following Andrews's directions, I took the faint track of the ration cart for seven or eight miles, and found a tank without any trouble. (Remember that this is a recital of what happened long before the date of our record.) Early next morning, Dan O'Connell joined me, and we crawled along for another five or six miles, on a still fainter track, marked only by a few trips of the contractor's wagonette. In the afternoon we struck a line of bored posts, and dumped twenty coils. In due time, I unyoked, and Dan led me to a new tank, half-full of horribly alkaline water. Thence, after arranging to meet me in the morning, he cut across to his own boundary hut, six or eight miles away.

Next day, still following the line of posts, we dropped the rest of the wire; and, before Dan left me, I made him repeat again and again his directions for finding a gilgie, which he knew to be full of first-class water, and which I ought to strike about sunset. Next day I would reach the station in good time, thus completing a loop journey of thirty-odd miles in four days.

Dan had impressed me as a person likely to be of considerably more account in the estimation of his Maker than of his fellow-products; and, having previously studied men of the same description, I now accepted this involuntary sentiment as the only way of accounting for something not unfamiliar in his voice and bearing. A man of average stature, with a vast black beard, and guileless blue eyes, set off by a powerful Armagh accent. Evidently unobservant, uncritical, and utterly destitute of devil in any form, it seemed that the Spirit of the Bog had followed him into the bush, preserving his noxious innocence and all-round ineptitude in their pristine integrity. Naturally, he had taken a slight local colour, but this seemed to express the limit of his susceptibility to altered conditions.

Yet he twice startled me by the breadth and exactness of his information—once when America was mentioned, and he glanced at the character and policy of each President, from Washington to Van Buren; and again, when he spoke of the Massacre of Cawnpore, almost as if he had been there at the time. Also, an unconscious familiarity with the Bible and Shakespear was noticeable in his conversation, though he was evidently a Catholic of the Catholics.

When I complimented him on his erudition, he remarked, with amusing incompatibility of dialect and manner, "Mebbe it 's thrue fur ye. Me father hed consitherable mains, so he hed; an' A har'ly ivver done a han's turn, furbye divarsion, to A come out here." However, you will now understand why I made him repeat his topographical notes half a dozen times before I let him go.

Just at sunset I struck the partly-plain patch of sixty or eighty acres, where the gilgie ought to be. I unyoked with despatch, then left the bullocks, and rode round, looking for a clump of mallee, which would indicate the immediate neighbourhood of the water. No use. I could find no mallee anywhere. Night came on—richest starlight, though, of course, dark in the scrub—and still I objurgated round, and purposely scattered the bullocks to search for themselves, and anathematised in all directions, and consigned the whole vicinity to the Evil One, for lack of that clump of mallee. Hour after hour passed; the bullocks from time to time trying to clear off for the distant Lachlan, and I spending half my time in using them as divining rods, and the other half in execrating back and forward in search of that mallee. It was about midnight when I gave it best. I must have struck the wrong spot. Now—would it be advisable to make a bee-line to the station at once, with the bullocks loose?—or to wait for morning and take the wagon with me? The distance was eight or ten miles.

I was standing near the edge of the open scrub, with the reins

over my arm. The mare was famished and exhausted. The bells
were almost silent, for the bullocks stood still in the agony of thirst.
The weather was hot; and they had barely sipped the alkaline water
at last camp. I was absently observing one white bullock close by,
when, with a low bellow, he suddenly darted forward eight or ten
yards, and began drinking at the gilgie. That bellow was answered
from all sides; and in two minutes his nineteen mates were sharing
the discovery. Meanwhile, I had let Fancy go amongst them, after
putting on her bell, and taking off the saddle and bridle. I had
done with her for the night. And I knew that the water was good,
for all the beasts stood on the brink, and drank without wetting
their feet.

But how had the first bullock found the water, after he and his
mates had passed it a dozen times, and within a few yards? This
was worth investigating at once. So, before thinking about supper,
I went to the exact spot where the beast had been standing, and
there saw the stars reflected in the water. Of course, if it had been
anything like a permanent supply, the sound of frogs or yabbies
would have guided the beasts to it at once. But even wild cattle
can no more scent water than we can, though they make better use
of such faculties as they possess. I have tested the supposition
deliberately and exhaustively, time after time; and this instance is
cited, not controversially, but because it has to do with the present
memoir.

However, next morning—after verifying the tracks of the thirsty
bullocks so near the gilgie that it seemed a wonder they had n't
walked into it—I looked for the clump of mallee. I don't believe
there was a stick of it within miles; but there was a clump of yarran where it should have been. A stately beefwood, sixty feet high,
with swarthy column furrowed a hand-breadth deep, and heavy
tufts of foliage like bundles of long leeks in colour and configuration—the first beefwood I had seen since leaving the homestead—
stood close to the water, making a fine landmark; but Dan's sense
of proportion had selected the adjacent bit of yarran; and—as I
told the breakfast-party—he had never concerned himself to know
the difference between yarran and mallee.

"Curious combination of a fool and a well-informed man,"
remarked Ward.

"Is he either of the two?" asked Broome. "My belief, he shams
both."

"Easy matter to sham foolishness," observed Williamson. "Not
so easy to sham information."

"Any relation to the late Liberator?" I asked.

"Dan O'Connell 's only his nickname," replied Andrews. "His proper name is Rory O'Halloran."

"Rory O'Halloran!" I repeated. "I thought I had met him before, but could n't place him. And so Rory has found his way here?"

"Well, he was brought here," replied Andrews. "Twelve or fourteen years ago he turned up at Moogoojinna, down Deniliquin way, and froze to the station. Then when Arbuthnot settled this place— five years ago now—Spanker brought Rory with him, and he 's been here ever since. Got married at Moogoojinna, a year or two before leaving, to a red-hot Protestant, from the same part of the globe as himself; but she stayed at Moogoojinna for her confinement, and only came up four years ago, after Dan was settled in the Utopia paddock. Good woman in her way; but she spends her time in a sort of steady fury, for she came to Moogoojinna with the idea of collaring something worth while. So Spanker says; and he was there at the time. Seems she did n't want Dan, and Dan did n't want her, but somehow they were married before they came to an understanding. He 's very good to her, in his own inoffensive way; and she leads him a dog's life. One kid. Likely you knew him on Moogoojinna. According to his own account, he came straight through Vic., only stopping once, when he chummied for a few weeks with a squatter that took a fancy to him and treated him like a long-lost brother. Grain of salt just there."

"Not necessarily," I replied. "I can verify his statement to the letter, for I was that land-cormorant." And I straightway unfolded to the boys an earlier page of Dan O'Connell's history——

It was about thirteen years before. At that time I was really suffering the embarrassment of riches, though the latter consisted only of those chastening experiences which daily confront adventurers of immature judgment and scanty resources, on new selections. The local storekeeper, however, was keeping me supplied with the luxuries of life—such as flour, spuds, tea, sugar, tobacco —whilst turkeys and ducks were to be had for the shooting, and kangaroos for the chasing. The storekeeper had also taken charge of my land license, for safety, and occasionally presented documents for my signature, making me feel like some conscious criminal, happily let off for the present with a caution.

One summer evening, whilst dragging myself home from work, I encountered a young fellow, who, I flattered myself, resembled me only in age. Soft as a cabbage in every way, he was footsore and weary, as well as homesick and despondent to the verge of tears.

In one hand he carried a carpet bag, and in the other a large bundle, tied up in a coloured handkerchief. In his conversation he employed the Armagh accent with such slavish fidelity as to make it evident that he regarded any other form of speech as showing culpable ignorance or offensive affectation. His name was Rory O'Halloran.

Of course, I offered him the rugged hospitalities of my hut. In the morning, perceiving that his feet showed startling traces of the hundred-and-twenty-mile walk from Melbourne, I constrained him to rest for a few days. But the poor fellow had a painfully outspoken scruple against eating the damper of idleness; so, as soon as he was able to get his boots on without supplication for Divine support, he started to help me with my work.

Soon our acquaintance ripened to intimacy; and I learned something of his history. Like the majority of us, he was the scion of an ancient family. He was the youngest of eleven, all surviving at latest advices (praise God). Seven of these had swarmed to America, and were doing well (glory be); two remained in their native hive, with full and plenty (Amen); whilst he and his brother Larry had staked their future on the prosperity of Australia (God help us).

His father must have been a man of wealth and position, as he apparently spent his whole time in following the hounds, shooting pheasants, and catching salmon, with the other gentlemen. But just before Rory left home, his father and mother had withdrawn from society. And here the narrator's sudden reticence warned me not to inquire into the details of the old couple's retirement.

Larry, it appeared, had been doing Victoria and Riverina for five or six years, with magnificent, though unspecific, results. Anyway, he had franked Rory to Port Melbourne pier by passage warrant; but seemed to have made no provision for further intercourse. And Rory, having walked the streets of Melbourne for two whole days without finding any trace of Larry, had concluded that he must be in Riverina, and that it would be a brave notion to slip over, and take the defaulter by surprise. Hence his present pilgrimage.

Poor Rory, in spite of his willingness, was naturally awkward with splitters' tools, nor did he know how to harness a horse. All this, he explained to me, was a penalty adherent to people who, by reason of their social-economic position, are emancipated from manual labour. But when a heavy, soaking pour of summer rain brought the ground into fencing condition, I noticed that he could handle the spade with a strength and dexterity rarely equalled within my observation.

"You 're a Catholic—are n't you, Rory?" I speculated, one evening, struck by the simple piety of some asinine remark he had made.

A startled look of remonstrance and deprecation was his only reply. However, as it has always been my rule to seek information at first hand, I tried, in a friendly and confidential way, to draw him out respecting certain of his Church's usages and tenets, which I knew to be garbled and falsified by Protestant bigotry. But it was evident that throughout every fibre of his moral nature there ran a conviction that the mere mention of Purgatory or Transubstantiation would be fatal to our friendship. And he, at all events, would be no party to the unmasking of that great gulf which hereditarily divided us.

[It may be worth while, before we go any farther, to inquire into the nature and origin of this gulf—not merely for the sake of information, but because it is a question which affects the moral health of our community.

When Australia was first colonised, any sensible man might have foreboded sorrel, cockspur, Scotch thistle, &c., as unwelcome, but unavoidable, adjuncts of settlement. A many-wintered sage might have predicted that some colonist, in a fit of criminal folly, would scourge the country with a legacy of foxes, rabbits, sparrows, &c. But a second and clearer-sighted Jeremiah could never have prophesied the deliberate introduction of hydrophobia for dogs, glanders for horses, or Orangeism for men. Yet the latter enterprise has been carried out—whether by John Smith or John Beelzebub, by the Rev. Jones or the Rev. Belphegor, it matters not now. Some one has carried his congenial virus half-way round the globe, and tainted a young nation.

It is no question of doctrine. There is a greater difference between the Presbyterian and Episcopalian creeds than between the latter and the Catholic. But in tracing sectarian animosities back to their source, you may always expect to crash up against Vested Interests. For instance, the great Fact of the English Reformation was the confiscation of Church property. Afterward, a Protestant England submitted peaceably to the Inquisition; but when Mary proposed restitution of the abbey tenures—whoop! to your tents, O Israel! The noble army of prospective martyrs could n't conform to that heresy; and the stubborn Tudor had to back down. Again, Wesleyanism tapped the offertory of Episcopalianism, and thus earned the undying hatred of that Church—though in point of doctrine, the two are practically identical. But the prejudice of the Irish Protestant against the Irish Catholic has the basest origin of all.

The English and Scotch colonists drafted into Ulster by Elizabeth, James I, Cromwell, and William III, always evinced a tendency to become Irish in the second generation. The reason is plain. Devil-worship—the cult of Fear—was the territorial religion of Ireland; and, in this bitter fellowship, native Catholic and acclimatised Protestant sank their small sectarian differences. The almighty and eternal Landlord, of course, was the Power who had to be placated by tribute and incense, approached on all fours, and glorified in the highest.

We don't know much of the non-political history of Ireland during the 18th century, and indeed there is not much to be known. An Irish Parliament, consisting solely of landlords and their nominees, legislated as men do when the personal equation is allowed to pass unchecked. Meanwhile the agent collected such rents as he could get, with an occasional charge of slugs thrown in gratis: and the finest peasantry in the world slaved, starved, lied, stole, attended the means of grace, got drunk as often as possible, married and gave in marriage, harnessed itself to the landlord's carriage whenever that three-bottle divinity deigned an avatar, and hoarded up its pennies for the annual confiscation. Broadly speaking, it rendered unto Cæsar the things that were Cæsar's, and unto God the things that were God's—social-economic conditions being so arranged that Cæsar's title covered everything except an insignificant by-product of atrophied souls.

However, we are concerned only with Ulster, where the native element of population, oblivious to Thrift, and instinctively loyal to anything in the shape of supremacy, had become alloyed with an ingredient derived from the most contumacious brood at that time in Western Europe, namely, the so-called Anglo-Saxon—a people unpleasantly apt in drawing a limit-line to aggression on its pocket, and by no means likely to content itself with an appeal to the Saints or the Muses. But was there no sectarian line of cleavage?—was there no party spirit abroad, seeing that, for the alleged safety of the Protestant population, the Catholics lived under severe penal laws? Well——

'We hold the right of private judgment in matters of religion to be equally sacred in others as in ourselves; and, as men, as Christians, and as Protestants, we rejoice in the relaxation of the penal laws against our Roman Catholic fellow-subjects; and we believe the measure to be fraught with the happiest consequences to the union and prosperity of Ireland.'

That is part of a resolution carried with only two dissentient voices in a meeting composed of the delegates of 143 corps of Ulster Volunteers, numbering 25,000 men. The meeting was held at Dungannon, Tyrone, in 1782. The Volunteers were tenants who, in 1778, had spontaneously enrolled themselves for defence against foreign invasion; Protestants only were eligible, as the possession of arms, except by special license, was prohibited to Catholics. Yet by a curious paradox—the American War being then in progress—the feeling of the Irish Protestant was strongly revolutionary, while the Irish Catholic, true to his fatal instinct of illogical veneration, was distinctly loyalist. Nevertheless, the bond of a common nationality had by this time overborne sectarian estrangement; and never before nor since has Ireland seen a time when the professors of those hostile creeds got drunk together in such amity. This is a historical fact which cannot be too often repeated.

'Probably at no period since the days of Constantine,' says the accomplished and trustworthy Lecky, 'was Catholicism so free from domineering and aggressive tendencies as during the Pontificates of Benedict XIV and his three successors.' This covers a period extending from 1740 to 1775; and we know that cycles of ecclesiastical polity never close abruptly. The Catholic was first to perceive that 'when lenity and cruelty play for a kingdom, the gentler gamester is the soonest winner.'

But the Volunteers—armed and organised without the invitation or concurrence of Government—now began to propose reforms in parliamentary representation, amendments in internal legislation, a relaxation of trade restrictions, &c. So it was time for the man with a stake in the country to think about doing something.

Divide and govern! A good idea, though not a new one! And, providentially, here was the latent spark of religious dissent, ready to respond to the foulest breath ever blown from the lips of Greed. In 1785 the spark was first fanned into flame, with the best results; then, the satisfactory working of the experiment being assured, the first Orange Lodge was formally inaugurated at Loughlea, Armagh, in 1795—exactly 105 years after the dethronement and expulsion of James II, and 93 years after the death of William of Orange.

Patronised by noblemen, gentlemen, clergymen, and intermediary pimps of substantial position, the institution naturally appealed to the highest sentiments (which is saying extremely little) of a Protestant half-population forced into servility by agrarian conditions. Soon it became self-supporting, and waxed mighty in the land, feeding itself with fresh vendetta from each recurring 12th of July.

Observe its origin well. The profound cunning of a propertied class, operating with sinister purpose on the inevitable flunkeyism of a dependent class, per medium of that moral kink in human nature which makes sectarian persecution an act of worship, generated an accordant monster. Hence any L.O.L. convocation, however slenderly attended, may fitly be called a monster meeting.

The domestic history of the movement in its palmy days—the brutal and cowardly baiting of a penalised class; the boorish insult to ideals held sacred by sensitive devotees; the deliberate cultivation of intra-parochial blood-feud; the savage fostering of hate for hate's own sake; the thousand squalid details of affray, ambuscade, murder, maltreatment, malicious injury to property— these, happily or unhappily, rest on fast-perishing oral tradition alone. But the whole record, though not the most flagrant in modern history, is undeniably the vilest. 'Who,' asks Job, 'can bring a clean thing out of an unclean?' And his answer is superfluous.

A fixed resolution to avoid the very appearance of digression in these annals prevents my referring to various sporadic Irish combinations of the 18th century—Whiteboys, Steelboys, Oakboys, Peep-o'-day Boys, Defenders—some Catholic, some Protestant, some mixed; but each representing an inarticulate protest against agrarian or ecclesiastical aggression. Notice, however, that the customary dragging in of these irrelevancies, to confuse the main issue, is not to be wondered at, seeing that Orangeism itself is based, in a large, general way, on the Bible. But again, what fanatical lunacy or class-atrocity of Christendom was ever based on anything else?

O Catholic and Protestant slaves of dogma! Zealots, Idumæans, partisans of ye know not what! Fools all!—whooping for your Ananus, your John of Giscala, your Simon of Bargioras; and fighting amongst yourselves, whilst the invincible legionaries of Science advance confidently on your polluted Temple! Small sympathy have ye from this Josephus.]

But Rory, poor fellow, had all the impressions of party spirit built into his moral system. It was a vital and personal fact to him, though only a historical truth to me, that this hereditary war of the Big-endians and Little-endians had been conducted by our own immediate forefathers. Strictly speaking, mind you, neither party cracked the egg—that too-dainty product being taboo for rent

—but they compromised by cracking each other's domes of thought. Rory could n't get away from the strong probability that my grandfather had overpowered his own contemporary ancestor in the name of the Glorious, Pious and Immortal Memory, and had chopped his head off with a spade. He was willing to let bygones be bygones; but——No more o' that, an thou lovest me!

Yet he showed a distinctly intelligent interest, as well as a complacent assent, when I pointed out to him the irony of the Orangeman's situation. England's original title to the over-rule of Ireland —and a perfectly valid one, as times went then—was the momentous bull of Pope Adrian IV, issued to Henry II, in 1155. And any private title to land in Ireland, traced back through inheritance, purchase, or what not, must lead to a Royal grant as its source; the authority for such grant being the Papal bull aforesaid; and the validity of the bull resting on the Pope's temporal power. Now, the Orangeman is prepared to die in his last hiding-place in vindication of the English domination, that rests on the Papal bull, that is warranted by the Pope's temporal power, that lay in the house that Peter built. To be sure, provided a title be safe, its value is not affected though it may have emanated from the Father of Lies himself. But we should frankly say so.

Rory's character was made up of two fine elements, the poetic and the prosaic, but these were not compounded. There was a dreamy, idealistic Rory, born of a legend-loving race; and there was a painfully parsimonious Rory, trained down to the standard of a model wealth-producer. The first was of imagination all compact, living in an atmosphere of charms, fairies, poetic justice, and angelic guidance: the second was primed with homely maxims respecting the neglected value of copper currency. Which reminds me——

We had been together about a week when the thresher came round. I had no crop of my own—the wild cattle having walked over the dog-leg fence, and eaten it (the crop, of course, not the fence)—but we both went to help a neighbour. I was deputed to sew the bags, and Rory to pull out the tailings and bag them up for sending through again. I noticed that the fan pulley of the machine was secured with a home-made key, projecting about two inches beyond the end of the shaft; and as this was close beside where Rory was kneeling at his work, I pointed it out to him as a thing that meant mischief to the unwary. Half an hour afterward, there was a yell from the vicinity of the fan, and I knew that the key had found Rory. The engine driver shut off at once, and I made for the fan, whipping out my pocket knife as I went. The key had snatched the sleeve of the young fellow's homespun linen shirt, midway between elbow and shoulder, twitching the strong fabric into a knot, and burrowing into the soft meat of his arm. Already the fan was pulled up, while the belt slipped and smoked on the drum pulley above. The blade of my knife was just touching the twisted nucleus of linen, when Rory exclaimed wildly,

"Aisy, Tammas! For marcy sake, don't! Can't ye take the shurt aff the nail without cuttin' it?"

At this moment, the engine driver threw the fan belt off, and Rory was soon liberated. His satisfaction at finding the garment almost uninjured was but slightly dashed by the bruise on his arm. The latter would heal of itself; the former would n't. But for the rest of the day he kept his eye on that key.

Among the few things he brought out with him from home was the old-fashioned habit of sleeping in his skin—a usage, by the way, more to be commended than the converse custom, practised by English coal-miners, of turning into the blankets and out again fully dressed, till the raiment, never removed, rots off by effluxion of time. Rory maintained that his system added considerably to the lifetime of a shirt.

However, one Sunday forenoon, while we were enjoying that second sleep which gives to the Day of Rest its true significance, the smouldering fire ate its way through the side of the log chimney, and caught a couple of hundred two-foot shingles, stacked in the angle outside. It was about half-past ten when Rory was awakened by a crackling sound close beside him; and the first sight he saw was a broad tongue of flame leaping in under the eave, and licking the rafter above his head.

He had heard of bush fires; and though he knew the locusts were starving on the surrounding plain, his roar of despair brought me to my feet on the floor. Immediately grasping the situation and a long-handled shovel, I called on him to bring a bucket of water. The barrel was empty, as a matter of course; and Rory cantered away down the road a quarter of a mile, to where a deep crab-hole —replenished by the rain before referred to—furnished our supply. But, in the panic of the moment, it escaped his observation that he was affording a scandalous spectacle to two spring-cart loads of assorted Cornish people, on their way to the local tabernacle. In fact, he had swooped up a bucket of water and turned back with it before he was aware that they had been close behind him all the time. His first thought was to squat down, taking cover behind the bucket; but, remembering the exigency of his errand, he girded up his fortitude—which was the only thing he had to gird—and faced the spring-carts, for the sake of my hut, as bravely as his ancestors had faced ear-cropping, and similar cajoleries, for the sake of the wan thrue Church. And there was no more joke about the later martyrdom than about the earlier. However, by the time he returned, I had thrown the burning shingles to a safer distance, and removed all the loose fire, so that the bucket of water made everything safe.

Owing to the fire being on the side of the hut furthest from the road, the church-goers never noticed it. Hence they assumed that Rory was casually bringing the water for domestic purposes; and their unavoidable inference placed the Irish Catholics on a lower moral plane than the Aborigines, by reason of their priests keeping them in ignorance. This misconception had acquired all the solidity of fact before it reached me; consequently, my explanation was received as a well-meant fib. Anyway, these details will give you some idea of Rory, in his natural state as a colonist.

After the first fortnight or so, I frankly told him that, though nothing would suit my own interests better than a lifelong extension of his assistance, I would n't advise him to stay, as there could be no wages forthcoming. I had absolutely no money, nor was I likely to have such a thing in my possession till the forty-acre paddock was fenced, ploughed and sowed, and the crop (if any) harvested and sold. Even then—taking the average of the district—I could n't expect a return of more than £100; and out of this I would have to pay off an accumulated shortage of about £200.

"It 's a quare, quare counthry, anyhow," sadly soliloquised the exile of Erin, after he had thought the matter over. "Wondhers 'll niver quit saisin'. At home, iv a body hed twenty English acres o' good lay lan', at a raisonable rent—let alone a graat farrum like thon—he need n't do a han's turn the year roun', beyant givin' ordhers; an' he would hev lavin's iv iverything, an' a brave shoot o' clo'es till his back, an' mebbe a gool' watch, furbye money in his pocket. Bates all! Bates all!"

But the anomalous and baffling nature of Australian conditions made Rory all the more reluctant to tear himself away from his present asylum—though its shelter seemed to resemble the shadow of a great deficit in an insolvent land.

So another fortnight passed, whilst each of us learned something from the other. I constantly endeavoured, by reminiscence and inference, to post him up in the usages of his adopted country; and he regaled me with the folk-lore of the hill-side where his ancestors had passively resisted extinction since the time of Japhet. Purposeless fairy tales and ghost stories made up his cheap repertory; with another class of legend, equally fatuous; but ah! how legitimately born of that auroral fancy, which ceases not to play above the grave of homely ambition, penury-crushed and dead! Legends whereof the unvarying motif was a dazzling cash advance made by Satan in pre-payment for the soul of some rustic dead-beat; delivery being due in seven years from date. And a clever repudiation of covenant, with consequent non-forfeiture of ensuing clip, always came as a climax; so that the defaulter lived happy ever after, while the outwitted speculator retired to his own penal establishment in shame and con-fusion of tail.

At last a queer thing happened. I received a letter, containing a bank draft for £2, from a friend to whom I had lent the money three years before, on the diggings. In case there might have been some mistake about the remittance, that draft was cashed before the post-master had missed me from the window, and I was on the way home before the bank manager thought I was clear of his porch. On the same evening, I placed one of the notes in Rory's hand, adjuring him not to let the storekeeper know anything about it, but to depart from me while he was safe.

He shrank from the note as from a lizard, while his lip quivered, and he tried to swallow his emotion down. Then ensued mutual expostulation, which he terminated by producing a knitted purse, which might have belonged to his grandfather—or to Brian Boru's grandfather, for that matter—and disclosing a hidden treasure of seven shillings, two sixpences, and ten coppers. I nearly hit him in the mere fury of pity. Ultimately, however, my superior force of character told its tale, and we added the note to his reserve fund.

I got him started next morning. I gave him my Shakespear as a keepsake, with a billy and pannikin, and a few days' rations. I made up his swag scientifically while he lay heart-broken on his bunk; then I walked with him to the Echuca road. So he sorrowed his way northward, in renewed search of his brother Larry; and, as I watched his diminishing figure, I prayed that he might be enticed into the most shocking company in Echuca, and be made fightably drunk, and fall in for a remembersome hammering, and get robbed of everything, and be given in charge for making a disturbance, and wind up the adventure with a month in Her Majesty's jail. It seemed to me that no milder dispensation of Providence would satisfy his moral requirements. Drastic, but such is life.

I had a letter from him a month afterward, but as the postmark

was hopelessly illegible, and as he had omitted to head the com-
munication with any address, and as he referred to the place where
he was working as 'the station,' mentioning no names except those
of his fellow-workmen, I had to withhold the response for which his
forlorn soul craved.

"Takes a lot of different sorts of people to make a world," observed
Williamson, referring to the hero of my reminiscences.

"Original remark," commented Ward. "And it seems to me that
people 's as much alike as sheep; and Dan 's just one of the flock.
I always speak of a man as I find him."

"Another original remark," said Broome. "But there 's greater
fools than Dan—if you only knew where to drop across them."

"Original remark, number three," put in Andrews, who was five
years older than any of the boys. "You 're all chaps of great experience."

"Speaking of Dan, as you call him," said I; "by the foot we
recognise the Hercules; and if he knows as much about all other
historical subjects as he does about Cawnpore and the American
Presidents, he must have ripened into an extraordinary man. But
then, an extraordinary man should have learned the difference
between mallee and yarran in five years of solid scrub-observation."

"Well, you are gauging him by a standard that 's foreign to his
class of mind," replied Andrews. "If he had been as strange to that
gilgie as you were, and had got the same directions he gave you, he
would have found it first shot. When a certain class of bushman
says 'mallee', he means any sort of scrub except lignum; and when
he says 'mulga', he means any tree except pine or currajong. Same
mental slovenliness in women. A woman will tell a yarn that no
man can make head or tail of, but it 's as clear as day to any other
woman. And if you tell a woman a yarn, as it ought to be told,
she 'll think she understands it, and you 'll think so too, if she says
nothing. But if she chances any remark about it, you 'll see that the
correctness of style has carried it over her head."

"Speaking of style reminds me that Dan 's a bit of an author,"
remarked Williamson. "One day I was in his place, and he casually
showed me a page of some treatise he 's on of evenings. And, my
word, the style was grand. Knocks Ouida into a cocked hat."

"Well, I am glad to hear that," I observed. "Useful sort of man
on the station, too, I should imagine?"

"Average, or better," replied Andrews. "Nothing brilliant, but
careful and trustworthy. Revolves in his orbit without a what-you-
may-call-'im."

"Perturbation," I suggested. "How far is his hut from here?"

"Twelve mile. Let 's see—six or eight mile north-west of where you dropped the first lot of wire that time."

"Can't I take him on the way to Mulppa?"

"Yes; but don't trust him for directions beyond his own place. We 'll give you the geography. Better put up at his place to-night, and you 'll reach Mulppa in good time to-morrow evening. And look out for that dog of yours when you get in range of Dan's place. He 's great on strychnine; and the station gets the benefit of it in two ways—he keeps his paddock clear of dingoes, and he never has a scalp to sell."

By this time, breakfast was concluded; and in two minutes the combined topographical knowledge of the young fellows had laid down the best route to Mulppa, via Dan's hut.

Then a short official interview with Mr. Spanker, followed by a long, desultory gossip, brought me another couple of hours nearer the final reward of my orthodox upbringing. In another hour, my horses were saddled, and I was having a drink of tea and a bit of brownie in the men's hut.

A few minutes afterward, Cleopatra was shaking this refreshment well down by means of the exercise with which he habitually opened the day's work. But this was to be accepted in the same spirit as the abusive language of a faithful pastor. It was all in the contract. I had made a rule of backing him only on loose sand-hills, or in soft swamps, for the first fortnight. By that time, an amicable understanding had been established between us, at an expense of only three spills—once through an unexpected change of tactics; once through my own negligence; and once in spite of my best endeavours, for the faithless swamp was dry. I dare say I might have gradually weaned him from his besetting sin, but I did n't want to be pestered with people borrowing him.

However, before midday I was out on the ration-cart track, along which I had started with the wire, nearly three years before. Here and there the marks of the wagon were still identifiable, where the long team and heavy load had cut off corners of the winding track.

Presently the heavy wheel-marks diverged to the right, and disappeared in the all-pervading scrub. Then the faint track became suddenly fainter, where half the scanty traffic branched off to the left, in the direction of Lindsay's paddock.

It is not in our cities or townships, it is not in our agricultural or mining areas, that the Australian attains full consciousness of his own nationality; it is in places like this, and as clearly here as at the centre of the continent. To me the monotonous variety of this interminable scrub has a charm of its own; so grave, subdued, self-centred; so alien to the genial appeal of more winsome landscape, or the assertive grandeur of mountain and gorge. To me this wayward diversity of spontaneous plant life bespeaks an unconfined, ungauged potentiality of resource; it unveils an ideographic prophecy, painted by Nature in her Impressionist mood, to be deciphered aright only by those willing to discern through the crudeness of dawn a promise of majestic day. Eucalypt, conifer, mimosa; tree, shrub, heath, in endless diversity and exuberance, yet sheltering little of animal life beyond half-specialised and belated types, anachronistic even to the Aboriginal savage. Faithfully and lovingly interpreted, what is the latent meaning of it all?

Our virgin continent! how long has she tarried her bridal day! Pause and think how she has waited in serene loneliness while the deltas of Nile, Euphrates, and Ganges expanded, inch by inch, to spacious provinces, and the Yellow Sea shallowed up with the silt of winters innumerable—waited while the primordial civilisations of Copt, Accadian, Aryan and Mongol crept out, step by step, from palæolithic silence into the uncertain record of Tradition's earliest fable—waited still through the long eras of successive empires, while the hard-won light, broadening little by little, moved westward, westward, round the circumference of the planet, at last to overtake and dominate the fixed twilight of its primitive home—waited, ageless, tireless, acquiescent, her history a blank, while the petulant moods of youth gave place to imperial purpose, stern yet beneficent—waited whilst the interminable procession of annual, lunar and diurnal alternations lapsed unrecorded into a dead Past, bequeathing no register of good or evil endeavour to the ever-living Present. The mind retires from such speculation, unsatisfied but impressed.

Gravely impressed. For this recordless land—this land of our lawful solicitude and imperative responsibility—is exempt from many a bane of territorial rather than racial impress. She is committed to no usages of petrified injustice; she is clogged by no fealty to shadowy idols, enshrined by Ignorance, and upheld by misplaced homage alone; she is cursed by no memories of fanaticism and persecution; she is innocent of hereditary national jealousy, and free from the envy of sister states.

Then think how immeasurably higher are the possibilities of a

Future than the memories of any Past since history began. By comparison, the Past, though glozed beyond all semblance of truth, is a clinging heritage of canonised ignorance, brutality and baseness; a drag rather than a stimulus. And as day by day, year by year, our own fluid Present congeals into a fixed Past, we shall do well to take heed that, in time to come, our own memory may not be justly held accursed. For though history is a thing that never repeats itself—since no two historical propositions are alike—one perennial truth holds good, namely, that every social hardship or injustice may be traced back to the linked sins of aggression and submission, remote or proximate in point of time. And I, for one, will never believe the trail of the serpent to be so indelible that barefaced incongruity must dog the footsteps of civilisation.

Dan O'Connell's ten-by-five paddock lay end-on to my route; his hut being about midway down the line of fence. On striking the corner of the paddock, I went through a gate, and was closing and securing it behind Bunyip and Pup, when I became aware of a stout-built, black-bearded man on a fat bay horse, approaching along the inside of the fence.

"Rory?" said I inquiringly.

"Well-to-be-shure! A ken har'ly crarit it, Tammas!" exclaimed the evergreen, grasping my proffered hand, while his face became transformed with delight.

"You 're so much changed," said I—"so manly and sunburnt, and bearded like the patriarchs of old—that I did n't know you when I brought that wire. But I wonder how you failed to recognise me, considering that you heard my name."

"Och, man dear! A thought ye wur farmin' in Victoria," he replied. "An' Collins is a purty common name, so it is; an' A did n't hear yer Chris'n name at all at all. But ye 'll stap wi' me the night, an' we 'll hev a graat cronia about oul' times."

"That 's just what I was looking forward to, Rory. Which way are you going now?"

"No matther, Tammas. A 'll turn back wi' ye, an' we 'll git home a brave while afore sundown."

So we rode slowly side by side along the narrow clearing which extended in endless perspective down the line of fence. After giving Rory a sketch of the vicissitudes and disasters which had imparted an element of variety to the thirteen preceding years of my life, I yielded myself to the lulling influence of his own history during the same period. As you might expect, he glanced lightly over all points of real interest, and dwelt interminably on the statistics of the station—such as the percentage of lambs for each year since the stock was put on; the happily decreasing loss by dingoes; the average clip per head, and all manner of circumscribed pastoral shop.

I reined our conversation round to the future prospects and possibilities of the region wherein his lot was cast, and tried to steer it along that line. But he merely took the country as he found it, and left things at that. It had never occurred to him that a physical revolution was already in progress; that the introduction of sheep meant the ultimate extirpation of all trees and scrubs, except the inedible pine; and that the perpetual trampling of those sharp little hoofs would in time caulk the spongy, absorbent surface; so that these fluffy, scrub-clad expanses would become a country of rich and spacious plains, variegated by lakes and forests, and probably enjoying a fairly equable rainfall.

I have reason to remember that I quoted Sturt's account of the Old Man Plain as a desert solitude of the most hopeless and forbidding character. But, as I pointed out, settlement had crept over that inhospitable tract, and the Old Man Plain had become a pastoral paradise, with a possible future which no man could conjecture. Then I was going on to cite instances, within my own knowledge and memory, of permanent lakes formed in Northern Victoria, and a climate altered for the better, by mere settlement of a soil antecedently desiccated and disintegrated by idle exposure to the seasons. But I had brought round the subject of exploration; and again Rory amazed me by the extent and accuracy of his information.

Glancing from Sturt to Eyre, he firmly, yet temperately, held that the expedition carried out by this explorer along the shores of the Great Australian Bight was the ablest achievement of its kind on record; and he forthwith proceeded to substantiate his contention by a consecutive account of the difficulties met and surmounted on that journey. Also he expatiated with some severity on the slightness of public information with respect to Eyre's exploit.

He listened with kindly toleration whilst I adverted to the excellent work of more recent explorers, whose discoveries had made the Transcontinental telegraph line a feasible undertaking. But his discursive mind ricochetted off to the laying of the Transatlantic cable, in '65; and he dwelt on that epoch-marking work with such minuteness of detail, and such confident mastery of names, dates, and so forth, that I half-resented—not his disconcerting fund of information, but his modest reticence on other subjects of interest. It is a morally upsetting thing, for instance, to discover that the unassuming Londoner, to whom you have been somewhat loosely explaining the pedigrees of the British Peerage, has spent most of his life as a clerk in the Heralds' College.

But I noticed a growing uneasiness in Rory's manner, despite his efforts towards a free-and-easy cordiality. At last he said deprecatingly:

"We 're about a mile aff the house now, Tammas. A must go roun' be a tank thonder, an' that manes lavin' ye yer lone. Jist go sthraight on, an' ye 'll come till the horse-paddock fence, wi' a wee gate in the corner, an' the house furnent ye. An' ye might tell hursel' A 'll be home atoast sundown."

He shook up his horse, and dived through the scrub at an easy trot, whilst I went on down the fence. Before I had gone three-quarters of a mile, my attention was arrested by the peculiar apple-green hue of a tall, healthy-looking pine, standing about a hundred and fifty yards from the fence. Knowing that this abnormal deviation in colour, if not forthwith inquired into, would harass me exceedingly in after years, I turned aside to inspect the tree. It was worth the trouble. The pine had been dead for years, but every leafless twig, right up to its spiry summit, was re-clothed by the dense foliage of a giant woodbine, which embraced the trunk with three clean stems, each as thick as your arm. No moralist worthy of the name could fail to find a comprehensive allegory in the tree; but I had scarcely turned away from it before my meditations were disturbed——

Ten or fifteen yards distant, under the cool shade of a large, low-growing wilga, I observed a man reclining at ease. A tall, athletic man, apparently, with a billy and water-bag beside him, and nothing more to wish for. When I caught sight of him, he was in the act of settling himself more comfortably, and adjusting his wide-brimmed hat over his face.

My first impulse was to hail him with a friendly greeting, but a scruple of punctilio made me pause. The clearing of Rory's horse-paddock was visible here and there through gaps in the scrub; even the hut was in sight from my own point of view; the sun was still a couple of hours above the horizon; and the repose of the wilga shade was more to be desired than the activity of the wood-heap. To everything there is a time and a season; and the tactical moment for weary approach to a dwelling is just when fades the glimmering landscape on the sight, and all the air a solemn stillness holds. So, after a moment's hesitation, my instinctive sense of bush etiquette caused me to turn stealthily away, and seek the wicket gate which afforded ingress to Rory's horse-paddock. But I want you to notice that this decision was preceded by a poise of option between two alternatives. Now mark what followed, for, like Falstaff's story, it is worth the marking.

[Each undertaking, great or small, of our lives has one controlling alternative, and no more. To illustrate this from the play of *Hamlet:* You will notice that, up to a certain point of time, the Prince governs his own destiny—at least, as far as the Ghost's commission is concerned, and this covers the whole drama. He is master and umpire of his circumstances, so that when two or more lines of action, or a line of action and a line of inaction, appear equally efficacious, he can select the one which appears to be of least resistance. But subsequent to that point of time, he is no longer the arbiter of his own situation, but rather the puppet of circumstances. There are no more divergent roads; if he desires to leave the one he has chosen, he must break blindly through a hedge of moral antagonisms. His alternatives have become so lopsided that practically there is only one course open. The initial exercise of judgment was not merely an antecedent to later developments of the plot; it was a Rubicon-crossing, which has committed the hero to a system of interlaced contingencies; and the tendency of this system bears him away, half-conscious of his own impotence, to where the rest is silence. The turning-point is where Hamlet engages the Players to enact the Murder of Gonzago.

A major-alternative may create and enclose all the secondary alternatives of after life. A minor-alternative may exhaust itself in one minute, or less, leaving its indelible, though imperceptible, scar on the experimenter, and, through him, on the world in which he lives. The major-alternative is the Shakespearean 'tide in the affairs of men,' often recognised, though not formulated. In any case, each alternative brings into immediate play a flash of Free-will, pure and simple, which instantly gives place—as far as that particular section of life is concerned—to the dominion of what we call Destiny. The two should never be confounded. "Who can control his fate?" asks the ruined Othello. No one, indeed. But every one controls his option, chooses his alternative. Othello himself had independently evolved the decision which fixed his fate, recognising it as such an alternative. Thus:—

> Put out the light, and then—Put out the light?
> If I quench thee, thou flaming minister,
> I can again thy former light restore,
> Should I repent me;—but once put out thy light,
> Thou cunning'st pattern of excelling nature,
> I know not where is the Promethean heat
> That can thy light relume. When I have plucked thy rose,
> I cannot give it vital growth again;
> It needs must wither.

Also he perceives that it is a major-alternative which confronts him; and he contrasts this with the supposititious minor-alternative of extinguishing the lamp. But how often do we accept a major-alternative, whilst innocently oblivious to its gravity!

In *Macbeth*, the alternatives are very obvious. The interest of the play centres on the poise of incentive between action and non-action, and the absolute free-will of election. But that election once made, we see—and the hero himself acknowledges—a practical inevitableness in all succeeding atrocities which mark his career as king.

Such momentous alternatives are simply the voluntary rough-hewing of our own ends. Whether there 's a Divinity that afterwards shapes them, is a question which each inquirer may decide for himself. Say, however, that this postulated Divinity consists of the Universal Mind, and that the Universal Mind comprises the aggregate Human Intelligence, co-operating with some Moral Centre beyond. And that the spontaneous sway of this Influence is toward harmony—toward the smoothing of obstacles, the healing of wounds. In the axiom that 'nature reverts to the norm,' there is a recognition of this restorative tendency; and the religious aspect of the same truth is expressed in the proverb that 'God is Love.' For the grass will grow where Attila's horse has trod, while that objectionable Hun himself is represented by a barrow-load of useful fertiliser. But say that this always comes about by law of Cause (which is Human Free-will) and Effect (which is Destiny) —never by sporadic intervention. Yet a certain scar, tracing its origin to an antecedent alternative, will remain as the signet of that limitation under which the Divinity works—the limitation, namely, of Destiny, or the fixed issue of present effect from foregone cause; such cause having been perpetually directed and re-directed by recurring operation of individual Free-will, exercised, independently, by those emanations from the Moral Centre which, by courtesy, we call reasonable beings.

Vague? Yes. Well, put it in parable form. A young man has reached an absolute poise of incentive. He tosses a shekel. 'Head —I go and see life; tail—I stay at home. Head it is.' The alternative is accepted; whereupon Destiny puts in her spoke, bringing such vicissitudes as are inevitable on the initial option. In due time, another alternative presents itself, and the poise of incentive recurs. The Prodigal spits on a chip, and tosses it. 'Wet—I crawl back home; dry—I see it out. Wet it is.' So he goes, to meet the ring, and the robe, and the fatted calf. His latter alternative has taken him home; and a felicitous option on the old man's part has given him a welcome. But the earlier alternative is following him up, for the farm is gone! The old man himself cannot undo the effect of the foregone choice.

Or put it in allegorical form. The misty expanse of Futurity is radiated with divergent lines of rigid steel; and along one of these lines, with diminishing carbon and sighing exhaust, you travel at schedule speed. At each junction, you switch right or left, and on you go still, up or down the way of your own choosing. But there is no stopping or turning back; and until you have passed the current section there is no divergence, except by voluntary catastrophe. Another junction flashes into sight, and again your choice is made; negligently enough, perhaps, but still with a view to what you consider the greatest good, present or prospective. One line may lead through the Slough of Despond, and the other across the Delectable Mountains, but you don't know whether the section will prove rough or smooth, or whether it ends in a junction or a terminus, till the cloven mists of the Future melt into a manifest Present. We know what we are, but we know not what we shall be.

Often the shunting seems a mere trifle; but, in reality, the switch is that wizard-wand which brings into evidence such corollaries of life as felicity or misery, peace or tribulation, honour or ignominy, found on the permanent way. For others, remember, as well as for ourselves. No one except the anchorite lives to himself; and he is merely a person who evades his responsibilities.

Here and there you find a curious complication of lines. From a junction in front, there stretches out into the mist a single line and a double line; and, meantime, along a track converging toward your own, there spins a bright little loco., in holiday trim, dazzling you with her radiant head-lights, and commanding your admiration by her 'tractive power. Quick! Choose! Single line to the next junction or double line to the terminus? A major-alternative, my boy! "Double line!" you say. I thought so. Now you 'll soon have a long train of empty I's to pull up the gradients; and while you snort and bark under a heavy draught, your disgusted consort will occasionally stimulate you with a 'flying-kick'; and when this comes to pass, say Pompey told you so. To change the metaphor: Instead of remaining a self-sufficient lord of creation, whose house is thatched when his hat is on, you have become one of a Committee of Ways and Means—a committee of two, with power to add to your number. Dan O'Connell, for instance, had negotiated this alternative, and, in the opinion of the barracks, had made his election in a remiss and casual way.

And as with the individual, so with the community. Men, thinking and acting in mass, do not (according to the accepted meaning of the phrase) follow the line of least resistance. The myriad-headed monster adopts the alternative which appears to promise such a line, but Its previsions are more often wrong than right; and, in such cases, the irresistible momentum of the Destiny called into being by Its short-sighted choice drives It helplessly along a line of the greatest conceivable resistance. Is n't history a mere record of blundering option, followed by iron servitude to the irremediable suffering thereby entailed? Applied to the flying alternative, the 'least resistance' theory is gratuitously sound; beyond that, it is misleading. However, all this must be taken as referring back to my own apparently insignificant decision not to disturb the masterly inactivity of that sundowner under the wilga. Mere afterthoughts, introduced here by reason of their bearing on this simple chronicle.]

As a matter of fact, I approached Rory's neat, two-roomed hut speculating as to why he had purposely left me to feel my own way. I soon formed a good rough guess. A neatly-dressed child, in a vast, white sun-bonnet, ran toward me as I came in sight, but presently paused, and returned at the same pace. On reaching the door I was met by a stern-looking woman of thirty-odd, to whom I introduced myself as an old friend of Mr. O'Halloran's.

"Deed he hes plenty o' frien's," replied the woman drily. "Are ye gunta stap the night?"

"Well, Mr. O'Halloran was kind enough to proffer his hospitality," I replied, pulling the pack-saddle off Bunyip. "By the way, I 'm to tell you that he 'll be home presently."

"Nat a fear but he 'll be home at mail-time. An' a purty house he 's got fur till ax a sthranger intil."

"Now, Mrs. O'Halloran, it 's the loveliest situation I 've seen within a hundred miles," I replied, as I set Cleopatra at liberty. "And the way that the place is kept reflects the very highest credit upon yourself." Moreover, both compliments were as true as they were frank.

"Dacent enough for them that 's niver been used till betther. There's a dale in how a body 's rairt."

"True, Mrs. O'Halloran," I sighed. "I 'm sure you must feel it. But, my word! you can grow the right sort of children here! How old is the little girl?" My custom is to ask a mother the age of her child, and then express incredulity.

"Oul'er nor she 's good. She was five on the thurteenth iv last month."

"No, but seriously, Mrs. O'Halloran?"

"A 'm always sayrious about telling the thruth." And with this retort courteous the impervious woman retired into her house, while I seated myself on the bucket-stool against the wall, and proceeded to fill my pipe.

"We got six goats—pure Angoras," remarked the little girl, approaching me with instinctive courtesy. "We keep them for milkin'; an' Daddy shears them ivery year."

"I noticed them coming along," I replied. "They 're beautiful goats. And I see you 've got some horses too."

"Yis; three. We bought wan o' them chape, because he hed a sore back, fram a shearer, an' it 's nat hailed up yit. Daddy rides the other wans. E-e-e! can't my Daddy ride! An' he ken grow melons, an' he ken put up shelves, an' he knows iverything!"

"Yes; your Daddy 's a good man. I knew him long, long ago, when there was no you. What 's your name, dear?"

"Mary."

"She 's got no name," remarked the grim voice from the interior of the house. And the mild, apologetic glance of the child in my face completed a mental appraisement of Rory's family relations.

Half an hour passed pleasantly enough in this kind of conversation; then Rory came in sight at the wicket gate where I had entered. Mary forgot my existence in a moment, and raced toward him, opening a conversation at the top of her voice while he was still a quarter of a mile distant. When they met, he dismounted, and, placing her astride on the saddle, continued his way with the expression of a man whose cup of happiness is wastefully running over.

I had leisure to observe the child critically as she sat bareheaded beside Rory at the tea-table, glancing from time to time at me for the tribute of admiration due to each remark made by that non-pareil of men.

She was not only a strikingly beautiful child, but the stamp of child that expands into a beautiful woman. In spite of her half-Anglican lineage and Antipodean birth, there was something almost amusing in the strong racial index of her pure Irish face. The black hair and eye-brows were there, with eyes of indescribable blue; the full, shapely lips, and that delicate contour of chin which specially marks the highest type of a race which is not only non-Celtic but non-Aryan.

It is not the Celtic element that makes the Irish people a bundle of inconsistencies—clannish, yet disjunctive; ardent, yet unstable; faithful, yet perfidious; exceeding loveable for its own impulsive love, yet a broken reed to lean upon. It is not the Celt who has made Irish history an unexampled record of patience and insubordination, of devotion and treachery. The Celt, though fiery, is shrewd, sensible, and practical. It has been truly said that Western Britain is more Celtic than Eastern Ireland. But the whole Anglo-Celtic mixture is a thing of yesterday.

Before the eagle of the Tenth Legion was planted on the shore of Cantium—before the first Phœnician ship stowed tin at the Cassiterides—the Celt had inhabited the British Islands long enough to branch into distinct sub-races, and to rise from palæolithic savagery to the use of metals, the domestication of animals, and the observance of elaborate religious rites. Yet, relatively, this antique race is of last week only. For, away beyond the Celt, palæontology finds an earlier Brito-Irish people, of different origin and physical characteristics. And there is little doubt that, forced westward by Celtic invaders, of more virile type, and more capable of organisation, that immemorial race is represented by the true Irish of to-day. The black hair, associated with deep-blue eyes and a skin of extreme whiteness, found abundantly in Ireland, and amongst the offspring of Irish emigrants, are, in all probability, tokens of descent from this appallingly ancient people. The type appears occasionally in the Basque provinces, and on the Atlantic coast of Morocco, but nowhere else. Few civilised races inhabit the land where the fossil relics of their own lineal ancestors mark the furthest point of human occupancy; yet it would seem to be so with the true Irish. In what other way can this anomalous variety of the human race be accounted for? Ay, and beyond the earliest era noted by ethnography, this original Brito-Irish race must have dif-

ferentiated itself from the unknown archetype, and, by mere
genealogical succession, must have fixed its characteristics so
tenaciously as to persist through the random admixture of con-
quests and colonisations during countless generations. 'God is
eternal,' says a fine French apothegm, 'but man is very old.'

And very new. Mary O'Halloran was perfect Young-Australian.
To describe her from after-knowledge—she was a very creature of
the phenomena which had environed her own dawning intelligence.
She was a child of the wilderness, a dryad among her kindred
trees. The long-descended poetry of her nature made the bush
vocal with pure gladness of life; endowed each tree with sympathy,
respondent to her own fellowship. She had noticed the dusky aspect
of the ironwood; the volumed cumuli of rich olive-green, crowning
the lordly currajong; the darker shade of the wilga's massy foliage-
cataract; the clearer tint of the tapering pine; the clean-spotted
column of the leopard tree, creamy white on slate, from base to
topmost twig. She pitied the unlovely balah, when the wind sighed
through its coarse, scanty, grey-green tresses; and she loved to contemplate the silvery plumage of the two drooping myalls which,
because of their rarity here, had been allowed to remain in the
horse-paddock. For the last two or three springs of her vivacious
existence, she had watched the deepening crimson of the quondong,
amidst its thick contexture of Nile-green leaves; she had marked
the unfolding bloom of the scrub, in its many-hued beauty; she had
revelled in the audacious black-and-scarlet glory of the desert pea.
She knew the dwelling-place of every loved companion; and, by
necessity, she had her own names for them all—since her explora-
tions were carried out on Rory's shoulders, or on his saddle, and
technicalities never troubled him. To her it was a new world, and
she saw that it was good. All those impressions which endear the
memory of early scenes to the careworn heart were hers in their
vivid present, intensified by the strong ideality of her nature, and
undisturbed by other companionship, save that of her father.

This brings us to the other mark of a personality so freshly
minted as to have taken no more than two impressions. Rory was
her guide, philosopher, and crony. He was her overwhelming ideal
of power, wisdom, and goodness; he was her help in ages past, her
hope for years to come (no irreverence intended here; quite the
reverse, for if true family life existed, we should better apprehend
the meaning of 'Our Father, who art in heaven'); he was her
Ancient of Days; her shield, and her exceeding great reward.

A new position for Rory; and he grasped it with all the avidity of a love-hungered soul. The whole current of his affections, thwarted and repulsed by the world's indifference, found lavish outlet here.

After tea, Rory took a billy and went out into the horse-paddock to milk the goats—Mary, of course, clinging to his side. I remained in the house, confiding to Mrs. O'Halloran the high respect which Rory's principles and abilities had always commanded. But she was past all that; and I had to give it up. When a woman can listen with genuine contempt to the spontaneous echo of her husband's popularity, it is a sure sign that she has explored the profound depths of masculine worthlessness; and there is no known antidote to this fatal enlightenment.

Rory's next duty was to chop up a bit of firewood, and stack it beside the door. Dusk was gathering by this time; and Mrs. O'Halloran called Mary to prepare her for the night, while Rory and I seated ourselves on the bucket-stool outside. Presently a lighted lamp was placed on the table, when we removed indoors. Then Mary, in a long, white garment, with her innocent face shining from the combined effects of perfect happiness and unmerciful washing, climbed on Rory's knees—not to bid him good-night, but to compose herself to sleep.

"Time the chile was bruk aff that habit," observed the mother, as she seated herself beside the table with some sewing.

"Let her be a child as long as she can, Mrs. O'Halloran," I remarked. "Surely you would n't wish any alteration in her."

"Nat without it was an altheration fur the betther," replied the worthy woman. "An' it 's little hopes there is iv hur, consitherin' the way she 's rairt. Did iver anybody 'hear o' rairin' childher' without batin' them when they want it?"

"You bate hur, an' A 'll bate you!" interposed Rory, turning to bay on the most salient of the three or four pleas which had power to rouse the Old Adam in his unassertive nature.

"Well, A 'm sure A was bate—ay, an' soun'ly bate—when A was lek hur; an' iv A did n't desarve it then, A desarved it other times, when A did n't git it."

An obvious rejoinder rose to my mind, but evidently not to Rory's, for the look on his face told only of a dogged resolution to continue sinning against the light. He knew that his own contumacy in this respect would land his soul in perdition, and he deliberately let it go at that. Brave old Rory! Never does erratic man appear to such advantage as when his own intuitive moral sense rigorously overbears a conscientiousness warped by some fallacy which he still accepts as truth.

Yet the mother loved the child in her own hard, puritanical way. And, in any case, you are not competent to judge her, unless you have to work for your living, instead of finding somebody eager to support you in luxury for the pleasure of your society; unless, instead of marrying some squatter, or bank clerk, or Member of Parliament, you have inadvertently coupled yourself to a Catholic boundary man, named nothing short of Rory O'Halloran.

The embittered woman retired early, and without phrases. As she did so, I casually noticed that the bed-room was bisected by a partition, with a curtained doorway.

"Ever try your hand at literature, Rory?" I presently asked, remembering Williamson's remark.

"Well, A ken har'ly say No, an' A ken har'ly say Yis," replied Rory, with ill-feigned humility. "A 've got a bit iv a thraytise scribbled down, furbye a wheen o' other wans on han'. A thought mebbe"—and his glance rested on the angel-face of the sleeping child—"well, A thought mebbe it would do hur no harrum fur people till know that hur father—well—as ye might say—Nat but what she 'll hev money in the bank, plaze God. But A 'll lay hur down in hur wee cot now, an' A 'll bring the thrifle we wur mentionin'."

He tenderly carried the child into the first compartment of the bed-room, and, soon returning, placed before me about twenty quarto sheets of manuscript, written on both sides, in a careful, schoolboy hand. The first page was headed, *A Plea for Woman*.

"My word, Rory, this is great!" said I, after reading the first long paragraph. "I should like to skim it over at once, to get the gist of the argument, and then read it leisurely, to enjoy the style. And that reminds me that I brought you an *Australasian*. I 'll get it out of my swag, and you can read it to kill time."

But it became evident that he could n't fix his mind on the newspaper whilst his own literary product was under scrutiny. The latter unfolded itself as a unique example of pure deduction, aided by utter lack of discrimination in the value of evidence. It was all synthesis, and no analysis. A certain hypothesis had to be established, and it was established. The style was directly antithetical to that curt, blunt, and simple pronouncement aimed at by innocents who deceive no one by denouncing Socialism, Trades-Unionism, &c., over the signature of 'A Working Man.' But the Essay.

I am debarred from transcribing it, not only because of its length, but because——

"Rory, you must let me take a copy of this."

"Well, Tammas, A 'm glad it plazes ye; right glad, so A am; but A thought till—till"——

"Spring it on the public—so to speak?"

"Yis."

"Well, I 'll faithfully promise to keep the whole work sacred to your credit. And if ever I go into print—which is most unlikely—I 'll refer to this essay in such a way as to whet public curiosity to a feather edge. Again, if anything should happen to this copy, you 'll have mine to fall back upon."

"A 'll thrust ye, Tammas. God bless ye, take a copy any time afore ye go."

The object of the essay was to prove that, at a certain epoch in the world's history, the character of woman had undergone an instantaneous transformation. And it was proved in this way:

The two greatest thinkers and most infallible authorities our race has produced are Solomon and Shakespear.

Solomon's estimate of woman is shockingly low; and there is no getting away from the truth of it. His baneful evidence has the guarantee of Holy Writ; moreover, it is fully borne out by the testimony of ancient history, sacred and profane, and by the tendency of the Greek and Roman mythologies. Examples here quoted in profusion.

The fact of woman's pre-eminent wickedness in ancient times is traceable to the eating of the apple, when Eve, being the more culpable, was justly burdened with the heavier penalty, namely, a preternatural bias toward sin in a general way.

On the other hand, Shakespear's estimate of woman is high. And justly so, since his valuation is conclusively endorsed by modern history. Examples again quoted, in convincing volume, from the women of Acts down to Mrs. Chisholm and Florence Nightingale.

Now how do you bring these two apparently conflicting facts into the harmony of context? Simply by tracing the Solomon-woman forward, and the Shakespear-woman backward, to their point of intersection, and so finding the moment of transition. It is where the Virgin says:

'My soul doth magnify the Lord, and my spirit hath rejoiced in God my Saviour. For He hath regarded the low estate of His handmaiden; for, behold! from henceforth all generations shall call me blessed.'

This prophecy has not only a personal and specific fulfilment, as pointing to the speaker herself, but a transitive and general application, as referring to her sex at large. There you have it.

But no mere abstract can do justice to the sumptuous phraseology of the work, to its opulence of carefully selected adjective, or to the involved rhetoric which seemed to defeat and set at naught all your petty rules of syntax and prosody. Still less can I impart a notion of the exhaustive raking up of ancient examples and modern instances, mostly worn bright by familiarity with the popular mind, but all converging toward the conclusion striven for, and the shakiest of them accepted in childlike faith. Integrally, that essay conveyed the idea of two mighty glaciers of theory, each impelling its own moraine of facts toward a stated point of confluence— represented by a magnificent postulate—where one section, at least, of the Universal Plan would attain fulfilment, and the Eternal Unities would be so far satisfied. There was something in it that was more like an elusive glimmer of genius than an evidence of understanding, or, still less, of cleverness. Remarkable also, that, though the punctuation was deplorable, every superb polysyllable was correctly spelled. But as a monument of wasted ingenuity and industry, I have met with nothing so pathetic. A long term of self-communion in the back country will never leave a man as it found him. Outside his daily avocation, he becomes a fool or a philosopher; and, in Rory's case, the latter seemed to have been superimposed on the former.

At ten o'clock, I hunted him to bed. I had plenty of blank forms in my writing-case, and on these I took a preliminary copy of *A Plea for Woman*. This occupied about three hours. Then, not feeling sleepy, I took down one of four calico-covered books, which I had previously noticed on a corner shelf. It was my own old Shakespear, with the added interest of marginal marks, in ink of three colours, neatly ordered, and as the sand by the sea-shore innumerable. I put it back with the impression that no book had ever been better placed. The next volume was a Bible, presented by the Reverend Miles Barton, M.A., Rector of Tanderagee, County Armagh, Ireland, to his beloved parishioner, Deborah Johnson, on the occasion of her departure for Melbourne, South Australia, June 16, 1875. The third book was a fairly good dictionary, appendixed by a copious glossary of the Greek and Roman mythologies. The fourth was Vol. XII of Macmillan's Magazine, May to October, 1865.

Opening the latter book at random, I fell upon a sketch of Eyre's expedition along the shores of the Great Australian Bight. In another place was a contribution entitled 'A Gallery of American Presidents.' The next item of interest was an account of the Massacre of Cawnpore. And toward the end of the volume was a narrative of the Atlantic Telegraph Expedition. Of course, there were thirty or forty other articles in the book, but they were mostly strange to me, however familiar they might be to Rory.

Hopeless case! I thought, as I blew out the lamp and turned into my comfortable sofa-bed. If this morepoke's Irish love of knowledge was backed by one spark of mental enterprise, he might have half a ton of chosen literature to come and go on. And here he is, with his pristine ignorance merely dislocated.

When I woke at sunrise, Rory was kindling the fire, with the inseparable Mary squatted beside him in her nightgown. After putting on the kettle, he dressed the little girl, and helped her to wash her face. By this time, I was about; and Mary brought me a blank form, which I had dropped and overlooked the night before.

"Keep it till you learn to write, dear," said I.

"She ken write now," remarked Rory, with subdued exultation. "Here, jewel," he continued, handing her a pencil from the mantel-piece—"write yer name nately on that paper, fur Misther Collins till see."

The child, tremulous with an ecstatic sense of responsibility, bent over her paper on the table for a full minute, then diffidently pushed it across to me; and I read, in strong Roman capitals, the inscription, MRAY, with the M containing an extra angle—being, so to speak, a letter and a half.

"Ye 're wake in spellin', honey," remarked her father merrily; "an' the M 's got an exthry knuckle on it."

"It 's right enough," I interposed. "Could n't be better. Now, Mary, I 'll keep this paper, and show it to you again when you 're a great scholar and a great poetess. See if I don't."

The entrance of Mrs. O'Halloran cut short this nonsense; and Rory went out to milk the goats, accompanied, of course, by Mary.

After breakfast, we took our bridles and went out toward where the five horses were feeding together, the inevitable child pattering along by Rory's side.

"You have a lot to be thankful for," I remarked.

"Blessed be His Name!" thought Rory aloud; and I continued,

"You must make up your mind to send her away to school in another four or five years."

"Iv coorse," replied Rory sadly.

"A convent school, mind. None of your common boarding schools for a child like Mary."

Rory's only reply was a glance of gratitude. My stern admonition would be a moral support to him in the coming controversy.

"You mentioned some other literary work that you have on hand?" I remarked inquiringly.

"Yis; A 've jotted down a few idays. Now, Tammas—where was the Garden of Aden supposed to be?"

"My word, Rory, if a man could only disclose that to the world, he would command attention. However, one theory is that it was on the lost continent of Atlantis; another, that it was in the Valley of Cashmere. There are many other localities suggested, but I think the one which meets most favour is the Isle of Kishm, in the Straits of Ormuz, at the entrance to the Persian Gulf."

"Will ye repate that, Tammas, iv ye plaze."

I briefly rehearsed such relevant information as I possessed, whilst Rory kidnapped the geographical names and imprisoned them in his note-book, trusting to his memory for the rest.

"Oul' Father Finnegan, at Derryadd, useteh argie that the Garden iv Aden hed been furnent the Lake o' Killarney; an' no one dar' conthradict him," he remarked, with a smile. "But people larns till think fur theirselves when they 're out theyre lone. An' afther consitherin' the matter over, A take this iday fur a foundation: The furst Adam was created in a sartin place; then he sinned in a sartin place. An' when the Saviour (blessed be His Name!) come fur till clane the wurrld o' the furst Adam's sin, He hed till be born where the furst Adam was created; an' He hed till die where the furbidden fruit was ait. An' A 've gethered up proofs, an' proofs, an' proofs—How far is it fram Jerusalem till Bethlehem, Tammas?"

"Nearly six miles."

"A knowed the places must be convanient. Now ye mind where the Saviour (blessed be His Name!) says, 'all the blood shed on earth, fram the blood iv righteous Abel'—and so on? Well, 'earth' manes 'land': an' it 's all as wan as if He said, 'shed on the land.' An' what land? Why, the Holy Land. An' the praphets lived there when the Fall was quite racent; an' hear what they say:—"

(Here he gave me some texts of Scripture, which I afterward verified—and I would certainly advise you to do the same, if you can find a Bible. They are, Isaiah li, 3; Ezekiel xxviii, 13—xxxi, 9-18—xxxvi, 35; Joel ii, 3.)

"Rory, you 're a marvel," I remarked with sincerity. "And, by the way, if there 's anything in the inspiration of Art—if the Artist soars to truth by the path which no fowl knoweth—your theory may find some support in the fact that it was a usage of the Renaissance to represent the skull of Adam at the foot of the cross."

"Ay—that!" And Rory's note-book was out again. "Which artists, Tammas?"

"Martin Schoen—end of 15th century, for one. Jean Limousin —17th century—for another. Albert Dürer—beginning of 16th century—in more than one of his engravings. However, you can just hold this species of proof in reserve till I look up the subject. I won't forget."

"God bless ye, Tammas! Would it be faysible at all at all fur ye till stap to the morrow mornin', an' ride out wi' me the day?"

"Well—yes."

"Blessin's on ye, Tammas! Becos A 've got four more idays that ye could help me with. Wan iday is about divils. A take this fur a foundation: There 's sins fur till be done in the wurrld that men 'on't do; an' divils is marcifully put in the flesh an' blood fur till do them sins. 'Wan iv you is a divil,' says the Saviour (blessed be His Name!) 'He went to his own place,' says Acts—both manin' Judas. An' there 's a wheen o' places where Iago spakes iv himself as a divil. An' A 've got other proofs furbye, that we 'll go over wan be wan. It 's a mysthery, Tammas."

"It is indeed." Whilst replying, I was constrained to glance round at the weather; and my eye happened to fall on the creeper-laden pine, a quarter of a mile away. Suddenly a strange misgiving seized me, and I asked involuntarily, "Do you have many swagmen calling round here?"

"Nat six in the coorse o' the year," replied Rory, too amiable to heed the impolite change of subject. "Las' time A seen Ward," he continued, after a moment's pause, "he toul' me there was a man come to the station wan mornin' airly, near blin' wi' sandy blight; an' he stapped all day in a dark skillion, an' started again at night. He was makin' fur Ivanhoe, fur till ketch the coach; but it 's a sore ondhertakin' fur a blin' man till thravel the counthry his lone, at this saison o' the year. An' it 's quare where sthrangers gits till. A foun' a swag on the fence a week or ten days ago, an' a man's thracks at the tank a couple o' days afther; an' the swag 's there yit; an' A would think the swag an' the thracks belonged till the man wi' the sandy blight, barr'n this is nat the road till Ivanhoe."

"My word, Rory, I wish either you or I had spoken of this when you came home last night. Never mind the horses now. Give me your bridle, and take Mary on your back."

As we went on, I related how I had seen the man reclining under the tree; and Rory nodded forgivingly when I explained the scruple which had withheld me from making my presence known.

"He must 'a' come there afther ten o'clock yisterday," observed Rory; "or it would be mighty quare fur me till nat see him, con-sitherin' me eyes is iverywhere when A 'm ridin' the boundhry."

"But he was n't near the boundary. I had turned off from the fence to see that dead pine with the big creeper on it."

"Which pine, Tammas?"

"There it is, straight ahead—the biggest of the three that you see above the scrub. You notice it 's a different colour?"

" 'Deed ay, so it is. A would n't be onaisy, Tammas; it 's har'ly likely there 's much wrong—but it 's good to make sartin about it."

No effort could shake off the apprehension which grew upon me as we neared the fence. But on reaching it I said briskly:

"Stay where you are, Rory; I 'll be back in half a minute." Then I crushed myself through the wires.

Fifteen or twenty paces brought me to the spot. The man had changed his position, and was now lying at full length on his back, with arms extended along his sides. His face was fully exposed— the face of a worker, in the prime of manhood, with a heavy moustache and three or four weeks' growth of beard. So much only had I noted at first glance, whilst stooping under the heavy curtain of foliage. A few steps more, and, looking down on the waxen skin of that inert figure, I instinctively uncovered my head.

The dull eyes, half-open to a light no longer intolerable, showed by their death-darkened tracery of inflamed veins how much the lone wanderer had suffered. The hands, with their strong bronze now paled to tarnished ochre, were heavily calloused by manual labour, and sharply attenuated by recent hardship. The skin was cold, but the rigidity of death was yet scarcely apparent. Evid-ently he had not died of thirst alone, but of mere physical exhaus-tion, sealed by the final collapse of hope. And it seemed so strange to hear the low voices of Rory and Mary close by; to see through occasional spaces in the scrub the clear expanse of the horse-pad-dock, with even a glimpse of the house, all homely and peaceful in the silent sunshine. But such is life, and such is death.

Rory looked earnestly in my face as I rejoined him, and breathed one of his customary devotional ejaculations.

"Under the big wilga, just beyond that hop-bush," said I, in an indifferent tone. "Stay with me, Mary dear," I continued, taking out my note-book. "I 'll make you a picture of a horse."

"But A 'm aiger fur till see the pine wi' the big santipede on it," objected the terrible infant.

"Nat now, darlin'," replied Rory. "Sure we 'll come an' see the pine when we 've lavin's o' time; but we 're in a hurry now. Stap here an' kape Misther Collins company. Daddy 'll be back at wanst."

He kissed the child, and disappeared round the hop-bush. Then she turned her unfathomable eyes reproachfully on my face, as I sat on the ground.

"A love you, Tammas, becos ye spake aisy till my Daddy. But O!"—and the little, brown fingers wreathed themselves together in the distress of her soul—"A don't want till go to school, an' lave my Daddy his lone! An' A don't want till see that pitcher iv a horse; an' A 'on't lave me Daddy."

I weakly explained that it was a matter of no great importance whether she went to school or not; and that, at worst, her Daddy could accompany her as a schoolmate. Presently Rory returned.

"Mary, jewel, jist pelt aff, lek a good chile, an' see if the wee gate 's shut." Mary shot off at full speed; and he continued gravely, "Dhrapped aff at the dead hour o' the night, seemin'ly. God rest his sowl! O, Tammas! iv we 'd only knowed!"

"Ay, or if I had only spoken to him! He must have got there yesterday morning. Likely he had heard the cocks crowing at your place before daylight, and was making for the sound, only that the light beat him, and he gave it best five minutes too soon."

"Ah! we 're poor, helpless craythurs, Tammas! But A s'pose A betther see Misther Spanker at wanst?"

"No," I replied; "you stay and do what you can. I 'll ride back, and see Mr. Spanker. How far is it to where that swag is on the fence?"

"About—well, about seven mile, as the crow flies."

"Better have it here. Now we 'll catch the horses. Come on, Mary! Take her on your back, Rory; we must hurry up now."

I have already exceeded the legitimate exactions of my diary-record; but the rest of the story is soon told. Mr. Spanker, as a Justice of Peace, took the sworn depositions of Ward, Andrews,

Rory, and myself. In the man's pockets were found half-a-dozen letters, addressed to George Murdoch, Mooltunya Station, from Malmsbury, Victoria; and all were signed by his loving wife, Eliza H. Murdoch. Two of the letters acknowledged receipt of cheques; and there was another cheque (for £12 15s., if I remember rightly) in his pocket-book, with about £3 in cash. He was buried in the station cemetery, between Val English, late station storekeeper, who had poisoned himself, and Jack Drummond, shearer, who had died —presumably of heart failure—after breaking the record of the district. Such is life.

CHAPTER III

FRI. NOV. 9. Charley's Paddock. Binney. Catastrophe.

WHAT fatality impelled me to fix on the 9th, above all other days in the month? Why did n't I glance over the record of each 9th, before committing myself by a promise to review and annotate the entries of that date? For, few and evil as the days of the years of my pilgrimage have undeniably been, the 9th of November, '83, is one of those which I feel least satisfaction in recalling. Moreover, I incur a certain risk in thus unbosoming myself, as will become apparent to the perfidious reader who hungrily shadows me through this compromising story. But it may be graven with a pen of iron, that, at my age, no man shirks a promise, or tells a fib, for the first time; and so, 'Sad, but Strong'—the family motto of the Colonnas, that offshoot of our tribe which settled in Italy in the year One—I answer to my bail.

One reservation I must make, however. For reasons which will too soon become manifest, it is expedient to conceal the exact locality of the unhappy experience now about to be disclosed; but I think I shall be on the safe side in setting forth that it was somewhere between Echuca and Albury.

Any person who happens to have preserved the files of the —— *Express* may find, on the second page of the issue of Nov. 12th, the following local intelligence:—

LUNATIC AT LARGE!

On the night of Friday last the inhabitants of —— were thrown into a state of excitement which may better be imagened than described by the appearance of a lunatic *in puris naturalibus* whose mania was evidently homicidal. During the earlier portion of the night the unfortunate man was seen from time to time by quite a number of people in places many miles apart. Some of the pleasure-seekers returning from the picnic held by the Sunday School Teachers' Re-union (noticed elsewhere in our columns) saw him scuttling along the three-chain road at a breakneck pace, others saw him dodging behind trees or endeavouring to conceal himself in scrub. At about 9 o'clock in the evening one of the picnic party, an athlete of some repute, made a plucky and determined attempt to capture the madman, and succeeded in overpowering him. This accomplished *secundem artem,* an impulse of humanity prompted Mr. K——

(for as some of our readers have already guessed, the gentleman referred to was Mr. K——, of the firm of D—— and S——, Drapers, ——) to divest himself of part of his own clothing for the benefit of his prisoner. The latter, when Mr. K—— attempted to force the clothing upon him, rent the air with horrible shrieks heard by many others of the party, and by exertion of the unnatural strength which insanity confers, broke from his captor and escaped. Mr. K—— humorously comments on the difficulty of hoiding a nude antagonist. If we were inclined to be facetious on the subject we might suggest that *mens sana in corpore sano* is not an infallible rule. Late in the evening the maniac *horresco referrens* made a furious attack on the residence of Mr. G—— who was unfortunately absent at the time. Mrs. G—— with the splendid courage which distinguishes the farmer's wife, kept him at bay till some wild impulse drove him to seek "fresh fields and pastures new." The black trackers (who were brought on the scene on Saturday afternoon) have found his tracks in Mr. A——'s flower garden close to the parlour window, and also around Mr. H——'s homestead. The trackers aver that he is accorpanied by a large kaugaroo dog. It is a matter of congratulatiou that he has so far failed in effecting an entrance to any habitation. The police are scouring the neighbourhood and though the thunderatorm of Saturday night has unfortunately placed the trackers at fault, we trust soon to chronicle a clever capture, "a consummation devoutly to be wished." Various surmises are afloat regarding the identity of the lunatic but to our mind the suggestion of Inspector Collins, of the N.S.W. Civil Service appears most tenable: On Saturday afternoon when the excitement was at its height this gentleman called at our office, and in course of conversation on the all-absorbing topic prouounced his opinion that the lunatic is no other than the late escapee from Beechworth Asylum! Anent his mysterious disappearance at some time late on Friday night Mr. Collins snpposes that he must have drowned himself in the river, and advances many ingenious and apparently conclusive arguments in support of both his hypotheses.

Notwithstanding the ingenuity and conclusiveness of those arguments, the chain of fatalities which has headed this story with the entry of Nov. 9th brings the reluctant secret to light: I was that homicidal maniac.

The second page of the newspaper just quoted will be also found to contain, in another column, the following local item:—

We regret to learn that on the morning of Saturday last Mr. Q—— lost a valuable stack of hay by fire. The conflagration was detected almost immediately on its breaking out but no steps could be taken to check the progress of the "devouring element." It might be reasonably expected that Mr. Q——'s well-deserved popularity would be a sufficient safeguard against such barbarous incendiarism, but of a truth there are people now at large who ought to be in "durance vile." At the moment of our going to press we are happy to add that the police have a clue, and will soon no doubt unearth the cowardly perpetrator of this un-British outrage, and drag him forth to condign punishment.

However, the perpetrator in question, being even more cunning than cowardly, took special order that the police should not unearth him; and here he sits in his temporary sanctum, inviting them to

come on with what is left of their clue—though at the same time
keeping, like Sir Andrew, o' the windy side o' the law, by putting
initials and dashes in place of full names, and by leaving the exact
locality unspecified. Drag me forth to condign punishment! My
word! Drag a barrister.

Now for my narrative. Charley V——, a boundary rider on
B—— Station, N.S.W., is one of my very oldest acquaintances.
Away back in the procuratorship of Latrobe, two angels, in wreaths
of asphodel, had almost simultaneously deposited Charley and
myself on the same station; respectively, in the hut of a stock-
keeper, and in the hut of a petty overseer. Together, as the seasons
passed, we had looked forward to the shearing, the foot-rotting, and
the lambing; and together we had watched the lagoon for the
bunyip. We had aimed our little reed-spears at the same mark,
we had whirled our little boomerangs over the same big tree, and
we had been welted an equal number of times for crossing the river
on the same slippery log.

Whatever may be the development of my own inner nature,
Charley, at least, walks faithfully in the moral twilight which his
early training vouchsafed to him. His fidelity to B—— Station is
like that which ought to distinguish somebody's wife—I forget
whose, but no matter. The mere ownership of the property is a
matter of perfect indifference to Charley. When the place changes
hands, he is valued and sold as part of the working plant, without
his concern, and almost without his knowledge; owners may come,
and owners may go, but he virtually goes on for ever. His little
hut, three or four miles north from the Murray, is the very head-
quarters of hospitality. He has some hundreds of pounds lent out
(without interest or security) though his pay is only fifteen shillings a week—with ten, ten, two, and a quarter—and he is anything
but a miser. Many people would like a leaf out of his book. It is
my privilege to be able to furnish this, though in a sort of ambiguous way, having received the information in confidence. Here it is:

In a bend, on the north bank of the Murray, a few miles from
Charley's hut, is a tract, about a hundred acres in extent, of fine
grass land, completely isolated by billabongs, reed-beds, dense
scrub, and steep ridges of loose sand. At the time I write of, it
was impossible to ride to this island of verdure, and no white man
could track a horse through the labyrinth that led to it. Once
placed in that spot, no horse would ever try to get away. This is
all the information I feel justified in giving.

During the afternoon of the 9th, I was sitting on a log, in the shade of a tree, on the north bank of the river, about a mile from that secluded Eden, and four or five from Charley's hut. I had camped at dusk on the previous evening; and the equipment of my two horses, with other impedimenta, was lying about. A small damper was maturing under the handful of fire, and a quart pot of tea was slowly collecting a scum of dirt which made it nothing the worse to a man of my nurture. Pup was reposing on my possom rug, and Cleopatra and Bunyip were in Eden, per favour of the kindly scoundrel who held that property by right of discovery, and who, in spite of some reluctance on my part, had made me free of it. Along with my two horses were ten or twelve others, all strangers, and in various stages of ripening for rewards.

Owing to the broken character of the country, the N.S.W. river-road lay three or four miles north of Charley's very private pro-perty; but a short cut, impassable during the winter, and imprac-ticable at any time to wheeled vehicles, saved about three miles in ten, and passed within a mile of the property. It was beside this pad that I was camped.

The refined leisure of the day had been devoted chiefly to the study of my current swapping-book—*Edwards on Redemption*—and now, half-stifled by the laborious blasphemy of the work, I was seeking deliverance from the sin of reading it by watching the multitudes of white cockatoos through my binocular, and piously speculating as to their intended use.

Presently, sweeping the ground-line with the glass, I noticed, crossing an open place, about a mile away, the figure of a swag-man approaching from the west—that is, coming up the river. I kept the glass in his direction, and whenever he disappeared I was on the watch, and caught him again as he came in sight, tramping wearily along in the roasting sun. That swagman had a history, highly important, at all events, to himself. He had been born; he lived; he would probably die—and if any human being wants a higher record than that, he must work for it. This man's personal value, judged by the standard which I, for one, dare not disown, was certainly as high as that of the average monarch or multi-mil-lionare. But was I as much interested as I would have been had one of these personages been approaching my camp in state? And if not, why not?

I immediately filled and lit a mighty German meerschaum, an ally of established efficiency in ethical emergencies such as this. Then laying the pipe, so to speak, on the scent of the swagman, I attempted a clairvoyant rear-glance along his past history, and essayed a forecast of his future destiny, in order to get at the valuation presumably placed upon him by his Maker. But the pipe, being now master of the position, gently seduced my mind to a wider consideration, merely using the swagman as a convenient spring-board for its flight into regions of the Larger Morality. This is its hobby—caught, probably, from some society of German Illuminati, where it became a kind of storage-battery, or accumulator, of such truths as ministers of the Gospel cannot afford to preach.

Ah! (moralised the pipe) the man who spends his life in actual hardship seldom causes a trumpet to be blown before him. He is generally, by heredity or by the dispensation of Providence, an ornament to the lower walks of life; therefore his plea, genuine if ungrammatical, is heard only at second-hand, in a fragmentary and garbled form. Little wonder, then, that such a plea is received with felicitous self-gratulation, or passed with pharisaical disregard, by the silly old world that has still so many lessons to learn—so many lessons which none but that unresisting butt of slender-witted jokers can fitly teach, and which he, the experienced one, is usually precluded from teaching by his inability to spell any word of two syllables. Yet he has thoughts that glow, and words that burn, albeit with such sulphurous fumes that, when uttered in a public place, they frequently render him liable to fourteen days without the option.

And even though he be not a poor rogue hereditary; even though he may once have tasted the comfort ambiguously scorned of devils; even though his descent into Avernus be, like that of Ulysses or Dante, temporary and incidental, you need n't expect him, on reaching the upper air, to be the prophet, spokesman, and champion of the Order whose bitter johnny-cake he has eaten. You must n't be surprised to find him reticent, not to say mendacious, respecting details which he may regard as humiliating. A sort of Irish pride will probably lead him to represent that he had abundant, though unavailable, resources during the period of his perdition. For one or the other of these reasons—orthographical inability, or Irish pride—the half is never told; therefore, as a rule, the reading public is acquainted only with sketchy and fallacious pictures of that continuous, indurating hardship which finally sends reluctant Hope after her co-tenants of the box.

And further, of this, my son, be admonished (continued the pipe): The more bitter the hardship, the more unmixed and cordial is the ignominy lavished by the elect upon the sufferer—always provided the latter is one of the non-elect, and more particularly if he is a swagman. Yet this futureless person is the man who pioneers all industries; who discovers and unearths the precious ores; whose heavy footprints mark the waterless mulga, the wind-swept plains, and the scorching sand; who leaves intaglio impressions of his mortal coil on the wet ground, at every camp from the Murray to the Gulf; and whose only satisfaction, in the cold which curls him up like cinnamon bark—making him nearly break his back in the effort to hold his shoulders together—is the certainty that in six months he will scrape away the hot surface sand, in order to sleep comfortably on the more temperate stratum beneath; he is the man who, with some incoherent protest and becoming invective, metaphorically makes a Raleigh-cloak of himself, to afford free and pleasant passage for the noblest work of God, namely, the Business Man.

The successful pioneer is the man who never spared others; the forgotten pioneer is the man who never spared himself, but, being a fool, built houses for wise men to live in, and omitted to gather moss. The former is the early bird; the latter is the early worm. Like Rosalind's typical traveller, this worm has rich eyes and poor hands—the former often ophthalmic, the latter always brown and wrinkled, and generally dirty. Life is too short to admit of repeated blunders in the numeration of beans, and this being his one weak point, the dram of ale does its work. And so, neither as pharisee nor publican, but rather as the pharisee's shocking example, and the publican's working bee, he toils and swears his hour upon the stage, and then modestly departs to where the thrifty cease from troubling, and the thriftless be at rest. Little recks he then for lack of storied urn or animated bust, little that for him no minstrel raptures swell; for his animated busts are things of the past, and there never was anything of the swell about him.

Heaven help him! that nameless flotsam of humanity! (mused the pipe). Few and feeble are his friends on earth; and the One who, like him, was wearied with his journey, and, like him, had not where to lay his head, is gone, according to His own parable, into a far country. The swagman we have always with us——And comfortable ecclesiasticism marks a full stop there, blasphemously evading the completion of a sentence charged with the grave truth, that the Light of the world, the God-in-Man, the only God we can ever know, is by His own authority represented for all time by the poorest of the poor. Yet whosoever fails to recognise in the marred visage of any social derelict the image of Him who was despised and rejected of men—whosoever resents not the spectacle of that image weighted down by fraternal neglect and oppression till a human heart pulses with no higher aspiration than that which prompts a persecuted animal to preserve its life for further persecution—such a person, I say, can have no place among the Architect's workmen, being already employed on the ageless Babel-contract.

This special study of hardship (resumed the pipe, after a pause) leads naturally to the generic study of poverty; for, as the greater includes the less, poverty includes hardship, along with disfranchisement, social outlawry, proud man's contumely, and so forth; entirely without reference to the moral worth of the person most concerned. In a word, poverty is, in the eyes of the orthodox Christian, a hell in the hand, better worth avoiding than two hells in the book, which latter may be only figurative after all.

But the great institution of poverty (ruminated the pipe) is too often referred to in this large, loose way. There are two kinds—or rather, the condition exhibits two opposite extremes of moral quality. There is a voluntary poverty, which is certainly the least base situation you can occupy whilst you crawl between heaven and earth, and which is not so rare as your sordid disposition might lead you to imagine. There is also a compulsory poverty, shading down from discontented to contented. And, paradoxical as it may appear, the contented sub-variety is the opposing pole to voluntary poverty. The discontented sub-variety is the perpetual troubler of the world, by reason of its aiming only at changing the incidence of hardship, and suceeding fairly well in its object. Touching the contented sub-variety—well, possibly the Hindoo language might do justice to its vileness; the English falls entirely short. Compulsory-contented poverty is utterly, irredeemably despicable, and, by necessity, ignorantly blasphemous—not because its style of glorifying God is to place His conceded image exactly at the plough-horse level, but because it teaches its babies, from the cradle upward, that a capricious Mumbo-Jumbo has made pollard-bread for them, and something with a French name for its white-headed boy; moleskins, tied below the knee, for them, and a bell-topper for the favourite of the family; the three R's for them, and the classics, ancient and modern, for the vessel chosen to honour; illicit snake-juice for them, and golden top for the other fellow. The adherents of this cult vote Conservative, work scab, and are rightly termed the "deserving poor," inasmuch as they richly deserve every degree of poverty, every ounce of indignity, and every inch of condescension they stagger under. But their children don't deserve these things. And just mark the slimy little word-shuffle which, in order to keep the 'deserving poor' up to their work, pronounces upon them the blessings obviously adherent only to that unquestionable guarantee of unselfish purpose, namely, voluntary poverty. A subtle confusion of issues; but the person who homilises on the blessings of compulsory poverty should be left talking to the undefileable atmosphere.

Yet do I cling (continued the pipe) to Plato's beautiful thought, that no soul misses truth willingly. In bare justice to brave, misguided Humanity; in daily touch with beings in so many respects little lower than the imagined angels; in dispassionate survey of history's lurid record of distorted loyalty staining our old, sad earth with life-blood of opposing loyalty, while each side fights for an idea; in view of the zeal which fires the martyr-spirit to endure all that equal zeal can inflict; in contemplation of the ever-raging enmity between the seed of the woman and the seed of the serpent, the Ormuzd and the Ahriman in man; in view even of that dismal experiment indifferently termed 'making the best of both worlds,' and 'serving God and Mammon'—in view of all these things, I cannot think it is anything worse than a locally-seated and curable ignorance which makes men eager to subvert a human equality, self-evident as human variety, and impregnable as any mathematical axiom. And this special brand of ignorance is even more rampant amongst those educated asses who can read Kikero in the original than amongst uneducated asses who know not the law, and are cursed.

Remember (pursued the pipe, with a touch of severity) that Science apprehends no decimal of a second adequate to note, on the limitless circle of Time, the briefness of a centenarian's life; and yet the giddiest pitch of human effrontery dares not carry beyond the incident of death any vestige of a social code now accepted as good enough to initiate a development which, according to your own showing, goes on through changing cycles till some transcendent purpose is fulfilled. The 'love of equality'—that meanest and falsest of equivocations—sickens and dies, and the inflated lie of a social privilege based on extraneous conditions collapses, under the strict arrest of the fell sergeant, Death. If we seek absolute truth—which can never be out of place—surely we shall find it beyond the gates which falsehood cannot pass. And here we find it conceded by all; for as material things fade away, human vision clears, and truth becomes a unit.

Osiris's balances weighed impartially the souls of Coptic lord and slave, before the pyramids rose on Egypt's plains; austere Minos meted even justice to citizen and helot, while the sculptured ideals of Attica slept in Pentelican quarries; Brahmin and Sudra, according to deeds done in the body—strictly according to deeds done in some body—awake beyond the grave to share æons of sorrowful transmigration, and final repose; Nirvana awaits the Buddhist high and low alike; Islamism sternly sends all mankind across the sharp-edged Bridge, which the righteous only cross in safety, while wicked caliph and wicked slave together reel into the abyss below. The apotheosis of pagan heroes rested on personal merit alone. No eschatology but that of High Calvinism anticipates, in the unseen world, anything resembling the injustice of a civilisation which, of set purpose, excludes from the only redemption flesh and blood can inherit, that sad rear-guard whose besetting sin is poverty. Yet John Knox's wildest travesty of eternal justice never rivalled in flagrancy the moving principle of a civilisation which exists merely to build on extrinsic bases an impracticable barrier between class and class: on one side, the redemption of life, education, refinement, leisure, comfort; on the other side, want, toil, anxiety, and an open path to the Gehenna of ignorance, baseness, and brutality. Holy Willie's God, at least, heaps no beatitude on successful greed; and your Christian civilisation does so. Dare you deny it?

Chastened by contemplation of levelling mortality, awed into truth by the spectacle of a whole world made kin by that icy touch of nature, the belated soul seeks refuge in a final justice which excludes from natural heirship to the external home not one of earth's weary myriads. Your conception of heavenly justice is found in the concession of equal spiritual birthright, based on the broad charter of common humanity, and forfeitable only by individual worthlessness or deliberate refusal. Why is your idea of earthly justice so widely different—since the principle of justice must be absolute and immutable? Yet while the Church teaches you to pray, 'Thy will be done on earth, as it is done in heaven,' she tacitly countenances widening disparity in condition, and openly sanctions that fearful abuse which dooms the poor man's unborn children to the mundane perdition of poverty's thousand penalties. Is God's will so done in heaven? While the Church teaches you to pray, 'Thy Kingdom come,' she strikes with mercenary venom at the first principle of that kingdom, namely, elementary equality in citizen privilege. Better silence than falsehood;

better no religion at all—if such lack be possible—than one which concedes equal rights beyond the grave, and denies them here.

I wish you to face the truth frankly (continued the pipe), for, heaven knows, it faces you frankly enough. Ecclesiastical Christianity vies with the effete Judaism of olden time as a failure of the first magnitude. Passing over what was purely local and contemporaneous, there is not one count in the long impeachment of that doomed Eastern city but may be repeated, with sickening exactitude, and added emphasis, over any pseudo-Christian community now festering on earth. Chorasin and Bethsaida have no lack of antitypes amongst you. Again has man overruled his Creator's design. The mustard seed has become a great tree, but the unclean fowls lodge in its branches. The symbol of deepest ignominy has become the proudest insignia of Court-moths and professional assassins, but it is no longer the cross of Christ. Eighteen-and-a-half centuries of purblind groping for the Kingdom of God finds an idealised Messiah shrined in the modern Pantheon, and yourselves 'a chosen generation,' leprous with the sin of usury; 'a royal priesthood,' paralysed with the cant of hireling clergy; 'a holy nation,' rotten with the luxury of wealth, or embittered by the sting of poverty; 'a peculiar people,' deformed to Lucifer's own pleasure by the curse of caste; while, in this pandemonium of Individualism, the weak, the diffident, the scrupulous, and the afflicted, are thrust aside or trampled down.

And whilst the world's most urgent need is a mission of sternest counsel and warning, from the oppressed to the oppressor, I witness the unspeakable insolence of a Gospel of Thrift, preached by order of the rich man to Lazarus at his gate—a deliberate laying on the shoulders of Lazarus a burden grievous to be borne, a burden which Dives (or Davis, or Smith, or Johnson; anything—anything—but Christ's brutal 'rich man') hungry for the promised penalty, will not touch with one of his fingers. The Church quibbles well, and palters well, and, in her own pusillanimous way, means well, by her silky loyalty to the law and the profits, and by her steady hostility to some unresisting personification known as the Common Enemy. But because of that pernicious loyalty, she has reason to complain that the working man is too rational to imbibe her teachings on the blessedness of slavery and starvation. Meanwhile, as no magnanimous sinner can live down to the pseudo-Christian standard, unprogressive Agnosticism takes the place of demoralised belief, and the Kingdom of God fades into a myth.

Yet there is nothing Utopian (pleaded the pipe) in the charter of that kingdom—in the sunshiny Sermon on the Mount. It is no fanciful conception of an intangible order of things, but a practical, workable code of daily life, adapted to any stage of civilisation, and delivered to men and women who, even according to the show-ing of hopeless pessimists, or strenuous advocates for Individual-istic force and cunning, were in all respects like ourselves—deliv-ered, moreover, by One who knew exactly the potentialities and aspirations of man. And, in the unerring harmony of the Original Idea, the outcome of that inimitable teaching is merely the con-summation of prophetic forecast in earlier ages. First, the slenderest crescent, seen by eyes that diligently searched the sky; then, a broader crescent; a hemisphere; at last, a perfect sphere, discovered by the Nazarene Artisan, and by him made plain to all who wish to see. But from the dawn of the ages that orb was there, waiting for recognition, waiting with the awful, tireless, all-conquering patience for which no better name has been found than the Will of God.

History marks a point of time when first the Humanity of God touched the divine aspiration in man, fulfilling, under the skies of Palestine, the dim, yet infallible instinct of every race from eastern Mongol to western Aztec. 'The Soul, naturally Christian,' re-sponds to this touch, even though blindly and erratically, and so from generation to generation the multitudes stand waiting to wel-come the Gospel of Humanity with palms and hosannas, as of old; while from generation to generation phylactered exclusiveness takes counsel against the revolution which is to make all things new. And shall this opposition—the opposition by slander, conspiracy, bribery, and force—prevail till the fatal line is once more passed, and you await the Titus sword to drown your land in blood, and the Hadrian-plough to furrow your Temple-site?

I think not (added the pipe, after a pause). I think not. For a revolt undreamt of by your forefathers is in progress now—a revolt of enlightenment against ignorance; of justice and reason against the domination of the manifestly unworthy. The world's brightest intellects are answering one by one to the roll-call of the New Order, and falling into line on the side championed by every prophet, from Moses to the 'agitator' that died o' Wednesday. Inconceivably long and cruel has the bondage been, hideous beyond measure the degradation of the disinherited; but I think the cycle of soul-slaying loyalty to error draws near its close; for the whole armoury of the Father of Lies can furnish no shield to turn aside the point of the tireless and terrible PEN—that Ithuriel-spear which, in these latter days, scornfully touches the mail-clad demon of Privilege, and discloses a swelling frog.

Contemporaneous literature (continued the pipe thoughtfully) is our surest register of advance or retrogression; and, with few exceptions indeed, the prevailing and conspicuous element in all publications of more than a century ago is a tacit acceptance of irresponsible lordship and abject inferiority as Divine ordinances. Brutal indifference, utter contempt, or more insulting condescension, toward the rank and file, was an article of the fine old English gentleman's religion—'a point of our faith,' as the pious Sir Thomas Browne seriously puts it—the complementary part being a loathsome servility toward nobility and royalty. In that era, the most amiable of English poets felt constrained to weave into his exquisite Elegy an undulating thread of modest apology for bringing under notice the short and simple annals of the Vaisya caste. Later, Cowper thought poverty, humility, industry, and piety a beautiful combination for the wearer of the smock frock. Even Crabbe blindly accepted the sanctified lie of social inequality. And this assumption was religiously acquiesced in by the lower animal himself—who doubtless glorified God for the distinctly unsearchable wisdom and loving-kindness manifested in those workhouse regulations which separated his own toil-worn age from the equal feebleness of the wife whose human rights he should have died fighting for when he was young. And, as might be expected, this strictly gentlemanly principle looms larger in your forefathers' prose than in their poetry. At last, Burns and Paine flashed their own strong, healthy personalities on the community, marking an epoch; and from that day to this, the Apology of Humanity acquires ever-increasing momentum, and ever-widening scope. Now, if social-economic conditions fail to keep abreast with the impetuous, uncontrollable advance of popular intelligence, the time must come when, with one tiger-spring, the latter shall assail the former; and the scene of this unpleasantness (concluded the infatuated pipe) is called in the Hebrew tongue, Armageddon.

The swagman approached, plodding steadily along, with his billy in one hand and his water-bag in the other; on his shoulder, horse-shoe fashion, his forty years' gathering; and in his patient face his forty years' history, clearly legible to me by reason of a gift which I happily possess. I was roused from my reverie by some one saying:

"How fares our cousin Hamlet? Come and have a drink of tea, and beggar the expense."

"Good day," responded Hamlet, still pursuing his journey.

"Come on! come on! why should the spirit of mortal be proud?"

"Eh?" And he stopped, and faced about.

"Come and have a feed!" I shouted.

"I 'll do that ready enough," said he, laying his fardel down in the shade, and seating himself on it with a satisfied sigh.

I rooted my damper out of its matrix, flogged the ashes off it with a saddle-cloth, and placed it before my guest, together with a large wedge of leathery cheese, a sheath-knife, and the quart pot and pannikin.

"Eat, and good dich thy good heart, Apemantus," said I cordially. Then, resuming my seat, I took leisure to observe him. He was an every-day sight, but one which never loses its interest to me —the bent and haggard wreck of what should have been a fine soldierly man; the honest face sunken and furrowed; the neglected hair and matted beard thickly strewn with grey. His eyes revealed another victim to the scourge of ophthalmia. This malady, by the way, must not be confounded with sandy blight. The latter is acute; the former, chronic.

"Coming from Moama?" I conjectured, at length.

"Well, to tell you the truth, I ain't had anything since yesterday afternoon. Course, you of'en go short when you 're travellin'; but I 'm a man that don't like to be makin' a song about it."

"Would n't you stand a better show for work on the other side of the river?"

"Eh?"

"Is n't the Vic. side the best for work?" I shouted.

"Yes; takin' it generally. But there 's a new saw-mill startin' on this side, seven or eight mile up from here; an' I know the two fellers that owns it—two brothers, the name o' H——. Fact, I got my eyes cooked workin' at a thresher for them. I 'm not frightened but what I 'll git work at the mill. Fine, off-handed, reasonable fellers."

"Would n't it suit you better to look out for some steady work on a farm?"

"Very carm. Sort o' carm heat. I think there 's a thunderstorm hangin' about. We 'll have rain before this moon goes out, for a certainty. She come in on her back—I dunno whether you noticed?"

"I did n't notice. Don't you find this kind of weather making your eyes worse?"

"My word, you 're right. Not much chance of a man makin' a

rise the way things is now. Dunno what the country 's comin' to.
I don't blame people for not givin' work when they got no work to
give, but they might be civil"——he paused, and went on with his
repast in silence for a minute. It required no great prescience to
read his thought. Man must be subject to sale by auction, or be a
wearer of Imperial uniform, before the susceptibility to insult
perishes in his soul. "I been carryin' a swag close on twenty year,"
he resumed; "but I never got sich a divil of a blaggardin' as I got
this mornin'. Course, I 'm wrong to swear about it, but that 's a
thing I ain't in the habit o' doin'. It was at a place eight or ten
mile down the river, on the Vic. side. I was n't cadging, nyther. I
jist merely ast for work—not havin' heard about the H——s till
after—an' I thought the bloke was goin' to jump down my throat.
I did n't ketch the most o' what he said, but I foun' him givin' me
rats for campin' about as fur off of his place as from here to the
other side o' the river; an' a lagoon betwixt; an' not a particle o'
grass for the fire to run on. Fact, I 'm a man that 's careful about
fire. Mind you, I did set fire to a bit of a dead log on the reserve,
but a man has to get a whiff o' smoke these nights, on account o'
the muskeeters; an' there was no more danger nor there is with
this fire o' yours. Called me everything but a gentleman."

"Possess your soul in patience. You have no remedy and no
appeal till we gather at the river."

"O, I was in luck there. Jist after I heard about this saw-mill—
bein' then on the Vic. side—I foun' a couple o' swells goin' to a
picnic in a boat; an' I told them I wanted to git across, an' they
carted me over, an' no compliment. Difference in people."

"I know the H——s," I shouted. "When did you hear about
them starting this saw-mill?"

"O! this forenoon. I must ast you to speak loud. I got the
misfortune to be a bit hard o' hearin'. Most people notices it on
me, but I was thinkin' p'r'aps you did n't remark it. It come
through a cold I got in the head, about six year ago, spud-diggin'
among the Bungaree savages."

"I 'm sorry for you."

"Well, it was this way. After the feller hunted me off of his
place this mornin', who should I meet but a young chap an' his
girl, goin' to this picnic, with a white horse in the buggy. Now,
that 's one o' these civil, good-hearted sort o' chaps you 'll sometimes git among the farmers. Name o' Archie M——. I dunno
whether you might n't know him; he 's superintender o' the E——
Sunday School. Fact, I 'd bin roun' with the H——'s thresher at

his ole man's place four years runnin'; so when he seen me this mornin', it was, 'Hello, Andy!—lookin' for work?' An' the next word was, 'Well, I 'm sorry we ain't got no work for you'—or words to that effect—'but,' says he, 'there 's the H——s startin' a saw-mill fifteen or twenty mile up the river, on the other side. They won't see you beat,' says he; 'but if you don't git on with them,' says he, 'come straight back to our place, an' we 'll see about something,' says he. So I 'm makin' my way to the saw-mill."

"Well, I hope you 'll get on there, mate."

"You 're right. It 's half the battle. Wust of it is, you can't stick to a mate when you got him. I was workin' mates with a raw new-chum feller las' winter, ringin' on the Yanko. Grand feller he was—name o' Tom—but, as it happened, we was workin' sub-contract for a feller name o' Joe Collins; an' we was on for savin', so we on'y drawed tucker-money; an' beggar me if this Joe Collins did n't git paid up on the sly, an' travelled. So we fell in. Can't be too careful when you 're workin' for a workin' man. But I would n't like to be in Mr. Joe Collins's boots when Tom ketches him. Scotch chap, Tom is. Well, after bin had like this, we went out on the Lachlan, clean fly-blowed; an' Tom got a job boundary ridin', through another feller goin' to Mount Brown diggin's; an' there was no work for me, so we had to shake hands. I 'd part my last sprat to that feller."

"I believe you would. But I 'm thinking of Joe Collins. To a student of nominology, this is a most unhappy combination. Joseph denotes sneaking hypocrisy, whilst Collins is a guarantee of probity. Fancy the Broad Arrow and the Cross of the Legion of Honour woven into a monogram!"

"Rakin' style o' dog you got there. I dunno when I seen the like of him. Well, I think I 'll be pushin' on. I on'y got a sort o' rough idear where this mill is; an' there ain't many people this side o' the river to inquire off of; an' my eyes is none o' the best. I 'll be biddin' you good day."

"Are you a smoker?" I asked, replenishing my own sagacious meerschaum. "Because you might try a plug of this tobacco."

Now that man's deafness was genuine, and I spoke in my ordinary tone, yet the magic word vibrated accurately and unmistakably on the paralysed tympanum. Let your so-called scientists account for that.

"If you can spare it," replied the swagman, with animation. "Smokin 's about the on'y pleasure a man 's got in this world; an' I jist used up the dust out o' my pockets this mornin'; so this 'll

go high. My word! Well, good day. I might be able to do the
same for you some time."

"Thou speakest wiser than thou art 'ware of," I soliloquised as I
watched his retreating figure, whilst lighting my pipe. "As the
other philosopher, Tycho Brahe, found inspiration in the gibberish
of his idiot companion, so do I find food for reflection in thy casual
courtesy, my friend. Possibly I have reached the highest point of
all my greatness, and from that full meridian of my glory, I haste
now to my setting. From a Deputy-Assistant-Sub-Inspector—with
the mortuary reversion of the Assistant-Sub-Inspectorship itself—
to a swagman, bluey on shoulder and billy in hand, is as easy as
falling off a playful moke. Such is life."

The longer I smoked, the more charmed I was with the rounded
symmetry and steady lustre of that pearl of truth which the swagman had brought forth out of his treasury. For philosophy is no
warrant against destitution, as biography amply vouches. Neither
is tireless industry, nor mechanical skill, nor artistic culture—if
unaccompanied by that business aptitude which tends to the survival of the shrewdest; and not even then, if a person's *mana* is off.
Neither is the saintliest piety any safeguard. If the author of the
Thirty-seventh Psalm lived at the present time, he would see the
righteous well represented among the unemployed, and his seed in
the Industrial Schools. For correction of the Psalmist's misleading
experience, one need go no further down the very restricted stream
of Sacred History than the date of the typical Lazarus. Continually
impending calamities menace with utter destitution any given man,
though he may bury his foolish head in the sand, and think himself
safe. There lives no one on earth to-day who holds even the
flimsiest gossamer of security against a pauper's death, and a
pauper's grave. If he be as rich as Crœsus, let him remember
Solon's warning, with its fulfilment—and the change since 550 B.C.
has by no means been in the direction of fixity of tenure. Where
are one-half of the fortunes of twenty years ago?—and where will
the other half be in twenty years more? Though I am, like Sir
John, old only in judgment and understanding, I have again and
again seen the wealthy emir of yesterday sitting on the ash-heap
to-day, scraping himself with a bit of crockery, but happily too
broken to find an inhuman sneer for the vagrants whom, in former
days, he would have disdained to set with the dogs of his flock. I
could write you a column of these emirs' names. And if there is
one impudent interpolation in the Bible, it is to be found in the
last chapter of that ancient Book of Job. The original writer con-

ceived a tragedy, anticipating the grandeur of the *Œdipus at Colonos*, or *Lear*—and here eight supplementary verses have anti-climaxed this masterpiece to the level of a boys' novel. 'Also the Lord gave Job twice as much as he had before,' &c., &c. Tut-tut! Job's human nature had sustained a laceration that nothing but death could heal.

Is there any rich man who cannot imagine a combination of cir-cumstances that would have given him lodgings under the bridge? —that may still do so, say, within twelve months? Setting my knighthood and my soldiership aside, I can imagine a combination that would have quartered me in that airy colonnade—nay, that may do so before this day week; and my view of the matter is, that if I become not the bridge as well as another, a plague of my bringing up! We are all walking along the shelving edge of a precipice; any one of us may go at any moment, or be dragged down by another.

And this is as it ought to be. Justice is done, and the sky does not fall. For, from a higher point of view, the Sabians and Chal-deans of the present day don't dislocate society; they only alter the incidence of existing dislocation; and all this works steadily to-wards a restoration—if not of some old Saturnian or Jahvistic Paradise-idyll, at least of a Divine intention and human ideal. Vicissitude of fortune is the very hand of 'the Eternal, not our-selves, that maketh for righteousness,' the manifestation of the Power behind moral evolution; and we may safely trust the har-mony of Universal legislation for this antidote to a grievous dis-ease; we may rest confident that whilst this best of all possible worlds remains under the worst of all possible managements, the solemn threat of thirty-three centuries ago shall not lack fulfilment —the poor shall never cease out of the land. And no man knows when his own turn may come. But all this is strictly conditional.

Collective humanity holds the key to that kingdom of God on earth, which clear-sighted prophets of all ages have pictured in colours that never fade. The kingdom of God is within us; our all-embracing duty is to give it form and effect, a local habitation and a name. In the meantime, our reluctance to submit to the terms of citizenship has no more effect on the iron law of citizen recipro-city than our disapproval has on the process of the seasons; for see how, in the great human family, the innocent suffer for the guilty; and not only are the sins of the fathers visited upon the children, but my sins are visited upon your children, and your sins upon some one else's children; so that, if we decline a brotherhood of mutual blessing and honour, we alternatively accept one of mutual injury and ignominy. Eternal justice is in no hurry for recognition, but flesh and blood will assuredly tire before that principle tires. It is precisely in relation to the palingenesis of Humanity that, to the unseen Will, one day is said to be as a thousand years, and a thousand years as one day. A Divine Idea points the way, clearly apparent to any vision not warped by interest or prejudice, nor darkened by ignorance; but the work is man's alone, and its period rests with man.

My reason for indulging in this reverie was merely to banish the thought of my late guest. (Of course, my object in recording it here is simply to kill time; for, to speak like a true man, I linger shivering on the brink of the disclosures to which I am pledged. I feel something like the doomed Nero, when he stood holding the dagger near his throat, trying meanwhile to screw his courage to the sticking-place by the recitation of heroic poetry. Trust me to go on with the narrative as soon as I choose.)

I did n't want to think of Andy personally. Intuition whispered to me that the swagman, who would have parted his last sprat to a former mate, had n't that humble coin in his pocket; whilst pursepride hinted that I had four sovereigns and some loose silver in mine—not to speak of £8 6s. 8d. waiting for me in Hay. If I had allowed my mind to dwell on these two intrusive intimations, they would have seemed to fit each other like tenon and mortice; though when the opportunity of making the joint had existed, a sort of moral laziness, together with our artificial, yet not unpraiseworthy, repugnance to offering a money gift, had brought me out rather a Levite than a Samaritan. In mere self-defence, I would have been constrained to keep up a series of general and impersonal reflections till the swagman lost his individuality—say, five or six hours —but I was rescued from this tyranny by the faint rattle of a buggy on the other side of the river. Idly turning my glass on the two occupants of the vehicle, I recognised one of them as a familiar and valued friend—a farmer, residing five or six miles down the river, on the Victorian side. I rose and walked to the brink as the buggy came opposite.

"Hello! Mr. B——," I shouted.

"Hello! Collins. I thought you were way back. When did you come down? Why did n't you give us a call?"

"Could n't get across the river without sacrifice of dignity and comfort."

"Yes, you can; easy enough. You can start off now. I 'm going across here with Mr. G——, to see some sheep, but I 'll be back toward sundown. I 'll tell you how you 'll manage: Follow straight down the road till you come to the old horse-paddock, nearly opposite our place; then turn to your left, down along the fence——"

"No use, Mr. B——. I want to get away to-morrow; and you know when we get together——"

"Yes; I know all about that. But you must come, Collins. There 's a dozen things I want your opinion about."

"Indeed I appreciate your sensible valuation of me as a referee, Mr. B——, but I must still decline. I wish I had gone this morning; it 's too late now."

"Well, I 'll feel disappointed. So will Dick. By-the-by, Dick L—— has turned up again. He 's at our place now. He 's off next week—to Fiji, I suspect."

"Where has he been this last time?"

"You would n't guess. He 's been in the Holy Land. Poked about there for over six months."

"At Jerusalem?"

"Yes; he 's been a good deal in Jerusalem. He lived in Jericho for a month; but he spent most of his time at different places up and down the Jordan."

"Did he meet many Scotchmen wandering along that river?"

"I suppose he would meet a good many anywhere—but why there particularly?"

"Well, Byron tells us that on Jordan's banks the arab Campbells stray."

"I don't take."

"Neither do I, Mr. B——."

"But I 'm perfectly serious, Tom; I am, indeed. I thought you would like to have a yarn with Dick. His descriptions of the Holy Land are worth listening to."

"Say 'Honour bright'."

"Honour bright, then. I say, Collins—did you ever have reason to doubt my word?"

"No; but I always get demoralised out back. Where were you saying I could get across the river?"

"I thought that would fetch the beggar," I heard B—— remark to his companion. And he was right. It would fetch the beggar across any river on this continent.

Dick L——, Mrs. B——'s brother, was a mine of rare information and queer experiences. Educated for the law, his innate honesty had shrunk from the practice of his profession, and he had taken to rambling as people take to drink, turning up at irregular intervals to claim whatever might be available of the £12 10s. per quarter bequeathed to him by his father. His strong point was finding his way into outlandish places, and getting insulted and sat on by the public, and run in by the police. Apart, from this speciality, he was one of the most useless beings I ever knew (which is saying a lot). Some men, by their very aspect, seem to invite confidence; others, insult; others, imposition; but Dick seemed only to invite arrest. When well-groomed, he used to be arrested in mistake for some bank defaulter; when ragged, he was sure to be copped for shop-lifting, pocket-picking, lack of lawful visible, or for having in his possession property reasonably supposed to have been stolen. Therefore, honest as he was, he had been, like Paul, in prisons frequent. But, thanks to his forensic training, these interviews with the majesty of the law seemed homely and grateful to him. He could converse with a Bench in such terms of respectful camaraderie, yet with such suggestiveness of an Old Guard in reserve, that his innocence became a supererogatory merit. Besides which, he had been, in a general way, a servant of servants in every quarter of the globe, and had been run out of every billet for utter incompetency; often having to content himself with a poor halfpennyworth of bread to this intolerable deal of sack. So he enjoyed (or otherwise) opportunities of seeing things that the literary tourist never sees; and, being a good talker, and, withal, a singularly truthful man, he was excellent and profitable company after having been on the extended wallaby.

"Where were you saying I could get across the river, Mr. B——?"

"You know the old horse-paddock fence? Well, follow that down to the river, and just at the end of it you 'll find a bark canoe tied to the bank. Bark by name, and bark by nature. And you 'll see a fencing wire lying in the river, with the end fastened to a tree. When you haul the wire up out of the water, you 'll find the other end tied to a tree on this bank. Very complete rig. And, I say, Collins; mind you slacken the wire down from this end after you get across, on account of steamers, and snags, and so forth. The canoe 's dead certain to be on your side of the river. It belongs to a couple of splitters, living in the horse-paddock hut; and they only use it to come across for rations, or the like of that. Well, we 'll be off, Mr. G——. I 'll see you again this evening, then, Collins."

The buggy rattled away through the red-gums. I packed my

things in a convenient hollow tree, and started off down the river, followed by the slate-coloured animal that constantly loved me although I was poor. About half-way to the horse-paddock, I was overtaken and passed by Arthur H——, one of the two brothers reported to be starting the saw-mill; and I afterward remembered that, though we saluted each other, and exchanged impotent critic-isms on the weather, I had by this time obtained such ascendency over the meddlesome and querulous part of my nature that I had never once thought of asking him if he had met Andy.

It must have been near six in the afternoon when I made my way down the steep bank to where the aptly-named bark was tied up. I soon pulled the slack of the wire out of the bed of the river, and made all fast. Then it occurred to me that I might have a smoke whilst pulling across. My next thought was that I could economise time by deferring this duty till I should resume my journey, with both hands at liberty. Forthwith, I squatted in the canoe, and got under way, leaving Pup to follow at his own convenience.

In a former chapter I had occasion to notice a great fact, namely, that the course of each person's life is directed by his ever-recur-ring option, or election. Now let me glance at two of my own alternatives, each of which has immediate bearing on the incident I am about to relate:

Three weeks ago (from the present writing) I had open choice of all the dates in twenty-two diaries. I actually dallied with that choice, and inadvertently switched my loco. on to the line I am now faithfully, though reluctantly, following. The doom-laden point of time was that which marked the penning of my determina-tion; for a perfectly-balanced engine is more likely to go wandering off a straight line than I am to fail in fulfilment of a promise.

Another indifferent-looking alternative was accepted when my guardian angel suggested a smoke while crossing the river, and I declined, on the plea of haste. A picaninny alternative, that, you say? I tell you, it proved an old-man alternative before it ran itself out. The filling and lighting of my pipe would have occupied three or four minutes, and I should have seen an impending danger in time to guard against it. But I shunted on to the wrong line, and nothing remained but to follow it out to a finish. You shall judge for yourself whether even your own discretion and address could have carried the allotted trip to a less unhappy issue.

Hand over hand along the wire, I had wobbled the bark to the middle of the stream, when I noticed, not fifty yards away, a dead tree of twelve or fifteen tons displacement, *en route* for South Australia. Being about nineteen-twentieths submerged, and having no branches on the upper side, it would have passed under the wire but for a stump of a root, as thick as your body, standing about five feet above the surface of the water, on its forward end. In remarking that the tree was ong root, I merely mean to imply such importance in that portion of its substance that it might rather be viewed as a root with a tree attached than as a tree with a root attached. This is the aspect it still retains in my mind.

There was not half enough time to pull the bark ashore and sink the wire, so I did the next best thing I could. As the log approached, I carefully rose to my feet, and held the wire high enough to clear the root. Nearer it came; it would pass the bark nicely within three or four feet; a few seconds more, and the root would glide underneath the wire——

Pup had remained yelping and dancing on the bank for a few minutes after my embarkation—the kangaroo dog having a charcoal burner's antipathy to the bath—but at last becoming desperate, he had plunged in, and was rapidly approaching whilst I judiciously gauged the height of the root, and meanwhile balanced the unsteady bark under my feet. When the root was within six inches of the wire, Pup's chin and forepaws were on the gunwale; in three seconds more, I was clinging with one hand to the root, the other still mechanically holding the tightening wire; Pup was making for the log; and the splitters' bark had gone to Davy Jones's locker. In another half-minute, the wire parted, and Pup and I were deck passengers, ong root for the land of the Crow-eaters.

I was no more disconcerted than I am at the present moment. I would go on to B——'s as if nothing had happened; and put up with the inconvenience of swimming the river in the morning. In the meantime, though I was well splashed, all the things in my pockets were dry. I particularly congratulated myself on the good fortune of having been so close to the root at the Royal Georgeing of my bark. My bark—well, strictly speaking, it was the splitters' bark; but accidents will happen; and I was certain that not a soul had seen me turn off the main road toward the river.

My clothes were of the lightest. I took them off, and tied them in my handkerchief. I pounded a depression in the package to fit the top of my head, and bound it there with my elastic belt, holding the latter in my teeth. You must often have noticed that the chief difficulty of swimming with your clothes on your head arises from the fore-and-aft surging of the package with each stroke. But nothing could have been more complete than my arrangements as

I slid gently into the water, and paddled for the Cabbage Garden shore.

When I had gone a few yards, my faithful companion, now left alone on the log, raised his voice in lamentation, after the manner of his sub-species.

"Come on, Pup!" I shouted, without looking round; and the next moment I felt as if a big kangaroo dog had catapulted himself through twenty feet of space, and lit on my package.

After returning to the surface and coughing about a pint of water out of my nose and ears, I looked uneasily round for my cargo. It was nowhere to be seen. I swam back to the log, and stood on it to get a better view. Good! there was the white, rounded top, an inch above the water, ten yards away. As I swam toward it, a whirlpool took it under. I dived after it, struck it smartly with the crown of my head; and eventually returned to the log, whence I watched for its re-appearance above the slowly-swirling water. It never re-appeared.

Following the sinuosities of the river, this must have been a mile and a half below the splitters' crossing-place; and time had been passing, for there was the setting sun, blazing through a gap in the timber, and its mirrored reflection stretching half a mile of dazzling radiance along a straight reach of the river.

Now, though the Murray is the most crooked river on earth, its general tendency is directly from east to west. Would n't you, therefore—if you were on a floating log, remote, unfriended, melancholy, slow; standing, like the Apollo Sauroctones, with your hand on the adjacent stump, and, to enhance your resemblance to that fine antique, clad in simplicity of mien and nothing else—if you were sadly realising the loss of your best clothes, with all the things in the pockets, including a fairly trustworthy watch—if, in addition to this, the patient face of the spratless swagman was rising before you till you involuntarily muttered "O Julius Cæsar! thou art mighty yet!" and the nasty part of your moral nature was reminding you that you might have had anything up to four-pounds-odd worth of heavenly debentures; whereas, having failed to put your mammon of unrighteousness into celestial scrip, to await you at the end of your pilgrimage, you were now doubly debarred from retaining it in your pilgrim's scrip, by reason of having neither scrip nor mammon—under such circumstances, I say, would n't you be very likely to take the sunset on your left, and swing for the north bank, without doing an equation in algebra to find out which way the river ought to run? That is what I did. It never occurred to my mind that Victoria could be on the north side of New South Wales.

After shouting myself hoarse, and whistling on my fingers till my lips were paralysed, I brought Pup into view on the south, and supposedly Victorian, bank, opposite where I had landed. By the time I had induced him to take the water and rejoin me, the short twilight was gone, and night had set in, dark, starless, hot, and full of electricity.

And the mosquitos. Well, those who have been much in the open air, in Godiva costume, during opaque, perspiring, November nights, about Lake Cooper, or the Lower Goulburn, or the Murray frontage, require no reminder; and to those who have not had such experience, no illustration could convey any adequate notion. Hyperbolically, however: In the localities I have mentioned, the severity of the periodical plague goads the instinct of animals almost to the standard of reason. Not only will horses gather round a fire to avail themselves of the smoke, but it is quite a usual thing to see some experienced old stager sitting on his haunches and dexterously filliping his front shoes over a little heap of dry leaves and bark.

To return. The recollection of much worse predicaments in the past, and the reasonable anticipation of still worse in the future, restored that equilibrium of temper which is the aim of my life; and I felt cheerful enough as I welcomed my dripping companion, and, taking a leafy twig in each hand to switch myself withal, started northward for the river road, which I purposed following eastward to where the pad branched off, and then running the latter to my camp. Once clear of the river timber, and with the road for a base, the darkness, I thought, would make little difference to me.

After half an hour's gliding through heavy forest, and cleaving my way through spongy reed-beds, and circling round black lagoons, alive with the 'plump, plump' of bullfrogs, and the interminable 'r-r-r-r-r' of yabbies, I found the river on my right, with a well-beaten cattle-track along the bank. Here was something definite to go upon. By keeping straight on, I must soon strike the old horse-paddock fence, where the splitters used to keep their bark; and in an hour and a-half more, I would be at my camp.

But the discerning reader will perceive, from hints already given, that, by following the cattle track, with the river on my right, I was unconsciously travelling westward on the Victorian side, instead of eastward on the New South Wales side. If the sky had cleared for a single instant, a glance at the familiar constellations would have set me right.

After half a mile, the cattle-track intersected a beaten road, with the black masses of river timber still on the right, and a wire fence on the left—as I found by running into it. Everything seemed unfamiliar and puzzling; but I followed the road, looking out for landmarks, and zealously switching myself as I went along.

Soon I heard in front the trampling of horses, and men's voices in jolly conversation. I aimed for the sounds, and, after running against a loose horse, feeding leisurely on the grass, I distinguished through the hot, stagnant darkness the approaching forms of three men riding abreast.

"Good evening, gentlemen," said I politely, switching myself as I spoke. "Could you give me some idea of the geography"—— I got no farther, for a colt that one of the fellows was riding suddenly shied at me, and followed up the action by bucking his best. Upon this, the loose horse presented himself, cavorting round in senseless emulation, while the other two horses swerved and tried to bolt. All this took place in half a minute.

The rider of the colt was taken by surprise, but he was plucky. Though losing not only his stirrups but his saddle with the first buck, he spent the next couple of minutes riding all over that colt, sometimes on his ears, and sometimes on his tail. But this sort of thing could n't last—it never does last—so, after hanging on for about twenty seconds by one heel the fellow dismounted like a barrow-load of sludge. During this time, I saw nothing of the two other men, but I could hear them trying to force their excited horses toward the spot where I was skipping round, ready to catch the colt on the moment of his discharging cargo.

On making the attempt, I missed the bridle in the dark; and away shot the colt in one direction, and the loose horse in another.

"I bet a note Jack 's off," said a voice from the distance.

"Gosh, you 'd win it if it was twenty," responded another voice from the ground close by.

"There goes his moke!" said the first voice. "Come and jam the beggar against the fence, or he'll be off to glory." And away clattered the two horsemen after the wrong horse; Jack following on foot.

Noticing their mistake, I cantered hopefully after the colt, thinking to obtain a favourable introduction to Jack by restoring the animal; but in a few minutes I lost the sounds, and abandoned the pursuit. Then, after supplying myself with fresh switches, I resumed my fatal westward course.

More voices, a short distance away, and straight in front. Judging them to come from some vehicle travelling at a slow walk along the edge of the timber, I posted myself behind a tree, and waited as patiently as the mosquitos permitted.

"Now you need n't scandalise one another," said a pleasant masculine voice. "You 're like the pot and the kettle. You 're both as full of sin and hypocrisy as you can stick. Six of one, and half-a-dozen of the other. I would n't have believed it if I had n't seen it with my own eyes. You 've disgraced yourselves for ever. Who the dickens do you think would be fool enough to marry either of you after the way you 've behaved yourselves to-day?"

"Well, I 'm sure we 're not asking you to marry us," piped a feminine voice.

"Keep yourselves in that mind, for goodness' sake. I 'm disgusted with you. Why, only last Sunday, I heard your two mothers flattering themselves about the C—— girls knowing too much; and I 'll swear you 've both forgot more than the C—— girls ever knew. You 're as common as dish-water."

"O, you 're mighty modest, your own self," retorted a second feminine voice.

"It 's my place to be a bit rowdy," replied the superior sex. "It 's part of a man's education. And I don't try to look as if butter would n't melt in my mouth. You 're just the reverse; you 're hypocrites. 'Woe unto you hypocrites!' the Bible says. But it 's troubling me a good deal to think what your mothers 'll feel, now that you 've come out in your true colours."

"But you would n't be mean enough to tell?" interrupted one of the sweet voices.

"I always thought you were too honourable to do such a thing, Harry," remarked the other.

"Well, now you find your mistake. But this is not a question of honour; it 's a question of duty."

"O, you 're mighty fine with your duty! You 're a mean wretch. There!"

"I 'll be a meaner wretch before another hour's over. Go on, Jerry; let 's get it past and done with."

"But, Harry—I say, Harry—don't tell. I 'll never forgive you if you do."

"Duty, Mabel, duty."

"What good will it do you to tell?" pleaded the other voice.

"Duty, Annie, duty. On you go, Jerry, and let 's get home. This is painful to a cove of my temperament."

During this conversation, I had become conscious of standing on a populous ant-bed; and, not wishing to lose the chance of an interview with Harry, I had retreated in front of the buggy till a second tree offered its friendly cover. Jerry's head was now within two yards of my ambush, and, peeping round, I could make out the vague outline of the figures in the buggy.

"Well, I 'll tell you what I 'll do," said Harry, stopping the horse: "If each of you gives me a kiss, of her own good will, I 'll promise not to tell. Are you on? Say the word, for I 'll only give you one minute to decide."

"What do you think, Mabel?" murmured one of the voices.

"Well, I 've got no—— But what do you think?"

"I think it 's about the only thing we can do. We would never be let come out again."

There was perfect silence for a minute. My tree was n't a large one, and the near front wheel of the buggy was almost against it. Not daring to move hand or foot, I could only wish myself a rhinoceros.

"Come on," said one of the voices, at last.

"Come on how?" asked Harry innocently. "Look here: the agreement is that each of you is to give me a kiss, of her own good will. I 'm not going to move."

"O, you horrid wretch! Do you think we 're going to bemean ourselves? You 're mighty mistaken if you do."

"Go on, Jerry." And the buggy started.

"We 're not frightened of you now," remarked one of the voices complacently, whilst I threw myself on the ground, and rolled like a liberated horse. "If you dare to say one single word, we 'll just expose your shameful proposal. You mean wretch! you make people think it 's safe to send their girls with you, to be insulted like this. O, we 'll expose you!"

"Expose away. And don't forget to mention that you both agreed to the shameful proposal. I 'll tell your mothers that I made that proposal just to try you, and you consented on condition of me keeping quiet. You 're both up a tree. 'Weighed in the balances, and found wanting. Mene, Mene, Tekel Upharsin.' Go on, Jerry, and let 's have it over."

"What do you think, Annie?" asked one of the voices, whilst I made for my third tree.

"He 's the meanest wretch that ever breathed," replied the other vehemently. "And I always thought men was so honourable!"

"Live and learn," rejoined the escort pithily.

"O, Harry!" panted one voice, "I seen a white thing darting across there!"

"Quite likely," replied Harry. "When a girl 's gone cronk, like you, she must expect to see white things darting about. But I 'll give you one more chance."

"I think we better," suggested one of the voices.

"There 's nothing else for it," assented the other.

By this time, the buggy had disappeared in the darkness. I heard it stop; then followed, with slight intervals, two unsyllabled sounds.

"Over again," said Harry calmly. "You both cheated."

The sounds were repeated.

"Over again. You 'll have to alter your hand a bit—both of you —or we 'll be here all night. Slower, this time."

Once more the sounds were repeated; then the buggy started, and Harry's voice died away in the distance to an indistinct murmur, as he reviled the girls for this new exhibition of their shamelessness.

Whilst undecided whether to follow the buggy any further, I saw a light on the other side of the road. Making my way toward it, I crossed a log-and-chock fence, bounding a roughly ploughed fallow paddock, and then a two-rail fence; wondering all the while that I had never noticed the place when passing it in daylight. At last, a quarter of a mile from the road, a white house loomed before me, with the light in a front window. I opened the gate of the flower garden, and was soon crouched under the window, taking stock of the interior.

A middle-aged woman was sitting by the table, darning socks; and at the opposite side of the lamp sat a full-grown girl, in holiday attire, with her elbows on the table and her fingers in her hair, reading some illustrated journal; while a little boy, squatted behind the girl's chair, was attaching a possum's tail to her improver.

Like Enoch Arden (in my own little tin-pot way) I turned silently and sadly from the window, for I was n't wanted in that company. I thought of going round to the back premises in search of a men's hut; but before regaining the gate, I trod on a porcupine cactus, and forgot everything else for the time. Then, as I lay on the ground outside the gate, caressing the sole of my foot, and comforting myself with the thought that a brave man battling with the storms of fate is a sight worthy the admiration of the gods, a white dog came tearing round from the back yard, and rushed at me like a coming event casting its shadow before.

"Soolim, Pup!" I hissed. That was enough. Pup's colour rendered him invisible in the dark, and his stag-hound strain made him formidable when he was on the job. The office of a chucker-out has its duties, as well as its rights; and in half a minute that farm dog found that one of these duties demanded a many-sided efficiency with which Nature had omitted to endow him. He found that, though the stereotyped tactics of worrying, and freezing, and chawing, were good enough as opposed to similar procedure, they became mere bookish theories when confronted with the snapping system. Eviction becomes tedious when the intruder's teeth are always meeting in the hind quarters of the ejecting party; and the latter can neither get his antagonist in front of him, nor haul off to investigate damage.

Of course, I fanned the flame of discord as well as I could, hoping that some one of my own denomination would come out to see what was the matter. But no: the parlour door opened, Mam came out to the gate, and, in the broad bar of light extending from the door, I saw her pick up a clod, and aim it at the war-clouds, rolling dun. I was crouching some yards away to one side, but the clod crumbled against my ear. Then the storm of one-sided battle went raging round the back premises, as the farm dog returned to tell Egypt the story. Mam retreated from the gate in haste, and for a minute or two there was a confused clatter of voices in the house, and some opening and shutting of doors. Then all was silent again. Presently Pup returned, and accompanied me back to the road, carrying something which I ascertained to be a large fowl, plucked and dressed in readiness for cooking.

Musing on the difficulties of this Wonderland, into which, according to immemorial usage, I had been born without a rag of clothes, I waited for Pup whilst he ate his fowl, and then again pressed forward, alert and vigilant, as beseemed a man scudding under bare poles through an apparently populous country, which by right ought to have been a sheep-run, with about one selection every five miles.

I had managed to put another mile between myself and my camp, when two horsemen met and passed me at a canter, singing one of Sankey's Melodies. I made a modest appeal, but they did n't hear me, and so passed on, unconscious of their lost opportunity.

Then I saw, a long way ahead, the lamps of an approaching vehicle, and at the same time, I heard, close in front, the trampling of horses, and voices raised in careless glee. I headed straight for the horses. As I neared them, the laughing and chatting ceased, and I was about to open negotiations when a woman's awe-stricken voice asked,

"Wha-what 's that white thing there in front?"

Before the last syllable had left her lips, that white thing was receding into the darkness, like a comet into space. The party stopped for a minute, and then went on, conversing in a lower tone.

More pilgrims of the night. This time, the slow footfalls of horses, and a low, inarticulate murmur of voices, out in front and a little to the left, gave me fresh hope. Warned by past failures, I thought best to forgo the erect posture to which our species owes so much of its majesty. I therefore dropped on all-fours and went like a tarantula till I distinguished two horses walking slowly abreast, jammed together; the riders presenting an indistinct outline of two individuals rolled into one; and it was from this amalgamation that the low, pigeon-like murmurs proceeded. An instinct of delicacy prompted me to pause, and let the Siamese twins pass in peace; but, unfortunately, I happened to be straight in the way, and just as I started to creep aside, one of the horses extended his neck, and, with a low, protracted snore, touched me on the back with the coarse velvet of his nose. Then followed two quick snorts of alarm; the horses shied simultaneously outward, while down on the ground between them came two souls with but a single thud, two hearts that squelched as one. In spite of the compunction and sympathy I felt, modesty compelled me to glide unobtrusively away, leaving the souls to disentangle themselves and catch their horses the best way they could.

By this time, the buggy lamps had approached within fifty yards. Knowing how dense the outside darkness would appear to anyone in the vehicle, I made a circuit, and got round to the rear. It was a single-seated buggy, with a white horse, travelling at a walk; and, in the darkness behind the lamps, two figures were discernible. I followed a little, to hear them introduce themselves. They did so as follows:—

"Now, Archie; I 'll scream."

"My own sweetest"——

"Letmego! O,youwon'tletmego!"

Why, the district was fairly bristling with this class of people! I had never seen anything like it, except in the Flagstaff Gardens, when I was in Melbourne.

"My precious darling! My sweetest"——

"I 'lltellmotherIwill! O!"

"My sweetest, my beautiful"——

"O! I don'tloveyoudear! Idon'tloveyounow! Andyouwon'tlet-mego!"

"There, then, sweetest. Kiss me now."

"Yes, Archie, my precious love."

There was more of it, but it fell unheeded on my ears. I paused, and thought vehemently. The white horse in the buggy, and Archie M——, Superintendent of the E—— Sunday School, with his girl! No wonder I had met so many people, and all going in the same direction. They were the sediment of the picnic party, returning from their orgy. Here was the lost chord. The whole truth flashed upon me. Now, the solid earth wheeled right-about-face; east became west, and west, east. I recognised the Victorian river road, because I saw things as they were, not as I had imagined them—though, to be sure, I still saw them as through a glass, darkly.

My worldly-wise friend, let us draw a lesson from this. If you have never been bushed, your immunity is by no means an evidence of your cleverness, but rather a proof that your experience of the wilderness is small. If you have been bushed, you will remember how, as you struck a place you knew, error was suddenly superseded by a flash of truth; this without volition of judgment on your part, and entirely by force of a presentation of fact which your own personal error—however sincere and stubborn—had never affected, and which you were no longer in a position to repudiate. It has always been my strong impression that this is very much like the revelation which follows death—that is, if conscious individuality be preserved; a thing by no means certain, and, to my mind, not manifestly desirable.

But if, after closing our eyes in death, we open them on an appreciable hereafter—whether one imperceptible fraction of a second, or a million centuries, may intervene—it is as certain as anything can be, that, to most of us, the true east will prove to be our former south-west, and the true west, our former north-east. How many so-called virtues will vanish then; and how many objectionable fads will shine as with the glory of God? This much is certain: that all private wealth, beyond simplest maintenance, will seem as the spoils of the street gutter; that fashion will be as the gilded fly which infests carrion; that 'sport' will seem folly that would disgrace an idiot; that military force, embattled on behalf of Royalty, or Aristocracy, or Capital, will seem like—— Well, what will it seem like? Already, looking, or rather, squinting, back along our rugged and random track, we perceive that the bloodiest battle ever fought by our badly-bushed forefathers on British soil —and that only one of a series of twelve, in which fathers, sons, brothers, kinsmen, and fellow-slaves exterminated each other—was fought to decide whether a drivelling imbecile or a shameless lecher should bring our said forefathers under the operation of I Samuel, viii. (Read the chapter for yourself, my friend, if you know where you can borrow a Bible; then turn back these pages, and take a second glance at the paragraphs you skimmed over in that unteachable spirit which is the primary element of ignorance—namely, those reflections on the unfettered alternative, followed by rigorous destiny.)

Much more prosaic were my cogitations as I followed the buggy, keeping both switches at work. According to the best calculation I could make, I had ten or twelve miles of country to re-cross, besides the river; and, having no base on the Victorian side, it was a thousand to one against striking my camp on such a night. Of course, I might have groped my way to B——'s place; but if you knew Mrs. B——'s fatuous appreciation of dilemmas like mine, you would understand that such a thing was not to be thought of. I preferred dealing with strangers alone, and preserving a strict incognito. However, a pair of —— I must have, if nothing else— and that immediately. The buggy was fifteen or twenty yards ahead.

"Archie M——!" said I, in a firm, penetrating tone.

The buggy stopped. I repeated my salute.

"All right," replied Archie. "What 's the matter?"

"Come here; I want you."

The quadrant of light swept round as the young fellow turned his buggy.

"Leave your buggy, and come alone!" I shouted, careering in a circular orbit, with the light at my very heels.

"Well, I must say you 're hard to please, whoever you are," remarked Archie, stopping the horse. "Hold the reins, sweetest."

"Who is it?" asked the damsel, with apprehension in her tone.

"Don't know, sweetest. Sounds like the voice of one crying in the wilderness." And the light flashed on him as he felt downward for the step.

"Don't go!" she exclaimed.

"Never mind her, Archie!" I called out. "She 's a fool. Come on!"

"What on earth 's the matter with you?" asked Archie, addressing the darkness in my direction.

"I 'm clothed in tribulation. Can't explain further. Come on! O, come on!"

"Don't go, I tell you, Archie!" And in the bright light of the off lamp, I saw her clutch the after part of his coat as he stood on the foot-board.

"I must go, sweetest"——

"Good lad!" I exclaimed.

"I 'll be back in a minute. Let go, sweetest."

"Don't leave me, Archie. I 'm frightened. Just a few minutes ago, I saw a white thing gliding past."

"Spectral illusion, most likely. There was a hut-keeper murdered here by the blacks, thirty years ago, and they say he walks occasionally. But he can't hurt you, even if he tried. Now let go, sweetest, and I 'll say you 're a good girl."

"Archie, you 're cruel; and I love you. Don't leave me. Fn-n-n, ehn-n-n, ehn-n-n!" Sweetest was in tears.

"This is ridiculous!" I exclaimed. "Come on, Archie; I won't keep you a minute. The mountain can't go to Mahomet; and to state the alternative would be an insult to your erudition. Come on!"

"O, Archie, let 's get away out of this fearful place," sobbed the wretched obstruction. "Do what I ask you this once, and I 'll be like a slave the rest of my life."

"Well, mind you don't forget when the fright 's over," replied Archie, resuming his seat. "That poor beggar has something on his mind, whoever he is; but he 'll have to pay the penalty of his dignity."

"Too true," said I to myself, as Archie started off at a trot; "for the dignity is like that of Pompey's statue, 'th' austerest form of naked majesty'—a dignity I would gladly exchange for what Goldsmith thoughtlessly calls 'the glaring impotence of dress'."

I followed the buggy at a Chinaman's trot, thinking the thing over, and switching myself desperately, for the night was getting hotter and darker, and mosquitos livelier. You will bear in mind that I was now retracing my way.

Keeping on the track which skirted the river timber—the cool, impalpable dust being grateful to my bare feet—I heard some people on horseback pass along the parallel track which ran by the fence. Demoralised by the conditions of my unhappy state, I again paused to eavesdrop. Good! One fellow was relating an anecdote suited to gentlemen only. Thanking Providence for the tendency of the yarn, I darted diagonally across the clearing to intercept these brethren, and was rapidly nearing the party, when Pup, thinking I was after something, crossed my course in the dark. I tripped over him, and landed some yards ahead, in one of the five patches of nettles in the county of Moira. By the time I had cleared myself and recovered my equanimity, the horsemen had improved their pace, and were out of reach.

A few minutes afterward, I became aware of the footfalls of a single horse, coming along behind me at a slow trot. I paused to make one more solicitation. When the horseman was within twenty yards of where I stood, he pulled up and dismounted. Then he struck a match, and began looking on the ground for something he had dropped. The horse shied at the light, and refused to lead; whereupon, after giving the animal a few kicks, he threw the reins over a post of the fence close by, and continued his search, lighting fresh matches. Assuming an air of unconcern, so as to avoid taking him by surprise, I drew nearer, and noted him as a large, fair young man, fashionably dressed.

"Good evening, sir," said I urbanely.

With that peculiar form of rudeness which provokes me most, he flashed a match on me, instead of replying to my salutation.

"Are you satisfied?" I asked sardonically, switching myself the while, and still capering from the effect of the nettles.

He darted towards his horse, but before he reached the bridle my hand was on his shoulder.

"What do you want?" he gasped.

"I want your ——," I replied sternly. "I 'm getting full up of the admiration of the gods; I want the admiration of my fellow-men. In other words, I 'm replete with the leading trait of Adamic innocence; I want the sartorial concomitants of Adamic guilt. Come! off with them!" and with that I snapped the laces of his balmorals; for he had sunk to the ground, and was lying on his back. "And seeing that I may as well be hanged for a whole suit as for a pair of ——, I 'll just take the complete outer ply while my hand 's in; leaving you whatever may be underneath. Let me impress upon you that I don't attempt to defend this action on strictly moral grounds," I continued, peeling off his coat and waist-coat with the celerity of a skilful butcher skinning a sheep for a bet. "I think we may regard the transaction as a pertinent illustration of Pandulph's aphorism—to wit, that 'He who stands upon a slippery place, makes nice of no vile hold to stay him up.' When the hurly-burly 's done, I must get you to favour me with your address, so that"—— Here my antagonist suddenly gave tongue.

During an eventful life, I have frequently had occasion to observe that when woman finds herself in a tight place, her first impulse is to set the wild echoes flying; whereas, man resists or submits in silence, except, perhaps, for a few bad words ground out between his teeth. Therefore, when the legal owner of the —— which I was in the act of unfastening, suddenly splintered the firmament with a double-barrelled screech, the thought flashed on my mind that he was one of those De Lacy Evanses we often read of in novels; and in two seconds I was fifty yards away, trying to choose between the opposing anomalies of the case. A little reflection showed the balance of probability strongly against a disguise which I have never met with in actual life; but by this time I heard the clatter of horses' feet approaching rapidly from both sides. The prospective violation of my incognito by a hap-hazard audience made my position more and more admirable from a mythological point of view, so I straightway vaulted over the fence, and lay down among some cockspurs.

Within the next few minutes, several people on horseback came up to the scene of the late attempted outrage. I can't give the exact number, of course, as I could only judge by sound, but there might have been half a dozen. A good deal of animated conversation followed—some of it, I thought, in a feminine voice—then the whole party went trampling along the fence, close to my ambush, and away out of hearing.

The mosquitos were worse than ever. I pulled two handfuls of crop to replace the switches I had thrown away on attempting to cajole the Chevalier d'Eon out of his ——. My mind was made up. I would solicit this impracticable generation no longer. I would follow the river road for eight or ten miles, and then wait in some secluded spot for the first peep of daylight. I began to blame myself for not having gone straight on when Archie unconsciously gave me my longitude. To get home in the dark was, of course, entirely out of the question; all that I could do was to aim approximately in the right direction.

I was pacing along at the double, when a lighted window, a couple of hundred yards from the road, attracted my attention. Like Frankenstein's unhappy Monster, I had a hankering, just then, for human vicinity; though, like It, I met with nothing but horrified repulse. You will notice that Mrs. Shelley, with true womanly delicacy, avoids saying, in so many words, that the student omitted to equip his abnormal creation with a pair of ——. But Frankenstein's oversight in this matter will, I think, sufficiently account for that furtive besiegement of human homes, that pathetic fascination for the neighbourhood of man, which so long refused to accept rebuff. With ——, man is whole as the marble, founded as the rock, as broad and general as the casing air. Without ——, unaccommodated man is no more but such a poor, bare, forked animal as thou art. The —— standard is the Labarum of modern civilisation. By this sign shall we conquer. Since that night by the Murray, methinks each pair of —— I see hanging in front of a draper's shop seems to bear aright, *IN HOC SIGNO VINCES!* scrolled in haughty blazonry across its widest part. And since that time, I note and condemn the unworthy satire which makes the somnambulistic Knight of La Mancha slash the wine skins in nothing but an under garment, 'reaching,' says one of our translations, 'only down to the small of his back behind, and shorter still in front; exposing a pair of legs, very long, and very thin, and very hairy, and very dirty.' Strange! to think that man, noble in reason, infinite in faculty, and so forth, should depend so entirely for his dignity upon a pair of ——. But such is life.

Approaching the house, I judged by the style of window curtains that the light was in a bedroom. I made my way to the front door, and knocked.

"Who 's there?" inquired a discouraging soprano.

"A most poor man, made tame by Fortune's blows," I replied humbly. "Is the boss at home?"

"Yes!" she exclaimed, in a hysterical tone.

"Would you be kind enough to tell him I want him?"

"Clear off, or it 'll be worse for you!" she screamed.

"It can't be much worse, ma'am. Will you please tell the boss I want him?"

"I 'll let the dog loose!—that 's what I 'll do! I got him here in the room with me; and he 's savage!"

"No more so than yourself, ma'am. Will you please tell the boss I want him?"

"Clear off this minute! There 's plenty of your sort knockin' about!"

"Heaven pity them, then," I murmured sorrowfully; and I went round to the back yard, in hope of finding something on the clothesline, but it was only labour lost.

I was on my way back to the road when I saw another lighted window. The reason I had seen so few lights was simple enough. As a rule, farmers' families spend their evenings in the back dining room; and the front of the house remains dark until they are retiring for the night, when you may see the front bedroom window lighted for a few minutes.

Turning toward the new beacon, I waded through a quarter of a mile of tall wheat, which occasionally eclipsed the light. When I emerged from the wheat, the light was gone. However, I found the house, and went prowling round the back yard till I roused two watch-dogs. These faithful animals fraternised with Pup, while I prospected the premises thoroughly, but without finding even an empty corn-sack, or a dry barrel with both ends out.

In making my way back to the road, I noticed, far away in the river timber, the red light of a camp-fire. This was the best sight I had seen since sunset. Some swagman's camp, beyond doubt. I could safely count on the occupier's hospitality for the night, and his help in the morning. If he had any spare ——, I would borrow them; if not, I would, first thing in the morning, send him cadging round the neighbourhood for cast-off clothes, while I sought ease-with-dignity in his blanket. This was not too much to count on; for I have yet to find the churlish or unfeeling swagman; whereas, my late experience of the respectable classes had not been satisfactory. At all events, the fire would give me respite from the mosquitos.

Encouraged by this brightening prospect, I crossed the road and entered on the heavy timber and broken ground of the river frontage. But all preceding difficulties, in comparison with those which now confronted me, were as the Greek Tartarus to the Hebrew Tophet. So intense was the darkness in the bush that I simply saw nothing except, at irregular intervals, the spark of red fire, often away to right or left, when I had lost my dead reckoning through groping round the slimy, rotten margins of deep lagoons, or creeping like a native bear over fallen timber, or tacking round clumps of prickly scrub, or tumbling into billabongs. I could show you the place in daylight, and you would say it was one of the worst spots on the river.

Still, in pursuance of my custom, I endeavoured to find tongues in the mosquitos (no difficult matter); books in the patches of cutting-grass; sermons in the Scotch thistles; and good in everything. Light and Darkness!—aptest of metaphors! And see how the symbolism permeates our language, from the loftiest poetry to the most trifling colloquialism. 'There is no darkness but ignorance,' says the pleasantest of stage fools; 'in which thou art more puzzled than the Egyptians in their fog.' And what many-languaged millions of passably brave men have sympathised with Ajax in his prayer—not for courage or strength; he had those already—not for victory; that was outside the province of his interference—but for light to see what he was doing.

No obligatory track so rugged but man, if he be any good at all, may travel it with reasonable safety, in a glimmer of light. And no available track so easy but man, however capable, will blunder therein, if he walks in darkness; nay, the more resolute and conscientious he is, the more certainly will he stub his big toe on a root, and impale his open, unseeing eye on a dead twig, and tread on nothing, to the kinking of his neck-bone and the sudden alarm of his mind.

And Light, which ought to spread with precisely the rapidity of thought, is tardy enough, owing solely to lack of receptivity in its only known medium, namely, the human subject. But—and here is the old-man fact of the ages—Light is inherently dynamic, not static; active, not passive; aggressive, not defensive. Therefore, as twice one is two, the momentum of Light, having overborne the Conservatism of the Palæolithic, Neolithic, and other unpronounceable ages, has, in this 19th century, produced a distinct paling of the stars, with an opaline tint in the east. And, as a penny for the first nail, twopence for the second, fourpence for the third, and so on, amounts to something like a million sterling for the set of horse-shoes, so the faint suggestion of dawn observable in our day cannot do otherwise than multiply itself into sunshine yet. Meantime, happy insect is he whose luminosity dispels a modicum of the general darkness, besides shedding light on his own path as he buzzes along in philosophic meditation, fancy free——

Here I trod on something about as thick as your wrist—something round and smooth, which jerked and wriggled as my weight came upon it. I rose fully three feet into the air without conscious effort, and thenceforth pursued my difficult way with a subjective discontent which, I fear, did little honour to my philosophy; thinking, to confess the truth, what an advantage it would be if man, figuratively a mopoke, could become one in reality when all the advantage lay in that direction; also, feeling prepared to wager my official dignity against a pair of —— that Longfellow would never have apostrophised the welcome, the thrice-prayed-for, the most fair, the best-beloved Night, if he had known what it was to work his passage through pitch-black purgatory, in a state of paradise-nudity, with the incongruity of the association pressing on his mind. Ignorance again; but such is life.

It was about three-quarters of a mile from the edge of the timber to the fire; and I should think it took me an hour to perform the journey. It was a deserted fire, after all, and nearly burnt out; but I soon raised a good smoke, and had relief from the mosquitos. The passage from the road had given me enough of exploring for the time; so I parted the fire into three lots, and, piling bark and rubbish on each, lay down between them, to enjoy a good rest, and think the thing over thoroughly.

It may surprise the inexperienced reader to know that I had often before found myself in a similar state of nature, and in far more prominent situations. I had repeatedly found myself doing the block, or stalking down the aisle of a crowded church, mid nodings on, and had wakened up to find the unsubstantial pageant faded, and my own conspicuousness exchanged for a happier obscurity. So, throughout the trying incidents of the evening I have recalled, the hope of waking up had never been entirely absent from my mind; and now, as I lay drowsing, with Pup beside me, and not a mosquito within three yards, it occurred to me that if I did n't get out of the difficulty by waking up, I would get out of it some other way. Philosophy whispered that all earth-born cares were not only wrong, but unprofitable. Though I had inadvertently switched my little engine on to the wrong line when I postponed my intended smoke, and had so lost the clothes which evidently went so far toward making the man, it would be true wisdom to accept the consequent kismet, and wait till the clouds rolled by. The end of the section could n't be far ahead. Sufficient unto the day—— And I dropped asleep.

Here the record properly ends. I have faithfully recounted the events of the 9th of November, at what cost to my own sensibilities none but myself can ever know. But the one foible of my life is amiability; and, from the first, I had no intention of breaking off abruptly when my promise was fulfilled, leaving the reader to con-clude that I woke up at my camp, and found the whole thing a dream. The dream expedient is the mere romancist's transparent shift—and he is fortunate in always having one at command, though transparency should, of course, be avoided. The dream-expedient vies in puerility with the hero's rescue of the heroine from deadly peril—a thing that has actually happened about twice since the happily-named, and no less happily extinct, Helladotherium dis-ported itself on the future site of Eden. I am no romancist. I repudiate shifts, and stand or fall by the naked truth.

Therefore, though legal risk here takes the place of outraged sen-sibility, I shall proceed with the record of the next day, till my loco. reaches the end of the current section. By this large-hearted order of another herring, the foolish reader will be instructed, the integrity of narrative preserved, and the linked sacrifice long drawn-out. And if, in the writing of annotations yet to come, the exigencies of annalism should demand a repetition of this rather important favour, I may be trusted to grant it without fishing for compliments, or in any way reminding the recipient of his moral indebtedness. I can't say anything fairer than that.

It was good daylight when I woke, a little chilled and smarting, but otherwise nothing the worse. Let me endeavour to describe the scene which I stealthily, but carefully, surveyed during the next few minutes. The Victorian river road, running east and west, lay about three-quarters of a mile to the south. North and west, I could see nothing but heavy timber and undergrowth. The eastern prospect was more interesting. Within twenty yards of my lair, a long, deep lagoon lay north and south, the intervening ground being covered with whipstick scrub. Beyond the lagoon, a large promontory of red soil, partly cultivated and partly ringed, projected northward from the road into the State Forest. Beyond this, still eastward, the river timber again came out to the road.

A roomy homestead, with smoke issuing from one of the chimneys, stood almost opposite my point of observation, and about a hundred yards distant, whilst a garden occupied the space between the house and the lagoon. At the north side of the garden, the lagoon was divided by a dry isthmus. The nearer boundary fence of the farm, half-buried in whipstick scrub, ran north and south along the edge of the lagoon, the lower line of garden-fence forming part of it; and a gate opposite the isthmus afforded egress to the river frontage.

Again, opposite my fire, but considerably to the right, a deep, water-worn drain came down from the table-land into the lagoon; and between this drain and the house stood a little, old, sooty-looking straw-stack, worn away with the Duke-of-Argyle friction of cattle to the similitude of a monstrous, black-topped mushroom. The stack was situated close to the drain, something over a hundred yards from the house, and about the same distance from my camp. The paddock intersected by the drain was bare fallow— that is, land ploughed in readiness for the next year's sowing. There were several other old straw-stacks on different parts of the farm, but they have nothing to do with this record.

Away beyond the farm, two or three miles up the main road, and just to the right of the river timber, I recognised the F——'s Arms

Hotel. B——'s place lay beyond, and to the right, but shut out of view by a paddock of green timber. The sight of the pub.—a white speck in the distance—suggested to my mind an expedient, which, however, I had to dismiss.

We read that Napoleon Bonaparte, on the eve of signing his first abdication, walked restlessly about, with his hands behind his back, muttering, "If I only had a hundred thousand men!" Similarly, as I contemplated that pub., I muttered, "If I only had a handful of corks!" Ay, if! My prototype wanted the men to abet him in maintaining his Imperial dignity, whilst I wanted the corks to assist me in carrying-out an enterprise attempted by a good many people, from Smerdis to Perkin Warbeck, namely, the personation of Royalty. Something similar, you see, even apart from the fact that neither of us found any truth in Touchstone's statement, that 'there is much virtue in an if.'

Nice customs curtsey to great kings. Jacky XLVIII, under whose mild sway I have spent many peaceful years, wears clothes exactly when it suits his comfort. When his royal pleasure is to emulate the lilies of the field, he simply goes that way; thus literally excelling Solomon in all his glory. The Evolution of Intelligence has stripped him of every other prerogative; but there its stripping-power ends, and his own begins. European monarchs will do well to paste a memorandum of this inside their diadems, for, let them paint an inch thick, to this favour they must come at last. However, that is *their* business. My own Royal master can still do no wrong in arraying himself in any one of his three changes of attire —the put-on, the take-off, or the go-naked—and if I could only counterfeit his colour for a few hours, I would stalk majestically to my camp, caparisoned in the last-named regalia, and protected by the divinity that doth hedge a king. But I had no corks.

The homestead was cheerful with voices which reached my ambush clearly, though unintelligibly, through the still morning air. At last I saw a woman advance toward the edge of the fallow, and stand for a minute facing the direction of the old straw-stack; then she looked over her shoulder toward the house, and called out,

"Can any of you see Jim comin' with that horse? Father 'll be ready in a minute, and then there 'll be ructions."

A little boy climbed the garden fence, and stood on the corner post.

"Not comin' yet, Mam."

Mam went back to the house, and the boy followed her. Here was my opportunity. The topography of the place was so perfectly suited to the simplest plan of campaign that it may suggest to the suspicious reader a romancist's shift, diaphanous as the 'woven wind' of Dacca. Let me repeat, then, that such a flimsy thing is entirely out of my line, and would have been so even at that time.

Availing myself of the abundant cover of whipstick scrub, I made my way down to the lagoon, swam silently across, darted along the drain in a stooping position, till I could 'moon' the house with the old stack, and finally took my post in a convenient recess on the side of the stack farthest from the house. Sure enough, there was a cattle-track across the fallow, and a culvert on the drain close to my refuge. Jim would soon be coming down that track toward the house. And, as my unhappy condition might appear more compatible with the nature of an alien than of a Britisher, I would accost him with a slight foreign accent, state my difficulty, and ask him *pour l'amour de Dieu*, to bring me a pair of his ——. My name would be Frongswaw Bongjoor.

I sat down with my back against the stack to recover breath, for already Jim was in sight, approaching at an easy gallop, and in two minutes was within fifty yards. Then hope for a season bade the world farewell, and a cold shiver ran down my spine. Horror-stricken, but without moving from my niche, I desperately tore down handfuls of Irish feathers from the overhanging eave, to form a sort of screen; for 'Jim' was a magnificent young *woman,* riding barebacked, *à la* clothes-peg; the fine contour of her figure displayed with an amazonian audacity which seemed to make her nearly as horrid as myself. My brow was wet with honest sweat whilst, from the poor concealment already described, I watched her swing the horse aside from the culvert, and send him at the drain: and, with that danger-begotten fascination by trifles which, in situations like mine, you must often have experienced, I noticed her pliant waist spring in easy undulation to the horse's flying leap. And so, with that thick cable of platted hair flapping and surging down her back, she vanished from the scene. She was a phantom of delight, when first she gleamed upon my sight; but the revulsion of feeling was one of the quickest and fullest I ever experienced.

It was some minutes before I became my own philosophic self again. Then I crept to the corner of the stack, and reconnoitred the homestead. Near the back-door, Jim had just saddled the horse, and, with the near flap resting on her head, was taking up the slack of the girth with her teeth, whilst her left hand, grasping the rein close to the horse's mouth, prevented the animal from taking a piece out of her. Presently Dad trotted out of the house and took possession of the horse, while she stepped back a pace. Then she seemed to say something of great pith and moment, for Dad paused, evidently questioning her. At last he returned hastily into the house, leaving the horse again in her charge.

I made an effort to concentrate my remnant of faith on a double event, namely, that he would n't delay long, and that he would come my way when he started. He, at least, was a man and a brother. I would interview him as he passed, and——

Faith scored. He did n't delay long, and he came my way straight. But he came on foot, and he came with a gun; speaking over his shoulder to Jim as he bustled past. Even in the distance, I fancied her attitude was that of a girl who had imprudently set in motion a thing that she was powerless to stop.

I could n't believe in the reality of the spectacle. But the illusion was there, palpable enough; and it consisted chiefly of a determined-looking man hurrying toward the stack, his right hand on the lock of a long duck gun, his left partly along the barrel, and the cheek of the stock resting against his hip. Beyond doubt he was after something, and beyond doubt he meant mischief. I glanced behind me, and round the expanse of bare fallow, but there was n't even a magpie in sight. At the same time, the sportsman's general bearing, his depressed head and downward vigilance, showed that he was stalking ground game, and was n't interested in anything perched on the stack. This was apparent to me by the time he had got within thirty or forty yards, and was holding the gun ready to clap to his shoulder. Also I noticed that several other women had joined Jim, and were watching his progress. Having now approached within point-blank range, he deployed to the left, in order to outflank whatever he was after.

Of course, you would have rushed him; you would have wrenched the gun from his grasp, and broken it across your knee; you would have despoiled him of his ——, and cuffed him home with ignominy. Yes, I know. So would I.

What I actually did, however, was to make two kangaroo-rat springs, which landed me in the bottom of the drain. I called to mind that, less than half-way down to the lagoon, I had noticed a deep, narrow, miniature ravine, eaten into one side of the drain by a tributary channel, and well sheltered by the foliage of large docks, now run up to seed. In thirty seconds, I was rustling into this friendly cover. There my confidence speedily returned, and, raising my head among the seeding stems, I noted the guerilla tactics of that white savage.

Still holding his weapon at the ready, he had circled round the stack till his view commanded all its recesses. Then he looked up and down the drain, peered under the culvert, and cast his eye across the fallow in every direction. Apparently satisfied, he threw the gun on his shoulder, and started off toward the lower end of the garden. I saw him disappear in the whipstick scrub, between the garden and the lagoon; then I backed out into the drain.

But I could gain nothing by staying there, and just as little by going back to my camp; whereas from the stack I could see any advantage that might offer itself, either about the house or across the lagoon. And, logically, the stack ought now to be one of the safest places in the province. So I returned to my old post, and, almost hopelessly, brought one eye to bear on the homestead.

I was just in time to catch occasional glimpses of Dad's head above the foliage of the fruit trees, as he rode down along the farther side of the garden to the dry crossing in the lagoon; and presently I saw him go up the opposite bank, and disappear in the scrub. Another instance of erratic shunting on my part. If I had stayed at my camp, I might have accosted him on neutral ground, without his gun, and with his mind unpoisoned by any of Jim's hysterical imaginings. What on earth had she told him about me? She had certainly told him something.

Just at this moment, the sun, which had risen behind a dense bank of clouds, suddenly burst forth. The colourless monotony of the scene flashed into many-tinted loveliness under the magic pencils of golden light; and, against the sombre background of river timber, a pair of white ——, hanging, with other drapery, on a line between the house and garden, leaped out in ravishing chiaro-oscuro!

A lifelong education, directing the inherent loyalty of human nature, invests anything in the shape of national or associational bunting with a sacredness difficult to express in words. Loyalty to something is an ingredient in our moral constitution; and the more vague the object, the more rabid will be our devotion to the symbol. Any badge is good enough to adore, provided the worshipper has in some way identified the fetish with himself—anything, from the standard of St. George to the 'forky pennon' of Lord Marmion; from the Star-spangled Banner to the Three Legs of the Isle of Man.

Now, with insignia, as with everything else, it is deprivation only that gives a true sense of value; and, speaking from experience, I

maintain that even the British Flag, which covers fabulous millions
of our fellow-worms, dwindles into parochial insignificance beside
that forky pennon on the farmer's clothes-line, which latter covers,
in a far more essential manner, one-half of civilised humanity.
Rightly viewed, I say, that double-barrelled ensign is the proudest
gonfalon ever kissed by wanton zephyrs. Whoop! *Vive les* ——!
Thou sun, shine on them joyously! ye breezes, waft them wide!
Our glorious *Semper eadem*, the banner of our pride.

There was no time to lose. The bifurcated banner might be taken
into the house at any moment. In the meantime, several sharp-eyed
women were unwittingly maintaining a sort of dog-in-the-manger
guard over their alien flag. The —— to him who can wear them,
thought I.   I must give this garrison an *alerte*, though I should
have to sacrifice the old straw-stack. 'T is dangerous when the baser
nature comes between the pass and fell incensed points of mighty
opposites: the old straw-stack is the baser nature; the mighty opposites are the meteor-flag and myself.

Few men, I think, have a healthier hatred of incendiarism than
I have. This hatred dates from my eleventh year, or thereabout;
when I was strongly impressed by a bush-fire which cleaned the
grass off half the county. The origin of that fire still remains a
mystery, though all manner of investigation was made at the time;
one of the most diligent inquirers being a boy of ten or twelve,
who used to lie awake half the night, wondering what could be done
to a person for trying to smoke a bandicoot out of a hollow log,
without thinking of the dead grass.

But now it was a choice between the old straw-stack and my
citizenship, and the former had to go. I am aware, of course, that
the Law takes no cognisance of dilemmas like mine, and has no
manly scruple against raking up old grievances that would be
better forgotten; but, as I said before, Come on with your clue.

Embittered though I was by Abraham's idea of hospitality, I still
felt some lingering scruple as my order of battle unfolded itself in
detail. Every great operation, as well as every small or middle-
sized one, consists of details, as a circle consists of degrees; and
the person responsible for the grand enterprise must unavoidably
be responsible for its most uninviting detail.   The details of a
death-penalty, for instance, are revolting enough; and here you
must judge not according to the appearance, but judge righteous
judgment. You must perceive that the white hands of the ultra-
respectable judge are the hands which reeve the noose; which adjust
the same round the neck of the man (or woman); which pull down

the night-cap; which manipulate the lever; and which, if necessary, grip the other person's ankles, and hang on till he is dead—
dead—dead—and the Lord has mercy on his soul. It is as unreasonable to despise M. de Melbourne, or M. de Sydney, for his little
share in a scragging operation as it would be to heap contumely on
comp. or devil because of this somewhat offensive paragraph.

Having, in the present instance, no subordinate to carry out my
details, I realised their unpleasantness, even whilst speciously justifying the enterprise as a whole. Further provocation was required
to overcome my aversion to the dirty work; and this provocation
was forthcoming in ample measure.

I had withdrawn from the corner of the stack into my nook, to
lay a few plans, and to hastily review the ethics of the matter;
now I crept back to feast my eyes once more on the ——, before
making my *coup-de*-clothes-line. But another object met my sight
first; and I nearly fainted. When I recovered myself, a few minutes
later, I was in the lagoon. I dare n't swim across, for I would have
been in full view from the stack. A cluster of leafy reeds, growing
in two feet of water, and the same depth of slimy, bubble-charged
mud, was the nearest cover; and in the midst of this I cowered,
hardening my heart against society, and watching Jim herself as
she tripped blithely past the end of the stack, and looked into my
recess. It seemed incredible; and yet, in spite of the cold and
misery and difficulty of the situation, I could n't wake up to find
myself in my possum-rug.

I always make a point of believing the best where women are
concerned, and I had been prepossessed in Jim's favour; yet it now
seemed to me that if she had been worthy of her high calling, she
would have brought that pair of white —— off the line, with,
perhaps, a supplementary garment or so, and modestly left them
in the drain, instead of thus seeking further occasion against me.
She looked under the culvert, across the paddock, and toward the
lagoon, as Abraham had done, then walked round the stack, and
finally returned home by the lower end of the garden, even pausing
to look over the picket fence, and scanning right and left as she
entered the whipstick scrub.

Enough, and to spare, thought I. These barbarians have given
me the sign of their Order; now let me respond with the counter-
sign. Not without practical protest shall I die a nude fugitive on
their premises; and not if I can help it shall the post-mortem people
find the word —— written on my heart.

The intervening garden and whipstick scrub effectually concealed my movements from the enemy as I recrossed the lagoon, and made my way with all speed to the unfurnished lodgings I had occupied on the preceding night. There I selected a piece of thick bark, about the size of your open hand, and solid fire for half its length. I swam the lagoon with this in my teeth, and in a few minutes more had buried it in the broken, half-decayed straw at the base of the stack. Then I returned along the drain, but instead of crossing the lagoon, sneaked through the thick fringe of whipstick scrub to the lower end of the garden, and there waited for something to happen.

I had to wait a good while. The old straw-stack was n't in sight from my post; and I began to think I should have to get another piece of bark, when I heard a youngster's voice squeak out,

"Oo, Mam! th' ole straw-stack 's a-fier!"

Then followed sundry little yelps of surprise from the women; and, after giving them a start of a minute or two, I went loping round the left-hand side of the garden, and into the back yard. Before the enemy's vanguard reached the stack, I had captured the flag that braved a thousand years, and applied it to its proper use. I also made free with another banner, which I tucked into the former. I was like the man who wrapped his colours round his breast, on a blood-red field of Spain.

Glancing into the combined kitchen and dining-room, I saw a row of wooden pegs along the wall, with several coats and hats hanging thereon. I appropriated only an old wide-awake, shaped like a lamp-shade, even to the aperture at the top; and from three pairs of boots under the sofa, I chose the shabbiest. Astonished, like Clive, at my own moderation, I next rummaged all the most likely places in search of a pipe and tobacco, but without avail. I even extended my researches into the pantry, and thence into the sacred precincts of the front parlour. But the tobacco-famine raged equally everywhere. The place was a residence, but by no stretch of hyperbole could you call it a home.

The side window of the parlour looked toward the conflagration; and there I counted four women, one half-grown girl, and a little boy. Three of the women, to judge by their gestures, were laughing and joking, whilst the fourth, and most matronly, was talking to the others over her shoulder as she turned her steps toward the house.

Then I bethought myself of Dugald Dalgetty's excellent rule respecting the provant, and re-entered the kitchen. Early though it was, the breakfast-things had been cleared away; so I took the lid off the boiler under the safe, in search of the cake which ought to be kept there. But the house was afflicted with cake-famine too. However, having no time to fool-away, and being constitutionally anything but an epicure, I just helped myself to the major part of a dipper of milk which stood on the dresser, then secured a scone and a generous section of excellent potted head from the safe.

Eating these out of my hand, I departed without ostentation; reflecting that it was better to be at the latter end of a feast than the beginning of a quarrel; and pervaded by a spirit of thankfulness which can be conceived only by those who have undergone similar tribulation, and experienced similar relief. Relief! did I say? The word is much too light for the bore of the matter.

There is a story—bearing the unmistakable earmark of a lie, and evidently not a translation from any other language—to the effect that once a British subject, in a foreign land, was taken out to be shot, just for being too good. Pinioned and blindfold, he stood with folded arms, looking with haughty unconcern down twelve rifle-barrels, all in radial alignment on his heart of oak. Twelve foreign eyes were drawing beads on the dauntless captive, and twelve foreign fingers were pressing with increasing force on the triggers, when a majestic form appeared on the scene, and, with the motion of a woman launching a quilt across a wide bed, the British Consul draped the prisoner from head to foot in the Union Jack! That's all. The purpose of the lie is to convey the impression that it is a grand thing to be covered by the flag of Britain; but give me the forky pennon before referred to, and keep your Union Jack.

Cardinal Wolsey, you may remember, as a consequence of putting his trust in princes, found himself at last so badly treed that his robe and his integrity to heaven were all he dared now call his own. The effect was a peace above all earthly dignities. So with me, but in larger beatitude. Having my —— and my integrity to heaven, I found myself overflowing with the sunny self-reliance of the man that struck Buckley.

And before you join the hue-and-cry against the 'barbarous incendiary' of the —— *Express,* just put yourself in my place, and you won't fail to realise what a profitable transaction it was to get a *puris naturalibus* lunatic clothed and in his right mind by the sacrifice of a mere eyesore on a farm. The old straw-stack wasn't worth eighteen pence, but I would gladly have purchased its destruction with as many pounds—to be paid, say in nine monthly instalments. To be sure, it didn't belong to me; but then, neither did the splitters' bark. So there you are.

Crossing the dry place in the lagoon, I dived into the whipstick scrub and turned northward, intending to get across the river as soon as possible, and follow up the New South Wales side to my camp. I should have been—well, not exactly happy; having taken degrees in philosophy which place me above a state fit only for girls—I should have been without a ripple on my mirrored surface, but I was n't. Serenely sufficient as I felt, and fit for anything, some ingredient seemed lacking in my fennel-wreathed goblet. There was a vacant chair somewhere in my microcosm. I knew I was forgetting something—but how could that be, when, in the most restricted sense of the word, I had nothing to forget?

Thus musing, I had gone through half my provant; now I turned round to give the rest to——Ah! where was Pup? I knew he had followed me on my first journey up the drain, but I had n't seen him since, and had been too busy to notice his absence. He would probably be at the farmhouse. I must get my clothes changed, and look after him.

It was about a mile and a half northward to the river. Before reaching it, I saw, crossing the flat in the direction of the Victorian river road, a swagman whom I recognised in the distance as my friend Andy. In casual surprise—for, as you may remember, I had last seen him on the New South Wales side, eight or ten miles away, and going in the opposite direction—I went on without exchange of greeting. Shortly afterwards, I came plump upon Abraham, sitting on his horse, and talking to a young fellow with an axe on his shoulder. I respectfully swerved aside, not wishing, in this particular case, to come under the provisions of that unsound rule which judges a man by the clothes he wears.

Presently I became aware of the jingle of a horse-bell, and the smoke of a camp-fire; and, close to the river, I found a tilted spring-cart, near which an elderly man, with tattooed arms, sat on a log, enjoying his after-breakfast smoke. Now, if I had only known this a couple of hours earlier!

After the usual civilities, I reinforced my provant by a pannikin of tea, some fried fish, and a slice off the edge of a damper which rivalled the nether millstone in more than one respect; thus assuring myself that I had attained Carlyle's definition of a man: 'An omnivorous biped, that wears ——.' Meanwhile, in response to my host's invitation to tell him what I was lagged for, I explained that I was travelling; my horses were on the other side of the river; I had come across to see a friend, had been bushed all night, and wanted to get back.

He could manage the river for me, he said. He followed fishing and duck-shooting for a living; but there was so many informers about these times that a man had to keep his weather-eye open if he wanted to use a net or a punt-gun. People need n't be so particular, for there was ole Q—— had been warning and threatening him yesterday, and here was the two young Q——s out this morning at the skreek of daylight, falling red-gum spars to build a big shed, and the ole (man) out on horseback, picking the best saplings on the river. Ole Q—— was a J.P. His place was just across the flat, with a garden reaching down to the lagoon. Q—— himself was the two ends and the bight of a sanguinary dog.

After breakfast, the old fellow furnished me with smoking-tackle, and paddled me across the river. During the passage, for want of something else to say, I mentioned to him that I had seen Andy crossing the flat, apparently from his camp. He explained that the swagman had been on his way to a new saw-mill, the day before, but had met one of the owners, who told him the mill would n't start till after harvest, and promised him work on the farm in the meantime. So Andy, on his return journey, had seen the outlaw's fire in the dusk; and, after some one-sided conversation across the river, the latter had ferried him over, and entertained him for the night. I mention this merely to show with what waste of energy the so-called sundowner often hunts for work, particularly if he happens to be the victim of any physical infirmity.

On reaching the north bank, I reminded the old fellow that I wanted to return by-and-by to look after a dog I had lost when I was bushed; and he promised to bring his skiff for me when I would sing-out.

In a couple of hours I was at my camp. In another fifteen minutes I was arrayed in my best and only. Shortly afterward, my horses were equipped, and Cleopatra, being in fine trim, was bucking furiously in the sand-bed where I had mounted. In an hour and a half more, I had unsaddled and hobbled both horses on a patch of good grass, nearly opposite where the spring-cart stood. My persecuted acquaintance, in response to my coo-ee, appeared with his skiff, and ferried me over. Then I hurried across the flat, to the residence of Mr. Q——. A man loses no time when such a dog as Pup is at stake.

It could n't have been later than half-past-one when I walked up along the garden fence, and approached the door of the kitchen. A modest-looking and singularly handsome girl had just filled a bucket of water at the water-slide, and was hammering the peg into the barrel with an old pole-pin. I recognised her as Jim, and forgave her on sight.

"Good day to you, ma'am," said I affably. "Sultry weather is n't it? I 'm looking for a big blue kangaroo dog, with a red leather collar. Answers to the name of 'Pup'."

She hesitated a moment. "You better see my father. He 's at dinner. Will you come this way, please."

I followed her into the parlour. In passing through the kitchen, I noticed that dinner was over, and a second young woman—apparently the original owner of my boots—was disposing the crockery on the dresser. In the parlour, Mr. Q——, a man of overpowering dignity, redolent of the Bench, and, as I think, his age some fifty, or by 'r lady, inclining to three-score, was dining in solitary grandeur, waited on by young woman number three. Lucullus was dining with Lucullus.

"Good day, sir," said I, with a respectful salaam. "Have I the honour of addressing Mr. Q——?"

"Your business, sir?" he replied, surveying me from head to foot.

"I 'm looking for a dog I lost last night, or this morning; a big blue kangaroo dog, with a"——

"Are you sure he's your dog?"

"Perfectly sure, Mr. Q——."

"How did you come in possession of him?"

"I bought him eight months ago. Am I right in assuming that he 's on your prem"——

"Steady, my good man. Who are you? What 's your name?"

"I must apologise for not having given my name at first. My name is Collins—of the New South Wales Civil Service. I 'm Deputy-Assistant-Sub-Inspec"——

"And what leads you to imply that I 've got your dog?"

"Information received."

"Leave the apartment, Naomi," said the magistrate loftily. "Now, Mr. Collins," he continued, pouring out a glass of wine, and holding it between his eye and the light; "I want to ask you"—he drank half the wine, set the glass on the table, and leisurely wiped his mouth with his serviette—"I want to ask you"—he paused again, pursed his lips, and placed his forefinger against his temple —"I want to ask you how you come to imply that the dog is here? 'Information received' was your statement. Be precise this time, Mr. Collins. I 'm waiting for your answer."

"I had my information from a man who saw the dog on your premises, Mr. Q——."

"Very good, indeed! At what time did he see the dog? Be punctual, Mr. Collins. Punctuality implies truth."

"About sunrise, I think."

"You think! Are you sure?"

"Well, yes; I 'm sure."

"Describe your informer, please."

"Describe him! If I described him ever so accurately, you would n't know him from Adam," I replied sharply, and withal truthfully. "Is my dog here, Mr. Q——? If he is, I 'll take him, and go. I don't want to be trying your patience after this fashion."

"Steady, Mr. Connell. Was your informer a man about my height?"

"I have no idea of your height, Mr. Q——."

"Was he a man about your own height? We 'll get at it presently."

"You 've got at it first try. I should say you 've struck his height to about a sixteenth of an inch."

"Sunburnt face? Skulking, fugitive appearance generally?"

"Your description 's wonderfully correct, Mr. Q——. You might, without libel, call him a sansculotte."

"I 'm seldom far out in these matters. How was he dressed?"

"In a little brief authority, so far as I remember. But is my dog——"

"Do you imply a sarcasm?" inquired the J.P. darkly. "I would n't do so if I was you. I 'm not thinking about your dog. You and your dog! I 'm thinking about a valuable stack of hay I had burnt this morning; and you 've give me a clue to the incendiary." He paused, to let his words filter in. "You done it without your knowledge, Mr. O'Connell," he continued pompously, again holding up his glass to the light.

In the silence that ensued, I could hear the murmur of the girls' voices about the house, and the irregular ticking of two clocks; while there dawned on my mind an impression that somebody had fallen in the fat.

"I'm sorry to hear of your loss, Mr. Q——," I remarked, at length.

"So far as the loss goes, that gives me no inconvenience, though it might break a poorer man. I been burnt out, r—p and stump, by an incendiary, when I was at Ballarat"——

"Ah!" said I sympathetically, but my sympathy was with the other party——

"And then I could afford to offer a hundred notes for the apprehension of the offender, before the ashes was cold."

"But might n't this last affair be an accident, Mr. Q——? A horse treading on a match for instance? I think you ought to make strict inquiries as to whether any horse, or cow, or anything, passed by the stack shortly before the fire was noticed."

"I know my own business, Mr. O'Connor," he replied severely. "I been the instigation of bringing more offenders, and vagabonds, and that class of people, to justice than anybody else in this district. If I 'd my way, I 'd stamp out the lawless elements of society."

"I admire your principles, Mr. Q——; and you may count upon my assistance in this matter. By-the-way, there are two illicit red-gummers down here"——

"I was talking to you about this stack-burning affair," interposed the beak. "I 'm annoyed over it. I been on the wrong lay, so to speak, all this morning; but that never lasts long with me. I got the perpetrator in my eye now, in his naked guilt; and, take my word for it, Mr. Connor, I 'll bring him to book. I 'll make an example of him. I 'll make him smoke for it. It was an open question this forenoon; but to show how circumstantial evidence sort of hems in a suspected party—why, here I can lay my hand on the very man; and, what 's more, he can't get out of it. I can point out the very mark of his body, where he slep' at a fire among the whipstick scrub, just across that lagoon. And a party I'm acquainted with seen him yesterday afternoon, some distance up the river, on the other side; and I seen him this morning, crossing the flat here, more or less about the time the fire was noticed. What do you think of that for circumstantial evidence, Mr. Connelly? And in addition to this, I can point out his incentive—which I prefer to hold in reserve for the present. He might think his incentive justifiable; but the Bench might differ with him." And El Corregidor held me with his glittering eye while he sipped his wine.

"I beg your pardon, Mr. Q——," said I, clearing my throat. "I can't help taking a certain interest in this matter. Would it be impertinent in me to ask who the person was that saw the suspected incendiary up the river on yesterday afternoon?"

"I 've no objection to answer your question, Mr. Conway. I quite expect you to take a strong interest in the matter. In fact, I 'll require to know something of your whereabouts after you leave my premises. I think you 'll be wanted over this affair. The party

that seen the incendiary yesterday was Mr. H——, of H——
Brothers."

"Mr. Charles H——?" I inquired casually.

"No; Mr. Arthur H——. Very respectable man, having personal knowledge of the incendiary." Again the J.P. sipped his
wine; and the girls' voices murmured, and the clocks ticked, and
the hens clucked in the yard; also, the magpies tootled beyond the
lagoon, and a couple of axes sounded faintly across the flat; and I
even heard, through the open window, the noise of some old back-
delivery chattering through a crop of hay on an adjacent farm.
"Give me your address," continued Mephistopheles, replenishing
his glass. "Writing-material on the side table."

I wrote my name and official title, giving our departmental office
in Sydney as a fine loose postal address, and laid the paper on the
table beside the magnate. It reminded me of old times, when my
Dad used to send me to bring him the strap. It was time to shake
my faculties together, for ne'er had Alpine's son such need.

"I 've made a study of law, myself, Mr. Q——," I remarked
thoughtfully. (This was perfectly true, though, in the urgency of
the moment, I omitted to add that my researches had been confined
to those interesting laws which govern the manifold operations of
Nature.) "I 've made a special study of law; and I think you will
agree with me that a successful criminal prosecution is a Pyrrhic
victory at best. At worst—that is, if you fail to prove your case;
and, mind you, it 's no easy matter to prove a case against a well-
informed man by circumstantial evidence alone—if you fail to
prove your case; then it 's his turn, for malicious prosecution;
and you can't expect any mercy from him. When you think your
case is complete, you find the little hitch, the little legal point, that
your opponent has been holding in reserve. Now, you 're a gentleman of substance, Mr. Q——. You 're a perfect target for a man
that has studied law." I paused, for I noticed the Moor already
changing with my poison. "By heaven! I 'd like to have a shot at
you for a thousand!" I continued, eyeing him greedily.

"One of the obstacles in a position like mine is the thing you
just implied, Mr. Connellan," responded the waywode, almost
deferentially. "Same time, this case ought to be followed up, for
the sake of the public weal. As valuable as the stack was, I don't
give that for it." And he snapped his finger and thumb.

"You may be morally certain of the identity of the scoundrel,
but your proofs require to be legally impregnable," I continued,
pressing home where he had disclosed weakness of guard. "I know

a very respectable man—a Mr. Johnson—who dropped something over a thousand in a case similar to this. The scoundrel was a deep subject; and he got at Johnson for false imprisonment. These roving characters can always get up an *alibi*, if they 're clever. Excuse my meddling in this case, Mr. Q——, but you've interested me strongly. You have evidence that this suspected incendiary was seen somewhere down the river yesterday—or up the river was it? —and you saw him somewhere here, this morning. Very well. Would the two descriptions of dress and deportment tally exactly with each other, and with the appearance of the person whom, independently of that evidence, you know to be the perpetrator— I mean the scoundrel of the camp-fire? Consider the opening for an *alibi* there! You hold the incentive in reserve, I think you said? Pardon me—is it a sufficient one?"

"It don't take much incentive to be sufficient for a vagabone without a shirt to his back!" replied the ratepayer, suddenly boiling-over.

"True," I conceded; "but, 'Seek whom the crime profits,' says Machiavelli. What profit would it be to such a scoundrel to do you an injury, Mr. Q——?"

"The propertied classes is at the mercy of the thriftless classes," he remarked, with martyr-pride.

"But incendiarism! Mr. Q——," I urged in modest protest. "Why, the whole country lives by the farmer; and I 'm sure"——

"We won't argy the matter, Mr. Collingwood," replied my antagonist, lowering his point. "Possibly I won't trouble you any further over this affair. Your business keeps you on the move," he continued, looking at the paper beside him; "and it might be difficult to effect service. You want your dog. Go into the kitchen; inquire for Miss Jemima, and tell her I authorise her to give you the dog. And a very fine dog he is."

"Thank you, Mr. Q——. Good day."

"Good day," replied the boyard, acknowledging my obeisance by a wave of his hand.

It was a near thing, but I had scored, after all. You can't beat the pocket-stroke. Passing through the kitchen, I met the graceful Jim.

"Are you Miss Jemima?" I asked, in the tone you should always use towards women.

A dimple stole into each beautiful cheek as she nodded assent.

"Well, Mr. Q—— authorises Miss Jemima to give me the kangaroo-dog."

"Come this way, then, please." There was a slight flush of vexation on the girl's face now. And, indeed, it was scarcely fair of
Dogberry, when his own soft thing had fallen through, to make
Jim cover his dignified retreat. With deepening colour, she led
the way to the stable, and opened a loose-box, disclosing Pup,
crouched, sphynx-like, with a large bone between his paws. The
red collar was gone; and he was chained to the manger by a
hame-strap. Of course, I did n't blame the franklin, nor do I
blame him now; rather the reverse. There seems something touching and beautiful in the thought that respectability, at best, is
merely poised—never hard home; and that our clay will assert
itself when a dog like Pup throws himself into the other scale.
But I could feel the vicarious crimson spreading over Jim's forehead and ears as I unbuckled the hame-strap, whilst vainly ran-
sacking my mind for some expression of thanks that would n't
sound ironical. A terrible tie of sympathetic estrangement bound
this sweet scapegoat and me asunder, or divided us together; and
each felt that salvation awaited the one who spoke first, and to the
point—or rather, from the point. All honour to Jim; she paced——

"You call him 'Pup'," observed the girl girlishly. "He 's a big
pup."

"His proper name is 'The Eton Boy'," replied the wretch wretch-
edly. And neither of us could see anything in the other's remark.

But the tension was relaxed; and, leaving the stable together, we
gravely agreed that a thunderstorm seemed to be hanging about.
Still a new embarrassment was growing in the girl's face and voice,
even in the uneasy movement of her hands. At last it broke out——

"I s'pose you have n't had any dinner?"

"Don't let that trouble you, Miss Q——."

"Father 's not himself to-day," she continued hastily. "He blames
us for burning an old straw-stack; and I 'm sure we never done it.
Mother's been at him to burn it out of the way this years back, for
it was right between the house and the road; and it was '78 straw,
rotten with rust. But I 'm glad we did n't take on us to burn it, for
father 's vowing vengeance on whoever done it; and he 's awful at
finding out things."

"Mr. Q—— mentioned it to me," I replied, with polite interest.
"But don't you think it seems a most unlikely thing for a stranger
to do? Perhaps some of your own horses or cattle trod on a match
that Mr. Q—— had accidentally dropped there himself?"

"That could n't be; for father never allows any matches about

the place, only them safety ones that strikes on the box. And he
hates smoking. My brothers has to smoke on the sly."

"Have you many Irish people about here, Miss Q——?"

"None only the Fogartys; and they 're the best neighbours we
got."

"And was nobody seen near the stack before the fire broke out?"

"Not a soul. I was past there myself, not twenty minutes before
we seen the fire; but I was going middling smart, and I did n't see
anybody—nothing only Morgan's big white pig, curled under the
edge of the stack, that always jumps out of the sty, and comes
over here, and breaks into our garden. Well, father 's always
threatening to shoot that pig; and me, never thinking, I told him
it was there; and he got his gun and went after it; and us in a
fright for fear he would find it, but he did n't. Then when we seen
him well out of sight, I went over to the stack quietly, to shoo the
pig home, but it was gone; and there was no sign of fire then, and
nobody in sight. Then my sisters and me was just starting out to
the milking-yard, and mother had begun to take the things off the
line, when little Enoch seen the fire. We could n't make it out at
all; and I examined up and down the drain for boot-marks, but
there was none. And just before you come, I picked up the track
of the horse I was riding, to see if his feet had struck fire on anything; but I was as wise as ever."

"Ah! the horse was shod, Miss Q——?"

"No; he 's barefooted all round. Well, he trod on a piece of
a brick, near the corner of the garden; but the fire never travelled
from there. It's very unaccountable."

"Very. I wonder would there have been such a thing as a broken
bottle anywhere about the stack, Miss Q——? The sun came out
unusually strong this morning, I noticed; and it 's a well-known
scientific fact that the action of the solar rays, focussed by such a
medium as I have suggested, will produce ignition—provided, of
course, that the inflammable material is in the angle of refraction."

"I don't know, sir," she replied reverently.

"Why, gold has been melted in four seconds, silver in three, and
steel in ten, under the mere influence of the sun's heat-rays, con-
centrated by a lens"—she shivered, and I magnanimously withheld
my hand. "If this hypothesis should prove untenable," I continued
gently, "we may assume spontaneous ignition, produced by chemical combination. Nor are we confined to this supposition. Silex
is an element which enters largely into the composition of wheaten
straw; and it is worthy of remark that, in most cases where fire

is purposely generated by the agency of thermo-dynamics, some form of silex is enlisted—flint, for instance, or the silicious covering of endogenous plants, such as bamboo, and so forth. A theory might be built on this."

"It seems very reasonable, sir," she murmured. "Anyway, I 'm glad the old stack 's out of the road. The place looks a lot cleaner."

"Well, I won't keep you out in the sun," said I reluctantly. "Good-bye, Miss Q——. And I 'm very much obliged to you."

"Oh, don't mention it! I 'm sure we 're very happy to"——she hesitated, blushing desperately.

"Well, good-bye, Miss Jemima."

"Good-bye," she murmured, half-extending her hand.

"I might see you again, some time," I remarked, almost unconsciously, as our fingers met.

"I hope so," she faltered.

"Good-bye, Jim," said I, slowly releasing her hand.

"Good-bye." The word sounded like a breath of evening air, kissing the she-oak foliage.

Then the maiden with the meek brown eyes, and the pathetic evidence of Australian nationality on her upper lip, returned to her simple duties. And the remembrance of Mrs. Beaudesart came down on me like a thousand of bricks. Such is life.

But my difficulties were over for the time being. My loco. had jolted its way over the rough section, carrying away an obstruction labelled V.R., and had reached the next points. I was still two or three days ahead of my official work; and there had happened to be a stray half-crown in the pocket of the spare oriflamme I had unfurled at my camp. Should I push on to Hay on the strength of that half-crown, draw my £8 6s. 8d., and send my clothier a guileful letter, containing a money-order for, say, thirty shillings? This would test his awfulness at finding out things, besides giving myself, morally, a clean bill of health. Or should I first walk across to B——'s and get Dick L—— to shift some of my inborn ignorance *re* Palestine?

I decided on the latter line of action, and followed it with—— Well, at all events, I have the compensating consciousness of a dignity uncompromised, and a nonchalance unruffled, in the face of Dick's really interesting descriptions of South-eastern Tasmania. Concerning my lapse of engagement on the previous evening, I merely remarked that the default was caused by circumstances over which &c.

I spent a couple of days, besides Sunday, at B——'s place; while the fisherman kept an eye on my horses. I helped B—— to work out a new and rotten idea of a wind-mill pump; Dick handing me things, and holding the other end. On the first afternoon, a couple of hours after my arrival, I drove into —— for some blacksmith work; and, whilst it was being done, I looked in at the *Express* office, and had a gossip with Archimedes on the topics of the day.

And now, whilst duly appreciating the rectitude of soul which has carried me through this trying disclosure, you will surely condone the obscurity in which I have been compelled to envelop all names used herein.

CHAPTER IV

*SUN. DEC. 9. Dead Man's Bend. Warrigal Alf **down**.
Rescue twice. Enlisted Terrible Tommy.*

Now what would your novelist rede you from that record, if he had
possession of my diary? Something mysterious and momentous, no
doubt, and probably connected with buried treasure. Yet it is only
the abstract and brief chronicle of a fair average day; a day happy
in having no history worth mentioning; merely a drowsy morning,
an idle mid-day, and a stirring afternoon. Life is largely composed
of such uneventful days; and these are therefore most worthy of
careful analysis.

How easy it is to recall the scene! The Lachlan river, filled by
summer rains far away among the mountains, to a width of something like thirty yards, flowing silently past, and going to waste.
Irregular areas of lignum, hundreds of acres in extent, and eight
or ten feet in height, representing swamps; and long, serpentine
reaches of the same, but higher in growth, indicating billabongs
of the river. The river itself fringed, and the adjacent low ground
dotted, with swamp box, river coolibah, and red-gum—the latter
small and stunted in comparison with the giants of its species on
the Murray and Lower Goulburn. On both sides of the river, far
as the eye can command, extend the level plains of black or light-
red soil, broken here and there by clumps and belts of swamp box,
now cut off from the line of the horizon by the quivering, glassy
stratum of the lower atmosphere.

And where the boundary fence of Mondunbarra and Avondale
crosses the plain, is seen a fair example of the mirage—that
phenomenon so vaguely apprehended in regions outside its domain,
and so little noticed where repetition has made it familiar. But
there it is; no smoky-looking film on the plain, no shimmering
distortion of objects in middle-distance, but, to all appearance, a
fine sheet of silvery water, two hundred yards distant, about the
same in average width, and half-a-mile in length from right to
left. Both banks are clearly defined; irregular promontories jut

far out into the smooth water from each side; and the boundary fence crosses it, post after post, in diminishing perspective, like any fence standing in shallow, sunlit water. The most critical and deliberate examination can no more detect evidence of phantasy in the unreal water than in the real fence.

The mirage is one of Nature's obscure and cheerless jokes; and in this instance, as in some few others, she is beyond Art. She even assists the illusion by a very slight depression of the plain in the right place. In fact, an artist's picture of a mirage would be his picture of a level-brimmed, unruffled lake; also, the most skilful word-painter, in attempting to contrast the appearance of water with that of its fac-simile, would become as confused and hazy as any clergyman taxed to differentiate his creed from that of the mollah running the opposition. And Nature, in taking this mirthless rise out of the spectator, never repeats herself in the particulars of distance, area, or configuration of her simulacre; it may be a mere stripe across the road—the brown, sinuous track disappearing beneath its surface, to re-appear on the opposing shore—it may be no larger than a good gilgie; or it may be the counterfeit presentment of a sheet of water, miles in extent, though this last is rare.

A hot day is not an imperative condition of the true mirage; but the ground must be open plain, or nearly so; the atmosphere must be clear, and the ground thoroughly dry. It is worthy of notice that horses and cattle are entirely insusceptible to the illusion. Another fact, not so noteworthy in view of the general perversity of inanimate things, is, that you never see a mirage when you are watching for it to decide an argument. It always presents itself when you have no interest in it. In this quality of irredeemable cussedness it resembles the emu's nest. No one ever found that when he was looking for it; no one ever found it except he was in a raging hurry, with a long stage to go, and no likelihood of coming back by the same route.

To complete the picture—which I want you to carry in your mind's eye—you will imagine Cleopatra and Bunyip standing under a coolibah—standing heads and points, after the manner of equine mates; each switching the flies and mosquitos off his comrade's face, and shivering them off such parts of his own body as possessed the requisite faculty. And in the centre of a clear place, a couple of hundred yards away, you may notice a bullock-wagon, apparently deserted; the heavy wool-tarpaulin, dark with dust and grease, thrown across the arched jigger, forming a tent on the body, and falling over the wheels nearly to the ground, yet displaying the outline of the Sydney pattern—which, as every school-girl knows, differs from that of Riverina.

In the foreground of this picture, you may fancy the present annalist lying—or, as lying is an ill phrase, and peculiarly inapplicable just here—we 'll say, reclining, pipe in mouth on a patch of pennyroyal, trying to re-peruse one of Ouida's novels, and thinking (ah! your worship 's a wanton) what a sweet, spicy, piquant thing it must be to be lured to destruction by a tawny-haired tigress with slumbrous dark eyes. No such romance for the annalist, poor man.

Such, then, was my benevolent and creditable allotment, such my unworthy vagary, at the time this record opens. I had camped in the Dead Man's Bend late on the previous evening, had wakened-up a little after sunrise, and turned out a little after eleven. Then a dip in the river, to clear away the cobwebs, and a breakfast which, if not high-toned in its accessories, was at least enjoyed at a fashionable hour, had made me feel as if I wanted a quiet smoke out of the gigantic meerschaum which I unpack only on special occasions, and something demoralising to read.

But the austere pipe resented this unworthy alliance so strongly that, for peace sake, I had to lay aside the literary Dead-Sea-apple. Then I remembered the official letter I had received on the previous day. I had merely glanced over it before acting on the orders it contained; now I re-opened the document, and pharisaically contemplated the child-like penmanship and Chaucer-like orthography of my superior officer:—

Sydney 28/11/83

Mr T Collins
    Dr sir

    Haveing got 3 months leave of Absence you are hereby requested to be extra atentive to the Interests of the Dept not haveing me to reffer to in Cases of difeculty or to receive instructions from me which is not practicacable on account of me being in the other Colonys. I write this principaly to acquaint you Communication from Mr Donaldson Mr Strong Mr Jeffrey representatives will meet you at Poondoo on monday 10 prox re matter in dispute. Keep this apointment without fail comunnicate with central Office pending further Orders from me.

                Ynnnnnnnnly
                R Wmlnlnllnn

I was now on my way to keep the 'apointment.' I was still about twenty miles from Poondoo; and the next day would be 'monday 10 prox.' I intended to start again at about two o'clock; so I had still a couple of hours to spend in what civilians call rest, and soldiers, fatigue; whilst studying such problems as might present themselves for solution. Pup was safe by my side, and I had nothing to trouble myself about. A thought of the transitoriness and uncertainty of life did occur to me, as it has done to thinkers and non-thinkers of all ages; but I deftly applied the reflection to my superior officer, and so turned everything to commodity.

The unfortunate young fellow, I thought, is a confirmed invalid, sure enough. A trip round the colonies may liven him up a bit, or, on the other hand, it may not; and, if he returns, it is to be hoped that kind hands will soothe his pillow, and so forth; and when, with dirges due, in sad array, they have performed the last melancholy offices, I trust that some one will be found to dress, with simple hands, his rural tomb. I would do it myself, for, as the poet says, 'Ah, surely nothing dies but something mourns.' A sweet fancy, but not so filling as the cognate reflection——

"Ha-a-ay!"

Somebody calling from the other side of the river; probably some forlorn and shipwreck'd brother, looking for his mates—— The cognate reflection, namely, that nothing withdraws but it leaves room for a successor. And this successor—thus favoured by a Providence which has kindly supervised the fall of the antecedent sparrow—will be entitled to live in a four-roomed weatherboard house, with the water laid-on, and a flower-garden up to the footpath, and a few silver-pencilled Hamburgs in the back yard, and everything comfortable. Ah, me! it is the thought of the dove——

"Ha-a-a-ay!"

Peace! peace! Orestes-like, I breathe this prayer. Thy comrades are sleeping; go sleep thou with them.——The thought of the dove that has suggested this fairy picture of the dovecote. And something tells me that Jim Quarterman is not likely to forget a certain cavalier who called one day about a dog. Doubtless her memory holds him enshrined as a person of scientific attainments and courtly address; offering a contrast, I trust, to the uninteresting hayseeds who have come under her purview. And will he not come again? Yea, Jim, mystery and revelation as thou art! he will come again, to lay at thy shapely and substantial feet the trophy of an——

"Ha-a-a-ay!"

Ay, lay thee down and roar——Of an Assistant-Sub-Inspectorship. Ah, Jim! tentatively beloved (so to speak) by this solitary, but by no means desolate, heart!—setting aside the rises I would

take out of thy artlessness, and the way I would whip thy simplicity with my fine wit till thou wert as crestfallen as a dried
pear—I confess a spontaneous thought associated with the mental
carte-de-visite of thy wholesome avoirdupois. No less, indeed, than
the psychological recognition of an angel-influence——

"Ha-a-a-a-a-ay!"

In vain! in vain! strike other chords! You can call spirits from
the vasty deep; but will they come when you do call for them?——
An angel-influence, tangible, visible, audible, which would make
Jordan the easiest of all roads to travel by thy side. Peerless Jim!
crowning triumph of Darwinian Evolution from the inert mineral,
through countless hairy and uninviting types! how precious the
inexplicable vital spark which, nevertheless, robs thy sculptured
form of all cash Gallery-value; and how easy to read in that gentle
personality a satisfying comment on the concluding lines of *Faust*:

> The Woman-Soul leadeth us
> Upward and on.

A double meaning there, by my faith! Alas! poor little Jim! go
thy ways, die when thou wilt; for Maud Beaudesart comes——

"Ha-a-a-a-a-ay!"

Rest, rest, perturbed spirit. By thy long grey beard and glittering eye, now wherefore stop 'st thou me?—For Maud Beaudesart
comes o'er my memory as doth the raven o'er the infected house.
Get thee to a nunnery, Jim. The chalk-mark is on my door; for
Mrs. B. has no less than three consecutive husbands in heaven—
so potently has her woman-soul proved its capacity for leading
people upward and on. Methinks I perceive a new and sinister
meaning in the Shakespearean love-song:—

> Come away, come away, death;
> And in sad cypress let me be laid.
> Fly away, fly away, breath;
> I am slain by a fair, cruel maid.

Nicely put, no doubt; but the importance of a departure depends
very much on the——

"Ha-a-a-a-a-a-ay!"

No appearance, your worship. Call for Enobarbus; he will not
hear thee, or, from Cæsar's camp, say 'I am none of thine.'——
On the value of the departed. For instance, when a man of property departs, he leaves his possessions behind—a fact noticed by
many poets—and the man himself is replaced without cost. When
a well-salaried official departs—such as a Royal Falconer, or a

Master of the Buckhounds, or an Assistant-Sub-Inspector—he perforce leaves his billet behind; and we wish him *bon voyage* to whichever port he may be bound. But when a philosopher departs in this untimely fashion, he leaves nothing——

"Ha-a-a-a-a-a-a-a-ay!"

And echo answers, 'Ha-a-a-a-ay!' Authority melts from you, apparently.—Leaves nothing but a few rudimentary theories, of no use to anyone except the owner, inasmuch as no one else can develop them properly; just a few evanescent footprints on the sands of Time, which would require only a certain combination of age and facilities for cohesion to mature into Mammoth-tracks on the sandstone of Progress. All on the debit side of Civilization's ledger, you observe. Consequently, he does n't long to leave these fading scenes, that glide so quickly by. And when the poet holds it truth that men may rise on stepping-stones of their dead selves to higher things, he is simply talking when he ought to be sleeping it off in seclusion. I understand how a man may rise on the stepping-stone of his defunct superior officer to higher things; but his dead self—it won't do, Alfred; it won't do. But hark! that heavy sound breaks in once more, as if the clouds its echo would repeat.——

"Ha-a-a-a-a-a-a-a-ay!"

Who is he whose grief bears such an emphasis? whose phrase of sorrow makes the very lignum quiver in sympathy? It may not be amiss to look round and see.

So I turned my head, and saw, on the opposite side of the river, about eighty yards away, a man on a grey horse. I rose, and advanced toward the bank.

"Why, Mosey," said I, "is that you? How does your honour for this many a day? Where are you camped?"

"Across here. Tell Warrigal Alf his carrion's on the road for Yoongoolee yards, horse an' all; an' from there they 'll go to Booligal pound if he ain't smart. I met them just now."

"Where shall I find Alf?"

"Ain't his wagon bitin' you—there in the clear? You ain't a bad hand at sleepin'—no, I 'm beggared if you are. I bin bellerin' at you for two hours, dash near."

"Who has got the bullocks, Mosey?"

"Ole Sollicker."

"Could n't you get them from him yourself?"

"I did n't try. I was glad to see them goin'; on'y I begun to think after, thinks I, it 's a pity o' the poor misforchunate carrion walkin' all that way, free gracious for nothin'; an' p'r'aps a trip to Booligal pound on top of it; an' them none too fat. But I 'm glad for Alf. I hate that beggar. I would n't len' him my knife to cut up a pipe o' tobacker, not if his tongue was stickin' out as long as yer arm. I was n't goin' to demean myself to tell him about his carrion, nyther; on'y I knowed your horses when I seen them; an' by-'n'-by I spotted you where you was layin' down, sleepin' fit to break yer neck; an' I bin hollerin' at you till I'm black in the face. I begun to think you was drunk, or dead, or somethin'—bust you." And with this address, which I give in bowdlerised form, the young fellow turned his horse, and disappeared through a belt of lignum.

I walked across to the bullock-wagon. The camp had a strangely desolate and deserted appearance. Three yokes lay around, with the bows and keys scattered about; and there was no sign of a camp-fire. Under the wagon lay a saddle and bridle, and beside them the swollen and distorted body of Alf's black cattle-dog— probably the only thing on earth that had loved the gloomy misanthrope. I lifted the edge of the hot, greasy tarpaulin, and looked on the flooring of the wagon, partly covered with heavy coils of wool-rope, and the spare yokes and chains.

"A drink of water, for God's sake!" said a scarcely intelligible whisper, from the suffocating gloom of the almost air-tight tent.

I threw the tarpaulin back off the end of the wagon, and ran to the river for a billy of water. Then, vaulting on the platform, I saw Alf lying on his blankets, apparently helpless, and breathing heavily, his face drawn and haggard with pain. I raised his head, and held the billy to his lips; but, being in too great a hurry, I let his head slip off my hand, and most of the water spilled over his throat and chest. He shrank and shivered as the cool deluge seemed to fizz on his burning skin, but drank what was left, to the last drop.

"Now turn me over on the other side, or I 'll go mad," he whispered.

He shuddered and groaned as I touched him, but, with one hand under his shoulders, and the other under his bent and rigid knees, I slowly turned him on the other side.

"Would n't you like to lie on your back for a change?" I asked.

"No, no," he whispered excitedly; "my heels might slip, and straighten my knees. Another drink of water, please."

I brought a second billy of water, but he turned from it with disgust.

"If you could make a sort of an effort, Alf," I suggested.

He treated me to a half-angry, half-reproachful look, and turned away his face. I rose to my feet, and rolled back the tarpaulin half-way along the jigger, for the heat was still suffocating.

"Is there anything more I can do for you just now, Alf?" I asked presently.

"More water." I gave him a drink out of a pannikin; and, as I laid his head down again, he continued, in the same painful whisper, and with frequent pauses, "Have you any idea where my bullocks are?—I was trying to keep them here—in this corner of Mondunbarra—and they 're reasonably safe unless—unless the Chinaman knows the state I 'm in—but if they cross the boundary into Avondale—Tommy will hunt them over the river, and—Sollicker will get them."

It must be remembered that Alf was camped at the junction of three runs: Yoongoolee lay along the opposite side of the river, whilst on our side, Mondunbarra and Avondale were separated by a boundary fence which ran into the water a few yards beyond where the wagon stood. The fence, much damaged by floods, was repaired merely to the sheep-proof standard. The wagon was in Mondunbarra.

"They 're across the river now, Alf. Mosey Price told me so, not twenty minutes ago."

"Across the river!" hissed Alf, half-rising and then falling heavily back, whilst a low moan mingled with the furious grinding of his teeth. "They 've got into Avondale, and Tommy has hunted them across! May the holy"——&c., &c. "Never mind. Let them go. I 've had enough of it. If other people are satisfied, I 'm sure *I* am."

"Who is she?" I thought; and I was just lapsing into my Hamlet-mood——

"Collins!"

"Yes, Alf."

"Would you be kind enough to lift my dog into the wagon? I have n't been able to call him lately, but he won't be far off."

"Bad news for you, Alf. The poor fellow got a bait somewhere, and came home to die. He 's lying under the wagon, beside your saddle."

The outlaw turned away his face. 'Short of being Swift,' says Taine; 'one must love something.' (Ay, and short of being too morally slow to catch grubs, one must hate something. See, then, that you hate prayerfully and judiciously.)

While I was thinking that every minute's delay would make my journey after the bullocks a little longer, Alf suddenly looked round.

"You need n't stay here," said he sharply—thin blades of articulation shooting here and there through his laboured whisper, as the water he had drunk took effect on his swollen tongue. "If you would come again in an hour, and give me another turn-over, you would be doing more for me than I would do for you. What day is this?"

"Sunday, December the ninth."

He pondered awhile. "I 've lost count of the days. What time is it?"

"Between one and two, I should think. My watch is at the bottom of the Murray."

"Afternoon, of course. I think I ought to be dead by this time to-morrow. What 's keeping you here? I want to be alone."

"Don't talk nonsense, Alf. I 'll pull you through, if I can only hit the complaint. Have you any symptoms?"

"I don't know. I don't know. I was gradually getting worse and worse for a week, or more; but still able to yoke up a few quiet bullocks to shift the wagon every day; till at last, one night, I just managed to climb in here, to get away from the mosquitos. I don't know what night it was, or how the time has passed since then. Just look at my arms, if you have any curiosity; but don't dare to prescribe for me. I had enough of your doctoring at the Yellow Tank—blast you!"

Without heeding his reminiscence, which has no connection with the present memoir, I untied an old boot-lace which fastened one of his wrist-bands, and drew up the sleeve. The long, sinewy arm, now wet and clammy from the effect of the water he had drunk, was helpless and shapeless, round and rigid; the elbow-joint set at a right-angle, and extremely sensitive to pain.

"There," said he, with a quivering groan; "the other arm is just the same, and so are my knees and ankles; and my head 's fit to burst; and I 'm one mass of pains all over. It 's all up with me, Collins. Now I only ask one favour of you—and that is to get out of my sight."

"I 'll be back in two or three hours, Alf," said I, rising. "Keep your mind as easy as possible, and see if you can doze off to sleep."

So I returned to my own camp, and, with all speed, caught and equipped Cleopatra. Then, after chaining Pup in a shady place, I stowed some smoking-tackle in the crown of the soft hat I wore; then shed apparel till I was like the photo. of some champion athlete; finally, I stuck the spare clothes, with the rest of my riches, among the branches of a coolibah, out of the way of the wild pigs. The next moment, I was in the saddle, and Cleopatra, after perfunctorily illustrating Demosthenes's three rules of oratory:—the first, Action; the second, ditto; the third, ibid.—turned obediently toward the river, and was soon breasting the cool current, while, with one arm across the saddle, I steered him for the most promising landing-place on the opposite bank.

(Let me remark here, that the man who knows no better than to remain in the saddle after his horse has lost bottom, ought never to go out of sight of a bridge. He is the sort of adventurer that is brought to light, a week afterward, per medium of a grappling-hook in the hollow of his eye. Perhaps the best plan of all—though no hero of romance could do such a thing—is to hang on to the horse's tail. Also, never wait for an emergency to make sure that your mount can swim. Many a man has lost his life through the helpless floundering of a horse bewildered by first and sudden experience of deep water.)

My landing-place happened to be none of the best. After clearing the water, it required all Cleopatra's strength and activity to climb the bank. Having slipped into the saddle as he regained footing, I was lying flat against the side of his neck, to help his centre of gravity and give him a hold with his front feet, when he brushed under a low coolibah, and the spur of a broken branch or something started at the neck of the under-garment which I cannot bring myself to name, and ripped it to the very tail, nearly dragging me off the saddle. When we reached level ground, the vestment alluded to was hanging, wet and sticky, on my arms, like a child's pinny unfastened behind, or, to use a more elegant simile, like the front half of a herald's tabard. What I should have done was to have reversed the thing, and put it on like a jacket; but, being in a desperate hurry, and slightly annoyed by the accident, and not feeling the sun after just leaving the water, I whipped the rag off altogether, and threw it aside. In two seconds more, Cleopatra was stretching away, with his long, eager, untiring stride, towards Yoongoolee home-station, distant about sixteen miles.

Slackening speed now and then to cross creeks and rough places, I found myself following a pad, and noticed the fresh tracks of the bullocks, mile after mile. At last I heard across the lignum the jangle of a brass bell, and the 'plock, plock' of an iron frog, and presently my quarry appeared in sight a couple of hundred yards ahead.

To do the boundary-rider justice, he was driving the cattle quietly and considerately. He looked round on hearing the clatter of horse's feet, but my Mazeppa aspect seemed neither to surprise nor disconcert him. He was n't altogether a stranger to me. For several years I had known him by sight as a solid, phlegmatic man, on a solid, phlegmatic cob; and I suppose he had his own crude estimate of me, though we had never had occasion to exchange civilities.

But now, after a five miles' chase, the sight of the man acted on my moral nature as vinegar is erroneously supposed to act on nitre. I reined-up beside him. The Irresistible was about to encounter the Immovable; and, even in the excitement of the time, I awaited the result with scientific interest. When a collision of this kind takes place, it sometimes happens that the Irresistible bounces off in a more or less damaged state; at other times, the Immovable is scattered to the four winds of heaven in the form of scrap, while the Irresistible, slightly checked, perhaps, in speed, sails on its way. But you can never tell.

"Where are you taking these bullocks?" I demanded in a tone which, I am sorry to say, reflected as little credit on my politeness as on my philosophy.

"Steation yaads," he replied indifferently, and with a strong English accent.

"Did you take them off purchased land?" I asked, eyeing him keenly.

"Oi teuk 'e (animals) horf of 'e run," he remarked, rather than replied, without condescending to look at me.

"Do you know what day this is?" I inquired magisterially.

"Zabbath," he replied kindly.

"And do you know there 's a new act passed—'Parkes's Act,' they call it—that makes the removing of working-bullocks from pastoral leasehold, on Sundays, a misdemeanour, punishable by a term of imprisonment not exceeding twelve months, with or without hard labour?"

"Granny!" he remarked.

Driven back in disorder, I hurried up my second line.——

"Do you know who these bullocks belong to?" I inquired ominously.

Something akin to a smile flickered round the shaven lips of the descendant of Hengist as, contemplating the lop ears of his horse, he observedly contentedly,

"Ees, shure; an' 'hat 's f'r w'y Oi be a-teakin' of 'em."

"Well, Alf 's laid-up; not able to look after them"——

"Oi 've 'eard 'at yaan afoor."

—— "so I 've come to take them back, and leave them at his camp on Mondunbarra."

"Horrite. Oi wants wun-an'-twenty bob horf o' you afoor 'em (bullocks) tehns reaoun'."

"Will you have it now, or wait till you get it?" I asked, betrayed by the annoyance of the moment into a species of vulgarity unbecoming an officer and gentleman. "I don't mind paying you the money, provided it clears the bullocks for the future—not otherwise. In the meantime I 'm going to take them back—pay or no pay."

"Be 'e a-gwean to resky 'em?" he inquired, slightly reining his hippopotamus, and looking me frankly in the face, whilst an almost merry twinkle animated his small blue eyes.

"By no means," I replied suavely; and we rode together for a few minutes in silence.

I had wakened the wrong man. The Immovable had scored. simply because he was a person of one idea, and that idea panoplied in impenetrable ignorance. A compound idea, by the way: namely, that Alf's bullocks were going to the station yards, and that he, Fitz-Hengist, was taking them there. All this was apparent to me as I regarded him out of the corner of my eye.

"Foak bea n't a-gwean ter walk on hutheh foak," he remarked calmly.

"A gentleman against the world for bull-headedness," I sneered, aiming, in desperation, at the heel by which mother Nature had held him during his baptism in the thick, slab bath of undiluted oxy-obstinacy (scientific symbol, Jn Bl).

"Hordehs is hordehs," he argued, as the good arrow-point penetrated his epidermis, fair in the vulnerable spot.

I laughed contemptuously. "Fat lot you care for orders! A man in your position talking about orders! Get out!"

"Wot 's a (person) to diew?" The point was forcing its way through the sensitive second-skin, or cutis.

"Do!" I repeated, with increasing scorn. "Strikes me, you can do pretty well as you like on this station."

"Bea n't Oi a-diewin' my diewty?" he asked in wavering expostulation—the point now settling in the vascular tissues.

"It 's in the blood, right enough," I retorted, with insolent frankness, and still regarding him out of the corner of my eye. "I believe you 're Viscount Canterbury's brother, on the wrong side of the blanket."

"Keep 'e tempeh; keep 'e tempeh," said he deprecatingly, as the poison filtered through his system. "Zpeak 'e moind feear atwixt man an' man. Bea n't Oi a-diewin' wot Oi be a-peead f'r diewin'? Coomh!"

"Well, you are a rum character," I remarked, judiciously assisting the action of the virus. "I 'm surprised at a gentleman in your position making excuses like that. Do you know"—and my tones became soft and confidential—"something struck me that you were an Englishman." (Even this was n't too strong.) "I wish you were, both for my sake and your own. However, that can't be helped. Now, for the future, you 'll have the satisfaction of knowing that you had your own way, and that you walked a man's bullocks off to the yard while he was helpless. Yes, sir; I 'm glad you 're not an Englishman. But the sun 's too hot for my bare skin, so I must be getting back; and if I 've said anything to offend you, I 'm sorry for it, and I beg your pardon." Then, still regarding him out of the corner of my eye, I turned Cleopatra slowly round.

" 'Ole 'aad!" he snorted. "Oi calls 'e a (adj.) feul!"

With this sop to his own dignity, the boundary man slapped his Episcopalian charger round the barrel—not round the flank, for the animal had none—with his doubled cart-whip, and turned off the track at a right-angle, beckoning me to follow. When he had gone twenty yards, he pulled steadily on one rein and, so to speak, wore his ship of the plains round till we faced the cattle again—for I had simultaneously pirouetted Cleopatra on one hind foot.

"Fetch 'em back, Jack," said he authoritatively. "Put 'em weare 'e got 'em, an' leab'm boide. Iggerant (people) we be; dunno nuffik; carnt diew noffik roight."

The black collie was sitting where he had stopped on the instant that we had turned off; sitting with his head slightly canted to one side; one ear limp and pendant, the other partly erect, and with something like a smile on his expectant face. On hearing the order, he made a wide circuit round the cattle, and quietly turned them back along the track, where he followed them as before. Meanwhile, Sollicker sullenly slipped off his linen coat, and handed it to me with a low growl. I thanked him with great sincerity, and put it on.

But his glance at me as we fell-in behind the cattle seemed to demand further appreciation; and I was not slow to respond—

partly from a sense of obligation, but principally from a broadening hope of extended concession. I had already selected him as a singularly eligible guardian for Alf's bullocks; and I knew that if I could once get him to accept the trust, nothing short of dynamite would shift him. But the seduction of a direct-action, single-cylinder purpose is a contract not to be taken by any of your mushroom mental firms; and this was a large order. Of course, the diplomatic flunkey-touch of nature has served as a letter of introduction to the man; now I would follow up the national phase of this delicate point of contact.

"No use," I remarked doggedly. "I give it up. I can't find words. This is not a personal favour. It 's an evidence of the principle that makes an Englishman respected all over the world. All over the world, sir; for, you know, the sun follows the English drum-beat right round the earth. Now, I can't flatter you; I 'd see you in the bottomless pit first; I 'm above anything of that kind; it sort of sticks in my throat; but I can assure you that, in all my experience"——

" 'Ees, 'ees; 'at 's horrite; 'at 's horrite. Wot d' y' think o' thet (collie) f'r a dorg?"

There was impatience in the first half of the speech, and arrogance in the last. I eased off, and took the branch track.

"He just knocks spots off any dog I 've seen working cattle!" I burst-out. "But you can't beat the Scotch collie"——

"Scotch coolie be dang! Doan' 'e know a Smiffiel' coolie? Chork an' cheese, Oi calls 'em."

"Smithfield collie, of course! Did I say Scotch collie? Of course, the Smithfield collie has been in good hands for hundreds of years; and when you get the pure breed—Just look at that dog! How did you get such a dog as that? Bred him yourself, I suppose?"

"Noa," he replied good-naturedly. "Oi g'e 'e foor moor troys. Coomh!"

"Bought him a pup?"

"Troy ageean."

"Got him a present?"

"Troy ageean?"

"Found him?"

"Not dezackly. Troy ageean."

I shook my head hopelessly, though I could have suggested another title to the ownership of dogs—a very common one, too, and good enough till the proper person comes interfering. Boys' dogs are generally held under this tenure. My companion, seeing me at fault, remarked with elephantine waggishness,

" 'At (dog) coomed deaoun t' me f'm ebm!"

I assumed the look of a man who conceals staggering bewilderment under the transparent disguise of incredulity; and Sollicker, looking, like Thurlow, wiser than any man ever was, enjoyed my discomfiture as much as he was capable of enjoying anything. Then he proceeded with great deliberation to interpret his oracular utterance; but first, with a powerful facial exertion, he wrenched his mouth and nose to one side, inhaling vigorously through the lee nostril, then cleared his throat with the sound of a strongly-driven wood-rasp catching on an old nail, and sent the result whirling from his mouth at a butterfly on a stem of lignum—sent it with such accurate calculation of the distance of his object, the trajectory of his missile, and the pace of his horse, that the mucous disc smote the ornamental insect fair on the back, laying it out, never to rise again. This was but a ceremonious prologue, intended to deepen the impression of the coming revelation.

"Useter 'ev a 'oss Oi 'd ketch hanyweares. 'Wo, Bob!' 'n' 'ud stan' loike a statoot t' Oi 'd ketch 'e (animal), 'n' git onter 'im 'n' shove me hutheh 'osses in 'e yaad, 'n' ketch wich (one) Oi want. B't 'e doid hautumn afoor las'—leas'ways, 'e got 'ees 'oine leg deaoun a crack, an' cou'n't recoverate, loike; f'r 'e (beast) wur moo 'n twenty y'r ole, 'n' stun blin', 'e wur. Ahterwahs, by gully! Oi got pepper—follerin' ahteh me 'osses hevery mo'nin' afoot. Wet 'n' droy; day hin, day heaout; tiew, three, foor heaours runnin'; 'n' 'ey (horses) spankin' abeaout, kickin' oop 'er 'eels loike wun o'clock. 'Ed ter wark 'em deaoun afoot, loike."

"But why did n't you hobble them?"

His face reddened slightly. "Me 'obble my 'osses! Tell 'e wot, lad: 'at 's f'r w'y 'e C'lonian 'osses bea n't no good, aside o' Hinglish 'osses. Ain't got n' moor g—ts 'n a snoipe. G—ts shooked outen 'em a-gallerpin' in 'obbles. Tell 'e, Oi seed my (horses) a-gallerpin' foor good heaours, 'n' me ahteh 'em all 'e toime. Noo 'osses 'ud dure sich gallerpin' in 'obbles. Doan' 'e preach 'obbles ter me, lad. Oi got good 'osses; noo man betteh; 'osses fit f'r a gentleman; on'y C'lonian 'osses 'es C'lonian fau'ts—ahd ter ketch —'ell ter ketch. Fifteen monce—hevery day on it—wet 'n' droy; day hin, day heaout; tiew, three, foor heaours runnin'; 'n' 'ey (horses) spankin' abeaout, kickin' oop 'er 'eels loike wun o'clock, 'n' gittin' wuss 'n' wuss, steed o' betteh 'n' betteh. Toimes, Oi see me a'moos' losin' tempeh."

I turned away my face to conceal my emotion. Sollicker went on——

"Accohdin', wun mo'nin' las' winteh, heaout Oi goes, o' course; 'n' my 'osses 'ed n't n' moo 'rn stahted trampin' loike; 'n' hevery-think quiet 's zabbath, 'n' nubbody abeout f'r moiles; 'n' horf goos 'em 'osses loike billy-o; horf 'ey goos 'arf-ways reaoun' 'he paddick, 'n' inter 'e stockyaad, 'n' 'ere 'ey boides; 'n' 'at dorg a-settin' in 'e panel, a-watchin' of 'em, loike. Neaow, 'ow d'ye ceaount f'r 'at, lad? Doan' 'at nonpulse 'e? Coomh!"

"It does, indeed! You did n't put him on the horses?"

"Noa, s'elp me bob. Neveh clapped heyes honter 'im, not t' Oi seed 'im hahteh my 'osses, a-yaadin' of 'em f'r me. My Missus, she 'lows a hangel fetched 'e (dog) deaown f'm ebm! 'At 's w'y Oi calls 'm 'Jack'."

"I see!" said I admiringly. Which, the censorious reader will not fail to notice, marked a slight deflection from my moral code. "And he stayed with you, sir?"

"Follered hahteh me 'oss's 'eels heveh since. (Dog) dews hevery-think loike a Christian—heverythink b't tork. Hevery mo'nin', hit 's 'Cyows, Jack; we 's y' cyows?' An' horf goos Jack, 'ees hown self, 'n' fetches 'e cyows. Hahteh breakfas' hit 's ' 'Osses, Jack; fetch y' 'osses'. An' horf trots Jack, 'n' presinkly 'e 'osses be in 'e yaad, 'n' 'e (dog) a-settin' in 'e panel, a-watchin' of 'em."

"Beats all!" I murmured, thinking how the Munchausens run in all shapes; then, desiring to minister occasion to this somewhat clumsy practitioner, I continued, "I suppose you drop across some whoppers of snakes in your rounds, sir?"

"Sceace none. Hain't seed b't wun f'r tiew year pas'; 'n' 'e (reptile) wah n't noo biggeh 'n me w'ip-an'l."

"Grand horse you 're riding," I remarked, after a pause.

This neatly-placed comment opened afresh Sollicker's well of English undefiled; and another hour passed pleasantly enough, except that Alf's bullocks preyed on my mind, and I wanted them to prey on Yoongoolee instead. I therefore modestly opened my mouth in parable, recounting some half-dozen noteworthy reminiscences, as they occurred to my imagination, and always slightly or scornfully referring to the magnanimous and indomitable hero of my yarn as 'one of these open-hearted English fools,' or as 'an ass of a John Bull that had n't sense enough to mind his own business.' These apologues all seemed to point toward chivalrous succour of the helpless and afflicted as a conspicuous weakness of the English character; and Sollicker listened with a stolid approbation unfortunately altogether objective in character.

I never dealt better since I was a man. No one has dealt better since Antony harangued the Sollickers of his day on dead Cæsar's behalf; but I differed from Antony so largely in result that the comparison is seriously disturbed. There was no more spring in my auditor than in a bag of sand. The honest fellow's double-breasted ignorance stood solidly in the way, rendering prevarication or quibble, or any form of subterfuge, unnecessary on his part. He merely formed himself into a hollow square, and casually glanced at the impossibility of those particular bullocks loafing on his paddock. If they came across the river again, he would hunt them back into Mondunbarra—he would do that much—but Muster M'Intyre's orders were orders. Two bullock drivers (here a truculent look came over the retainer's face) had selected in sight of the very wool-shed; and now all working bullocks found loafing on the run were to be yarded at the station—this lot being specially noticed, for Muster M'Intyre had a bit of a derry on Alf.

By way of changing the subject, Sollicker became confidential. He had been in his present employ ever since his arrival in the country, ten years before, and had never set foot outside the run during that time. He was married, three years ago come Boxing Day, to the station bullock-driver's daughter; a girl who had been in service at the house, but could n't hit it with the missus. Muster M'Intyre wanted to see him settled down, and had fetched the parson a-purpose to do the job. He had only one of a family; a little boy, called Roderick, in honour of Muster M'Intyre. His own name (true to the 9th rule of the Higher Nomenology) was Edward Stanley Vivian—not Zedekiah Backband, as the novel-devouring reader might be prone to imagine—and his age was forty-four. If I knew anyone in straits for a bit of ready cash, I was to send that afflicted person to him for relief. He liked to oblige people; and his tariff was fifteen per cent. per annum; but the security must be unexceptionable.

I gave him some details of Alf's sickness, and asked whether he had any medicine at home—Pain-killer, by preference. I have great faith in this specific; and I 'll tell you the reason.

A few years before the date of these events, it had been my fortune to be associated, in arduous and unhealthy work, with fifteen or twenty fellow-representatives of the order of society which Daniel O'Connell was accustomed to refer to as 'that highly important and respectable class, the men of no property'—true makers of history, if the fools only knew, or could be taught, their power and responsibility. Occasionally one of these potential rulers and practical slaves would come to me with white lips and unsteady pace——

"I say, Tom; I ain't a man to jack-up while I got a sanguinary leg to stan' on; but I 'm gone in the inside, some road. I jist bin slingin' up every insect-infected sanguinary thing I 've et for the last month; an' I 'm as weak as a sanguinary cat. I must ding it. Mebbe I 'll be right to-morrow, if I jist step over to the pub., an' git"——

Here I would stop him, and endeavour to establish a diagnosis. But a man with the vocabulary of a Stratford wool-comber (whatever a wool-comber may be) of the 16th century—a vocabulary of about two hundred and fifty words, mostly obscene—is placed at a grave disadvantage when confronted by scientific terminology; and my patient, casting symptomatic precision to the winds, and roughly averaging his malady, would succinctly describe himself as sanguinary bad. That was all that was wrong with him. Nevertheless, having a little theory of my own respecting sickness, I always undertook to grapple with the complaint. I had noticed as a singular feature in Pain-killer, that the more it is diluted, the more unspeakably nauseous and suffocating it becomes; wherefore, my medicine chest consisted merely of a couple of bottles of this rousing drug. My practice was to exhibit half-a-dozen tablespoonfuls of the panacea in a quart of oxide of hydrogen (vulgarly known as water). When my patient had swallowed that lot, I caused him to lie down in some shady place till the internal conflagration produced by the potent long-sleever had subsided to cherry-red; and then sent him back to his work like a giant refreshed with new wine. I never knew one of those potentates to be sick the second time.

Sollicker did n't know whether his wife had any medicine, but we could see. Accordingly, when the twenty bullocks and the horse had landed themselves on Mondunbarra, close to Alf's camp, we started at a canter, and, after riding a couple of miles, pulled up at a comfortable two-roomed cottage, half-concealed by the drooping, silvery foliage of a clump of myall. Sollicker turned his moke loose in the paddock; I tied my horse to the fence; and we entered the house. A tall, slight, sunburnt, and decidedly handsome young woman, with a brown moustache, was replenishing the fire.

"Theas (gentleman) 'e be a-wantin' zoom zorter vizik f'r a zick man," remarked the boundary rider, taking a seat.

"D—d if I know whether I got any," replied his wife, with kindly concern, and with an easy mastery of expression seldom attained by her sex. "I 'll fine out in about two twinklin's of a goat's tail. Sit down an' rest your weary bones, as the sayin' is. I shoved the kettle on when I seen you comin'." She opened a box, and produced a small, octagonal blue bottle, which she held up to the light. "Chlorodyne," she explained; "an' there 's some left, better luck. Good thing to keep about the house, but it ain't equal to Pain-killer for straightenin' a person up." She handed me the bottle, and proceeded to lay the table. I endeavoured to make friends with Roddy, but he was very shy, as bush children usually are.

"He 's a fine little fellow, ma'am," I remarked. "How old is he?"

"He was two years an' seven months on last Friday week," she replied, with ill-concealed vainglory.

"No, no," said I petulantly. "What is his age, really and truly?"

"Jist what I told you!" she replied, with a sunny laugh. "Think I was tryin' to git the loan o' you? Well, so help me God! There!"

"Helenar!" murmured her husband sadly. And, as he spoke, an inch of Helenar's tongue shot momentarily into view as she turned her comely face, overflowing with merriment, toward me.

"My ole man was cut out for a archdeacon," she remarked. "I tell him it 's all in the way a person takes a thing. But it 's better to be that way nor the other way; an' he ain't a bad ole sort—give the divil his due. Anyway, that 's Roddy's age, wrote in his Dad's Bible."

I laid my hand on the boundary rider's shoulder. "Look here, sir," said I impressively: "you 're an Englishman, and you 're proud of your country; but I tell you we 're going to have a race of people in these provinces such as the world has never seen before." And, as I looked at the child, I drifted into a labyrinth of insoluble enigmas and perplexing hypotheses—no new thing with me, as the sympathetic reader is by this time well aware.

The boundary rider shook his head. "Noa," he replied dogmatically. "Climate plays ole Goozeb'ry wi' heverythink hout 'ere. C'lonians bea n't got noo chest, n' mo'n a greyhound." And he placed his hand on his own abdomen to emphasise his teaching. "W'y leuk at 'er; leuk at 'ee ze'f; leuk at 'e 'oss, ev'n. Ees, zhure; an' Roddy 'll be jist sich anutheh. Pore leetle (weed)!"

He took the child on his knee with an air of hopeless pity, and awkwardly but tenderly wiped the little fellow's nose. I was still lost in thought. We are the merest tyros in Ethnology. Nothing is easier than to build Nankin palaces of porcelain theory, which will fall in splinters before the first cannon-shot of unparleying fact.

What authority had the boundary man or I to dogmatise on the Coming Australian? Just the same authority as Marcus Clarke, or Trollope, or Froude, or Francis Adams—and that is exactly none. Deductive reasoning of this kind is seldom safe. Who, for instance, could have deduced, from certain subtly interlaced conditions of food, atmosphere, association, and what not, the development of those silky honours which grace the upper lip of the Australienne? No doubt there are certain occult laws which govern these things; but we have n't even mastered the laws themselves, and how are we going to forecast their operation? Here was an example: Vivian was a type Englishman, of his particular sub-species; his wife was a type Australienne, of the station-bullock-driver species; and their little boy was almost comically Scottish in features, expression, and bearing. Where are your theories now? Atavism is inadmissible; and fright is the thinnest and most unscientific subterfuge extant. The coming Australian is a problem.

Mrs. Vivian overwhelmed me with instructions concerning Alf, and frankly urged me to hurry back to his assistance. I paid little heed to her advice, for I knew he would soon come round; and in the meantime, my mind was fully occupied with his team. After drinking a cup of tea, I shook hands with her, and lingered at the door, looking at her husband, as he amused himself with Roddy.

"I 'll leave your coat on the fence, Mr. Vivian," said I at length.

"Horrite."

"You want to be as lively as God 'll let you," said the excellent woman, accompanying me to my horse. "I won't be satisfied till I see you off."

Very well, thought I; on your own head be it. So I took off the linen coat, and handed it to her.

"You should 'a' kep' on a inside shirt," she remarked kindly. "Them shoulders o' yours 'll give you particular hell to-morrow. Why, you 're like a boiled crawfish now. Hides like that o' yours," she added, testing with her finger and thumb the integument on my near flank, as I hastily placed my bare foot in the stirrup, "ain't worth a tinker's dam for standin' the sun." (For the information of people whose education may unhappily have been neglected, it will be right to mention that the little morsel of chewed bread which a tin-smith of the old school places on his seam to check the inconvenient flow of the solder, is technically and appropriately termed a 'tinker's dam.' It is the conceivable minimum of commercial value.)

The sun was still above the trees when I unsaddled Cleopatra at my camp, and resumed my clothes. The bullock-bells were ringing among the lignum, as the animals exerted themselves to make up for lost time.

"And how are we now?" said I, assuming a cheerful professional air, as I swung myself on the platform of the wagon. "I 've secured a drop of one of our most valuable antiphlogistics, which is precisely what you require, as the trouble is distinctly arthrodynic. You 'll be right in a couple of days."

"No, Collins," replied Alf gently; "I 'll never be right—in the sense you mean. I won't take any medicine. I 've done with everything. Help me to turn over again, please, and give me another drink of water. I want to tell you something."

After giving him a turn over, I took the billy and replenished it at the river. Before getting into the wagon again, I emptied the contents of Mrs. Vivian's bottle into half a pannikin-full of the oxide of hydrogen, and stirred the potion thoroughly with a stick. Then returning to my patient, I raised his head, and held the pannikin to his lips. He finished the draught, unconscious of its medicinal virtues; and I refolded the old overcoat which served as a pillow, and laid him down as gently as possible.

"The water seems to have a peculiar taste," he murmured. "I don't notice my sight failing yet, but my hearing is all deranged. I hear your voice through a ringing of bells, and a sound like a distant waterfall. I 'm just on the border-land, Collins. I 've very little more to suffer; and why should I come back, to begin it all again? How long is it since you left me?"

"From four to five hours, I think. I put your bullocks together; they 're close by."

"Well, now, I would n't have the slightest idea whether it was one hour or twelve. I 've been in the spirit-world since then, or a spirit has visited me here. I heard, plain and clear, the voice of a woman singing old familiar songs; and that voice has been silent in death for ten years—silent to me for three years before that. Thirteen years! That may not seem much to you; but what an age it seems to me! It was no dream, Collins; I saw everything as I see now, but I heard her glorious voice as I used to hear it in our happy days; and I felt that her spirit was bringing forgiveness at last. I 'm not a religious man, Collins; I don't know what will become of me after death; but God does, and that 's sufficient for me. I never believed on Him so devoutly as I do now that He has vindicated His justice upon me. I praise him for avenging an act of the blindest folly and heartlessness; and I thank Him that my punishment is over at last. There! Listen! No, it 's nothing. But it was a favourite song of hers; and while you were away I heard her sing it, with new meaning in every syllable. My poor love!"

"Alf, Alf," I remonstrated; "compose yourself, and go to sleep if you can." The tears of feebleness had accumulated in the hollows of his sunken eyes, and, not having the use of his hands, he was throwing his head from side to side to clear them away.

"Did you ever make a terrible mistake in life, Collins?" he asked, at length. Before I could reply, he resumed absently, "When I was a boy, away on the Queensland border, I knew a squatter—as fine a fellow as ever lived—and this man married some young lady in Sydney, and brought her to live on the station. A few months afterward, he came home unexpectedly at about two o'clock one morning, and found his place occupied by an intimate friend of his own —a young barrister, who was staying at the station as a guest. He managed to conceal his discovery; and, within the next few days, he got his friend to draw out a new will, by which he left everything, without reservation, to his wife. A day or two after completing the will, he took his gun and went out alone, turkey-shooting. He did n't come home that night; and next day one of the station hands found him at a wire fence, shot straight through the heart. Accidentally, of course. But we knew better."

"It might have been accidental, Alf," I suggested. "There 's a lot of supposition in the story."

"None, Collins. Before going out with his gun, he wrote a letter to my father, and sent it by a trustworthy blackfellow. My father got the letter about ten o'clock at night; and he had a horse run-in at once, and started off for the station through a raging thunder-storm, arriving next day only in time to see his friend's body before it was moved to the house. My father was terribly cut-up about it. He was manager of an adjoining station at the time.

"Now let me tell you another true story," pursued Alf dreamily. "Five years ago, I knew a man on the Maroo, a tank-sinker, with a wife and two children. The wife got soft on a young fellow at the camp; and everybody, except the husband, saw how things stood. Presently the husband began to circulate the report that he was going to New Zealand. In the meantime, he sent the two children to a boarding-school in Wagga. He was in no hurry. Afterward, he sold his plant to the station, and bade good-bye, in the most friendly way, to all hands, including the Don Juan. Then he started across the country to Wagga, alone with his wife, in a wagonette. Are you listening?"

"Attentively, Alf. But suppose I boil your billy, and"——

"Two years afterward, a flock was sold off the station I was speaking of, for Western Queensland; and one of the station men went with the drover's party, to see the sheep delivered. Curious coincidence: he met on the new station his old acquaintance, the tank-sinker, with his two children and a second wife. The tank-sinker told him that his first wife had died soon after leaving the Maroo, and that he had changed his mind about going to New Zealand. Am I making myself clear?"

"Yes; so far. You know the man you 're speaking of?"

"Slightly. I delivered goods to him once on the Maroo, and casually heard the scandal that was in the air. Well, the shearing came round on the Maroo just as the station man got back from Queensland; and while the adjoining station was mustering for the shed, a boundary man found, in the centre of one of the paddocks —in the loneliest, barrenest hole of a place in New South Wales— he found where a big fire had been made, and some bones burnt into white cinders and smashed small with a stick. He kicked the ashes over, and found the steel part of a woman's stays, and the charred heel of a woman's boot, and even a thimble and a few shillings that had probably been in her pocket. I was on the station at the time, waiting for wool, and saw the relics when the boundary man brought them in. There are queer things done when every man is a law unto himself."

"Supposition, Alf; and strained supposition at that. But why should you trouble your mind about these things?"

"There was no supposition on the station where the things were found, nor on the station the tank-sinker had left, when they compared notes. The things were found three or four miles off a bit of a track that led to Wagga; and there was 'a pine of a year and a half old growing in the ashes. But we 'll pass that story. I want you to listen to another."

"Some other time, Alf. I 'll make you a drink of tea, and"——

"When I was young," continued Alf doggedly, "I was very intimate with an American, a man of high principle and fine education. Best-informed man I ever knew. This poor fellow was a drunkard, occasional, but incorrigible. Misfortune had driven him to it. His wife was dead; his children had died in infancy; and at forty-five he was a hopeless wreck. He worked at my father's farm on the Hawkesbury for two or three years, and died at our place when I was about twenty-five, immediately before I left home"——

"I don't like to correct you, Alf," I interposed; "but I understood you to say that your father was a station-manager, on the Queensland border."

"Up to the time I was twenty-one or twenty-two. Then he bought a place on the Hawkesbury, intending, poor man! to spend the evening of his life indulging his hobby of chemistry, while I took the care of the place off his hands—for though I have two sisters, I was his only son. His great ambition was to bequeath some chemical discovery to future generations. But I demolished his castles in the air along with my own. It's no odds about myself; but my poor father deserved better, after all his work and worry. Ah, my God! we parted in anger; and now I don't know whether he's alive or dead!" The prodigal paused, and sighed bitterly.

"And your mother?" I suggested experimentally.

"She was an invalid for several years before I left home," replied Alf, his tone fulfilling my anticipation.

(Have you ever noticed that the prodigal son of real life, in nineteen cases out of twenty, speaks spontaneously and feelingly of his father, with, perhaps, a dash of reverent humour; whereas, to quote Menenius, he no more remembers his mother than an eight-year-old horse? This is cruel beyond measure, and unjust beyond comment; but, sad to say, it is true; and the platitudinous tract-liar, for the sake of verisimilitude, as well as of novelty, should make a memo. of it. Amongst all the hard-cases of my acquaintance, I can only think of one whose mother's unseen presence is a power, and her memory a holy beacon, shining, by-the-way, with a decidedly intermittent light. Unfortunately, a glance along the three 9ths yet to come shows me that this nobly spurious type of prodigal— Jack the Shellback, vassal of Runnymede Station—will not come within the scope of these memoirs.)

Alf dreamily resumed his inconsequent story: "However, this Charley Cross, or Yankee Charley, was an old Victorian digger. About twelve years before his death, he was working on Inglewood, with a mate that he would have trusted, and did trust, to any extent, and in any way. But it was the old, old story. He got a friendly hint, and watched, and watched, for weeks, without betraying any suspicion. At last he was satisfied. Then he carefully laid down his line of action, and followed it to the end. One day, his mate, sitting on the edge of the shaft, ready to put his foot in the rope, suddenly overbalanced, and went down head-foremost. Of course,

Cross was close beside him at the time, and no one else was in sight. Cross gave the alarm, and, in the meantime, went hand-under-hand down the rope, intending, like Bruce, to 'mak sicker'; for the shaft was only about forty feet deep. But it happened that the man's neck was broken in the fall. Cross forgave his wife, and never breathed a word of his discovery or his vengeance; but in spite of this, the woman seemed to live in fear and horror. During the next couple of years, luck favoured him, and he made an independence. He invested his money judiciously; but there 's no guarantee for domestic happiness—in fact, there 's no guarantee for anything. First, his two surviving children died of diphtheria; then his wife followed, dying, Cross assured me, of a broken heart. He sorrowed for her more deeply, perhaps, because she had cost him so dear; and this, no doubt, was what drove him to drink."

"Very probably," I replied. "But, Alf, this taxing of your mind is about as good for you just now as footballing or boxing. Are you a smoker?"

"No."

"That's what I feared. Now, take my advice, and give yourself absolute rest, while I boil"——

"One more story, Collins, as well authenticated as any of the three I have told. I knew a young fellow of between twenty-five and thirty"——

"This won't do," I interposed firmly, for he had become restless and excited. "Why should you allow your mind to dwell so exclusively on the manifestations of one particular phase of moral aberration, and, to do bare justice to womanhood, an exceedingly rare one—except among the very highest and the very lowest classes? Unless you handle such questions in a scientific spirit, you 'll find them—or unfortunately, you won't find them—envelop your reasoning faculties in a most unwholesome atmosphere. The perpetual brooding over any one evil, however fatal that evil may be, naturally side-blinds the mind into a narrow fanaticism which is apt to condone ten times as much wrong as it condemns; and you drift into the position of the man who strains at the moderate drinker, and swallows the usurer. We see this in the Good Templar, the Social Purity person, the Trades Unionist, and the moral faddist generally. Musonius Rufus sternly reminded Epictetus that there were other crimes besides setting the Capitol on fire."

"Have you done?" asked Alf, coldly but gently. "Let me tell you one more story while I 'm able. I 'll soon be silent enough.——

The man I 'm thinking of was a saw-mill owner. He had been married a couple of years, and had one child. I could n't say that he actually loved his wife; in fact, she was n't a woman to inspire love, though she was certainly good-looking. At her very best, there was nothing in her; at her worst, she was ignorant, and vain, and utterly unprincipled—no, not exactly unprincipled, but non-principled. She was essentially low—if you understand my meaning—low in her tastes and aspirations, low in her likes and dislikes, low in her thoughts and her language, low in everything. She may not have been what is called a bad woman, but—that miserable want of self-reverence—I can't understand how——Would you give me another drink, please?"

He drank very little this time. He had been speaking with an effort, and a haggard, hopeless look was intensifying in his face. I began to suspect a temporary delirium. The presentiment of impending death was unreasonable, though not ominous; so also with the determination to narrate irrelevant stories; but the incongruity of the two associated notions set me speculating in a sympathetic way.

"Alf," said I gravely; "it 's foolish to tax your memory for anecdotes now. Try if you can settle yourself to sleep. I 'm sure I 'll have great pleasure in exchanging yarns with you at some future time, when you 're more fit."

"Listen, Collins," he replied sullenly. "Our saw-mill owner got the inevitable glimpse of the truth. He was blind before; now he was incredulous. He condescended to play the spy, and he was soon satisfied. This time it was a Government official—clerk of the local Court—a blackleg vagabond, with interest at head-quarters—about the vilest rat, and certainly the vilest-looking rat, that ever breathed the breath of life. Our hero took no further notice of him than to terrify him into confession, and drive him into laying the blame on his paramour. And the amusing feature of the case was, that she, finding herself fairly run to earth, thought she had nothing to do but to turn from the evil of her ways, and take her husband's part against the other fellow. But no, no. Our hero, after thinking the matter over, took her into his confidence, without giving her any voice in the new arrangement. He sold-out to the best advantage, and divided the proceeds with her; reserving to himself enough to start him in a line of life that he could follow without the annoyance of being associated with anyone. All that he earned afterward, beyond bare expenses, he forwarded to her, to save or squander as she pleased; the only condition being that she should acknowledge each remittance, and answer, as briefly as possible, such questions as he chose to ask. She humbly assented to all this, evidently looking forward to forgiveness and reconciliation, somewhere in time or eternity. But, by God! she mistook her mark!" He laughed harshly, paused half-a-minute, and resumed,

"One restraint upon our hero was the thought of his little boy, only old enough to creep about, and incredibly fond of him; though this never softened him towards the worthless, cursed mother. Anyway, after about three years, the little boy died; and his heart was turned to stone. Still, through mere bitterness and obstinacy he followed the course he had adopted; meeting with a run of success that surprised himself. The very curse that was on him seemed to protect him from the mishaps that befell other men in his line of work; and he found life worth living for the sake of hating and despising the whole human race, including himself. There 's no pleasure like the pleasure of being a devil, when you feel yourself master of the situation, and—Now I 've done, Collins."

"That 's right. I 've been thinking how to fix things for you till you 're able to"——

"First, I have one question to ask you," persisted Alf. "You notice that all these men acted differently. Which of them acted right?—or did any of them? You know, there are two other courses open: to appeal to the law, or to pass the matter over quietly, for fear of scandal. Is either of these right? One course must be right, and all the others must be wrong."

By this time, I had made up my mind to humour him. "Well," I replied; "it happens that I have given the subject some thought, as I intend, if I can find time, to write a few words on the varied manifestations of jealousy in the so-called Shakespear Plays. You 're familiar with the plays, of course?"

"I 've read bits of them."

"Possibly you remember, then, that Posthumus, in *Cymbeline*, on receiving proofs of his wife's infidelity (we know her to be loyal, but that does n't affect his proofs) harbours not one thought of revenge toward the man who has supplanted him. Indeed, as an artistic illustration of Iachimo's immunity from retribution, Posthumus is afterward represented as disarming and sparing him in battle—a concession he would n't have made to an ordinary enemy. He looks to Imogen alone. Nothing but the sacrifice of her life will satisfy him. On the eve of the same battle, we find him, though seeking for death himself, still gloating over the handkerchief supposed to be stained with her life-blood. Very well. Now Troilus in *Troilus and Cressida*, is a man very much resembling Posthumus in temperament—brave, resolute, truthful, unsuspicious, and more liberally endowed with muscle than brains"——

"But this has nothing to do with it," interrupted Alf. "I was asking your opinion as to which of the four acted rightly?—or did any of them?"

"Yes, Alf; I 'm coming to that. I was going to remark that, though the temperamental conditions of Posthumus and Troilus are apparently so similar—apparently, mind—and their position as betrayed husbands so identical, we find them acting in directly opposite ways. Troilus entertains no thought of revenge upon his faithless wife; he gives his whole attention to the co-respondent. Now let us glance at Othello. Here is a man who, allowing for his maturer age, is much like the Briton and the Trojan in temperament, even to the extent of being more liberally endowed with muscle than"——

"But you 're not answering my question," moaned Alf. "Which of the four acted right?"

"Well," I replied; "I 'm afraid my conclusions won't have the rounded completeness we value so much in moral inferences unless I 'm allowed to empanel Leontes, in the *Winter's Tale*, as well as Othello, and thus work from a solid foundation. But we 'll see. I 'll put my answer in this way: A casual thinker might pronounce it impossible to lay down any hard-and-fast rule of conduct here, on account of necessary diversity in condition. He would, perhaps, argue that, though abstract Right is absolute and unchangeable, the alternative Wrong, though never shading down into Right, varies immeasurably in degree of turpitude; so that the action which is intrinsically wrong may be more excusable in one man than in another, or under certain conditions than under others. Now, I 'm not going to deny that it lies within our province, as rational beings, to classify wrongs, provided we do so from a purely objective stand-point. I shall endeavour to deal with that issue by-and-by. I merely notice"——

"Stop! stop!" interrupted Alf, rolling his head from side to side. "Answer my question!"

"Well, if you must have it like a half-raw potato, I give my vote in favour of Potiphar the Fourth, the saw-mill man. I don't see what better he could have done. It was n't the most romantic course, perhaps; but I 'm not a romantic person—rather the reverse —and it meets my approval."

"And your deliberate conviction is that he acted rightly—rightly, mind?"

"Assuredly he did. That is what I was driving at; but now you have to take my conclusion as an *ipse dixit*, rather than as a theorem. The misanthropy of the gentleman's after-life is another question, and one which would lead us into a different, and much wider, region of philosophy. But I think we 'll find it interesting to trace, step by step, from its genesis to its culmination, the involuntary process of thought which led each of your Potiphars, separately, to his independent action. We can't embark on this inquiry just now, Alf, for we shall have to grapple with the most minute and subtle shades of psychical distinction, and we shall have to deal largely in postulates; for though"——

"I want to tell you something, Collins," interrupted Alf, in a tone now free from all trace of the distraction and constraint which made it painful to listen to him. "Like poor Cross, I feel impelled to place my tragedy on record, but in one man's memory only. I trust entirely to your discretion. Did you know I was a married man?"

"No; I certainly did n't," I replied, recalling myself; for I had been half-listening to a sound in the lignum. But as he spoke there flashed across my mental vision the picture of his wife—a tawny-haired tigress, with slumbrous dark eyes; a Circe, whose glorious voice had been silent in death for ten years, and lost to him for three years longer. Hence, by some sequence worth tracing, the voluntary exile, the Ishmaelite occupation; the morbid, malevolent interest in the Messalinas at large; and the generally pervading smell of husks. This, let me tell you, is what comes of meddling with tawny-haired tigresses, who harass a man out of individuality, and then die or abscond, leaving him like the last cactus of summer.

"No young fellow could have started in life with a fairer prospect than I had," continued Alf, in a grave, composed tone. "But I was guilty of one deliberately fiendish and heartless action, and following upon that action, I made a mistake that nothing but death can absolve. I married a woman, who, I believe, was divinely assigned to me as a punishment. I 'll tell you the whole story"——

"Wait, Alf," said I hastily. "I must leave you for a few minutes. Do you want anything before I go?"

"Nothing, thank you. Don't stay long."

"You may be sure I won't. Try if you can go to sleep."

I jumped off the wagon. There was no time to lose. During the last few minutes, a peculiar cadence in the sound of Alf's bells had told me, just as surely as words could have done, that the bullocks were mustered, and travelling away. My horses were not far off; and, to save time, I took Alf's saddle and bridle from under his wagon. As I did so, I heard his voice, low and monotonous. I paused involuntarily.——

"O Molly! Molly, my girl!—my poor love!—my darling!"——

I hurried away, and put the saddle and bridle on Bunyip. Body o' me! I thought—can a tawny-haired tigress be called Molly? This must be seen into when I have time.

In a couple of minutes Bunyip had settled down to that flying trot which would have been an independence to anyone except myself. After clearing the lignum, I got a back elevation of the bullocks, half-a-mile out on the plain; and, rapidly overhauling them, I perceived that I should have to pit myself against the Chinese boundary rider this time. Consequently I felt, like Cassius, fresh of spirit and resolved to meet all perils very constantly.

"Our of my way, you Manchurian leper, or I 'll run over you!" I shouted gaily, as I swung round the cattle, turning them back.

"Muck-a-hi-lo! sen-ling, ay-ya; ilo-ilo!" remonstrated the unbeliever, drawing his horse aside to let them pass.

"You savvy, John," said I, suiting my language to his comprehension, while from my eye the Gladiator broke—"bale you snavel-um that peller bullock. Me fetch-um you ole-man lick under butt of um lug; me gib-it you big one dressum down. Compranny pah, John?" The Chinaman had turned back with me, and, as if he had been hired for the work, was stolidly assisting to return the cattle to the spot whence he had taken them.

"Why don't you speak for yourself, John?" I asked, thanklessly quoting from the familiar hexameter, and lighting my pipe as I spoke.

"Eulopean dam logue," responded the heathen in his blindness.

"In contradistinction to the Asiatic and the Australian, who are scrupulously honest," I observed pleasantly. "You savvy who own-um that peller bullock, John?"

"Walligal Alp," replied the pagan promptly. "Me collal him bullock two-tlee time to-molla, all li; two-tlee time nex day, all li."

"All li, John—you collar-um that peller bullock one more time, me manhandle you; pull-um off you dud; tie-um you on ant-bed, allee same spread-eagle; cut-um off you eye-lid; likee do long-a China; bimeby sun jump up, roast-um you eye two-tlee day; bull-dog ant comballee, eat-um you meat, pick-um you bone; bimeby you tumble-down-die; go like-it dibil-dibil; budgeree fire long-a that peller. You savvy, John?"

"Me tellee Missa Smyte you lescue," replied John doggedly. "All li; you name Collin; you b'long-a Gullamen Clown; all li; you killee me bimeby; all li." With this the discomfited Mongol turned his horse in the direction of Mondunbarra homestead, and, like a driver starting an engine when there is danger of the belt flying off, gradually worked up his pace to a canter, leaving me in possession of the field.

But in cases of this kind, there is only one thing worse than victory. I was fairly in a fix with Alf's bullocks. You must understand that these beasts had no legal right to be anywhere except travelling along the track, or floating down the river. If they scattered off the track—not being attended by some capable person— their owner would, there and then, and as often as this occurred, be liable for trespass; twenty times a day, if you like, and a shilling per head each time. If I wished to remove them across a five or ten-mile paddock, the only way I could legally do so would be by means of a balloon. The thousands of homeless bullocks and horses which carry on the land-transport trade had to live and work, or starve and work, on squatters' grass, year after year. So the right to live, being in the nature of a boon or benefaction, went largely by favour—like the slobbery salute imagined by poets—and poor Alf was no favourite with anyone.

The managers of all these three stations were out of reach; and besides, there was no great hope in appealing to any of them.

Yoongoolee homestead, across the river, was about sixteen miles distant; and Hungry M'Intyre, from what I knew of him, was little likely to make concessions to any member of the guild whose representatives had selected within sight of his wool-shed. Yoongoolee was avoided by all the floating population of the country, and particularly by those who could n't afford to be independent, forasmuch as there was nothing there but Highland pride, and Highland eczema and hunger. Most squatters have titles; M'Intyre had two, which were used indifferently; one of these was derived from the hunger, the other from the eczema.

And, of all Alf's enemies, perhaps the most inveterate was the Chinaman's boss, Mr. Smythe, managing partner of Mondunbarra. This gentleman, whose exclusiveness took the very usual form of excluding all considerations not tending to his own profit, and whose refinement manifested itself to the vulgar eye chiefly in cutting things fine about the station, had, a couple of years pre-

viously, taken Alf in the very act of running one of his own bullocks out of the station cattle. An altercation had ensued, followed
by a summons; and Alf had been mulcted in five shillings trespass,
with six guineas costs, besides having to travel seventy or eighty
miles to Court, and the same distance back to his wagon. This was
trying enough to a man of Alf's avaricious and irascible bent. It
had caused him to speak a word in private to Mr. Smythe; and,
from that time forward, the squatter hated the bullock driver considerably more than he hated sin, and feared him more than he
feared his reputed Maker.

Poor Smythe! the remembrance of him wings my soul with pity,
even now. He was parsimonious, cunning, pusillanimous, fastidious,
and hysterically excitable. He was cruelly sat-on by his inexorable
partner, M'Gregor; contemned by his social equals; hated by his
inferiors, and popularly known as the Marquis of Canton. His
only friend was his brother Bert, a quiet youth, who attended him
with Montholon-fidelity; and his appreciation of the cheap and
reliable Asiatic was passively recognised by a station staff of Joss-
devotees.

There was no use in my appealing to this gentleman, for, though
most men in his place would have accepted the opportunity of laying Alf under an obligation, I knew his unhappy moral organisation well enough to be certain that neither policy nor magnanimity
could intervene on behalf of a prostrate enemy. And to make matters more hopeless, Confucius would be just ahead of me, with his
story of forcible rescue, coupled with personal threats of the gravest
character.

Avondale remained. This station belonged to that grand old
colonist, Captain Royce, who governed the seigneury from his
Toorak mansion, like Von Moltke commanding an army from his
telegraph-office. The large-hearted patriarchal traditions of early
days were still current on the station; but that property had to pay,
and pay well, at the manager's peril. To illustrate this: Captain
Royce, in responding to 'Our Pastoral Interests,' never failed to
remark that no working beast had ever been impounded from Avondale. This, of course, conveyed the impression that it was a run
flowing with grass and water for distressed teams; but the unhappy
manager, watched and reported always by at least one narangy,
and ground, as you see, between the upper mill-stone of Royce the
munificent and the nether and much harder one of Royce the busi-
ness-man, had to transmute every blade of grass, or twig of cotton-
bush, into a filament of wool, or let somebody else have a try.

Consequently, the boundary riders of Avondale had strict orders to hunt all strays and trespassers across the frontiers of stations that did impound; so the fine old squatter-king got there just the same—also the carriers' teams and the drovers' horses.

One characteristic of Avondale was that the rank and file of the station were always treated with fatherly benevolence, and were never discharged. They gradually got useless by reason of mere antiquity, and, without actually dying, slowly mummified, and were duly interred in the cemetery at the homestead.

In view of the rigorous usages specified, it was no marvel that a deficiency in the Avondale clip of '83 had led to the resignation of Mr. Angus Cameron, and the installation of a new manager, a few weeks before the date of these incidents. But the appointment of a strange boundary rider to the paddock adjoining Alf's camp—an event which had taken place three or four months before the same date—seemed like a sudden angle and break in the corridor of Time.

Avondale home-station was nine miles distant. I had never met the new manager; but his name was Wentworth St. John Ffrench; and, by all accounts, he acted up to it. Popular rumour likened him to the man with the whole pound of tobacco, who had sworn against borrowing or lending. Mr. Ffrench could afford to be independent of such men as Alf, but could n't afford to establish a precedent for invalided carriers loafing on the run. Of course, you would n't look at the thing in that light; but then, your name is not Wentworth St. John Ffrench, and you would n't do for a manager of Avondale. You would have the run swarming with a most tenacious type of trespassers before you knew what you were doing. Moreover, the moral responsibility (if any) of the matter rested on Mondunbarra, not on Avondale.

Neither had I ever seen the new Avondale boundary man; but I was prejudiced against him also. It required no deep dive into the mysteries of Nomenology to augur ill from the nickname of 'Terrible Tommy.' The title was, of course, satirical; the man an imbecile and fickle windbag. Still, this name was better than the manager's.

Evidently, my only chance was to deal directly with some one of the boundary men. I had already failed to melt the musing Briton's eyes; and though I had, in a sense, prevailed over the Mongol, I could make no use of him; so I found myself hanging, as you might say, by one strand, that strand being Terrible Tommy.

I must enlist this man, I mentally concluded, as a willing accomplice; and, by my faith, I 'll do so before I leave him. I care not an he be the devil; give me faith, say I.

By this time, the sun was just setting. I left the bullocks near the boundary fence, turned Bunyip adrift, and placed the saddle and bridle where I could find them again. Then crossing into Avondale, I picked my way through a belt of tall lignum, sloppy with warm water, and alive with mosquitos; then on through scattered timber until, a mile from the fence, appeared the one-roomed abode of the man I wanted. I knew where to find the place, having stayed there one night when Bendigo Bill was in charge of the paddock. But now, nearing the house, how I wished I had that frank, good-hearted old Eureka rebel to deal with instead of the hard-featured, sandy-complexioned man whom I saw carrying home a couple of buckets of water on a wooden hoop. Our old friends, the Irresistible and the Immovable were about to encounter once more.

"Evening, sir," I cooed, with an urbanity born of the conditions already set down.

"Gude evenin' (Squire Western's expression!) Ye maun gang fairther, ye ken; fir fient haet o' sipper ye 'se hae frae me the nicht. De'il tak' ye, ye lang-leggit, lazy loun, flichterin' roun' wi' yir 'Gude evenin' sir!' an' a' sic' clishmaclaver. Awa' wi ye! dinna come fleechin' tae me! The kintra 's l—sy wi' sic' haverils, comin' sundoonin' on puir folk 'at henna mickle mair nir eneugh fir thir ain sel's. Tak' aff yir coat an' wark, ye glaikit—De'il tak' ye; wha' fir ye girnin' at?"

"Gude save 's!" I snarled; "wha' gar ye mak' sic' a splore? Hoo daur ye tak' on ye till misca' a body sae sair 's ye dae, ye bletherin' coof? Hae ye gat oot the wrang side yir bed the morn?—ir d' ye tak' me fir a rief-randy?—ir wha' the de'il fashes ye the noo? Ye ken, A was compit doon ayont the boondary, an' A thocht A wad dauner owre an' hae a wee bit crack wi' ye the nicht. A wantit tae ken wha' like mon yir new maunager micht be, an' tae speer twa-three ither things firbye; bit sin' yir sae skrunty, ye maun tak' yir domd sipper till yir ain bethankit ava, an' A 'll gang awa' bock till me ain comp. Heh!" And I turned away with unconcealed resentment and contempt.

"Haud a wee," said the boundary rider, setting down his buckets, and slapping the back of his neck. "Ye ken, A 'm sae owrecam wi' thir awfu' mustikies that whiles A canna—Bit cam awa' tae the biggin; cam awa' tae the biggin, an' rest yirsel'." The Irresistible had scored this time. Such is life.

I helped Tommy out of his embarrassment by an occasional 'Ay, mun,' interjected into his apologetic and cordial monologue; and so we reached the hut, where, after directing me to a seat, he filled a billy with some of the water he had brought, and hung it on the crook.

"An' wha' dae they ca' ye?" he asked, turning his back to the fire, and surveying me with a kindly interest which made me feel as uneasy as if I had been sleeping in a fowl-house.

"Tam Collins," I replied readily, though interrupted by a fit of coughing as I pronounced my surname.

"Ye 'll no be yin o' the M'Callums o' Auchtermauchtie?" he inquired eagerly. "A kent them weel."

I shook my head. "An' wha' dae they ca' yirsel'?" I asked.

"Tam Airmstrang—anither Tam, ye ken. An' whaur ye frae? Wha' pairt o' the kintra was ye born in syne?" A boggy-looking place for a man to carry his integrity safely across; however, I replied,

"Ye 'se aiblins be acquent wi' yon auld sang:—

> Braw, braw lads on Yarrow braes,
> That wander through the bloomin' heather.

Aweel, A was born on the braes o' Yarra. Ye ken, the time 's gane lang wi' me sin' A rin aboot the braes, an' pu'd the gowans fine. Ay, mun!"

"A-y-y, mun!" rejoined my companion, echoing my home-sick sigh. "D'ye ken—A wadna' thocht ye was a Selkirksheer mon. A wad hae thocht ye was frae Lanarksheer, ir aiblins frae"——

"Whaur micht ye be frae, yirsel'?" I interrupted desperately.

He seemed about to reply, but checked himself, and looked at me absently; then he turned to the fire, took his canister from the shelf, and mechanically measured out a handful of tea. He stood gazing into the fire till recalled to himself by the boiling of the billy; then a triumphant smile invaded his stern features; he took the billy off the crook, threw the tea into it, clapped both hands on my shoulders, and quoted with fine effect that lucid passage from Burns:—

> Bye attour, ma gutcher has
> A heigh hoose an' a leigh ane,
> A' firbye ma bony sel',
> The lad o' Ecclefechan!

Ha-ha-ha! The lad o' Ecclefechan, ye ken—no the lass o' Ecclefechan! Losh! A hae whiles laffit mysen gey near daft at yon!

The lad o' Ecclefechan!" He gave way to another burst of hilarity, in which I sincerely joined. "A henna' thocht aboot yon a towmond syne," he continued, wiping the dew of merriment from his eyes; "bit ye hae brocht it bock the nicht. The lad o' Ecclefechan! ha-ha-ha! Ay, mun; A 'm frae Ecclefechan, an' ma feyther afore me. Syne, A hae been a' ip an' doon Ayrsheer, frae yin fair till anither wi' nowte. Brawly dae A ken Mossgeil, an' Mauchline, an' Loughlea, an' the auld Brig o' Doon, firbye a wheen ither spotes ye 'se aiblins hear tell o'."

"Ye 'll hae seen Alloway Kirk?" I conjectured.

"Seen 't! ay," he replied magnificently. "A thocht naethin' o' 't!"

"Ye what?" I retorted, in the mere wantonness of power. "Ye hae seen yon auld hauntet kirk, whaur witches an' warlocks flang an' loupit, an' Auld Nick himsel' screwt his pipes an' gart them skirl, till roof an' rafters a' did dirl! ye hae keekit intil yon eerie auld ruin!—an' syne ye daunert awa', an' thocht naethin' o' 't! Be ma saul, Bobbie Birns didna' think naethin' o' 't! Heh!"

Tommy was now laying the table. He made no reply to my rebuke, but the forced and deprecating smile which struggled to his face showed that the Irresistible had scored again.

But one of the most unpleasant experiences I can now recall to mind was the sitting down with that unsuspecting fellow-mortal to his soda-bread and cold mutton, while I smiled, and smiled, and was a Scotchman. The easy victory, tested by that moral straightedge we all carry, made me feel as mean as a liveried servant; and when Tommy requested me to ask a blessing, and sat with his elbow on the table and his face reverently veiled by his hand, whilst I wove a protracted and incoherent grace from the Lowland vocabulary, I seemed to sink to the level of a prince's equerry. In fact, I would almost as soon make one of a crowd to hurrah for a Governor as go through such an ordeal again. My truthfulness—perhaps the only quality in which I attain an insulting pre-eminence—seemed outraged to the limit of endurance as I looked forward to the inevitable detection, soon or late, of the impromptu deception which, in spite of me, was expanding and developing like a snake-lie, or an election squabble.

However, I contented myself with directing the stream of conversation, and leaving the rest to Tommy. It transpired that he had been four months in his present situation, and only nine in the country altogether. He had got employment on Avondale by a lucky chance; and, though engaged only for six months, entertained hopes that he might be baptised into the billet, to the permanent exclusion of Bendigo Bill.

For menial employment on Avondale was like membership in a Church, only that, to the carnal mind, there was more in it; moreover, the initiation was attended with greater ceremony, and the possibility of expulsion was kept further in the background. Once admitted into Avondale fellowship, the communicant might turn out a white sheep or a black one; but he was still a sheep, whilst all outside the fold, white or black, as the case might be, were goats. This may be illustrated by the incident which had just given Tommy the footing of an unbaptised believer, provisionally admitted amongst the elect. He gave me the account, so far as it affected himself; and Bendigo Bill, sitting on the same kerosene-case, long afterward narrated the episode fully.

Two years before the date of this record, Bendigo Bill's mind, such as it was, had been disturbed by the discovery of gold at Mount Brown. As time went on, the occasional sight of northward-bound drays and pack-horses revived the old lunacy in its most malignant form, till the demonaic at last gave formal notice of his intention to leave the station, and push his fortune on the diggings. His resignation was in due course forwarded to Captain Royce; whereupon that potentate sent him a peremptory order to mind his paddock, and not make an infernal exhibition of himself. The demon quaked and collapsed for the time, and Bill, in his proper person, acquiesced with the humility customarily manifested by Avondale people when Captain Royce was conducting the other side of the argument. But the evil spirit was scotched, not killed; and Bill became a harmless melancholic, dwelling on old-time memories of the diggings, and gradually lying himself into the conviction that, if he had gone to Mount Brown, he could have told by the lay of the country, unerringly, and at the first glance, where the gold was.

Things being in this posture, there reached Avondale, in the winter of '83, a vague, intangible bruit of somebody expecting to hit it on Mount Brown; and, shortly afterward, Bill, in a vision of the night, found himself paddocking a bit of four-foot ground for a free, lively, six-inch wash, running something like ten ounces to the dish—rough, shotty, water-worn gold. Next night the dream was repeated, but with this addition, that the dreamer bent the point of his pick whilst hooking out of a sort of pocket in the pipe-clay a flat, damper-shaped nugget that he could hardly lift. The third night found the ground richer than ever; but Bill, knowing it

to be a dream, and having no way of permanently retaining the
gold he might get under such conditions, very wisely contented
himself with taking accurate observations of his landmarks, so that
he might know the place again when he saw it by daylight. Whilst
so engaged, his attention was attracted by two emus, which resolved
themselves, respectively, into Captain Royce and Mick Magee—the
latter being an old mate of his own, accidentally killed on the Jim
Crow, about fifteen years before. This made the assurance of the
thrice-repeated dream triply sure; for the emu is one of the luckiest
things a person can dream about; and its identification with Captain Royce was as good as an old boot thrown by that awesome
magnate; whilst its association with Mick Magee made the cup of
blessing overslop in all directions—Mick having been, in the days
of his vanity, a man that brought luck with him wherever he went,
particularly in shallow ground.

So Bill wiped from the tablet of his memory everything except
the picture of a place where two gullies met, after the fashion of
a Y, and formed a bit of a blind creek, running between low ranges
broken here and there by the outcrop of a hungry white quartz. His
dream intuitively conveyed the further knowledge that the surrounding country had been prospected for a few floaters, and the
creek, lower down, rooted-up for bare tucker, while this little spur
of made ground, between the prongs of the Y, remained intact—
and there was the jeweller's shop.

Again Bill, emboldened by the unholy afflatus caught from his
earlier life, gave notice to the manager; this time following up his
action by buying a horse and spring-cart from a tank-sinker, and
conditionally selling his own two horses. Then came Captain
Royce's ukase, to the effect that no man must be allowed to swag
the country, ragged and homeless, with the story in his mouth that
he had been boundary riding on Avondale for ten years. Therefore, Bill's notice was passed over with the contempt it merited.
But something must be done; so a six months' leave of absence was
granted; and the manager was instructed to employ, for that time
only, the first likely-looking stranger who presented himself—the
latter being clearly given to understand that he was only in the
loosest sense of the word an Avondale employé. If Bill returned
on the expiration of his furlough, he should be reinstated, and all
would be forgiven; if he failed to return, such default would be
taken as evidence of contumacy; excommunication would promptly
follow, and the station would thereby be acquitted of all responsibility touching any destitute old bummer who might swag the

country with the yarn that he had been boundary riding on Avondale for ten years. Captain Royce could be stern enough when he let himself out.

The emu-section of the dream being thus partly fulfilled, Bill clutched at a release in any form; and it happened that, simultaneously with the arrival of Captain Royce's mandate, came Tom Armstrong and his mate, Andrew Glover, from a job of ringing on the Yanko. The manager, being named Angus Cameron, plumped Tom into the vacancy, and supplied him with a couple of old station horses. Bill remained a few days longer, teaching Tom the routine of his work; then the manager slacked-off, and Bill harnessed his horse and fled northward—not because he disliked Avondale, but because he liked it so well that he was impatient to make Captain Royce such a bid for the property as that nabob could n't think of refusing, with any hope of luck afterward.

On my mentioning Alf's bullocks, Tom told me that he had heard bells among the lignum in the corner of Mondunbarra, a few nights before, and had next morning found twenty bullocks and a bay horse on the Avondale side of the fence. He knew that the Chow had passed them on to him to save trouble, so he immediately passed them back to the Chow. Next evening, his neighbour had re-delivered them to Avondale f.o.b., and in the morning, Tom returned them to Mondunbarra c.o.d. Next night, the untiring Asiatic had them back on Avondale o.r.; and in the morning, Tom did what he should have done at first—put them across the river on to the station from whose bourne no trespasser returned. The ensuing adventures of the bullocks you already know.

Tom had acquired, without any severe wrench of his finer feelings, the boundary man's hostility to the bullock driver, and was cultivating the same with all the energy of his race. His title, after all, was no more quizzical in its application than that of Ivan the Terrible; and to understand how nasty a station vassal can sometimes make himself, you must know a little concerning the manners none and customs beastly of the time and place wherein our scene is laid.

And, to my unspeakable disgust, I found that though Tom had never met Alf personally, the unfortunate outlaw was his Doctor Fell too. And the very spirit of Leviticus breathed in his tone as he informed me that gin he had umquhile kent the nowte belangit tae yon ill-hairtet raff, he wad hae whummelt them owre the burn (the Lachlan a burn! O, my country) lang syne, an' no fashit himsel' wi' ony sic' fiddle-fyke.

Nothing but extreme caution would do here. The brutal truth of my unwarranted solicitude for the sick man would certainly cause friction, and might spoil all. So, in a few well-chosen words, I informed Tom that there was a trifle between Alf and me; and he was sick, just when I wanted to keep him on his feet for a while. Would Tom (and my patois became so hideously homely that, for the reader's sake, I have to paraphrase it)—would Tom, as a personal favour to me, call round at Alf's camp, morning and evening, for a few days, and in the meantime keep his bullocks safe?

No answer. The silken bond of our nationality would n't stand such a strain. Then I slowly drew out my pocket-book, and, with the stifled sigh of a thrifty man, handed my compatriot one of the four one-pound notes which excluded me from the state of grace enjoyed by Lazarus; remarking, half-sullenly, that he could n't be expected to take all this trouble for nothing; and though I was a poor man like himself, it would pay me to get Alf at work again. And, considering that a bullock driver often has it in his power to do a good turn for a boundary man, would n't it be better, I suggested, for Tom to do all this on his own account, without a whisper concerning my interposition?

I had known better than to make such a proposition to Sollicker. That impracticable animal—who would have uncovered his head to receive backsheesh, as backsheesh, from a 'gentleman'—would have spurned my lubricant as an unholy thing; and woe to Alf's bullocks if he had caught them again! But I was n't surprised to find my *modus vivendi* accepted by this passive product of a social code fabricated and compiled in the nethermost pit—a code which, under the heading of Thrift, frankly teaches the poor to grind each other without scruple, whilst religiously avoiding all inquiry into the claims of the rich—a code, in fact, which makes the greasing of the fat pig a work holy unto the Lord. The keen selfishness of my proposal touched a kindred chord in poor Tom's bosom, the mettlesome casting of my sprat upon the waters, in sure hope of finding a mackerel after many days, awoke his admiration; whilst an immediate and prospective advantage to himself stood out through it all. Yet, under this crust of clannishness, cunning, and money-hunger, there lay a fine manhood. I saw the latter come to the surface a few months afterward. But that is another episode; and I must confine myself to the case before the Court.

Tom knew of an island among the lignum, where the bullocks would be safe; and he would put them there in the morning, after he had visited Alf. But I must take the bells off first. I thanked him with a sincerity out of all keeping with my accent, and shortly afterward drew the intolerable conference gently to a close. Upon the whole, I had impressed my host as a shrewd, well-informed person, too much taken-up with the cares of the world and the deceitfulness of riches to dwell upon personal memories of the auld kintra. I was touched to notice a certain disappointment and for-lornness in his manner as he accompanied me to the boundary fence, where we shook hands, and parted—each looking forward to the probability of meeting again, but with different degrees of longing.

And now, thought I, as I recovered Alf's saddle and bridle, heaven grant that that parting may be a Kathleen Mavourneen one; and let me have some other class of difficulty to deal with next time.

Thus, in the best of spirits, owing to the prospect of some smooth travelling on my main trunk line, after having traversed the steep and crooked section to which I had been committed by one touch of the switch two hours before, I made my way through the lignum to Alf's camp; guided partly by the instinct which we share unequally with the lower creation, and partly by the smell of the dead dog, zephyr-borne on the night air. After dragging the poor animal's body a little distance away, I vaulted into the wagon, and spoke cheerily to Alf.

No reply. I struck a match, and saw him sleeping the peaceful, dreamless sleep of a tired child. I lit a bit of candle I had noticed in the daytime, and sat down to note his progress in a professional way. His pulse was right, as I found by timing it with my own; and the hard swelling of the elbows seemed to have relaxed a little. The backs of his hands were pretty bad with the external scurvy known as 'Barcoo rot'—produced by unsuitable food and extreme hardship—but that had nothing to do with the complaint which had so strangely overtaken him. His breathing was gentle and regular, though his face was covered with gorged mosquitos. The healthy moistness of the skin showed that my prescription had operated as a sudorific, no less than as a soporific. Altogether, there was a marked diminution of what we call febrile symptoms; and, better still, he had managed to turn himself over since I left him.

I lit my pipe, and contemplated the unconscious outlaw. With-out being aggressively handsome, like Dixon or Willoughby, Alf, in his normal state, was a decidedly noble-looking man, of the so-called Anglo-Saxon type, modified by sixty or eighty years of Australian deterioration. His grandfather had probably been something like Sollicker; and the apprehensions of that discomfortable cousin were being fulfilled only too ruthlessly. The climate had played Old Gooseberry with the fine primordial stock. Physically, the Suffolk Punch had degenerated into the steeplechaser; psychologically, the chasm between the stolid English peasant and the saturnine, sensitive Australian had been spanned with that *facilis* which marks the *descensus Averni*.

But the question of racial degeneracy, past, present, or to come, troubled its victim very little as he lay there. Indeed, it had never troubled him much. He was one of those men who cannot learn to think systematically, but who make up their deficiency by feeling the more intensely. And now that the unseen Guide had given His beloved sleep, and the stern, defiant blue eyes were veiled, and the habitual frown smoothed from the fine forehead, I found something pathetic in the worn repose of the sleeper's face.

Presently, drifting into a philosophic mood, I placed my propositions in order, and, by the inductive system applicable in such cases, read his history like a book, right back to the time when, according to a popular, though rather tough, assumption, he had lain helpless and imbecile on his mother's knee, clad in a white garment about four feet long, and with a pulsating soft place on the top of the bald head which wobbled on his insufficient neck like a rain-laden rose on a weak stalk. Little dreamed that mother, poor mortal! when with tireless iteration she ticked off his extremities; —'This pig went to market; this pig stayed at home'—little did she dream, when she wiped the perpetual dribble from his mouth; when she poured all manner of unintelligible tommy-rot into his inattentive and conspicuous ears—little did she then dream that the blind evolution of events would transform her inexplicably valued baby into a scrap of floating wreckage on a sea of trouble; scarcely amounting to a circumstance in the vast and endless procession of his fellow-waifs.

Doubtless, he would soon be on his feet again, but to what end? Merely to resume the old persecuted life, still achieving, still pursuing, that strictly congruous penalty which waits upon the man whose life is one protracted challenge to a world wherein no person except the systematic and successful hypocrite has too many friends, or too good a character. Any fool can get himself hated, if he goes the right way to work; but the game was never yet worth a rap, for a rational man to play. This in clear view of the fact that most people lose more by their friends than by their enemies. But there are few sins more odious than ill-nature; and there 's nothing blessed about the persecution you undergo on that account. Your position is not heroic; at best, it is only pitiable; at worst, it is detestable. *Athanasius contra mundum* is grand only in cases where the snag is right, and the mundus wrong. Then persecution becomes the second-highest form of blessedness—the highest form, of course, being the ability to turn round and flatten-out the persecutor. Now, if Alf could open the windows of his understanding—— But then, one of the gravest disabilities in the leopard of thirty-five, or thereabout, is connected with the changing of his spots. Such is life.

With these reflections, I extinguished the candle, and left the wagon. The bullocks happened to be close by. After the manner of workers, they had collected themselves on a piece of open ground; some folded asleep, head to flank, while others lay chewing meditatively, reviewing the events of the day, and wondering what the morrow might bring forth. Amidst the reposing group stood the hardy bay horse, the world forgetting, by the world forgot; for, contrary to popular supposition, the horse has not half the innate sagacity of the ox, though he is to a much greater extent the creature of habit, and therefore appears more teachable.

By the light of a good half-moon, now declining in the west, I got the two bells off without much trouble, and threw them under the wagon. Then, in case the Confucian might be an earlier bird than the lad of Ecclefechan, I put the bullocks and horse across the boundary fence, carefully replacing the brush I had removed for their passage. From there I struck across to the sound of Cleopatra's bell, and brought my two most useful friends to where the most valuable was still chained-up. In ten minutes, I had packed my share of the things that make death bitter, and in another half-hour I had left Mondunbarra behind, and was well into Avondale, working out in my own mind an abstruse ethical problem, which would have no interest for the shallow-pated reader. And so ends the day.

But not the narrative. I am mindful of my promise. As hour after hour passed, the insecurity of Alf's situation grew upon me, till I could think of nothing else. Philosopher—seer, I might say —as it has pleased heaven to fashion me, I confess I could arrive at no definite forecast of the order which the outlaw's affairs would assume at the next turn of the kaleidoscope. But I knew that it was in the nature of the kaleidoscope to turn.

In due time, the stars dimmed and disappeared; the deep-blue of the south-eastern sky paled to a greenish tint, like the under side of a melon, changing slowly to an opaline hue; then imperceptibly succeeded a blush of shell-pink, presently shot with radial bars of dusky red; and now every object above the horizon stood vividly revealed through the limpid air—soon to be blurred, distorted, or entirely withdrawn from view. In the favourable interval of ten or fifteen minutes, I saw Poondoo homestead, six or eight miles ahead. In the intermediate distance appeared a moving dot, which, as I was travelling at a walk, brought my field-glass into use. Only an iron-grey man, in a pith hat, driving a pair of chestnuts in a buggy. No business of mine, I thought, in my human short-sightedness; and I was lowering the glass, when the figure of another traveller crossed its field. This last was a person bearing a startling resemblance to Mungo Park, inasmuch as he was evidently a poor white man, with no mother to bring him milk, no wife to grind his corn. The solitude of the place made the contrast between the two travellers impressive. I replaced the glass, thinking, with sorrow rather than conceit, that I could make a better world myself, with my eyes shut. There was no irreverence in the thought; the irreverence is on the part of any profane reader who forges the Creator's endorsement to that good old rule and simple plan which was, is, and ever shall be, the outcome of Individualism. But the good old rule, as you shall perceive, worked happily in this instance. Now try to imagine a writer of fiction deliberately inventing an incident which seems to strike at the very root of his own argument. Then you will have some idea of the annalist's stern veracity, as opposed to the mere expediency of the novelist.

I was within a quarter of a mile of the swagman when the buggy overtook him. The driver drew up to a walk, apparently yarning with Mungo; and I nearly tumbled off my horse when I saw him stop on the off lock, and wait whilst the swagman deposited bluey on the foot-board and himself on the seat. Then the chestnuts tossed their heads, and the buggy resumed its way, surging across the crab-holes like a canoe on rough water. My soul went forth in a pæan of joy, for, exactly as the perfect circle of a flying scrawl bespoke Giotto, this action bespoke Stewart of Kooltopa, now masquerading under a pair of strange horses. Here was my opportunity. Figuratively, I would put Alf in a basket, with a note pinned to his bib, and leave him on Stewart's door-step.

Those whose knowledge of the pastoral regions is drawn from a course of novels of the *Geoffrey Hamlyn* class, cannot fail to hold a most erroneous notion of the squatter. Of course, we use the term 'squatter' indifferently to denote a station-owner, a managing partner, or a salaried manager. Lacking generations of development, there is no typical squatter. Or, if you like, there are a thousand types. Hungry M'Intyre is one type; Smythe—petty, genteel, and parsimonious—is another; patriarchal Royce is another; Montgomery—kind, yet haughty and imperious—is another; Stewart is another. My diary might, just as likely as not, have compelled me to introduce, instead of these, a few of the remaining nine-hundred and ninety-five types—any type conceivable, in fact, except the slender-witted, virgin-souled, overgrown schoolboys who fill Henry Kingsley's exceedingly trashy and misleading novel with their insufferable twaddle. There was a squatter of the Sam Buckley type, but he, in the strictest sense of the word, went to beggary; and, being too plump of body and exalted of soul for barrow-work, and too comprehensively witless for anything else, he was shifted by the angels to a better world—a world where the Christian gentleman is duly recognised, and where Socialistic carpenters, vulgar fishermen, and all manner of undesirable people, do the washing-up.

Stewart, it must be admitted, was no gentleman. Starting with a generous handicap, as the younger son of a wealthy and aristocratic Scottish laird, he had, during a Colonial race of forty years, daily committed himself by actions which shut him out from the fine old title. He was in the gall of altruism, and in the bond of democracy. Amiable demeanour, unmeasured magnanimity, and spotless integrity, could never carry off the unpardonable sin in which this lost sheep-owner wallowed—the taint, namely, of isocratic principle. When a member of the classes takes to his bosom that unclean thing, in its naked reality, he thereby forfeits the title of 'gentleman,' and becomes a mere man. For there is no such thing as a democratic gentleman; the adjective and noun are hyphenated by a drawn sword. If the said unclean thing eats into its victim to the same extent that the wolf did into Baron Munchausen's sleigh-horse, the metamorphosed subject comes perilously near being what the Orientals call a dog of a Christian. For there is no such thing as a Christian gentleman, except as loosely distinguished from the Buddhist, Parsee, or Mahometan gentleman. Try the transposition: gentleman-Christian. And why not, since you have the gentleman-this-or-that? Taking the shifty, insidious title in its go-to-meeting sense, every Christian is *prima facie* a gentleman; taking it in its every-day sense, no 'gentleman' can be a Christian; for Christianity postulates initial equality, and recognises no gradation except in usefulness.

So Stewart was never, even by inadvertence, spoken of as a gentleman—always as a Christian. Three-score years of wise choice in the perpetually-recurring alternatives of life, had made the Golden Rule his spontaneous impulse; and now, though according to the shapen-in-iniquity theory, he must have had faults, no one in Riverina, below the degree of squatter, had proved sharp enough to detect them. It was considered bad form to express approval of anything he did. 'Stewart! Oh, he 's a (adj.) Christian!' That was all. He had reached a certain standard, and was expected to live up to it. Such is life.

By a notable coincidence, Stewart was rich. Not owing to his Christianity, bear in mind; but partly to a faculty for knowing by the look of a sheep, as it raced past, whether the animal was worth six-and-tenpence or seven shillings; partly to his being able to tell, by what was happening in some other quarter of the globe, how the wool-market was going to move; partly to his being connected with a thing that paid; partly to his knowing when he was well off, and leaving the reflected meat to the inverted dog in the water; partly to a stubborn crotchet which made him hold the giver of usury, as well as the taker, to be beyond the pale of mercy; partly to a fine administrative ability; partly to the avoidance of expensive habits—partly to all these combined, but chiefly to the fact that his *mana* never failed.

Anyway, he could afford to impart, in judicious assistance to deserving and undeserving people, more than the average squatter spends in usury and extravagance put together, and be better off all the while. An illustration may not be amiss here. I 'll tell you what I saw in the Mia-mia Paddock, on Kooltopa, during the autumn and winter of '83—that is, from six to nine months before the date of this discursive, yet faithful, record.

'83 was a bad year. The scanty growth of the '82 spring had been eaten off nearly as fast as it grew, and afterward the millions of stock had to live—like the Melbourne unemployed of later times —on the glorious sunshine. Then when the winter came, it brought nothing but frost; and the last state of the country was worse than the first. The mile-wide stock-route from Wilcannia to Hay was strewn with carcases of travelling sheep along the whole two hundred and fifty miles. On one part of the route, some frivolous person had stooked the dried mummies (they were lying so thick) in order that drovers and boundary men might have the pleasure of cantering on ahead to run the little mobs out of the way. And as human nature, thus sold, never grudges to others participation

in the sell, the stooks improved in size and life-likeness for weeks
and months. I remember noticing once, in passing along the fifty-
mile stretch of that route which bisects the One Tree Plain, that,
taking no account of sheep, I never was out of sight of dying cattle
and horses—let alone the dead ones. The famine was sore in the
land. To use the expression of men deeply interested in the matter,
you could flog a flea from the Murrumbidgee to the Darling. Or,
to put it in another way: the life of stock in Riverina was as cheap
as the life of the common person in the novels of R. L. Stevenson,
Rider Haggard, Rudyard Kipling, and some other modern classics.

Kooltopa, being the best of land, and lightly stocked, was an
exception; and thither flocked nearly all the uncircumcised of
Riverina, with their homeless bullocks and horses. Stewart was n't
the man to order them off, while ordering would have been of any
use; and in affairs of this nature, the squatter who hesitates is lost.
The time comes when grass-loafers will stand a lot of ordering off;
in extreme cases, such as the one under review, they are about equal
in tenacity to the Scythians or the Cimbri of olden times.

There was no end to them. Week after week, month after month,
they came stringing-in from seven-syllabled localities on all points
of the compass; some with sunburnt wives, and graduated sets of
supple-jointed, keen-sighted children—the latter, I grieve to admit,
distinctly affirming that disquieting theory which assumes evolution
of immigrating races toward the aboriginal type.

There was plenty of rough feed in the Mia-mia Paddock, and
there the tribes congregated to hold their protracted Feast of Taber-
nacles, their vast camp-meeting, which they by no means conducted
on religious lines. For the easy profanity, unconscious obscenity,
and august slang of the back country scented the air like myall;
whilst the aggregate repertory of *bonâ fide* anecdote and reminiscence was something worth while. No young fellow in that great
rendezvous dared to embellish his narrative in the slightest degree,
on pain of being posted as a double-adjective blatherskite; for his
audience was sure to include a couple of critical, cynical, iron-grey
cyclopedias of everything Australian—everything, at least, un-
tainted by the spurious and blue-moulded civilisation of the littoral.

An evangelist, collecting money for the support of an Aboriginal
mission, went fifty miles out of his way to give these unregenerate
brethren a word of exhortation. This good man—he probably never
had a sovereign which he regarded as his own; and, rest his soul!
he needs no money now—this good man afterward told me, with
tears of gratitude and sorrow in his eyes, that he got a fine collec-

tion in the Mia-mia, but no souls; and both clauses of his statement seemed to have the ring of truth.

Stewart sullenly avoided this gathering of the clans. He knew he was n't wanted there; and, as the paddock consisted chiefly of purchased land, he felt that the conventionalities were, in a sense, violated. But what could the people do? It was a miserable business altogether.

At last, moved by the report of the Mia-mia boundary rider, he drove slowly along the river frontage, and saw five miles of wagons, wagonettes, spring-carts, buggies, tents, women, children, dogs, cooking-utensils, and masculine laundry. He saw fellows patching tarpaulins, mending harness, making yokes, platting whips, fishing, pig-hunting, reading Ouida, yarning round fires, or trying to invent some new form of gambling; but he only saw their backs, and they did n't see him at all. He took a tour round the paddock, and found a racecourse duly laid out in a suitable place, with a few fellows training their bits of stuff for a coming event. Others were duck-shooting in the swamps, and others after turkeys on the plains, whilst a few diverted themselves by coursing rabbits on the sand-hills. And as for bullocks and horses—why, they were as grass-hoppers for multitude.

A closer examination brought to light his own sheep. Wild and shy, as paddocked merinos always are, these had withdrawn to the quietest places they could find, and were there making the best of a bad job. Stewart lost his temper, for once; and he that is without similar sin among the readers of this simple memoir is hereby authorised to cast the first stone.

He allowed the sun to go down upon his wrath. Next morning, he rallied up all his station hands; mustered the Mia-mia Paddock; distributed the sheep elsewhere over the run; and thus washed his hands of all responsibility touching the welfare of his guests.

Toward spring, he drove round the camps again, pausing here and there to give the trespassers a bit of his mind: "Now, boys; I must get you to shift. Lots of perishing teams not able to get down out of the back country till now, and all making for this paddock. Must leave a bit of grass for them when they come." And more to the same effect. So the settlement gradually broke-up, and things returned to their normal monotony.

But not altogether so. Some of the nomads wanted land, and had means to back their desire. Rambling leisurely over the station paddocks, with the county map for reference, these people saw where the most eligible allotments were, and presently picked the eyes out of the run; in some cases, shifting straight from their camps to their selections. Such is life.

Saint Peter, I should imagine, had narrowly watched the squatter's attitude when the Assyrian came down like a person flying from perdition. Afterward, he had noted with approval that the new selectors were treated with the same forbearance and benevolence they had formerly experienced as refugees. But not until he saw Stewart pounce on the incident of the mammoth surprise-party as a clinching argument against land-monopoly, did that austere janitor hang his keys on his thumb, to hunt-up, far back in his book, the page reserved in case of rich men. And still the metaphor of the camel and the needle's eye stands unimpaired. The difficulties vanish only when you attain some conception of what the Kingdom of God is—how much more to the purpose than pearly gates or jasper seas; how accordant with the Ormuzd in man; how premeditated in design; how indomitable in patience; and how needfully and inexorably guarded by the diminutive portal above referred to.

"Good morning, Collins."

"Good morning, Mr. Stewart. An early stirrer, by the rood."

"Yes; I have a (sheol) of a long stage before me to-day. Been travelling all night?"

"Only since about twelve. I camped yesterday in the Dead Man's Bend, on Mondunbarra. I 've been kept on the move since dinnertime, or so. Tell you how it came. I was lying in the shade of a tree, having a smoke, and thinking about one thing or another, when I heard some one calling from the other side of the river. It was Mosey Price; and he told me" &c., &c.

Stewart sighed, glanced toward the south-east, produced a cigarcase, took thence three cigars, handed one to me and another to Mungo Park, lit the third himself, then smoked listlessly and mechanically.

"Good," he remarked, throwing away the inch-long stump of his cigar, and gathering his reins. "What 's your name?" he continued, turning to the swagman.

"Bob Stirling," replied the African explorer. "I worked on Kooltopa, many years ago, but I don't suppose you remember me."

"I 'm not sure. However, I 'll find a nice comfortable week's work for you, at all events. Collins, I give you credit. You should have gone into politics. You 'd have made a d——d good diplomatist."

"I 'm glad you think so, Mr. Stewart. But the main body of the story has to come. You see, I was, in a sense, no farther forward than at first. Alf's bullocks were only respited, and briefly at that. So, as I was telling you, I left them against the boundary fence, and walked across to interview this Terrible Tommy. He was my last resource. I just met him carrying home a couple of buckets of water from the lagoon. 'Evening, sir,' says I, as sweet as sugar" &c., &c.

Stewart glanced at the blazing orb, now slowly climbing the coppery sky, sighed again, lit another cigar, and smoked impassively.

"D——d if I approve of your action in that instance, Collins," he remarked gravely, throwing away his second stump, and groping for something under the buggy-seat.

"Indeed, Mr. Stewart, I don't defend the action. I only endeavour to palliate it on the plea of necessity. And, if Adam fell in the days of innocency, what should poor Tom Collins do in the days of villainy?"

"Shakespear," observed the squatter approvingly, as he drew a bottle and glass from a candle-box under the seat. "Misquoted, though, unless my memory betrays me. But I look at the thing in this way—The Poondoo people put a couple of bottles of Albury into the buggy; and I think we can do one of them now, early as it is. When shall we three meet again? Eh? How is that for aptness? A Roland for your (adj.) Oliver.—I look at the thing in this way, Collins—But you must n't take anything on an empty stomach. I have some sandwiches here." He handed a couple to me, a couple to Bob, and reserved a couple for himself.—"I look at the thing in this way. I put myself in Tommy's place. Now, if any man presumed to play such a trick on me—why, d——n me, I should take it very ill. Now, Collins"——

"O, stop, please! don't fill that glass for me! I 'm very sensible of your disapproval, Mr. Stewart. I 'm more sorry than I can express—not in the way of penitence, certainly, but that I should be unfortunate enough to have incurred your displeasure. I wish you could put yourself in my place, instead of Tommy's.——Well, long life to you, Mr. Stewart, both for your own sake and the sake of the public."

"Thanks for the good wish, Collins, and to (sheol) with the flattery. I may tell you that I do put myself in your place, as well as in Tommy's. But, d——n it, you don't seem to be alive to the principle of the thing.——*You 're* not a blue-ribboner, I suppose?" And he tendered the replenished glass to Bob. "Bad hand you 've got, poor fellow. Severe accident apparently?"

"Sepoy bullet at Lucknow, sir. I was a lad of nineteen then; just joined."

"You 've been a soldier?"

"Yes, sir; I was an ensign in the Queen's 64th. We formed part of Havelock's column of relief." The placid, unassertive, incapable face told the rest of the poor fellow's story.

"You don't seem to be alive to the principle of the thing," repeated Stewart, turning again to me. "Your cosmopolitanism is a d——d big mistake. Every man has a nationality, remember; and though you 'll find many most excellent fellows of all races, yet, if you want the real thing, you must look"——

"May God bless you, Mr. Stewart!" murmured Stirling of Ours, raising the glass to his lips.

"Thank you, my friend.——You must look to Scotland for it. And, d——n it, man, this is the very nationality you have been fleering at. Of course, I don't dwell on the subject because I happen to be a Scotsman myself; only, I must say I should never have expected—But what do you think is the matter with Alf Morris?"

"Difficult to say. Some sort of arthrodynic complaint, I fancy; at all events, he 's badly gone in most of his joints."

"Poor devil!" soliloquised the squatter, filling the glass for himself. "He 's a bad lot—a d——n bad lot—a d——nation bad lot. Bitter, vindictive sort of man. You 're familiar, like myself, with Shakespear; now, Morris reminds me of Titus Andronicus.—Better luck, boys."

"Thank you, Mr. Stewart."

"Thank you, Mr. Stewart."

"This Titus, as you may remember, was expelled from Athens by the people, after they had elected him consul. They could n't stand his d——d pride. He took up his abode in a cave, and, for the rest of his life, met every overture of friendship with taunts and insults. Even in his epitaph, written by himself:—

> Here rests his head upon the lap of earth——

Now, d——n it, I committed those lines to memory—ay, forty-five years ago. I wish I could recall them."

"I think I can repeat the passage, Mr. Stewart," said I modestly:—

> Here lies a wretched corse, of wretched soul bereft;
> Seek not his name. A plague consume you wicked caitiffs left.
> Here lie I, Timon, who, alive, all living men did hate.
> Pass on, and curse thy fill, but pass, and stay not here thy gait.

"Good," replied the squatter—all his hurry forgotten in the fascination of profitless gossip. "Now there you have Morris to the very life. Hopeless d—d case!"

"But the misanthropy of the Shakespearean hero was not without cause, Mr. Stewart," I urged. "Given certain rigorous circumstances, acting on a given temperament, and you have a practically inevitable sequence—perhaps a pious faith; perhaps a philosophic calm; perhaps an intensified selfishness; perhaps a sullen despair —in fact, the variety of possible results corresponds exactly with the variety of possible circumstances and temperaments. In the case of the Greek misanthrope, the factor of temperament is first carefully stated; then the factor of circumstances is brought into operation; then the genius of the dramatist supplies the resultant revolution of moral being, in such a manner as to excite sympathy rather than reprobation. Reasoning from cause to effect, we see the inevitableness of the issue. But in Morris's case, we must reason from effect to cause. We see a certain outcome"——

"D—d unmistakably," muttered the squatter.

——"And it rests with us to account for this from prior conditions of temperament and circumstances. Then we shall have, so to speak, the second and third terms; and from these it won't be difficult, I think, to calculate the term which should antecede them, namely, temperament. Morris is a widower. His wife was a magnificent singer, and, in a general way, one of those tawny-haired tigresses who leave their mark on a man's life, and are much better left alone"——

"Has he any children?" asked Stewart.

"Well, no; these tawny-haired tigresses don't have children. Anyway, she died some ten years ago; but at the time of her death they had been separated for about three years."

"They could n't have been living long together; or else he married young," suggested Stewart.

"No, they were n't long together; but Alf is a man of peculiar moral constitution; he frets a lot over her memory; loves and hates her at the same time. Secondary to this, is a misunderstanding with his father, which caused Alf to clear off, leaving the old man to mind everything himself. Of course, I 'm only giving you the heads; and my information is derived from no random hearsay, but is obtained by an intransmissible power of induction, rare in our times."

"Thought as much!" muttered Stewart.

"It remains, then," I continued, "to determine the temperament which, acted upon by these circumstances, has given the result which is already before us. Now, I think that that temperament, though, perhaps, tending to the volcanic, must have been a sensitive and an amiable one; however it may have soured and hardened into misanthropy and avarice. We can't all be philosophers, Mr. Stewart."

"If there 's one thing I hate like (sheol)," replied the squatter gravely, "it is the quoting of Scripture as against my fellow-creature; but, d—n it, we are told that 'when the righteous man turneth away from his righteousness, and committeth iniquity all the days of his vanity which God giveth him under the sun, he shall be likened unto a foolish man that built his house upon the sand.' You know the rest. If we take upon us to judge Morris at all, we must judge him as he is. Your judgment is generous, but nonsensical; mine is rational, but churlish—d—d churlish." He paused, in evident discomfort, flicked a roley-poley with his whip, and continued. "You know, I had him on Kooltopa for a couple of months, bringing in pine logs, when Barker's sawing-plant was there. Well, without going into details——Capable fellow, too; fine combination of a cultivated man and an experienced rough-and-ready bushman. Strictly honest, also, I think—only for his d—nable disposition."

"Doctor Johnson liked a good hater," I suggested sadly, for it was evident that my unfortunate protégé had already, in his own peculiar way, recommended himself to Stewart.

You can imagine, by that circumstance alone, what a strong tincture of venom was held in solution by this feeble tenant of an hour. Indeed, if the matter had rested with the squatters, they would have starved him out of Riverina by industrial boycott. But the in-transport of wool, and the out-transport of goods, are cares that, as a rule, fall to the lot of the forwarding firms; and these resemble George IV., in having no predilections (though, let us hope, the similarity ceases here). Hence, the jolly good soul of a carrier, with lots of spring in him—the man who seldom buys any groceries, whose breath often smells like broached grog-cargo, and who makes a joke of camping for a few weeks with a load on his wagon—is very naturally passed over in favour of the misanthrope who neither asks nor gives quarter. And the personal popularity of the latter with his own guild is not enhanced by this preference.

"Doctor Johnson be d—d!" replied the squatter warmly. "What is his dictum worth? What the (sheol) entitled him, for instance, to sneer at the very element of population that has made Britain a

nation? You know what I allude to? Now, speaking with strict
impartiality, it strikes me d—d forcibly that the finest prospect
England ever saw is the road that leads from Scotland." He
checked himself, and continued in a gentler tone. "That just
reminds me of a very able article I read some time ago—I think it
was in *Blackwood's*. The writer proves that your Shakespear must
have imbibed his genius, to a great extent, in Scotland. He
grounds his argument partly—and I think, justly—on the fact that the best
play in the collection is a purely Scottish one. He makes a d—d
strong point, I remember, of the expression, 'blasted heath.' 'Say
from whence, upon this blasted heath you stop our way, making
night hideous?'——and so forth."

"Yes," I replied mechanically. And then, avoiding the eye of
the grand old saint, and hating myself as a buffoon, I continued,
"My own conjecture is that something must have occurred to irri-
tate the dramatist whilst he was writing that passage, and the
expression slipped from his pen unawares."

"Never!" replied Stewart. "No man under the influence of petty
irritation ever wrote anything like the passage where that expression occurs. Criticism is not your forte, Collins. The writer I 'm
speaking of sees a landscape photographed in those two words.
Pardon me for saying that your talent seems to run more in the line
of low-comedy acting. I don't like referring to it again, but d—n
it all, my interest in you personally makes me feel very strongly
over your interview with this Tom Armstrong."

"Indeed, Mr. Stewart, I can't tell you how sorry I am to have
fallen in your estimation. But you were speaking of Alf Morris
when I unfortunately drew you from the subject."

"Ay. To return to Morris. Do you know how he came to leave
the Bland country, some five or six years ago?"

"Well, yes," I replied reluctantly; "rates are a lot higher here
than there."

"Did you ever hear that he shot anyone? A boundary rider, for
instance?"

"The kernel of truth in that report, Mr. Stewart, is that he spoke
of a certain boundary rider as a man that deserved shooting."

"How do you know?"

"Well, in the first place, I 'm only allowing for fair average
growth in the report; and in the second place, when a person shoots
a boundary man, he 's not allowed to just change his district, and
go his way in peace."

"Sometimes he is. I 'll tell you how it happened with Morris."

And the man who had a profanely long stage before him settled into an easy position, his heels on top of the splash-board, and his arms behind the back of the seat, whilst Bob held the reins. "It was on Mirrabooka. O'Grady Brothers had owned the place for a few years; but they were careless and intemperate, great lovers of racehorses, and d—d extravagant all round"—

"Familiar faults with people named O'Grady," I remarked.

"You 're perfectly right. They got involved, and had to sell the place. Prescott bought it; and it was about a month after he had taken possession that the thing occurred. During the O'Gradys' time, the bullock drivers had made a d—d thoroughfare of the run, zigzagging from one tank to another, and passing close to the home station. Prescott determined to put a stop to this. He locked all the gates on the track, and secured the tanks with cattle-proof fences, and kept his men foxing the teams day and night; and along with all this, he prosecuted right and left. D—d hard on the bullockies, of course, and far from generous on Prescott's part; but it acted as a check; and in a couple of months the track was closed for good. However, just in the thick of the trouble, Morris crossed the run, and, of course, fared neither better nor worse than the rest. One evening he was seen taking down a fence and camping at a new tank, a couple of miles from the homestead; and at nine or ten o'clock that night he rode up to the station, and asked to see Mr. Prescott. When Prescott appeared, Morris drew him aside and told him, as cool as a d—d cucumber, that he wanted to make a deposition before him, as a magistrate, to the effect that he had just shot a man for attempting to remove his bullocks. Prescott refused to take the deposition just then; but he had a pair of horses put in a wagonette, and took the storekeeper with him, to accompany Morris to where the thing had happened. When they got there, d—n the sign of a body could they find; but Morris showed them the spot, and strictly charged them to note it well. Then he refused to have anything more to do with the d—d business, and went after his bells, while Prescott and the other fellow returned to the station, coo-eeing and listening as they went. They overtook the man on the way, with a revolver bullet-hole through his arm, and the bullet lodged in his side. Of course, he was one of the station men—I forget his name at the present moment, but it 's no matter. When they got the chap home, and found there was nothing dangerous, Prescott had his horse saddled at once, and followed the track till he came to Morris's wagon; from there he went to the bells, and found Morris minding his bullocks. They had a long conference, and Prescott went home. Next morning, Morris continued his journey; and when he unloaded—about sixty miles this side of Mirrabooka—he came right on to Riverina. Now, Collins; you put a d—d big value on your acumen, and your sagacity, and your penetration, and all the rest of it—What do you make of that story? Mind, I vouch for the truth of it."

"There 's a hitch somewhere, Mr. Stewart."

"Confess you 're at fault, d—n you!"

"I am at fault—for once."

"Good," replied the squatter complacently. "Now I 'll give you the key. When the O'Gradys sold the station, there was a £200 tank nearly finished, but not paid for; and somehow (d—d if I know how people can make such blunders!)—somehow this tank was overlooked in the valuation. Prescott considered that the terms of sale included the tank, the liability being still on the O'Gradys; while they imagined that the whole transaction was taken off their hands. If the truth must be told, Prescott tried to do a sharp thing, under the cloak of an oversight; and the O'Gradys checkmated him with a d—d sight sharper thing. In this way. Their last action, while the station remained in their power, was to transfer the tank to the Department, on condition that a section of land should be reserved round it. The Department accepted it on these terms, and struck the section off the Mirrabooka assessment; but Prescott got wind of the thing before it was gazetted, and was moving heaven and earth to secure the reserve, just at the time Morris camped there. How Morris came by this information beats the devil; but, of course, all he had to say to Prescott was, 'I caught some d—d scoundrel stealing my bullocks by night off the Government reserve close by here. I tried without effect to get them from him peaceably; and I was compelled to stop him by force. I was careful to ask him if he was a Government official; but, d—n it, he gave me an insulting answer; then, knowing him to be a cattle-thief at large, I shot him in the act of felony.' It did n't suit Prescott to stir-up the question of the reserve just at that time—so what the (sheol) could he do? And, in any case, Morris was within his legal rights; the reserve was as free to him as to Prescott; and, d—n it all, stock must be protected. Curious case altogether. Of course, Prescott afterward got the land secured quietly. But just think of the cold-blooded calculation and d—d unscrupulousness of Morris. He 's a man to be avoided, Collins."

"Well," I replied, baffled and hopeless, "I 've nothing more to say, except that, generally speaking, the man who ought to be avoided is just the sort of person that my own refractory nature clings to with the fellow-feeling which makes us wondrous kind. Therefore I 'll go away sorrowful—not because I have great possessions, for I certainly have n't—but because my last hope for Alf was that you might interest yourself in his present difficulty."

A half-inquiring, half-incredulous look crossed the frank face of the fine old believer, followed by one of his evanescent frowns.

"Why, d—n it, man, have n't I arranged that already with Bob here?" said he, resuming a normal position on the seat, and taking the reins from his companion's hand. "We 're going straight to the Dead Man's Bend. Never you fear; I 'll see Morris through."

"I 'll never forget your kindness, Mr. Stewart."

"Nonsense. But is n't it a most remarkable thing—what we 're too apt to call a mere coincidence? Here I find Bob footsore, through walking in bad boots; and while I 'm wondering what in the devil's name to do with him, you tell me of Morris; and I see immediately why Bob was placed in my way. It 's the legislation of an unsleeping Providence, Collins—nothing short of it. We meet with these Divine adjustments of circumstances every day of our lives, if we only choose to recognise them. Thinking over these things makes me feel devilish small in my own eyes, but all the more confident, knowing that not a sparrow falls to the ground without——Oh, d—n it! look where the sun has got to! Good-bye! I might n't see you again. I 've sold Kooltopa."

"Surely not!"

"Ay. Crowded-out. Going to Queensland. They 'll tell you about it at Poondoo. Good-bye."

"Good-bye, Mr. Stewart."

CHAPTER V

WED. JAN. 9th. Trinidad Pad., per Sam Young. Conclave.

INTRODUCTORY.—On the evening of Tuesday, the 8th, I had called officially at Mondunbarra homestead. No one was visible except Bert Smythe, the managing partner's younger brother, who was leaving the store, with a ring of keys on his finger. His icy response to my respectful greeting revived certain memories connected with the Chinese boundary man, and Warrigal Alf's bullocks, as related in last chapter. In the fewest words possible, Bert informed me that Mr. Smythe was in Melbourne, and would n't be back for another week. If I chose to leave the K form with himself, it would be filled up and posted to our Central Office immediately on Mr. Smythe's return. Which would save me the trouble of calling at the station again for some time. I gave him the K form, and he was moving away toward the barracks, when I asked him if he could let me have a bob's worth of flour and a bob's worth of tea and sugar. Without a word, he turned back to the store, and supplied the articles required, whilst I monologued pleasantly on the topics of the day. When I inquired where I would be likely to find a bit of grass, he glanced at my half-starved horses; and I honoured him for the evident accession of sympathy which dictated his ready reply. He informed me that the only available grass was to be found in the near end of Sam Young's paddock, and proceeded to give me directions that a child might follow. Fixing these in my mind, I went round by the slaughter-yard, to solicit from the Tungusan butcher a pluck for Pup; and, altogether, by the time I reached Sam Young's paddock, night had imperceptibly set-in. The atmosphere was charged with smoke—probably from some big fire among the spinifex, far away northward—and a nucleus of brighter light on the meridian showed the position of a gibbous moon. Yet the hazy, uniform light, disciplining the eye to its standard, seemed rather like a noonday dulled to the same shade. The temperature was perfect for comfort, so I fared well enough; whilst with respect to my horses, I could only hope that Bert had been unfaithful to his chief and clan.

Now for the record of Wednesday, the 9th:—

Just at sunrise, one glance round the vicinity brought me out of my possum-rug with an impression that there was nothing but roguery to be found in villainous man. The country on all sides was as bare as the palm of your hand; and my horses, a quarter of a mile away, were nibbling at the stumps of cotton-bush. Breakfast, however, was the first consideration, as I had n't bothered about supper on the previous night—though filling my water-bag at a tank on the way.

Whilst baking a johnny-cake of such inferior quality as to richly deserve its back-country designation, and meanwhile boiling my quart-pot on a separate handful of such semi-combustibles as the plain afforded, I found myself slowly approached by a Chinaman, on a roan horse. And though it is impossible to recognise any individual Chow, I fancied that this unit bore something more than a racial resemblance to the one from whom I had recovered Alf's bullocks. Moreover, he was riding the same horse.

"Mornin', John," said I condescendingly. "You scoot-um long-a home-station big one hurry."

"Lidee boundly," replied the early bird, in his mechanical tone. "Borak this you paddock, John?"

"My plully paddock, all li."

"You name Sam Young?"

"Paul Sam Young," corrected the boundary man. "You wantee glass you holse?—two-tlee day—goo' glass? Me lay you on, all li."

"It is the voice of a god, and not of a man!" I replied. "Have-um drink o' tea, Paul? Have-um bit o' du-pang? Where me find-um grass?"

"Tlinidad Paddock, all li—plurry goo' glass."

"How me fetch-um that peller?"

Paul dismounted, and, declining my meagre hospitality, gave me copious information respecting the Trinidad. The nearest corner of this paddock was only eight miles away; but it would be expedient to go round by certain tracks, making the distance twelve or fourteen miles. It was a small paddock—five by two—being portion of a five by ten, recently divided. There was no water in it. It was crossed by a shallow billabong, which had been dammed when the dividing fence was erected; but the first flood in the Lachlan had burst an opening in the embankment, so that even at the end of the previous winter there was no water in the paddock, except a drop of sludgy stuff in the excavation. Hence the grass. There was no stock in the Trinidid, and no one in charge. There were two station men, with a team of bullocks and scoop, cleaning out the dam and repairing the bank; but they would n't see anything. Also, Mr. Smythe was away in Melbourne, and would n't be back for another week. Of course, it took me about half-an-hour to Champollion all this information from the cryptical utterances of the friendly Asiatic.

"You allee same Christian," I remarked, packing away my breakfast-service. "You go long-a good place bimeby."

"Me Clistian allee same you," he replied, not without dignity. "Convelt plurry long time. 'Paul' Clistian name. Splink' wattel, all li."

With this he bade me a civil good-bye, and went his way. Then I saddled-up and started for the Trinidad; mentally placing Mr. Smythe, Bert, and myself, in one dish of the moral scale, and this undesirable alien in the other, with an unflattering upshot to the superior race.

And this conclusion was more than verified when I reached my destination. The grass was something splendid. Any island or peninsula of plain among the tall lignum would do for a camp; and there was a good waterhole about a mile away, with only a low, slack fence to cross.

Between one thing and another, it might have been about three in the afternoon when, with Pup reposing by my side, I finally settled down to an after-dinner smoke from the sage meerschaum often deservedly noticed in these annals.

The two greatest supra-physical pleasures of life are antithetical in operation. One is to have something to do, and to know that you are doing it deftly and honestly. The other is to have nothing to do, and to know that you are carrying out your blank programme like a good and faithful menial. On this afternoon, the latter line of inaction seemed to be my path of duty—even to the extent of unharnessing my mind, so that when any difficulty did arise, I might be prepared to meet it as a bridegroom is supposed to meet his bride. Therefore whenever my reasoning faculties obtruded themselves, I knapp'd 'em o' the coxcombs with a stick, and cry'd 'Down, wantons, down.' Briefly, I kept my ratiocinative gear strictly quiescent, with only the perceptive apparatus unrestrained, thus observing all things through the hallowed haze of a mental sabbath. There is a positive felicity in this attitude of soul, comparing most favourably with the negative happiness of Nirvana.

"Taking it easy, Tom?" conjectured a familiar voice.

"No, Steve," I murmured, without even raising my eyes. "Tea in the quart-pot there. What are you after? Or is someone after you?"

"Prospecting for a bite of grass."

"Well, you 've bottomed on the wash. Thought you were out to Kulkaroo, with salt?"

"Just getting down again, with a half-load of pressed skins. Bullocks living on box-leaves and lignum. Rode over to get the geography of this place by daylight. Saunders, the fencer, told me about it this morning. He 's got a ten-mile contract away on Poolkija, and he 's going out with three horses and a dray-load of stores for himself. Dray stopped on the road for the last week, with his wife minding it. Horses supposed to be lost in the lignum on Yoongoolee, and him hunting them for all he 's worth. Keeps them planted all day, and tails them here at night. He would n't have laid me on, only that he 's going to drop across them to-morrow morning, and shift."

"Anyone coming with you to-night?"

"Baxter and Donovan. It 's a good step to travel—must be ten or twelve mile—but this grass is worth it. Safe, too, from what I hear. Might get two goes at it, by taking the bullocks out at daylight, and planting them till night. However, I must get back, to meet the other chaps with the mob."

"Well, I 'll be here when you come."

Thompson turned his horse, and disappeared round a promontory of lignum. By this time, the sun was dipping, dusky red, toward the smoky horizon; so I addressed myself to the duties of the evening, which consisted in taking my horses and Pup to the water, and bringing back a supply for myself. Also, as a concession to the new aspect of things, I took the bell off Cleopatra.

Daylight had now melted into soft, shadowless moonlight; and the place was no longer solitary. Dozens of cattle were scattered round, harvesting the fine crop of grass; and Thompson, with his two confederates, joined me. During daylight, I had made it my business to find a secluded place, bare of grass, where a fire could be kindled without offending the public eye; and to this spot the four of us repaired to see about some supper.

Before the first match was struck, a sound of subdued voices behind us notified the coming of two more interlopers.

One of these was Stevenson, a tank-sinker, now on his way north-ward with twenty-two fresh horses—fresh, by the way, only in respect of their new branch of industry, for the draft was made-up entirely of condemned coachers from Hay, and broken-down cab-horses from Victoria.

The other arrival was a Dutchman, who brought his two ten-horse teams. A thrifty, honest, sociable fellow he was; yet nothing but the integrity of narrative could possibly move me to repeat his name. It was Helsmok, with the 'o' sounded long. The first time I had addressed him by name—many years before—a sense of deli-cacy had impelled me to shorten the vowel, also to slur the first syllable, whilst placing a strong accent on the second. But he had corrected me, just as promptly as Mr. Smythe would have done if I had called him Smith, and far more civilly. He had even softened the admonition by explaining that his strictness arose from a justi-fiable family pride, several of his paternal ancestors having been man-o'-war captains, and one an admiral—in which cases, the name would certainly seem appropriate. But some Continental surnames are sad indeed. The roll-call of Germany furnishes, perhaps, the most unhappy examples. There are *bonâ fide* German names which no man of refinement cares about repeating, except in a shearers' hut or a gentlemen's smoking-room.

"Shadowed you chaps," remarked Stevenson, replying to the bul-lock drivers' look of inquiry. And he also applied himself to the kindling of a small fire.

"Jis' missed my ole camp by about ten chain!" cheerfully observed Saunders, entering the arena with a billy in one hand and a small calico bag in the other. "I was makin' for her when I heard you (fellows) talkin'. More the merrier, I s'pose." And he set about making a third little fire.

"Gittin' out with loadin', Helsmok?" asked Donovan, while we waited the boiling of the billies.

"Yoos gittin' dan mit der las' wool," replied the Dutchman. "I make der slow yourney; but, by yingo, I mus' save der horses."

"Ought to change that name of yours, Jan," remarked Thomp-son, with real sincerity. "It 's an infernal name for children to hear."

"Literally so," commented Stevenson.

"Alter it to John Sulphur-Burnin'," suggested Baxter.

"How 'd Jack Brimstone-Reek do?" asked Donovan.

"Give it the aristocratic touch," proposed Stevenson. "Sign your-self Jean Fumée de l'Enfer."

"Why not the scientific turn?" I asked. "Make it Professor John Oxy-Sulphuret, F.R.S.—Foreigner Rastling for Selebrity."

"My idear 's Blue Blazes," put in Saunders bluntly.

"Tank you, yentlemen," replied the genial Mynheer. "Mineself, I enyoy der yoke. Bot I am brout of my name. Mit mine forefadders, it have strock der yolly goot fear of Gott into der Spaniar' und der English."

"No wonder," sighed Thompson, purposely misconstruing the honest vindication. "And it 'll have the same effect on anybody that considers it properly. But for that very reason, it's not a decent name."

"It is ein olt name, Domson," argued the Dutchman.

"Old enough," rejoined Thompson gloomily. "It was to the fore when Satan was slung out of heaven; and it 'll be going as strong as ever when we're trying to give an account of ourselves. It won't be a joking-matter then."

Nor was it any longer a joking-matter for our assembly. Soon, however, the billies were taken off the fires, and spiritual apprehension forthwith gave place to physical indulgence.

After supper, we adjourned to the open plain. The night was delicious; and for half-an-hour the congress was governed by that dignified silence which back-country men appreciate so highly, yet so unconsciously. Then the contemplative quiet of our synod was broken by the vigorous barking of Saunders's dog, at a solitary box tree, indicating a possum tree'd in full sight.

"Gostruth, that 'on't do!" muttered the fencer, hastily starting toward the dog. "That 's visible to the naked eye about three mile on a night like now."

"Recalls the most perfect pun within my knowledge," remarked Stevenson. "A lady, travelling by coach, had a pet dog, which annoyed her fellow-passengers till one of them remonstrated. 'I 'm surprised that you don't like my dog,' says the lady; 'he 's a real Peruvian.' 'We don't object to your Peruvian dog,' says the passenger, 'but we wish he would give us less of his Peruvian bark'."

Before our company had recovered from the painful constraint induced by this unfathomable joke, Saunders resumed his place, holding the dog by a saddle-strap taken from his own equator.

"Dead spit of my poor old Monkey," remarked Thompson sadly, as he caressed the dog. "Never felt the thing that 's on me more distinctly than when I lost poor Monkey."

"Well, I offered you a fiver for him," rejoined Donovan. "Never know'd a man to have luck with a thing that he 'd refused a good bid for. Picked up a bait, I s'pose?"

"Monkey would never have stayed with you," replied Thompson. "That dog would have broke his heart if he'd been parted from me. Tell you how I lost him. Last winter, when I was loaded-out for Kenilworth—where I met Cooper—you might remember it was dry, and frosty, and miserable, and the country as bare as a stockyard; and mostly everybody loafing on Kooltopa. Well, I dodged round by Yoongoolee, stealing a bite of grass here, and a bite there; and travelling by myself, so as not to be worth ordering-off the runs; and staying with the bullocks every night, and keeping them in decent fettle, considering.

"So, one evening, I left the wagon on that bit of red ground at the Fifteen-mile Gate, and tailed the bullocks down in the dark to sample the grass in Old Sollicker's horse-paddock. About eleven at night, when the first of them began to lie-down, I shifted the lot to an open place, so as to have them all together when they got full. I was in bodily fear of losing some of them among the lignum, in the dark; for it 's a hanging-matter to duff in a horse-paddock on Yoongoolee. I knew Old Sollicker was as regular as clockwork, and I was safe till sunrise; so I intended to rouse-up the bullocks just before daylight, to lay in a fresh supply. In the meantime, I settled myself down for a sleep."

"Where was the (adj.) dog?" asked Baxter.

"Rolled up in the blanket with me, I tell you; and we both slept like the dead"——

"Owing to having no fleas on you?" suggested Stevenson.

"Don't know what was the cause; but the thing that woke me was the jingle of a Barwell horse-bell on one side, and the rattle of a bridle on the other. Sure enough, there was the sun half-an-hour high, and Old Sollicker about thirty yards off; and here on the other side was his two horses dodging away from him; and me in a belt of lignum, half-way between; and my twenty bullocks, as bold as brass, all feeding together in the open, a bit to the left of the horses. It was plain to be seen that the old fellow had n't caught sight of the bullocks on account of the belt of lignum where I was planted; but he was making for an openish place, not twenty yards ahead of him, and when he got there it would be all up. So I grabbed hold of Monkey, and fired him at the horses. He was there! He went like a boomerang when I let him rip, and in two seconds he had the blood flying out of those horses' heels; and, of course, they streaked for the clear ground near the hut. As soon as I let the dog go, I turned my attention to Sollicker. At the first alarm, he stopped to consider; then, when the horses shot past him, with the dog eating their heels, he rubbed his chin for about two minutes—and me trusting Providence all I was able— then he gave a sort of snort, and said, 'Well, I be dang!' and with that he turned round and went toward his hut. That was the signal for me to clear; and in fifteen minutes I had all my stock in safety —bar poor Monkey; and I never saw him from that day to this."

"You (adj.) fool! why did n't you hunt for him?" asked Donovan.

"And did n't I hunt for him till I was sick and tired? I spent half that day hunting for him; and next morning I went back seven mile, and called at the hut to ask Mrs. Sollicker if her old man had seen a magpie steer, with a bugle horn, anywhere among the lignum; and when I got clear of the hut, I whistled till I was black in the face; and.still no dog. I hunted everywhere; and still no dog. Vanished out of the land of the living. That dog would never leave me while he had breath in his body; and when he did n't come back, after he had chivied the horses, I might have"——

"Sh-sh-sh!" whispered Stevenson. And, following the direction of his look, we discerned the approaching figure of a man on horseback.

"Ben Cartwright," observed Baxter, after a pause. "Anybody else comin', I wonder? Seems like as if people could n't fine a bit o' grass without the whole (adj.) country jumpin' it."

"I move that all trespassers ought to be prosecuted with the utmost vigour o' the (adj.) law," remarked Donovan aloud, as the new-comer dismounted and liberated his horse, a few yards away.

"We should certainly be justified in taking the opinion of the Court on a test case," added Stevenson. "Suppose we make an example of Cartwright? Oh, I beg your pardon!" For the intended sacrifice was just collapsing into an easy position beside the speaker.

"Been scoutin' for you (fellows) this last half-hour," he remarked sociably, but in the suppressed tone befitting time and place. "Seen samples o' your workin' plant, an' know'd who to expect. Heard the dog barkin' jis' now. Soft collar we got here— ain't it?"

"How did you find it?" asked Thompson.

"Know Jack Ling—at the Boree Paddick, about four mile out there? Well, I worked on his horse-paddick las' night, an' he follered me up this mornin', an' talked summons. But I ain't very fiery-tempered, the way things is jis' now; an' I got at the soft side o' the (adj.) idolator; an' he laid me on here. Reckoned I 'd mos' likely fine company."

"One good point about a Chow boundary man," observed Thompson. "So long as you don't interfere with his own paddock, he never makes himself nasty."

My own experience of the morning led me to endorse this judgment; wherefore, if John did n't exactly rise in the estimation of the camp, he certainly reduced his soundings in its detestation.

"Comin' down with wool?" asked Baxter.

"Comin' down without wool, or wagon, or any (adj.) thing," replied Cartwright. "Jist loafin' loose. Bullocks dead-beat. Left the wagon tarpolined at the Jumpin' Sandhill, a fortnit ago. Five gone out o' eighteen since then, an' three more dead if they on'y know'd it. Good for trade, I s'pose."

"Had any supper?" asked Thompson.

"Well, no. Run out o' tucker to-day, an' reckoned I 'd do till I foun' time to go to Booligal to-morrow."

While three or four of the fellows placed their eatables before Cartwright, Thompson remarked:

"You gave me a bit of a start. When I saw you coming, it reminded me of one time I got snapped by Barefooted Bob, on Wo-Winya, while M'Gregor owned the station. For all the world such a night as this—smoky moonlight, and as good as day. I 'd had a fearful perisher coming down with the last wool, and I was making for the Murray, by myself; stealing a bite of grass every night, and getting caught, altogether, five times between Hay and Barmah. Well, I knew there was rough feed in the Tin Hut Paddock; so I crawled along quietly, and loosed-out after dark, in that timber where the coolaman hole is. Then I sneaked the bullocks through the fence, and out past that bit of a swamp; and they had just settled down to feed, when I saw some one riding toward me.

" 'I 've got possession of some bullocks close handy here,' says he. 'Do you own them?'

" 'Yes,' says I; 'and, by the same token, *I* have possession.'

" 'Right you are,' says he. 'Court job, if you like. Your name 's Stephen Thompson. Good night.'

" 'Hold-on!' says I. 'On second thoughts, I have n't possession. But I think I know your voice. Are n't you Barefooted Bob? Where 's Bat?'

" 'Laying for Potter's horse-teams to-night,' says Bob. 'He 'll get them, right enough.'

" 'Come over to the wagon, and have a drink of tea,' says I.

" 'No, no,' says he; 'none of your toe-rag business. I 'll just stop with these bullocks till it 's light enough to count them out of the paddock.'

"So we stayed there yarning all night, and in the morning we settled-up, and he saw me out of the paddock. Nicest, civilest fellow you 'd meet; but no more conscience than that kangaroo-dog of Tom's. He and Bat had been four or five years away north toward the Gulf, and had just come down. M'Gregor used to keep them up to their work. Sent them away somewhere about the Diamantina, shortly after this affair; and now Bob"——

"Speak o' the divil," growled Baxter. "You done it, you blatherin' fool! Look behind you! Now there 's a bob a-head, or a summons, for every (individual) of us. Might 'a' had more sense!"

Thompson (as you will remember) had heard of Bob's decease, but had since learned the fallacy of the report. I was therefore, probably, the only person present who took for granted that M'Gregor's obnoxious familiar was so removed from further opportunity of mischief as to leave him a safe subject of conversation among people situated as we were. Hence the well-concealed disquietude of the company was nothing in comparison with my own perplexity—which, I trust, was no less successfully disguised. For it was Bob himself who had just ridden round a contiguous cape of lignum, and now, dismounting and throwing his reins on the ground, joined our unappreciative group. After folding his interminable legs in two places, and clasping his hands round his shins, this excrescence on society remarked, in basso profundo:

"Evenin', chaps."

"Evenin'," came in sullen, but general, response. Then Baxter queried indifferently:

"Same old lay?"

"Not me," replied the deep, low voice. "Every man to his work. My work 's mullockin' in a reservoy, with a new-chum weaver from Leeds for a mate, an' a scoop that 's nyther make nor form, an' the ten worst bullocks ever was yoked."

"Well, Bob," said I; "though you gave me a fright, I must congratulate you. I heard you were dead."

"Would n't mind if I was dead, Collins."

"Where 's Bat?" I asked.

"Gone to a better billet"—and the leonine voice deepened to hoarseness. "Restin' in the shadder of a lonely rock, as the Bible says. I buried him by my own self, way out back, eight or ten months ago. Many 's the time I wish I was with him, for I 'm dog-tired of everything goin'. Best-hearted feller ever broke bread, Bat was; an' the prittiest rider ever I seen on a horse. Yes; pore old chap 's gone. You 'd 'a' thought he was on'y asleep when"——

No further word was spoken for a couple of minutes. Then Stevenson asked:

"How long since you came down?"

"Five months since I left the Diamantinar. Grand grass there, an' most o' the road down. I come with some fats as fur as Wil-cannia; an' a drover took charge o' them there; an' my orders was to come on to Mondunbarra. I been here goin' on for three weeks, rasslin' with that reservoy, an' cursin' M'Gregor an' Smythe for bein' man-eaters, an' myself for bein' a born fool."

"Then why don't you leave?" asked Thompson.

"How can I leave without a settlin'-up?"

"An' why the (sheol) don't you git a settlin'-up?" asked Don-ovan.

"How 'm I goin' to git a settlin'-up, when M'Gregor don't know me from a crow, an' says Smythe 'll represent him in the mean-time; an' Smythe says his hands is tied on account of M'Gregor, or else he 'd dem soon give me the run. Nice way for a man to be fixed, after me breakin' my neck since I was fifteen, to make M'Gregor what he is. Eighteen solid years clean throwed away!"

"How did you fine us here, unless you was (adv.) well after somebody?" asked Baxter, still suspicious of the dog with a bad name.

"Well, I *am* after somebody. I 'm after ole M'Gregor—at least, I 'll be after him as soon 's I git this reservoy off o' my mind. Daresay I 'll git you to understand by-'n'-by. See: Jist when Smythe wanted this job fixed-up, he got a slant o' fourteen bullocks, sold at a gift, for debt; an' he thought that would be the cheapest way to git the work done; for he did n't want to engage any o' your sort, knowin' you 'd loaf on the grass, an' most likely make a song about it, an' be the instigation of no end o' trouble watchin' the place. Well, them fourteen was put in Sling Ho's paddick for a fortnit before I come; an' I could on'y muster ten; an' me an' this mate o' mine we made a start with that lot—not knowin' which was near-siders, nor off-siders, nor leaders, nor nothing. Nice con-tract. Anyway, jist before dark this evenin', I seen two o' the missin' ones in the 'joinin' paddick, so I rooted-up one o' my horses, an' fetched them in here. Then I heard a dog barkin' out this way, an' I thought I 'd come across to kill time; an' then I happened to hear a lot o' laughin' where them other blokes is camped"——

"Which other blokes?" asked Saunders.

"Dan Lister an' three Vic. chaps. Be about half-a-mile out there. Dan 's as sulky as a pig with these coves for foxin' him; an' they 're laughin' at him like three overgrown kids. They got twelve bullocks each. Dan tells me he dropped two out of his eighteen, comin' down from Mooltunya. Says one o' the Chinks laid him on to this bit o' grass. Two other fellers I met in the plain—strangers to me —they had the very same yarn. Them heathens think I 'm in charge here; an' they 're workin' a point to make me nasty with the chaps on the track. An' if I was in charge, that's jist the sort o' thing would put a hump on me. Sort o' off-sider for a gang o' Chinks! My word!"

"Bin many people workin' on this paddick lately?" asked Saunders innocently.

"Well, besides your three horses, there 's been an odd team now an' agen for the fortnit or three weeks I been here. Good many last night. Rallyin'-up to-night. No business o' mine. Too busy shiftin' mullock to know what 's goin' on. Way o' the world, I s'pose. Anyway, Smythe's gittin' a slant to come to an understandin' with M'Gregor about me; an' if it ain't satisfactory, there 'll be bad feelin' between us. I want to be kep' at my own proper work, or else sacked an' squared-up with—not shoved into a job like this the minit I show my face; with that young pup cheekin' me for callin' him 'Bert.' 'Mr. Smythe, if you please,' says he! Hope I 'll live to see him with a bluey on his back."

"Well-matched pair—M'Gregor an' Smythe," remarked Donovan thoughtfully. "Wonder which of the two (individuals) is worst in the sight o' God?"

"Toss-up," replied Bob. "Same time, there 's a lot o' difference in people, accordin' to the shape o' their head. There 's Stewart of Kooltopa; he don't demean his self with little things; he goes in for big things, an' gits there; an' he 's got the heart to make a proper use o' what money travels his road. Comes-out a Christian. Then there 's Smythe: his mind 's so much took-up with the tuppenny-thruppenny things that he can't see the big thing when it 's starin' him in the face. Can't afford to come-out anything but a pis-ant. Then there 's M'Gregor: he goes-in for big things an' little things, an' he goes-in to win, an' he wins; an' all he wins is Donal' M'Gregor's. Comes-out a bow constructor."

"Do you think he 'll shift Smythe from Mondunbarra, as he did Pratt from Boolka?" I asked.

"Ain't he doin' it all the time?" replied Bob. "He 's got Smythe frightened of him now, an' beginnin' to hate him like fury, besides. That 's M'Gregor's lay. By-'n'-by, Smythe 'll be dreamin' about him all night, an' wishin' he was game to poison him all day; an' when he feels enough haunted, M'Gregor 'll make him an offer, an' he 'll sell-out like a bird."

"I should be inclined to reverse the situation," remarked Stevenson. "I should make him glad to sell-out to me."

"My word, you 'd do a lot," replied Bob. "I seen smarter men nor you took-down through tryin' to work points on the same ole M'Gregor. Tell you what I seen on Wo-Winya, about three year ago—jist before me an' pore Bat was put on the Diamantinar. Feller name o' Tregarvis, from Bendigo, he selected a lot o' land on Wo-Winya, an' made-up his mind he 'd straighten M'Gregor. Bit of a Berryite, he was. Well-off for a selector, too; an' he done a big business back an' forrid to Vic. with cattle. Mixed lots, of course, with stags an' ole cows that no fence would hold. North of Ireland feller, name o' Moore, was managin' Wo-Winya at the time; an' M'Gregor was a good deal about the station, takin' a sort o' interest in this Tregarvis. Well, things was so arranged that the Cousin Jack's cattle was always gittin' into our paddicks; an' the rule was that his people had to come to the home-station to get leaf to hunt 'em; an' a man was sent along o' them as a percaution. An' generally, by the time they foun' the cattle, there was one or two o' the fattest o' them short."

"Remedy for that game," remarked Stevenson. "I should have laid a trap."

"Jist what Tregarvis done," rejoined Bob. "One day there was a stranger among our cattle—a fine big white bullock, an' Tregarvis's brand on him. We run this mob into the yard before dinner, to git a beast to kill, an' turned 'em all out agen, bar the white one; but he was in the killin'-yard all the afternoon. Dusk in the evenin', the white bullock was shot; an' jist in the nick o' time, when the head was slung in the pig-sty, an' the hide was hangin' on the fence, raw side up, who should pounce on us but ole Tregarvis, an' young Tregarvis, an' a trooper. No mistake, Moore looked a bit gallied on it; an' he hum'd an' ha'd, an' threatened to brain Tregarvis if he laid a hand on the hide. Anyhow, the trooper took charge o' the hide; an' both the Tregarvises struck matches an' examined the head in the pig-sty. Next mornin', a warrant was served on Moore; but, of course, he was bailed. Then the Court-day come on; an' Tregarvis swore to a knowledge that a white bullock of his was among the Wo-Winya cattle; an' he give evidence about the findin' o' the skin, an' swore to the head he seen in the pig-sty. An' young Tregarvis, he swore he was watchin' with a telescope, an' seen a white bullock o' theirs yarded with some more, an' all the rest turned-out; an' he kep' his eye on that white bullock all the afternoon; an' he heard the shot, an' went up with his ole man an' the trooper; an' he seen the raw hide hangin' on the fence, an' the head in the pig-sty, an' a couple o' fellers hoistin' the carkidge on the gallus. When the magistrate asked Moore if he wanted to make a statement, he said he was quite bewildered about it. He allowed he had picked the white bullock for killin', an' he had give the order; but he 'd swear the beast belonged to the station. So the hide was spread out on a bit o' tarpolin in the floor o' the Court; an' there was on'y one brand on it, an' that brand was M'Gregor's—D M G off-rump. Mind you, this is on'y what I was told. My orders was to keep clear till the case was over; an' it was on'y a day or two follerin' that me an' pore Bat got our orders for the Diamantinar. Anyhow, Moore whanged it on to Tregarvis for malicious prosecution; an' it cost the Cousin Jack a good many hundred before he was done with it. As for young Dick Tregarvis, he got four years for perjury; so they 'll be jist about lettin' him out now, if he 's got the good-conduct remission."

"Beast changed?" suggested Thompson.

"Yes. That was the idear. Some different dodge next time. Changed jist at dusk, an' shot the minit after. I had the station bullock all ready, before ever Tregarvis's one was yarded. Dead spit o' one another, down to the shape o' their horns—bar the brands, of course; Tregarvis's beast havin' N T near-shoulder, an' J H conjoined under half-circle off-ribs. I had him half-ways back to the paddick agen when Tregarvis thought he was identifyin' him in the killin'-yard. So he fell-in, simple enough. An' between one thing an' another, an' bein' follered-up like the last dingo on a sheep station, ole Tregarvis was glad to sell-out to M'Gregor, before all was over. Yes, Stevenson; Lord 'a' mercy on M'Gregor if you got a holt of him! My word!"

"Where the (adj. sheol) do you reckon on bein' shoved into when you croak, Bob?" asked Donovan, with a touch of human solicitude.

"Well," replied Bob pointedly, as he unfolded his long angles to

a perpendicular right line—"I got good hopes o' goin' to a place
where there 's no admittance for swearers. Ain't ashamed to say I
repented eight or ten months ago. Guarantee you fellers ain't heard
no language out o' my mouth since I set down here. Nor 'on't—
never again. Well, take care o' yourselves, chaps." And, without
further farewell, Bob removed his lonely individuality from our
convention.

"Anointed (adj.) savage," remarked Donovan, as the subject of
his comment receded into the hazy half-light of the plain, where his
horse was feeding.

"Uncivilised (person)," added Baxter.

"Well—yes," conceded Thompson. "Same time, he 's got the
profit of his unprofitableness, so to speak. Hard to beat him in the
back country. You 'd have to be more uncivilised than he is. And
I saw that very thing happen to him, four or five weeks ago, out
on Goolumbulla." Thompson paused experimentally, then continued, "Yes, I saw him put-through, till he must have felt a lot
too tall in proportion to his cleverness." Another tentative pause.
"But it took the very pick of uncivilisation to do it." A prolonged
pause, while Thompson languidly filled and lit his pipe. Still the
dignified indifference of the camp remained unruffled. Thompson
might tell his yarn, or keep it to himself. Once already during the
evening his tongue had run too freely. "What I 'm thinking about,"
he continued, in a tone of audible musing, "is that I forgot to tell
Bob, when he was here, that I had a long pitch with Dan O'Connell, three or four nights ago."

"Boundary man on Goolumbulla," I suggested apathetically.
"Got acquainted with Bob years ago, when he was making himself
useful on Moogoojinna, and Bob was making himself obnoxious on
Wo-Winya, or Boolka."

"No; they never met till four or five weeks ago," replied Thompson, with inimitable indifference, though now licensed to proceed
without damage to his own dignity. "Dan's an old acquaintance of
yours—is n't he? I heard your name mentioned over the finding of
a dead man—George something—had been fencing on Mooltunya
—George Murdoch. Yes."

Thompson told a story well. I verily believe he used to practise
the accomplishment mentally, as he sauntered along beside his
team. He knew his own superiority here; his acquaintances knew
it too, and they also knew that he knew it. Hence they were reluctant to minister occasion to his egotism.

"Speaking of Bob," he continued listlessly; "I met him in the hut, at Kulkaroo, on the evening I got there with the load. He was on his way down from that new place of M'Gregor's, where he 's been; and he had come round by Kulkaroo to see one of the very few friends he has in the world; but he lost his labour, for this cove had left the station more than a year before.

"However, we had been yarning for hours, and the station chaps were about turning-in, when we heard someone coming in a hurry. No less than Webster himself—first time he had been in the hut since it was built, the chaps told me afterward. He had a leaf of a memorandum-book in his hand; and says he:

" 'Child lost in the scrub on Goolumbulla. Dan O'Connell's little girl—five or six years old. Anybody know where there 's any blackfellows?'

"Nobody knew.

" 'Well, raise horses wherever you can, and clear at once,' says he. 'One man, for the next couple of days, will be worth a regiment very shortly. As for you, Thompson,' says he; 'you 're your own master.'

"Of course, I was only too glad of any chance to help in such a case, so I went for my horse at once. Bob had duffed his two horses into the ration paddock, on his way to the hut, and had put them along with my mare, so that he could find them at daylight by the sound of her bell. This started me and him together. He lent his second horse to one of the station chaps; and the three of us got to Goolumbulla just after sunrise—first of the crowd. Twenty-five mile. There was tucker on the table, and chaff for our horses; and, during the twenty minutes or so that we stayed, they gave us the outline of the mishap.

"Seems that, for some reason or other—valuation for mortgage, I 'm thinking—the classer had come round a few days before; and Spanker had called in every man on the station, to muster the ewes. You know how thick the scrub is on Goolumbulla? Dan came in along with the rest, leaving his own place before daylight on the first morning. They swept the paddock the first day for about three parts of the ewes; the second day they got most of what was left; but Spanker wanted every hoof, if possible, and he kept all hands on for the third day.

"Seems, the little girl did n't trouble herself the first day, though she had n't seen Dan in the morning; but the second day there was something peculiar about her—not fretful, but dreaming, and asking her mother strange questions. It appears that, up to this time, she had never said a word about the man that was found dead near their place, a couple of months before. She saw that her parents did n't want to tell her anything about it, so she had never showed any curiosity; but now her mother was startled to find that she knew all the particulars.

"It appears that she was very fond of her father; and this affair of the man perishing in the scrub was working on her mind. All the second day she did nothing but watch; and during the night she got up several times to ask her mother questions that frightened the woman. The child did n't understand her father going away before she was awake, and not coming back. Still, the curious thing was that she never took her mother into her confidence, and never seemed to fret.

"Anyway, on the third morning, after breakfast, her mother went out to milk the goats, leaving her in the house. When the woman came back, she found the child gone. She looked round the place, and called, and listened, and prospected everywhere, for an hour; then she went into the house, and examined. She found that the little girl had taken about a pint of milk, in a small billy with a lid, and half a loaf of bread. Then, putting everything together, the mother decided that she had gone into the scrub to look for her father. There was no help to be had nearer than the home-station, for the only other boundary man on that part of the run was away at the muster. So she cleared for the station—twelve mile—and got there about three in the afternoon, not able to stand. There was nobody about the station but Mrs. Spanker, and the servant-girl, and the cook, and the Chow slushy; and Mrs. Spanker was the only one that knew the track to the ewe-paddock. However, they got a horse in, and off went Mrs. Spanker to give the alarm. Fine woman. Daughter of old Walsh, storekeeper at Moogoojinna, on the Deniliquin side.

"It would be about five when Mrs. Spanker struck the ewe-paddock, and met Broome and another fellow. Then the three split out to catch whoever they could, and pass the word round. Dan got the news just before sundown. He only remarked that she might have found her own way back; then he went for home as hard as his horse could lick.

"As the fellows turned-up, one after another, Spanker sent the smartest of them—one to Kulkaroo, and one to Mulppa, and two or three others to different fencers' and tank-sinkers' camps. But the main thing was blackfellows. Did anybody know where to find a blackfellow, now that he was wanted?

"Seems, there had been about a dozen of them camped near the tank in the cattle-paddock for a month past, but they were just gone, nobody knew where. And there had been an old lubra and a young one camped within a mile of the station, and an old fellow and his lubra near one of the boundary men's places; but they all happened to have shifted; and no one had the slightest idea where they could be found. However, in a sense, everyone was after them.

"But, as I was telling you, we had some breakfast at the station, and then started for Dan's place. Seven of us by this time, for another of the Kulkaroo men had come up, and there were three well-sinkers in a buggy. This was on a Thursday morning; and the little girl had been out twenty-four hours.

"Well, we had gone about seven mile, with crowds of fresh horse-tracks to guide us; and we happened to be going at a fast shog, and Bob riding a couple or three yards to the right, when he suddenly wheeled his horse round, and jumped off.

"'How far is it yet to Dan's place?' says he.

"'Five mile,' says one of the well-sinkers. 'We're just on the corner of his paddock. Got tracks?'

"'Yes,' says Bob. 'I'll run them up, while you fetch the other fellows. Somebody look after my horse.' And by the time the last word was out of his mouth, he was twenty yards away along the little track. No trouble in following it, for she was running the track of somebody that had rode out that way a few days before—thinking it was her father's horse, poor little thing!

"Apparently she had kept along the inside of Dan's fence—the way she had generally seen him going out—till she came to the corner, where there was a gate. Then she had noticed this solitary horse's track striking away from the gate, out to the left; and she had followed it. However, half-a-mile brought us to a patch of hardish ground, where she had lost the horse's track; and there Bob lost hers. Presently he picked it up again; but now there was only her little boot-marks to follow."

"A goot dog would be wort vivty men dere, I tink," suggested Helsmok.

"Same thought struck several of us, but it did n't strike Bob," replied Thompson. "Fact, the well-sinkers had brought a retriever with them in the buggy; a dog that would follow the scent of any game you could lay him on; but they could n't get him to take any notice of the little girl's track. Never been trained to track children —and how were they going to make him understand that a child was lost? However, while two of the well-sinkers were persevering with their retriever, the other fellow drove off like fury to fetch

Dan's sheep-dog; making sure that we would only have to follow him along the scent. In the meantime, I walked behind Bob, leading both our horses.

"Give him his due, he's a great tracker. I compare tracking to reading a letter written in a good business hand. You must n't look at what's under your eye; you must see a lot at once, and keep a general grasp of what's on ahead, besides spotting each track you pass. Otherwise, you 'll be always turning back for a fresh race at it. And you must no more confine yourself to actual tracks than you would expect to find each letter correctly formed. You must just lift the general meaning as you go. Of course, our everyday tracking is not tracking at all.

"However, Bob run this little track full walk, mile after mile, in places where I would n't see a mark for fifty yards at a stretch, on account of rough grass, and dead leaves, and so forth. One thing in favour of Bob was that she kept a fairly straight course, except when she was blocked by porcupine or supple-jack; then she would swerve off, and keep another middling straight line. At last Bob stopped.

" 'Here 's where she slept last night,' says he; and we could trace the marks right enough. We even found some crumbs of bread on the ground, and others that the ants were carrying away. She had made twelve or fourteen mile in the day's walk.

"By this time, several chaps had come from about Dan's place; and they were still joining us in twos and threes. As fast as they came, they scattered out in front, right and left, and one cove walked a bit behind Bob, with a frog-bell, shaking it now and then, to give the fellows their latitude. This would be about two in the afternoon, or half-past; and we pushed along the tracks she had made only a few hours before, with good hopes of overtaking her before dark. The thing that made us most uneasy was the weather. It was threatening for a thunderstorm. At this time we were in that unstocked country south-east of the station. Suddenly Bob rose up from his stoop, and looked round at me with a face on him like a ghost.

" 'God help us now, if we don't get a blackfellow quick!' says he, pointing at the ground before him. And, sure enough, there lay the child's little copper-toed boots, where she had taken them off when her feet got sore, and walked on in her socks. It was just then that a tank-sinker drove up, with Dan and his dog in the buggy."

"Poor old Rory!" I interposed. "Much excited?"

"Well—no. But there was a look of suspense in his face that was worse. And his dog—a dog that had run the scent of his horse for hundreds of miles, all put together—that dog would smell any plain track of the little stocking-foot, only a few hours old, and would wag his tail, and bark, to show that he knew whose track it was; and all the time showing the greatest distress to see Dan in trouble; but it was no use trying to start him on the scent. They tried three or four other dogs, with just the same success. But Bob never lost half-a-second over these attempts. *He* knew.

"Anyway, it was fearful work after that; with the thunderstorm hanging over us. Bob was continually losing the track; and us circling round and round in front, sometimes picking it up a little further ahead. But we only made another half-mile or three-quarters, at the outside—before night was on. I daresay there might be about twenty-five of us by this time, and eighteen or twenty horses, and two or three buggies and wagonettes. Some of the chaps took all the horses to a tank six or eight mile away, and some cleared-off in desperation to hunt for blackfellows, and the rest of us scattered out a mile or two ahead of the last track, to listen.

"They had been sending lots of tucker from the station; and before the morning was grey everyone had breakfast, and was out again. But, do what we would, it was slow, slow work; and Bob was the only one that could make any show at all in running the track. Friday morning, of course; and by this time the little girl had been out for forty-eight hours.

"At nine or ten in the forenoon, when Bob had made about half-a-mile, one of the Kulkaroo men came galloping through the scrub from the right, making for the sound of the bell.

"'Here, Bob!' says he. 'We 've found the little girl's billy at the fence of Peter's paddock, where she crossed. Take this horse. About two mile—straight out there.'

"I had my horse with me at the time, and I tailed-up Bob to the fence. He went full tilt, keeping the track that the horse had come, and this fetched us to where a couple of chaps were standing over a little billy, with a lump of bread beside it. She had laid them down to get through the fence, and then went on without them. The lid was still on the billy, and there was a drop of milk left. The ants had eaten the bread out of all shape.

"But Bob was through the fence, and bowling down a dusty sheep-track, where a couple of fellows had gone before him, and where we could all see the marks of the little bare feet—for the stockings were off by this time. But in sixty or eighty yards this pad run into another, covered with fresh sheep-tracks since the little girl had passed. Nothing for it but to spread out, and examine the network of pads scattered over the country. All this time, the weather was holding-up, but there was a grumble of thunder now and then, and the air was fearfully close.

"At last there was a coo-ee out to the left. Young Broome had found three plain tracks, about half-a-mile away. We took these for a base, but we did n't get beyond them. We were circling round for miles, without making any headway; and so the time passed till about three in the afternoon. Then up comes Spanker, with his hat lost, and his face cut and bleeding from the scrub, and his horses in a white lather, and a black lubra sitting in the back of the buggy, and the Mulppa stock-keeper tearing along in front, giving him our tracks.

"She was an old, grey-haired lubra, blind of one eye; but she knew her business, and she was on the job for life or death. She picked-up the track at a glance, and run it like a bloodhound. We found that the little girl had n't kept the sheep-pads as we expected. Generally she went straight till something blocked her; then she 'd go straight again, at another angle. Very rarely—hardly ever—we could see what signs the lubra was following; but she was all right. Uncivilised, even for an old lubra. Nobody could yabber with her but Bob; and he kept close to her all the time. She began to get uneasy as night came on, but there was no help for it. She went slower and slower, and at last she sat down where she was. We judged that the little girl had made about seventeen mile to the place where the lubra got on her track, and we had added something like four to that. Though, mind you, at this time we were only about twelve or fourteen mile from Dan's place, and eight to ten mile from the home-station.

"Longest night I ever passed, though it was one of the shortest in the year. Eyes burning for want of sleep, and could n't bear to lie down for a minute. Wandering about for miles; listening; hearing something in the scrub, and finding it was only one of the other chaps, or some sheep. Thunder and lightning, on and off, all night; even two or three drops of rain, toward morning. Once I heard the howl of a dingo, and I thought of the little girl, lying worn-out, half-asleep and half-fainting—far more helpless than a sheep—and I made up my mind that if she came out safe I would lead a better life for the future.

"However, between daylight and sunrise—being then about a mile, or a mile and a half, from the bell—I was riding at a slow walk, listening and dozing in the saddle, when I heard a far-away call that sounded like 'Dad-dee!'. It seemed to be straight in front of me; and I went for it like mad. Had n't gone far when William-son, the narangy, was alongside me.

" 'Hear anything?' says I.

" 'Yes,' says he. 'Sounded like 'Daddy'! I think it was out here.'

" 'I think it was more this way,' says I; and each of us went his own way.

"When I got to where I thought was about the place, I listened again, and searched round everywhere. The bell was coming that way, and presently I went to meet it, leading my horse, and still listening. Then another call came through the stillness of the scrub, faint, but beyond mistake, 'Dad-de-e-e!'. There was n't a trace of terror in the tone; it was just the voice of a worn-out child, deliber-ately calling with all her might. Seemed to be something less than half-a-mile away, but I could n't fix on the direction; and the scrub was very thick.

"I hurried down to the bell. Everyone there had heard the call, or fancied they had; but it was out to their right—not in front. Of course, the lubra would n't leave the track, nor Bob, nor the chap with the bell; but everyone else was gone—Dan among the rest. The lubra said something to Bob.

" 'Picaninny tumble down here again,' says Bob. 'Getting very weak on her feet.'

"By-and-by, 'Picaninny plenty tumble down.' It was pitiful; but we knew that we were close on her at last. By this time, of course, she had been out for seventy-two hours.

"I stuck to the track, with the lubra and Bob. We could hear some of the chaps coo-eeing now and again, and calling 'Mary!' "——

"Bad line—bad line," muttered Saunders impatiently.

"Seemed to confuse things, anyway," replied Thompson. "And it was very doubtful whether the little girl was likely to answer a strange voice. At last, however, the lubra stopped, and pointed to a sun-bonnet, all dusty, lying under a spreading hop-bush. She spoke to Bob again.

" 'Picaninny sleep here last night,' says Bob. And that was within a hundred yards of the spot I had made-for after hearing the first call. I knew it by three or four tall pines, among a mass of pine scrub. However, the lubra turned off at an angle to the right, and run the track—not an hour old—toward where we had heard the second call. We were crossing fresh horse-tracks every few yards; and never two minutes but what somebody turned-up to ask

the news. But to show how little use anything was except fair
tracking, the lubra herself never saw the child till she went right
up to where she was lying between two thick, soft bushes that met
over her, and hid her from sight"——

"Asleep?" I suggested, with a sinking heart.

"No. She had been walking along—less than half-an-hour before
—and she had brushed through between these bushes, to avoid some
prickly scrub on both sides; but there happened to be a bilby-hole
close in front, and she fell in the sort of trough, with her head
down the slope; and that was the end of her long journey. It
would have taken a child in fair strength to get out of the place
she was in; and she was played-out to the last ounce. So her face
had sunk down on the loose mould, and she had died without a
struggle.

"Bob snatched her up the instant he caught sight of her, but we
all saw that it was too late. We coo-eed, and the chap with the bell
kept it going steady. Then all hands reckoned that the search was
over, and they were soon collected round the spot.

"Now, that little girl was only five years old; and she had walked
nothing less than twenty-two miles—might be nearer twenty-five."

There was a minute's silence. Personal observation, or trustworthy report, had made every one of Thompson's audience
familiar with such episodes of new settlement; and, for that very
reason, his last remark came as a confirmation rather than as an
over-statement. Nothing is more astonishing than the distances lost
children have been known to traverse.

"How did poor Rory take it?" I asked.

"Dan? Well he took it bad. When he saw her face, he gave one
little cry, like a wounded animal; then he sat down on the bilby-
heap, with her on his knees, wiping the mould out of her mouth,
and talking baby to her.

"Not one of us could find a word to say; but in a few minutes
we were brought to ourselves by thunder and lightning in earnest,
and the storm was on us with a roar. And just at this moment
Webster of Kulkaroo came up with the smartest blackfellow in that
district.

"We cleared out one of the wagonettes, and filled it with pine
leaves, and laid a blanket over it. And Spanker gently took the
child from Dan, and laid her there, spreading the other half of the
blanket over her. Then he thanked all hands, and made them wel-
come at the station, if they liked to come. I went, for one; but Bob
went back to Kulkaroo direct, so I saw no more of him till to-night.

"Poor Dan! He walked behind the wagonette all the way, crying softly, like a child, and never taking his eyes from the little shape under the soaking wet blanket. Hard lines for him! He had heard her voice calling him, not an hour before; and now, if he lived till he was a hundred, he would never hear it again.

"As soon as we reached the station, I helped Andrews, the store-keeper, to make the little coffin. Dan would n't have her buried in the station cemetery; she must be buried in consecrated ground, at Hay. So we boiled a pot of gas-tar to the quality of pitch, and dipped long strips of wool-bale in it, and wrapped them tight round the coffin, after the lid was on, till it was two ply all over, and as hard and close as sheet-iron. Ay, and by this time more than a dozen blackfellows had rallied-up to the station.

"Spanker arranged to send a man with the wagonette, to look after the horses for Dan. The child's mother wanted to go with them, but Dan refused to allow it, and did so with a harshness that surprised me. In the end, Spanker sent Ward, one of the narangies. I happened to camp with them four nights ago, when I was coming down from Kulkaroo, and they were getting back to Goolumbulla. However," added Thompson, with sublime lowliness of manner, "that 's what I meant by saying that, in some cases, a person 's all the better for being uncivilised. You see, we were nowhere beside Bob, and Bob was nowhere beside the old lubra."

"Had you much of a yarn with the poor fellow when you met him?" I asked.

"Evening and morning only," replied Thompson, maintaining the fine apathy due to himself under the circumstances. "I was away all night with the bullocks, in a certain paddock. Did n't recognise me; but I told him I had been there; and then he would talk about nothing but the little girl. Catholic priest in Hay sympathised very strongly with him, he told me, but could n't read the service over the child, on account of her not being baptised. So Ward read the service. His people are English Catholics. Most likely Spanker thought of this when he sent Ward. Dan did n't seem to be as much cut-up as you 'd expect. He was getting uneasy about his paddock; and he thought Spanker might be at some inconvenience. But that black beard of his is more than half white already. And —something like me—I never thought of mentioning this to Bob when he was here. Absence of mind. Bad habit."

"This Dan has much to be thankful for," remarked Stevenson, with strong feeling in his voice. "Suppose that thunderstorm had come on a few hours sooner—what then?"

There was a silence for some minutes.

"Tell you what made me interrupt you, Thompson, when I foun' fault with singin'-out after lost kids," observed Saunders, at length. "Instigation o' many a pore little (child) perishin' unknownst. Seen one instance when I was puttin' up a bit o' fence on Grundle—hundred an' thirty-four chain an' some links—forty-odd links, if I don't disremember. Top rail an' six wires. Jist cuttin' off a bend o' the river, to make a handy cattle-paddick. They'd had it fenced-off with dead-wood, twelve or fifteen years before; but when they got it purchased they naterally went-in for a proper fence. An' you can't lick a top rail an' six wires, with nine-foot panels"——

"You 're a bit of an authority on fencin'," remarked Baxter drily.

"Well, as I was sayin'," continued Saunders; "this kid belonged to a married man, name o' Tom Bracy, that was workin' mates with me. One night when his missus drafted the lot she made one short; an' she hunted roun', an' called, an' got excited; an' you could n't blame the woman. Well, we hunted all night—me, an' Tom, an' Cunningham, the cove that was engaged to cart the stuff on-to the line. Decent, straight-forrid chap, Cunningham is, but a (sheol) of a liar when it shoots him. Course, some o' you fellers knows him. Meejum-size man, but one o' them hard, wiry, deep-chested, deceivin' fellers. See him slingin' that heavy red-gum stuff about, as if it was broad palin'. Course, he was on'y three-an' twenty, an' fellers o' that age don't know their own strenth. His bullocks was fearful low at the time, on account of a trip he had out to Wilcanniar with flour; an' that 's how he come to take this job"——

"Never mind Cunningham; he 's dead now," observed Donovan indifferently.

"Well, as I was tellin' you," pursued Saunders, "we walked that bend the whole (adj.) night, singin' out 'Hen-ree! Hen-ree!' an' in the mornin' we was jist as fur as when we started. Tom, he clears-off to the station before daylight, to git help; an' by this time I 'd come to the conclusion that the kid must be in the river, or out on the plains. I favoured the river a lot; but I bethought me o' where this dead-wood fence had bin burnt, to git it out o' our road, before the grass got dry. So I starts at one end to examine the line o' soft ashes that divided the bend off o' the plain—an' har'ly a sign o' traffic across it yet. Had n't went, not fifteen chain, before I bumps up agen the kid's tracks, plain as A B C, crossin' out towards the plain. Coo-ees for Cunningham; shows him the tracks; an' the two of us follers the line o' ashes right to the other end, to see if the tracks come back. No (adj.) tracks. So we tells the missus; an' she clears-out for the plain, an' me after her. Cunningham, he collars his horse, an' out for the plain too. Station chaps turns-up, in ones an' twos; an' when they seen the tracks, they scattered for the plain too. Mostly young fellers, on good horses—some o' them good enough to be worth enterin' for a saddle, or the like o' that. Curious how horses was better an' cheaper them days nor what they are now. I had a brown mare that time; got her off of a traveller for three notes; an' you pass her by without lookin' at her; but of all the deceivin' goers you ever come across"——

"No odds about the mare; she 's dead long ago," interposed Thompson.

"About two o'clock," continued Saunders cheerfully, "I was dead-beat an' leg-tired; an' I went back to the tent, to git a bite to eat; an', comin' back agen, I went roun' to have another look at the tracks. Now, thinks I, what road would that little (wanderer) be likeliest to head from here? An' I hitches myself up on a big ole black log that was layin' about a chain past the tracks, an' I set there for a minit, thinkin' like (sheol). You would n't call it a big log for the Murray, or the Lower Goulb'n, but it was a fair-size log for the Murrumbidgee. I seen some whoppin' red-gums in Gippsland too; but the biggest one I ever seen was on the Goulb'n. Course, when I say 'big,' I mean measurement; I ain't thinkin' about holler shells, with no timber in 'em. This tree I 'm speakin' about had eleven thousand two hundred an' some odd feet o' timber in her; an' Jack Hargrave, the feller that cut her"——

"His troubles is over too," murmured Baxter.

"Well, as I was tellin' you, I begun to fancy I could hear the whimper of a kid, far away. 'Magination, thinks I. Lis'ns fit to break my (adj.) neck. Hears it agen. Seemed to come from the bank o' the river. Away I goes; hunts roun'; lis'ns; calls 'Hen-ree!'; lis'ns agen. Not a sound. Couple o' the station hands hap-pened to come roun', an' I told 'em. Well, after an hour o' searchin' an' lis'nin', the three of us went back to where I heard the sound. I hitches myself up on-to the log agen, an' says I:

" 'This is the very spot I was,' says I, 'when I heard it.' An' before the word was out o' my mouth, (verb) me if I did n't hear it agen!

" 'There you are!' says I.

" 'What the (sheol) are you blatherin' about?' says they.

" 'Don't you hear the (adj.) kid?' says I.

" 'Oh, that ain't the kid, you (adj.) fool!' says they, lookin' as wise as Solomon, an' not lettin'-on they could n't hear it. But for

an' all, they parted, an' rode roun' an' roun', as slow as they could
crawl, stoppin' every now an' agen, an' listenin' for all they was
worth; an' me settin' on the log, puzzlin' my brains. At last I hears
another whimper.

"'There you are again!' says I.

"An' one cove, he was stopped close in front o' the butt end o'
the log at the time; an' he jumps off his horse, an' sticks his head
in the holler o' the log, an' lets a oath out of him. Fearful feller
to swear, he was. I disremember his name jis' now; but he 'd bin
on Grundle ever since he bolted from his ole man's place, in Bul-
larook Forest, on account of a lickin' he got; an' it was hard to
best him among sheep; an' now I rec'lect his name was Dick—
Dick—it 's jist on the tip o' my (adj.) tongue"——

"No matter hees name," interposed Helsmok; "he have yoined
der graat mayority too."

"Well, as I was sayin'," continued the patient Saunders, "we
lis'ned at the mouth o' the holler, an' heard the kid whinin' inside;
an' when we sung-out to him, he was as quiet as a mouse. An' we
struck matches, an' tried to see him, but he was too fur along, an'
the log was a bit crooked; an' when you got in a couple o' yards,
the hole was so small you 'd wonder how he done it. Anyhow, the
two station blokes rode out to pass the word; an' the most o' the
crowd was there in half-an-hour. The kid was a good thirty foot
up the log; an' there was no satisfaction to be got out of him. He
would n't shift; an' by-'n'-by we come to the impression that he
could n't shift; an' at long an' at last we had to chop him out, like
a bees' nest. Turned out after, that the little (stray) had foun'
himself out of his latitude when night come on; an' he 'd got gump-
tion enough to set down where he was, an' wait for mornin'. He 'd
always bin told to do that, if he got lost. But by-'n'-by he heard
'Hen-ree! Hen-ree!' boomin' an' bellerin' back an' forrid across
the bend in the dark; an' he thought the boody-man, an' the bunyip,
an' the banshee, an' (sheol) knows what all, was after him. So he
foun' this holler log, an' he thought he could n't git fur enough
into it. He was about seven year old then; an' that was in '71—
the year after the big flood—an' the shearin' was jist about over.
How old would that make him now? Nineteen or twenty. He left
his ole man three year ago, to travel with a sheep-drover, name o'
Sep Halliday, an' he 's bin with the same bloke ever since. Mos'
likely some o' you chaps knows this Sep? Stout butt of a feller,
with a red baird. Used to mostly take flocks for truckin' at Deniliquin; but that got too many at it—like everything else—an' he

went out back, Cooper's Creek way, with three thousand Gunbar yowes, the beginnin' o' las' winter, an' I ain't heard of him since he crossed at Wilcanniar"——

"No wonder," I observed; "he 's gone aloft, like the rest."

There was a pause, broken by Stevenson, in a voice that brought constraint on us all:

"Bad enough to lose a youngster for a day or two, and find him alive and well; worse, beyond comparison, when he 's found dead; but the most fearful thing of all is for a youngster to be lost in the bush, and never found, alive or dead. That 's what happened to my brother Eddie, when he was about eight year old. You must remember it, Thompson?"

"Was n't my father out on the search?" replied Thompson. "Tom's father, too. You were living on the Upper Campaspe."

"Yes," continued Stevenson, clearing his throat; "I 've been thinking over it every night for these five-and-twenty years, and it seems to me the most likely thing that could have happened to him was to get jammed in a log, like that other little chap. Then after five years, or ten years, or twenty years, the log gets burned, and nobody notices a few little bones, crumbled among the ashes.

"I was three or four years older than Eddie," he resumed hoarsely; "and he just worshipped me. I had been staying with my uncle in Kyneton for three months, going to school; and Eddie was lost the day after I came home. We were out, gathering gum— four of us altogether—about a mile and a half from home; and I got cross with the poor little fellow, and gave him two or three hits; and he started home by himself, crying. He turned round and looked at me, just before he got out of sight among the trees; and that was the last that was ever seen of him, alive or dead. My God! When I think of that look, it makes me thankful to remember that every day brings me nearer to the end. The spot where he turned round is in the middle of a cultivation-paddock now, but I could walk straight to it in the middle of the darkest night.

"Yes; he started off home, crying. We all went the same way so soon afterward that I expected every minute to see him on ahead. At last we thought we must have passed him on the way. No alarm yet, of course; but I was choking with grief, to think how I 'd treated the little chap; so I gave Maggie and Billy the slip, and went back to meet him. I knew from experience how glad he would be.

"Ah well! the time that followed is like some horrible dream. He was lost at about four in the afternoon; and there would be about a dozen people looking for him, and calling his name, all night. Next day, I daresay there would be about thirty. Next morning, my father offered £100 reward for him, dead or alive; and five other men guaranteed £10 each. Next day, my father's reward was doubled; and five other men put down their names for another £50. Next day, Government offered £200. So between genuine sympathy and the chance of making £500, the bush was fairly alive with people; and everyone within thirty miles was keeping a look-out.

"No use. The search was gradually dropped, till no one was left but my father. Month after month, he was out every day, wet or dry; and my mother waiting at home, with a look on her face that frightened us—waiting for the news he might bring. And, time after time, he took stray bones to the doctor; but they always turned out to belong to sheep, or kangaroos, or some other animal. Of course, he neglected the place altogether, and it went to wreck; and our cattle got lost; and he was always meeting with people that sympathised with him, and asked him to have a drink—and you can hardly call him responsible for the rest.

"However, on the anniversary of the day that Eddie got lost, my mother took a dose of laudanum; and that brought things to a head. My father had borrowed every shilling that the place would carry, to keep up the search; and there was neither interest nor principal forthcoming, so the mortgagee—Wesleyan minister, I 'm sorry to say—had to sell us off to get his money. We had three uncles; each of them took one of us youngsters; but they could do nothing for my father. He hung about the public-houses, getting lower and lower, till he was found dead in a stable, one cold winter morning. That was about four years after Eddie was lost."

Stevenson paused, and restlessly changed his position, then muttered, in evident torture of mind:

"Think of it! While he was going away, crying, he looked back over his shoulder at me, without a word of anger; and he walked up against a sapling, and staggered—and I laughed!—Great God! —I laughed!"

That was the end of the tank-sinker's story; and silence fell on our camp. Doubtless each one of us recalled actions of petty tyranny toward leal, loving, helpless dependents, or inferiors in strength—actions which now seemed to rise from the irrevocable past, proclaiming their exemption from that moral statute of limitations which brings self-forgiveness in course of time. For an innate Jehovah sets His mark upon the Cain guilty merely of bullying or terrifying any brother whose keeper he is by virtue of superior strength; and that brand will burn while life endures. (Conversely —does such remorse ever follow disdain of authority, or defiance of power? I, for one, have never experienced it.)

Soon a disquietude from another source set my mind at work in troubled calculation of probabilities. At last I said:

"Would you suppose, Steve, that the finding of George Murdoch's body was a necessary incitement among the causes that led to the little girl's getting lost?"

"Domson 's ascleep," murmured Helsmok. "I tink dey all ascleep. I wass yoos dropp'n off mineself."

And in two minutes, his relaxed pose and regular breathing affirmed a kind of fellowship with the rest, in spite of his alien birth and objectionable name. But I could n't sleep. Dear innocent, angel-faced Mary! perishing alone in the bush! Nature's precious link between a squalid Past and a nobler Future, broken, snatched away from her allotted place in the long chain of the ages! Heiress of infinite hope, and dowered with latent fitness to fulfil her part, now so suddenly fallen by the wayside! That quaint dialect silent so soon! and for ever vanished from this earth that keen, eager perception, that fathomless love and devotion! But such is life.

Yet it is well with her. And it is well with her father, since he, throughout her transitory life, spoke no word to hurt or grieve her. Poor old Rory! Reaching Goolumbulla, after his sorrowful journey, his soft heart would be stabbed afresh by the sight of two picture-books, which I had posted a fortnight before. And how many memories and associations would confront him when he returned to his daily round of life! How many reminders that the irremediable loss is a reality, from which there can be no awakening! How many relics to be contemplated with that morbid fascination for the re-quickening of a slumbering and intolerable sense of bereavement! But the saddest and most precious of memorials will be those little copper-toed boots that she left along the way. Deepest pathos lies only in homely things, since the frailness of mortality is the pathetic centre, and mortality is nothing but homely.

Hence, no relic is so affecting as the half-worn boots of the dead. Thus in the funeral of that gold-escort trooper, when I was but little older than poor Mary. The armed procession—the Dead March— the cap and sword on the coffin—seemed so imposing that I forthwith resolved to be a trooper myself. That ambition passed away;

but the pathos of the empty boots, reversed in the stirrups of the led horse, has remained with me ever since.

From sad reflections, I seemed to be thus drifting into philosophic musing, when Helsmok shook me gently by the shoulder. A glance at the setting moon showed that I had been asleep, and that it was long past midnight. Here, therefore, ends the record of December the 9th; and you might imagine this chapter of life fitly concluded.

But sometimes an under-current of plot, running parallel with the main action, emerges from its murky depths, and causes a transient eddy in the interminable stream of events. Something of this kind occurred on the morning of the 10th.

"Collince," said the Dutchman softly. "Don' wake op der odder vellers—do no goot yoos now. I gone 'way roun' der liknum, und der bullock und der horse not dere. Notteen cronk, I hope. Mi 's well com anodder trip?"

I left my lair, and we walked out across the plain, followed by the faithful Pup. When we had ranged for an hour, in half-mile zig-zags, day began to break; and nothing had turned-up, except four of Stevenson's horses. But we heard, through the stillness of the dawn, a faint, far-away trampling of hoofs. We headed for the sound, and presently found ourselves meeting three or four dozen of mixed bullocks and horses, convoyed by five mounted Chinamen. We stood aside to let them pass. By this time, an advancing day-light enabled me to recognise the roan horse of Sam Young (also called Paul) with a rider who was more likely to be that proselyte than anyone else. At all events, he turned upon me the light of a countenance, broad, yellow, and effulgent as the harvest moon of pastoral poetry; and, like a silver clarion, rung the accents of that unknown tongue:

"Ah-pang-sen-lo! Missa Collin! sen-lo! Tlee-po' week, me plurry liah, all li; nek time, you plully liah, all li! Missa Smyte talkee you bimeby! Hak-i-long-see-ho! You lescue Walligal Alp bullock—eh? You killee me, by cli! Whe' you holse? Ling-tang-hon-me! My wuld, Tlinidad plully goo' glass, no feah! Hi-lung-sing-i-lo-i-lo!"

"Goo' molnin', Missa Helsmok!" chanted another yellow agony. "Nicee molnin', Missa Helsmok! Whaffoh you tellee me lah wintel you sclew my plully neck? Lak-no-ha-long-lee! Missa Smyte wakee you up—tyillin'-a-head you holse! Man-di-sling-lo-he!"

"Donder und blitzen!" retorted the Dutchman, striding toward the escort, which scattered at his approach. "Yomp off dem olt crocks, every man yack of you, und swelp mine Gott! I weel ponch der het of der vive of you altogedder mit, ef so moch der yudge seegs mons pot me into der yail bot!"

"Helsmok," said I, restraining him; "upon the heat and flame of thy distemper sprinkle cool patience. Let us accept the situation with dignity. Let us pit the honest frankness of the played-out Caucasian against the cunning of the successful Mongol." Then, addressing the Turanian horde, and adapting my speech to the understanding of our lowest types: "My word!" I exclaimed admiringly, "you take-um budgeree rise out-a whitepeller, John! Merrijig you! Borak you shift-um that peller bullock; borak you shift-um that peller yarraman. Whitepeller gib-it you fi' bob, buy-it opium. You savvy? Bale whitepeller tell-um boss. Bimeby whitepeller yabber like-it, 'Chinaman berry good'—yabber like-it, 'Comenavadrink, John'—yabber like-it, 'Chinaman brother b'long-a whitepeller.' You savvy, John?"

"Lak-hi-lo-hen-slung!" carolled a third Chow disdainfully. "You go hellee shut up! Eulopean allee sem plully whool! Lum-la-no-sun-hi-me!" And the raiders went on their way, warbling remarks to each other in their native tongue, while the discomfited foreign devils hurried toward their camp, to give the alarm.

But Baxter, Donovan, Thompson, and Saunders had already gone out to feast their eyes on the change which such a night would make in the appeaarnce of their stock. Stevenson was just getting on his feet, and feeling for his pipe. Cartwright was still asleep. It seemed a pity to disturb him. Sharply whetted to this form of self-indulgence by hardship that would have finished any civilised man, he had gently dozed off as the last bite of a copious and indigestible supper reached his emu-stomach, and had never moved since.

"Now who 'd 'a' thought them Chinks was so suddent?" he mused, as I woke him with the tidings. "Trapped! Gosh, what a slant I 'd 'a' had at that (fellow)'s horse-paddick, if I 'd on'y knowed! Cut-an'-dried, I be boun'. No good chewin' over it now, anyhow. After you with them matches, Stevenson; mine 's all done."

"Barefooted Bob 's mixed-up in this," remarked Stevenson, handing the matches. "Now, who would have suspected it, from his manner last night? But no one is to be trusted. Better take our saddles and bridles with us."

"In respect of imbecility and ignorance, I grant you," I replied. "But in respect of deliberate deceit, most men are to be trusted. By-the-way, there 's four of your frames left—out near those cooli-bahs."

"Stake the question on Bob," he suggested. "May as well catch them, and ride."

"So be it—to both proposals."

The sun was now above the indefinable horizon, looming blood-red through the smoky haze. All objects, even in the middle distance, showed vague and shadowy; but, knowing which way the marauders had taken their prey, we went after them, making a slight detour to secure the four horses. But we were just in time to discern a Chinese patrol tailing the same beasts toward a larger detachment, which was moving in the direction taken by the earlier draft. We followed; and, for my own part, even if I had not been personally interested, I should have judged it well worth going a mile to witness the strong situation which supplied a sequel to our homely little drama.

Precise and faithful execution, co-operating with masterly strategy, had realised one of the most magnificent hauls of assorted trespassers that I have been privileged to survey. I jotted down a memo. of the numbers. There were 254 head of overworked and underfed beasts—173 bullocks and 81 horses. These were in the custody of nine Mongolians, two Young-Australians, and two gentlemen—the latter being Mr. Smythe and Bert. Also, 7 bullocks and 3 horses left their bones in the paddock, as evidence of the bitter necessity which had prompted this illegal invasion of pastoral leasehold. There were (including myself) 23 claimants, present in person, or arriving by twos or threes. A few of these were ludicrously abashed; others were insolent; but the large majority observed a fine nonchalance, shading down to apathy. And Mr. Smythe, true to his order of mind, treated the first with outrageous contumely, the second with silent contempt, and the third with a respect born of vague disquietude and anxiety for the morrow. A squatter—just or unjust, generous or avaricious, hearty or exclusive, debonair or harsh—should be a strong man; this was a weakling; and my soul went forth in genuine compassion for him.

The three hours occupied in sorting-out and settling-up, furnished, perhaps, as varied and interesting experiences to me as to anyone else in the cast: first, a thrill of dismay, altogether apart from the drama; and afterward, the fortuitous cognisance of a bit of by-play in the main action.

My horses, of course, were among the captives; each of them with both hobble-straps buckled round the same leg. Early in the reception, whilst treating for them, I was fairly disconcerting Mr. Smythe with my affability, when that sudden consternation came over me. Where was Pup?

I put the two pairs of hobbles round Bunyip's neck, and saddled Cleopatra without delay. The gallant beast, as if he knew the need for despatch, bucked straight ahead till he merged into an easy gallop. A few minutes brought me to the camp; and my anxiety was dispelled. The chaps had hung their tucker-bags on some adjacent lignum, out of reach of the wild pigs, but at a height accessible to Pup. The absence of the owners, though desirable, would not have been absolutely necessary to the performance which followed, for a kangaroo-dag can abstract food with a motion more silent—and certainly more swift—than that of a gnomon's shadow on a sun-dial.

So I returned to the scene of interest, accompanied by Bunyip and Pup. Twelve or fifteen of the outlaws, having secured their saddle-horses, were sternly ordering the Chinamen to refrain from crowding the stock. The grass in this corner of the paddock was especially good; and these unshamed delinquents rode slowly through and through the mob, each vainly trying to identify and count his own; while now and then one would pass out to overbear some encroaching pagan by loud-spoken interrogations respecting a bay mare with a switch tail, or a strawberry bullock with wide horns—such ostentatious inquiry being accompanied by a furtive and vicious jabbing of evidence's horse, or evidence himself, with some suitable instrument. Yet batch after batch was withdrawn and paid for; while the red sun rose higher, and Mr. Smythe became impatient and crusty, by reason of the transparent dallying.

Helsmok, after protracted and patient sorting, brought out nineteen of his horses, and paid for twenty, besides his hack. He said he would have to borrow a whip from someone, to 'dost der yacket' of the impracticable animal that remained in the mob. Relevantly, one of the Chows had a stockwhip, the handle of which represented about six months' untiring work on a well-selected piece of myall. Helsmok had all along been pained by the incongruity of such a gem in such keeping; and now, having discharged his trespass-liability, the iron-wristed Hollander politely borrowed this jewel from its clinging owner, and so recovered his horse without difficulty. Then, when the bereaved boundary man followed him across the plain, intoning psalms of remonstrance, Helsmok, making a playful clip at a locust, awkwardly allowed the lash to curl once-and-a-half round the body of John's horse, close in front of the hind-legs. The cheap and reliable rider saved himself by the mane; but he let the stockwhip go at that.

Smythe—high-strung and delicate, in spite of his stock-keeper's rig-out—was taking little interest in anything except the shillings he collected. At last, with a heart-drawn sigh, he beckoned to his brother.

"You must meet me with the buggy, Bert, when this is over. I have a splitting headache. We can do without you now." Alas! what doth a station manager with splitting headaches? Answer, ye pastoralists!

Stevenson had just drafted and paid for his batch, when Bare-footed Bob stalked up, bearing an unmistakable scowl on his frank face, and a saddle on his shoulder.

"Did you receive my message last night, Bob?" demanded Smythe.

"Well," drawled Bob, "I could n't say whether it was las' night or this mornin'—but I got your message right enough."

"And why did n't you turn-up?"

"Why did n't I turn-up," repeated Bob thoughtfully. "P'r'aps you 'll be so good as to inform me if my work 's cleanin' out reservoys or mindin' paddicks?"

"But you should be loyal to your employ," replied Smythe severely.

"Meanin' I should n't turn dog?" conjectured Bob. "No more I don't. I ain't turnin' dog on anybody when I stick to my own work, an' keep off of goin' partners with opium an' leprosy. Same time, mind you, I 'd be turnin' dog on the station if I took advantage o' your message, to go round warnin' the chaps that was workin' on the paddick. Way I was situated, the clean thing was to stand out. An' that 's what I done."

Meanwhile, Stevenson had lingered to feel his pockets, sort his papers, examine his horse's legs, and so forth, while his draft spread out over the grass.

"You were right, and I was wrong," he remarked, aside to me. "Bob is trustworthy—ruthlessly so."

"Only in respect of conscience, which is mere moral punctilio, and may co-exist with any degree of ignorance or error," I replied. "I would n't chance sixpence on his moral sense—nor on yours, either."

"Thank-you, both for the lesson and the compliment. Don't forget to call round at my camp, any time you 're crossing Koolybooka. Good-bye."

"Are your bullocks here, Bob?" demanded Smythe.

"Horses too," replied Bob. "Ain't you lookin' at 'em?" But Smythe did n't know half-a-dozen beasts on the station; and Bob (as he afterward told me) was aware of his boss's weakness in Individuality.

"Take them and get to work then," retorted Smythe. "How many bullocks are you working?" he added, with sudden suspicion—his idea evidently being that Bob might wish to do a good turn to some of the bullock drivers.

"Well, I 'm workin' ten, but"——

" 'But!'——I 'll have no 'but' about it!" snapped Smythe. "Take your ten, and GO!"

"Right," drawled Bob, and he slowly strode toward one of his own horses.

"And look-sharp, you fellows!" vociferated Smythe. "This paddock must be cleared within fifteen minutes, or I shall proceed to more extreme measures."

Whereupon Thompson withdrew his lot, deliberately followed by four other culprits, whose names are immaterial. Meanwhile, Bob had some trouble in sorting out his ten—often slowly crossing and re-crossing the paths of Donovan and Baxter, in their still more arduous and long-drawn task. At last the eagle-eye of the squatter counted Bob's ten, accompanied by his spare horse, as he tailed the lot toward his camp; and the same aquiline optic tallied-off an aggregate of thirty-six to Baxter and Donovan—who, to my own private knowledge, had entered the paddock with thirty-four. This disposed of the whole muster.

Months afterward, when the two Mondunbarra bullocks had been swapped-away into a team from the Sydney side, I camped one night with Baxter and Donovan, who discussed, in the most matter-of-fact way, their own tranquil appropriation of the beasts. Each of these useful scoundrels had the answer of a good conscience touching the transaction. They maintained, with manifest sincerity, that Smythe's repudiation of the bullocks, and his subsequent levy of damages upon them as strangers and trespassers, gave themselves a certain right of trover, which prerogative they had duly developed into a title containing nine points of the law. Not equal to a pound-receipt, of course; but good enough for the track. And throughout the discussion, Bob's name was never mentioned, nor his complicity hinted at. Such is life.

CHAPTER VI

SAT. FEB. 9. Runnymede. To Alf Jones's.

Not much in that bill of fare, you think? Perhaps not. Nor was
Count Federigo degli Alberighi's falcon much of a banquet for the
Lady Giovanna, though that meagre catering cost a considerable
jar to the sensibilities of the impoverished aristocrat—accurately
represented, in this instance, by the writer of these memoirs. Of
course, I am committed to any narration imposed by my random
election of dates; but just notice that perversity, that untowardness,
that cussedness in the affairs of men, which brings me back to
Runnymede, above all places in the spacious south-western quarter
of the Mother Province. The unforeseen sequences of that original
option are masters of the situation, till they run their course—and
most tyrannical masters they are. They have tied me to a stake; I
cannot fly, but, bear-like, I must fight the course. Ay! your first-
person-singular novelist delights in relating his love-story, simply
because he can invent something to pamper his own romantic
notions; whereas, a similar undertaking makes the faithful chronicler squirm, inasmuch as——Oh! you 'll find out soon enough.

Five days before the date of this entry, I had received orders to
proceed at once to Runnymede, and there to complete an M form
which would in the meantime be forwarded from our Central Office
to Mr. Montgomery. Twelve hours' riding had brought me to the
station, but the document had not arrived, so there was nothing for
it but to wait till the next mail came in. That would be on the 9th.

Being a little too exalted for the men's hut, and a great deal too
vile for the boss's house, I was quartered in the narangies' barracks.

Social status, apart from all consideration of mind, manners, or
even money, is more accurately weighed on a right-thinking Australian station than anywhere else in the world.

The folk-lore of Riverina is rich in variations of a mythus, pointing to the David-and-Goliath combat between a quiet wage-slave
and a domineering squatter, in the brave days of old. With one
solitary exception, each station from the Murray to the Darling

claims and holds this legend as its own. On Kooltopa alone, the tables are turned, and the amiable Stewart makes a holy show of the truculent rouse-about. But on no station, not even on Kooltopa, has imagination bodied forth, or tradition handed down, any such vagary as might imply that a wage-slave saw the inside of the house or the barracks. And a narangy will always avoid your eye as he relates how, on some momentous occasion, the boss invited him to step in and take a seat. In the accurately-graded society of a proper station, you have a reproduction of the Temple economy under the old Jewish ritual. The manager's house is a Sanctum Sanctorum, wherein no one but the high priest enters; the barracks is an Inner Court, accessible to the priests only; the men's hut is an Outer Court, for the accommodation of lay worshippers; and the nearest pine-ridge, or perhaps one of the empty huts at the wool-shed, is the Court of the Gentiles. And the restrictions of the Temple were never more rigid than those of a self-respecting station. This usage, of course, bears fruit after its kind.

It was more than a mere custom with the mediæval baron—it was a large part of the religion which guided his rascally life—to wolf his half-raw pork in fellowship with his rouse-abouts; hence he could bash the latter about at pleasure; and they, in return, were prepared to die in his service. A good solid social system, in its own brutal and non-progressive way. The squatter, of course, cannot get back to the long table with the dogs underneath; but he ought to think-out some practicable equivalent to the baron's crude and lop-sided camaraderie—this having been a necessary condition of vassal loyalty in olden time. Without vassal loyalty, or abject vassal fear, the monopolist's sleep can never be secure. Domination, to be unassailable, must have overwhelming force in reserve —moral force, as in the feudal system, or physical force, as in our police system. The labour-leader, of accredited integrity and capability, though (so to speak) ducally weedy, has moral force in reserve; and we all know how he controls the many-headed. Also, the man glaringly destitute of integrity or capacity, but noticed as having a bullet-head, a square jaw, countersunk eyes, and the rest in proportion, is suspected of having the other kind of force in reserve; and we know how he escapes anything like wanton personal indignity in his intercourse with gentle or simple. Now, the only reserve-force adherent to station aristocracy resides in the manager's power to 'sack.'

The squatter of half-a-century ago dominated his immigrant servants by moral force—no difficult matter, with a 'gentleman' on one side and a squad of hereditary grovellers on the other. He dominated his convict servants by physical force—an equally easy task. But now the old squatter has gone to the mansions above; the immigrant and old hand to the kitchen below; and between the self-valuation of the latter-day squatter and that of his contemporary wage-slave, there is very little to choose. Hence the toe of the blucher treads on the heel of the tan boot, and galls its stitches. The average share of that knowledge which is power is undoubtedly in favour of the tan boot; but the preponderant moiety is just as surely held by the blucher. In our democracy, the sum of cultivated intelligence, and corresponding sensitiveness to affront, is dangerously high, and becoming higher. On the other hand, the squatter, even if pliant by disposition, cannot spring to the strain; social usage being territorial rather than personal; so here, you see, we have the two factors which should blend together in harmony—namely, the stubborn tradition of the soil, and the elastic genius of the 'masses'—divorced by an ever-widening breach. There are two remedies, and only two, available; failing one of these, something must, soon or later, give way with a crash. Either the anachronistic tradition must make suicidal concessions, or the better-class people must drown all plebeian Australian males in infancy, and fill the vacancy with Asiatics.

My acquaintance with Runnymede dated from about seven years before. Tracking three stray steers, I had reached the station at sunset. I had come more than sixty miles—nearly all unstocked country—in two days, and with only one chance meal. My horse was provokingly fagged; I was ragged by reason of the scrub, and dirty for lack of water: whilst an ill-spelled and ungrammatical order on Naylor of Koolybooka, for £28, was the nearest approach to money in my possession. I had left my cattle-tracks, and was approaching the home-station, when I met Mr. Montgomery himself. I told him my story. "Oh, well; go to the store and get your rations," said he disgustedly. "And, see—if those steers of yours are on the run, get them off as quick as possible. Fence-breakers, no doubt. Come! hurry-up, or the store will be closed!" The storekeeper measured me out a pannikin of dust into a newspaper, and directed me to the left-hand corner of the ram-paddock, as the best place for my horse. There, in the spacious Court of the Gentiles, I made a fire, worked up my johnny-cake on the flat top of the corner post, ate it hot off the coals, then lay down in swinophilosophic contentment, and read the newspaper till I could smell my hair scorching, and so to sleep.

My next visit to Runnymede took place about three years later. I had timed myself to draw-up to the station on a Saturday afternoon, with five-ton-seventeen of wire. Montgomery met me, as before. "You 're Collins, aren't you? I 've got the duplicate. We won't disturb your load till Monday. Shove your trespassers in the ration-paddock, and go and stop in the hut." I was rising in the world.

Next time I called at Runnymede, it was to inspect and verify the register which Montgomery was supposed to keep for my Department. Being now worthy of the Inner Court, I was told-off to sleep in the spare bed in Moriarty's room, and to sit at meat with the narangies, where we were waited on by a menial. If my social evolution had continued—if I had expanded, for instance, into a literary tourist, of sound Conservative principles—I would have seen the inside of the boss's house before I had done. But, as it happened, I withered and contracted from that point—simultaneously, mind you, with a perceptible diminution of my inherent ignorance and correlative uselessness. Such, however, is life.

But on the present occasion I had been quartered in the barracks for four whole days, as idle as a freshly-painted ship upon an ocean made iridescent by the unavoidable dripping and sprinkling of the pigment used. (A clumsy metaphor, but happily not my own.) This lethargy was inexcusable. I had three note-books filled with valuable memoranda for a series of Shakespearean Studies; and O, how I longed for a few days' untroubled leisure, just to break ground on the work. Those notes had been written in noisy huts, or by flickering firelight, or on horseback—written in eager activity of mind, and in hope of such an opportunity for amplification as I was now letting slip. But I have one besetting sin; and this Delilah, scissors in hand, had dogged me to Runnymede, and polled me by the skull. Nor could I plead inadvertence when I gravitated into the old familiar vice; but I left the consequences for an after-consideration. The opportunity was there, like an uncorked bottle under a dipsomaniac's nose, and that was enough. "One more," I kept saying to myself; "one more, and that 's the last; so sweet was ne'er so fatal."

According to the unhappy custom of besetting sins, this evil thing came upon me the moment I woke on the morning of the 9th. I slipped into my clothes, and started off along the horse-paddock fence toward a natural hollow, a mile from the station. Here twelve or fifteen years' continuous trampling by the worst-smelling of ruminants (bar the billy-goat) on ground theretofore untrodden except by blackfellows, birds, and marsupials, had developed a pond, sometimes a couple of acres in area, and eight feet deep in the middle, and sometimes dry. Full or dry, fresh or rotten, the pond was known as the 'swimming-hole.' At the time I speak of, the water was about half-gone, in both senses, and evaporating at the rate of an inch a day.

With a good supple stem of old-man saltbush I dispersed three snakes that lay around the margin, waiting for frogs; then I noticed my empty clothes lying on the bank, and found myself sliding through the lukewarm water, recklessly and wickedly discounting the prospective virility of another day; and there I remained till I thought it was time to go to breakfast.

Nothing but that integrity which springs from the certainty of being ultimately found-out, prompts me to the foregoing confession —a confession which I cannot but regard as damaging, from the literary, as well as from the moral, point of view. And for this reason.

During the last twenty or thirty years, the foremost humorist of our language has, from time to time, casually touched on the removal of natural and acquired dirt by means of bathing; but however lightly and racily this subject might leave his pen, it has been degraded into repulsiveness by the clumsy handling of imitators. Some things look best when merely implied in the dim background, and recent literature certainly proves this to be one of them. There is nothing dainty or picturesque in the presentment of a naked character washing himself; yet how few of our later novels or notes of travel are without that bit of description; generally set-off by an ungainly reflection on the dirt of some other person, class, or community. The noxious affectation is everywhere. Even the Salvation officer cannot now write his contribution to the *War Cry* without a detailed account of the bath he took on this or that occasion—a thing which has no interest whatever for anyone but himself. It would be much more becoming to wash our dirty skins, as well as our dirty calico, in private.

We might advantageously copy women-writers here. Woman, in the nature of things, must accumulate dirt, as we do; and she must now and then wash that dirt off, or it would be there still. (Like St. Paul, I speak as a man.) But the scribess never parades her ablutions on the printed page. If, for instance, you could prevail upon the whole galaxy of Australian authoresses and pen-women to attend a Northern Victoria Agricultural Show, in their literary capacity, you would see proof of this. Each would write her catalogue of aristocratic visitors, her unfavourable impressions *re* quality of refreshments, her sarcastic notice of other women's attire, and her fragmentary observations on the floral exhibits; but not one would wind-up her memoir with an account of the 'tubbing' she gave herself in the seclusion of her lodgings when the turmoil was over. Woman must be more than figuratively a poem if she can promenade a dusty show-yard for a long, hot afternoon without increasing in weight by exogenous accretion; but her soulfulness, however powerless to disallow dirt, silently asserts itself when that dirt comes to be shifted.

However, mere fidelity to fact brings me into the swim—in the figurative sense, as well as in the literal—and the sad consciousness of fellowship with men who 'tub' themselves on paper is added to the humiliation of the disclosure itself. In a word, just as I lost my vigour in the swimming-hole, I lose my individuality in the confession. But I don't lose my discrimination, nor my veracity. I don't call my evil good. In Physical Science, or in Pure Ethics— whoop! I am Antony yet!

Nature, by a kind of Monroe Doctrine, has allotted the dry land to man, and various other animals; the water to fish, leeches, etc.; the air to birds, bats, flies, etc.; the fire to salamanders, imps, unbaptised babies, etc.; and she strictly penalises the trespass of each class on the domain of any other. Naturally then, about sixteen raids, within four days, on an alien element, had stewed every atom of vigour out of my system, and quenched every spark of heroism.

Consider the child. He is the creature of instinct; and instinct— according to my late relative, Wilkie Collins—never errs, though reason often does so, as we know to our cost. Now, the picaninny knows what is good for him. Place him in proximity to a dust-hole or an ash-heap, and observe what takes place. He approaches it with that droll, yet pathetic, method of locomotion peculiar to his period of life—travelling on both hands and one knee, whilst with the big toe of the other hind-foot he propels himself along. In the very centre of the dirt, he deftly whirls into a sitting position, and proceeds to redeem the time, maintaining, meanwhile, that silence which is the perfectest herald of joy. Ormuzd the Good has inspired him with this inclination. But the Minister of Ahriman the Evil is not far off. The able-bodied mother seizes the mite of a bambino by the wrist, and carries him at arm's-length to the kitchen. It is to no purpose that he becomes alternately rigid and flaccid, lifting up his voice in clamorous protest, and making himself as heavy as a bag of shot. That misguided woman denudes him, washes him, rubs soap into his eyes, spanks him, re-arrays him, and sets him in a clean place, giving him a teaspoon to play with. Then she resumes her household work; whereupon Ormuzd whispers in the pledge's projecting ear, and that heaven-directed bimbo straightway turns his head toward the dust-hole, and, again illustrating the first clause of the Sphynx's not very complicated riddle, keeps the strictly noiseless tenor of his way, till Ahriman's priestess looks round to see the metaphors fulfilled, of the pup turning again to his ash-heap, and the papoose that was washed wallowing in the dust-hole. And so the pull-devil-pull-baker strife goes on to the last syllable of recorded time—not between mother and child, as you are prone to imagine, but between the two great principles of Good and Evil, so widely allegorised and personified, yet so uncertainly grasped, and so loosely defined. The result is sad enough: physically, not one in ten of us is what the doctor ordered, and, of course, brought; mentally, we are mostly fools; morally, we are, in a sense, little better than we ought to be. And such is life.

At breakfast, I remember, there occurred a slight misunderstanding between Mrs. Beaudesart, the housekeeper, and Ida, the white trash whose vocation was to wait on the narangies.

Mrs. Beaudesart was well-born. Don't study that expression too closely, or you'll get puzzled. Her father, Hungry Buckley, of Baroona—a gentleman addicted to high living and extremely plain thinking—had been snuffed-out by apoplexy, and abundantly filled a premature grave, some time in the early 'sixties, after seeing Baroona pass, by foreclosure, into the hands of a brainy and nosey financier. People who had known the poor gentleman when he was very emphatically in the flesh, and had listened to his palaver, and noticed his feckless way of going about things, were not surprised at the misfortune that had struck Buckley. Mrs. B. had then taken a small villa, near Sydney, where, in course of time, her son and daughter took positions of vantage, such as their circumstances allowed; each being prepared to stake his or her gentility (an objectionable word, but it has no synonym; and nasty things have nasty names) against any amount of filth that could be planked down by an aspiring representative of the opposite sex.

But young Mr. Buckley, who was something indefinite in a bank, presently ventured on a bit of blacksmith work, and being, by reason of hopeless impecuniosity, not worth lenient treatment, got a tenner hard. About the same time, Miss Buckley—then a singularly handsome young lady—became a veritable heroine of romance. A German prince, whose name I forget at the present moment, visited these provinces; and our Beatrix Esmond——Well, perhaps a reflected greatness is better than no greatness at all.

So, at all events, thought Mr. Lionel Fysshe-Jhonson, who married Miss Buckley on the strength of her celebrity. This young man in less than two years went to his reward; and his widow, after a seemly interval, reinforced her financial position by accepting the hand and heart of old Mr. Tidy, an aitchless property-owner, whose hobby was to collect his own rents. Bottoming on gold this time, she buried the old man within eighteen months, and paid probate duty on £25,000. After three years of something like life, she accepted the addresses of the Hon. Henry Beaudesart, a social refugee from Belgravia (wherever that may be). This was a gentleman of such refined tastes that it took over £10,000 a year to satisfy his soul-yearnings; so, when she buried him, after two years' trial, it was in the sure and certain hope that he would stay where he was put. This brought her to about the year '78. And the tide had turned.

For the next two years, the poor gentlewoman hung round the scene of her former glories, wearing garments that were out of fashion, and otherwise drinking to its very dregs the cup of bitterness which a heartless society holds to the lips of its deposed queen. The elegancies of life were necessities to her; but those elegancies would cost—to put it tangibly—the balance of profit accruing from the continuous labour of at least fifty average industrious women. And when the industrious women were not to the fore, where were the elegancies to come from? Where, indeed! It is a question which has broken many a gentler heart than Maud Beaudesart's, and will break many more. It is a cruel question; but not to put it would be more cruel still. For while this or that gentlewoman is in danger, no gentlewoman is safe. And the basest type of mind is that which gloats on the adversity of the world's spoiled child; the next basest is that which concentrates its sympathy on the same adversity; the least base, I think, is that which, goaded by a human compassion for all human distress, longs to get a lever under the order of things which necessitates the spoiling of any particular child.

Two or three years before the date of this record, Mrs. Montgomery, a distant relation and boarding-school friend of Mrs. Beaudesart, had met the latter in Sydney, and had brought her out to Runnymede. Montgomery, viewing the tenacious widow as a fixture, had insisted upon her having some definite status on the place, and she was therefore installed as housekeeper. Little wonder that the poor gentlewoman, remembering her own departed greatness, and chafing under the mild yoke of Mrs. Montgomery, used to make the handmaidens of the household wish themselves in Gehenna. Dionysius the Younger, shifted from his throne, opened a school, so that he might take it out of the boys. Such is life.

Levites, tribesmen, and Gentiles alike, used to poke fun at me over Mrs. Beaudesart; but the fact that they thought they knew my real standing, whereas they did n't, seemed to weigh so much in my favour as to make their banter anything but provoking. Yet my relations with the gentlewoman were painful enough. I 'll tell you exactly how we stood.

On my first official visit to Runnymede, whilst Montgomery and I stood talking in front of the store, Mrs. Beaudesart passed by. He detained her a moment to speak of my sleeping-accommodation, but first, with grave courtliness, introduced me to her as the last lineal descendant of Commander David Collins, R.N. Situated as I was, what could I say?—what would you have said? I had to fall in with the thing at the time; and having done so, of course, I had to live up to it; moreover this meant a good deal when I had to beat time with a woman like Maud. In spite of my chivalrous disinclination to flaunt superior descent in the face of a lady, our shuddersome intimacy deepened; and the necessity for keeping up my accompaniment seemed to grow more imperative as it became more difficult. But even at this distance of time, it soothes me to remember that I went through the ordeal without any sacrifice of veracity —partly by modest reticence touching my forebears, and the rest by a little diplomacy. For instance, in remarking that my grandfather, Sir Timothy Collins, had been well known in connection with the turf, I omitted to explain that he was allowed to obtain it only from a specified bog, and that his custom was to sell it at the stump for so much per donkey-load, to be taken out in spuds or oatmeal. Altogether, I got on better than you might expect. Meanwhile, some unhappy hitch in the Order of Things, as well as that strange fascination which accompanies danger of detection, kept dragging me to Runnymede on every pretext.

Another thing. Mrs. Beaudesart possessed a vast store of Debrett-information touching those early gentlemen-colonists whose enterprise is hymned by loftier harps than mine, but whose sordid greed and unspeakable arrogance has yet to be said or sung. Socially, she knew something fie-fie about most of our old nobility; and her class-sympathy, supported by the quasi-sacredness which invests aristocratic giddiness, lent tenderness of colour and accuracy of detail to some queer revelations. She could make me fancy myself in ancient Corinth.

And such was her hypnotic power, or my adaptability, that in the atmosphere of Runnymede I became a Conservative of the good old type, and actually enjoyed the communion of soul necessarily subsisting between a pedigreed lady and a pedigreed gentleman. We habitually spoke of the Montgomerys as of the wealthy lower orders, people of yesterday, and so forth; and because we took especial care to let nobody hear us, the jealousy of our inferiors manifested itself in that badinage so dear to the middle-class mind. 'Inferiors,' I say advisedly, for there was an indescribable something about us two when we got together, a something too subtle for expression in the vulgar tongue, which made us feel the station aristocracy to be a mere bourgeoisie, and ourselves the real Mackay. Of course, Montgomery had forgotten my high descent as soon as the words of introduction were out of his mouth; and I had begged the lady to conceal my gentilesse for the present; family pride causing me to be extremely sensitive on the subject of my low position. This was the only witchcraft I had used.

Ida, the handmaid of the barracks, was a common person. She certainly belonged to the same mammiferous division of vertebrata as Mrs. Beaudesart, but there the affinity ended with a jerk. In a word, she was the low-born daughter of a late poverty-stricken Victorian selector. Her father, after twelve years' manful struggle with a bad selection, had hanged himself in the stable; whereupon the storekeeper had sold the movables, and the mortgagee the farm. Runnymede was Ida's first situation. Her wages, month by month, went to the support of her broken-down mother, then living frugally in a country ownship, taking care of Ida's remaining brother, who had been knocked out of shape through getting run-over, in a painfully protracted way, by a heavy set of harrows. Her other brother had unfortunately sat down to eat his lunch on the wrong side of a partly-grubbed tree.

Altogether, poor Ida had very little to be thankful for. Personally, she was, without any exception, the ugliest white girl I ever saw. She measured about twice as long from the chin to Self-Esteem as from Benevolence to Amativeness; not one feature of her face was even middling; her skin was of a neutral creamy tint; and she had a straggly goatee of dirty white, with woolly side-boards of the same colour, in lieu of the short, silky moustache which is the piquant trade-mark of our country-women. Besides this, she was lame, on account of the back-sinew of one of her ankles having been cut through by a reaping-machine; and in addition to all this, the fingers of her left hand had been snipped to a uniform length, through getting into the feed of a chaff-cutter. Montgomery had picked her purposely for the barracks—so, at least, he told Mrs. Montgomery; so she told Mrs. Beaudesart, and so the latter told me. For myself, I often felt an impulse to marry the poor mortal; partly from compassion; partly from the idea that such an action would redound largely to my honour; and partly from the impression that such an unattractive woman would idolise a fellow like me.

The daughter of an unlucky selector is not taught to spare herself; and Ida was an untiring and conscientious worker. For the rest, she was a generous, patient, self-denying girl, transparently honest in word and deed; the gentle soul shining through its homely mask, like a candle in a bottle. Upon the whole, ugly, illiterate— and, above all, ill-starred, lowly, and defenceless—as she was, she would have made an admirable butt for the flea-power of your illustrated comic journal.

Mrs. Beaudesart abhorred Ida for her ugliness, for her vulgarity, for her simplicity, but chiefly for her name. (I can sympathise with the gentlewoman here—remembering how rancorously I once hated another boy because he came from the Isle of Wight.) Yet the two mammals' chronic state of friction was partly chargeable on Ida, who would answer back, in her own milk-and-water way. And, to add to the aggravation, she could n't answer back without crying.

Something had gone wrong, as usual, this morning; and Mrs. Beaudesart remained in the narangies' breakfast-room, mildly glowering into Ida's tear-stained face, and noting with polite deprecation the convulsive sobs which the sensitive girl vainly tried to repress before the young fellows. Beauty in distress is a favourite theme of your shallow romancists; but, to the philosophic mind, its pathos is nothing to that of ugliness in distress. At the best of times, poor Ida was heart-breaking; her sunniest smile wrung my soul with commiseration; and when the sympathy naturally accorded to helpless anguish was superimposed upon that which she claimed as her birthright, the pressure became intolerable. It had always been my consolation to think that she would yet be a bright and beautiful angel; and now I fell back for solace upon that thought—though how the thing was to be accomplished seemed a problem too vast for the grasp of a water-worn and partially dissolved understanding like mine.

"Remember, Mary, I reprimand you for your own good," murmured the lady. "Of course, brought up as you have been, you can't be expected to have the manners we look for in the servants of a well-conducted household; so when I consider it my duty to instruct you in the decencies of life, you must n't take it ill. People have to suffer for their ignorance, Mary, as well as for their faults. I know how you must feel it; but parents in the position that yours were in should send their children to service before they are too old for the necessary training."

"My parents done the best they could to keep theyre home together," protested the girl, in a choking voice.

"Speak grammatically, my dear. No doubt your parents did as you say, but my point is, that they forgot their position. Instead of accepting the fair wages and abundant food which society offers to their class, they joined the hungry horde that has cut up those fine Victorian stations. Part of the retribution justly falls on their children; part, of course, on themselves. Your father, I venture to say, often envied the life of the domestic animals on the station where he had selected. But he aimed at independence—independence! A fine word, Mary, but a poor reality. This idea of independence is much too common amongst people who, however poorly they may fare, are nevertheless better fed than taught. I 'm afraid you wilfully overlook the religious side of the question, Mary; the divine command to do our duty in that state of life in which it has pleased God to call us. Service is honourable"——

Here Ida sobbed out something that sounded like a rejoinder; and there was a harder ring in the lady's voice as she continued, without pausing:

"Yes, my dear; if your parents had known themselves, and had cheerfully remained in the position for which their birth and education fitted them, you would have been spared many humiliations, and it would have been better for your father, both in time and in eternity."

"O, can't you let him rest in his grave?" sobbed the girl.

"I have no wish to condemn him, Mary," replied the lady soothingly. "I assure you it is dreadful to me to realise the fate of that poor man, where the worm dieth not, and the fire is not quenched. I was only wishing to show you what a tempting of Providence it is for people of the lower classes to have notions above what their Maker intends for them. And you know how prone you are to forget your place—as you did this morning. Susan has the same fault, I 'm sorry to say; but I condone it to some extent in her. She has the advantage of good looks, and naturally expects to better her condition by marriage; but surely, Mary, one glance at yourself in the glass ought to show you the impropriety of counting upon any endowment of nature."

"Indeed, I know I 'm no beauty," blubbered Ida; and her tears rained hot and fast on the back of my neck, as she replaced my coffee-cup.

"Of course, you did n't make yourself," pursued the lady blandly; "but in view of your lack of personal attractions, you should endeavour to cultivate the modest and respectful demeanour which befits a sphere of life that you are likely to occupy permanently. No doubt it was good policy to transport yourself to a locality where the males of your own class are in such large majority; but the movement is still attended by certain disadvantages. A female whose looks approach repulsiveness should, at least, have a character beyond suspicion; and for any woman to run away from the neighbourhood where her doings are known, is not the way to inspire confidence. And though it has pleased God, for your own good, to remove the snare of beauty far from you, yet——Well, we must believe what we hear on good authority. Your master, before engaging you, should have made some inquiry regarding your antecedents, and not have left these things to leak-out. I wish I could hold you guiltless, Mary. Ask your own conscience whether you were justified in obtaining entry to an establishment like this. It places me in a very difficult"——

Here Ida turned, and, with blazing, tearless eyes, fearlessly fronted her fellow-mammal. The latter faltered, and paused. She had gone a step too far, and had trod on the lion's tail.

"What 's that you say, you wicked woman?" demanded Ida, in a calm voice, yet breathing heavily. "Ain't I miserable enough without you lyin' away my character? I 'll make you prove your words, as sure as you 're standin' there."

"You 're forgetting yourself!" replied the housekeeper haughtily, though still quailing before the girl's terrible plainness of speech and person.

"Am I, indeed? Well, we 'll both go straight to Mrs. Montgomery—she 's your missus as well as mine, she is—an' we 'll git her to write to a dozen people that knows me since I was n't as high as that windy-sill. I 'll make it hot for you, Mrs. Bodyzart, so I will."

"What impertinence!" ejaculated the lady, moistening her lips. "Leave the apartment, this instant, Mary; and send"——

"How dare you call me out o' my name?—for two pins, I 'd slap your face!" replied Ida, her voice rising to a hysterical scream. "You know what my proper name is, so you do! An' I won't leave the apartment to please you, so I won't! Think God made me for the likes o' you to wipe your feet on? Think I bin behavin' myself decent all my life, for you to put a slur on me? If I wanted to bemean myself, could n't I cast up somethin' you would n't like to be minded of? Ain't you ashamed o' yourself, you ole she-devil?"

"Gentlemen, I must apologise for my servant," said the housekeeper, with quiet dignity. "She seems to have taken leave of her senses. I trust you will overlook her rudeness. She knows no better."

"They can't help doin' me justice; an' that 's all I ask from anybody," rejoined Ida, looking appealingly round the table. "An' look here, Mrs. Bodyzart: I bin full up o' your nag-nag ever since I come to this house: an' I put up with it for the sake o' other people; but now you 've put a slur on my character; an' it 's me an' you for it. I ain't goin' to let this drop."

"I must withdraw, gentlemen," said the lady forbearingly. "Pray forget the unhappy scene you have been forced to witness; and let me beg of you, for this poor woman's sake, to leave all further pursuit of the matter entirely in my hands. Whilst she remains in this establishment, I must continue to shield her from the penalties to which she insists upon exposing herself. Come, Mary; dry your eyes, and attend to your duties. The time is coming when you will thank me for the discipline to which you are now subjected." And Mrs. Beaudesart retired, greater in defeat than in victory.

"I never expected anybody to put a slur on me," faltered Ida apologetically, after a minute's silence.

"Haud yir toang, lassie, fir Gode-sak," snarled the sheep-overseer, who was the senior of our company. "Be ma saul, an A hid ony say intil 't, A 'd whang the de'il oot o' ye baith wi' a stoke-whup."

"By George! you better not include Mrs. Beaudesart in your goodwill," remarked young Mooney gravely. "You 'll have Collins in your wool."

"Keep your temper, Collins," murmured Nelson. "I can imagine your feelings; but M'Murdo did n't think of you being here when he spoke."

"The de'il haet A care fir Collins, ony mair nir A dae fir yir ain sel', Nelson!" replied Mac defiantly. "Od! air ye no din greetin' the yet, lassie?" he continued, turning to Ida. "No anither pegh oot o' yir heed, ir bagode A 'll tak' ye in han'."

Ida dried her eyes, and with the more alacrity forasmuch as an approaching step crunched the gravel outside. It was Priestley, a bullock driver who had drawn up to the store on the previous evening; a decent sort of vulgarian, but altogether too industrious to get any further forward than the extreme tail-end of his profession.

Some carriers never learn the great lesson, that to everything there is a time and a season—a time for work, and a time for repose —hence you find the industrious man's inveterately leg-weary set of frames in hopeless competition with the judiciously lazy man's string of daisies. The contrast is sickening. Moreover, the same rule holds fairly well throughout the whole region of industry. But the Scotch-navigator can't see it. He is too furiously busy for eighteen hours out of the twenty-four to notice that, even in the most literal sense, loafing has a more intimate connection with bread-winning than working can possibly have. Such a man finds himself born unto trouble, as the sparks fly in all directions; but he is merely aware of undergoing a chastening process, just as the tethered calf is aware that he always turns a flying somersault when he impetuously charges in any direction away from his peg; and this simply because the man knows as much about the Order of Things as the calf knows about Euclid's definition of a radial line. The fact is, that the Order of Things—rightly understood—is not susceptible of any coercion whatever, and must be humoured in every possible way. In the race of life, my son, you must run cunning, reserving your sprint for the tactical moment. Priestley ran bull-headed. In consequence of being always at work, he could get very little work done; and, being pursuantly in a chronic state of debt and destitution, he got only the work that intermittently slothful men would n't take at the price. It is scarcely necessary to add that he had a wife and about thirteen small children, mostly girls.

"Mornin', chaps," said this plebeian, standing between the wind and our nobility, with a hand on each door-post. "Hope you 're enjoyin' yourselves. Say, Moriarty; I 'm waitin' to git that bit o' loadin' off."

"I 'll be with you in two minutes," replied the young storekeeper. "I know you always want to get away."

"Say, chaps," continued the bullock driver, advancing into the room, and glancing confidentially round the table, "think there's any use o' me stickin' up the boss for leaf to take the buggy-track to Nalrookar? See, I could make the Fog-a-bolla Tank to-night; an' there 's boun' to be a bit o' blue-bush, if not crows-foot, on them sand-hills. Then I 'd fetch Nalrookar to-morrow, easy. I got two-ton-five for there; an' I 'm thinkin' I 'll have a job to deliver it, if I can't git through your run. What do you think, chaps?"

"Why did n't you take this into consideration when you loaded?" demanded young Arblaster.

"Well, beggars ain't choosers," replied the apostle of brute force and ignorance. "Fact was, Arblaster, I bethought me what a lot o' work I 'd done for Magomery, one time or another, an' what good friends me an' him always was; an' I says to myself, 'Well, I 'll chance her—make a spoon, or spoil a horn.' That 's the way I reasoned it out. See, if I got to turn roun', an' foller the main track back agen to the Cane-grass Swamp, an' take the Nalrookar track from there, I won't fetch the station much short o' fifty mile; an' there ain't a middlin' camp the whole road. Everythin' et right into the ground. Starve a locust. 'Sides, I 'm jubious about the Convincer Sand-hill, even with half a load. Bullocks too weak."

"Well, it 's hardly likely the boss would let you cross the run," replied Arblaster. "He 'd be a d—d fool if he did."

"I 'm afraid there 's no use asking him, Priestley," added Nelson. "He won't make a thoroughfare of the run, at any price. For instance, when Baxter and Donovan delivered that well-timber in the Quondong Paddock, the other day, they were n't five mile from the main road—and a gate to go through—but he made them come right back by the station; thirty mile of a roundabout; and their cheques were n't forthcoming till they did it. No, Priestley; to ask Montgomery is simply to get a refusal; and to argue with him is simply to get insulted."

"Well, I s'pose I must worry through, some road," said the bullock driver resignedly, as he turned and went out.

"Fifty miles instead of twenty-two," remarked Mooney. "Hard enough case."

"And yet it 's necessary, in a sense," replied Nelson. "Same time, anybody except the like of Montgomery would spring a bit in a season like this. *I* could n't crush a poor, decent, hard-working devil like that. I 'd give him a thorough good blackguarding for calculating upon crossing the run; and then, as a matter of form,

I 'd send a man with him, to see him across. Well, I suppose we must go and get our *mot d' ordre*, boys."

So we left the breakfast-room to Ida. The four narangies, with the practical M'Murdo, went to the veranda of the boss's house for their day's orders; Moriarty, with a ring of keys in his hand, sauntered across to the store; and I managed to drag myself out to a seat built against the south side of the barracks, whence I torpidly surveyed the scene around, whilst listening to my vitality whistling out through four million yawning pores.

In an open shed, near the store—where two tribesmen were now assisting Priestley to unload—a travelling saddler and Salvationist, named (without a word of a lie) Joey Possum, was at work on the horse-furniture of the station; his tilted wagonette, blazoned with his name and title, JOSEPH PAWSOME, SADDLER, standing close by. Watching these lewd fellows of the baser sort at their sordid toil, my mind reverted to certain incidents of the preceding night, and so drifted into a speculation on the peculiar kind of difficulties which at certain times beset certain sojourners on the rind of this third primary orb. The incidents, of course, have nothing to do with my story.

But as the mere mention of them may have whetted the reader's curiosity, I suppose it is only fair to satisfy him.

The night in question seemed, from an astrological point of view, to be peculiarly favourable to the ascendancy of baleful influences. The moon hung above the western horizon, in her most formidable phase—just past the semicircle, with her gibbous edge malignantly feathered. Being now in the House of Taurus, she had overborne the benignant sway of Aldebaran, and was pressing hard on Castor and Pollux (in the House of Gemini). Also, her horizontal attitude was so full of menace that Rigel and Betelgeux (in Orion) seemed to wilt under her sinister supremacy. Sirius (in Canis Major), strongest and most malevolent of the astral powers, hung southwest of the zenith, reinforcing the evil bias of the time, and thus, from his commanding position, overruling the guardianship of Canopus (in Argo), south-west of the same point. Lower still, toward the south, Achernar seemed to reserve his gracious prestige, whilst, across the invisible Pole, the beneficent constellations of Crux and Centaurus exhibited the very paralysis of hopelessness. Worst of all, Jupiter and Mars both held aloof, whilst ascendant Saturn mourned in the House of Cancer.

Such was the wretched aspect of the heavens to my debilitated intelligence, as I slunk home from the swimming-hole, toward midnight. I was somewhat comforted to observe in Procyon a firmness which I attributed to the evident support of Regulus (in the House of Leo); but the most reassuring element in an extremely baleful horoscope was Spica (in the House of Virgo), scarcely affected by the moon's interference, and now ascending confidently from the eastern horizon.

Still, to my washed-out mind, there was something so hopeless in the lunar and stellar outlook that, for comfort, I turned my eyes toward the station cemetery, which was dimly in view.

There several shapeless forms, some white, and others of neutral hue, seemed to be moving slowly and silently amongst the dwellings of the dead, as if holding what you could scarcely call a carnival, in their own sombre way. The time, the place, the supermundane conditions, acting together on a half-drowned mind, gave to the whole scene a weird reality which writing cannot convey; so, after pinching myself to make sure I was awake, and doing a small sum in mental arithmetic to verify my sanity, I advanced toward the perturbed spirits, got them against the sky, and identified them as cattle, greedily stevedoring the long, dry grass.

It seemed a pity to turn the poor hungry animals out; yet I knew that somebody would have to suffer for it if Montgomery knew of anything trespassing here. But how had they got in, through seven wires—the upper one barbed—with rabbit-netting along the bottom?——

"Evenin', Collins."

"Evening, Priestley. Working the oracle?"

"Inclinin' that road. Dangerous—ain't it? Good job it 's on'y you. Nobody else stirrin'?"

"Not a soul. They 're as regular as clockwork on this station. How did you get in?"

"Took the hinges off o' the gate with my monkey-wrench. I 'll leave that all straight. Course, they 'll see the tracks by-'n'-by, an' know who to blame; but I 'll be clear by that time; an' I must guard agen comin' in contract with Runnymede till the st—nk blows off o' this transaction. Natural enough, Magomery 'll buck; but the ration-paddick's as bare as a stockyard; an' I can't ast the bullocks to die o' starvation."

"Certainly not, Priestley. Mind, it 's only four hours till daylight. Good night."

"Good night, ole man."

My way led me past a small, isolated stable, used exclusively for the boss's buggy-horses. Nearing this building, I heard a suppressed commotion inside, followed by soothing gibberish, in a very low voice. This was bad. Priestley's bullocks were within easy view; and Jerry, the groom, was a notorious master's man. I must have a friendly yarn with him.

"What's up with you this hour of the night, Jerry?" I asked, looking through the latticed upper-wall. "Uneasy conscience, I bet." Whilst speaking the last words, I distinguished Montgomery's pair of greys, tied, one in each back corner of the stable, whilst Pawsome's horses—a white and a piebald—were occupying the two stalls, and voraciously tearing down mouthfuls of good Victorian hay from the rack above the manger. Pawsome, silently caressing one of the greys, moved to the lattice on hearing my voice. "Sleight-of-hand work?" I suggested, in a whisper.

"Sort of attempt," replied the wizard, in the same key. "You gev me a start. All the lights was out two hours ago, an' I med sure everybody was safe."

"So they are. I 've only been down for a swim. Good-night, Possum."

"I say, Collins—don't split!"

"Is thy servant a dog, that he should do this great thing?"

"Second Kings," whispered the poor necromancer, in eager fellowship, and displaying a knowledge of the Bible rare amongst his sect. "God bless you, Collins! may we meet in a better world!"

"It won't be difficult to do that," I replied dejectedly, as I withdrew to enjoy my unearned slumber.

Now the night, replete with such sphere-music, was past, and the cares that infest the day had returned to everyone on the station, except myself and two or three equally clean, useless, and aristocratic loafers in the boss's house. Toby, the half-caste, was cantering away toward Clarke's, for the weekly mail. Priestley, at his wagon, was bullocking even more desperately than usual, with a view to getting out of sight of the station as soon as possible. Pawsome, repairing a side-saddle, on his extemporised bench, was softly crooning a familiar hymn, the sentiment of which seemed appropriate to himself, whilst the language breathed the very aroma of his social atmosphere:—

> Must I be carried to the skies
>   On flowery beds of ease,
> While others fought to gain the prize,
>   And sail'd through (adj.) seas?

In the veranda of the house, Mr. Folkestone, a young English gentleman of not less than two hundred-weight, lolled on a hammock, smoking a chibouque, and reading a magazine; while straight between us two aristocratic loafers, Vandemonian Jack, aged about a century, was mechanically sawing firewood in the hot, sickly sunshine. This is one of the jobs that it takes a man of four or five score years to perform ungrudgingly; and, to any illuminated mind, the secret of these old fellows' greatness is very plain. Bathing, though an ancient heresy, has been of strictly local prevalence, and, for the best of reasons, of transient continuance. Our relapse belongs to the present generation. Though our better-class grandsires understood no science unconnected with the gloves, a marvellous instinct taught them the unwholesomeness of sluicing away that panoply of dirt which is Nature's own defence against the microbe of imbecility, and which, indeed, was the only armour worn by the formidable Berserkers, from whom some of them claimed descent. We have done it however (at least, we say so), whilst our social inferiors have held on to the old-time religion (at least, we say so, here again); wherefore——

"I say, Mr. Collins," faltered Ida, breaking in on my reflections, "I picked up this little buckle aside o' your b——d; it 's come off o' the back o' your tr——rs. I 'll sew it on for you any time, for I notice you 're bothered with them slippin' down. O, Mr. Collins!" —and the poor unlovely face was suddenly distorted with anguish and wet with tears—"ain't Mrs. Bodyzart wicked to put a slur on me like that? There ain't one word o' truth in it; I 'd say the same if I was to die to-night; an' you may believe me or believe me not, but I 'm tellin' the truth. Far be it, indeed!"

"Hush! Stop crying, Ida! Don't look round—Mrs. Beaudesart's watching you from the window, over there. You poor thing! you should n't trouble yourself over what anybody says. Did you feed Pup this morning?"

"I give him a whole milk-dish full o' scraps; but if people tells the truth, there 's nobody in the world can say black is the white o' my eye; an' you may believe me or believe me not"——

"You 'll need to give Pup a drink, Ida."

"He 's got a dish o' good rain-water aside him; but if people would on'y consider"——

"True—very true. Now go away, dear, and don't come fooling about me, or you 'll give her liberty to talk."

The girl limped back to the scene of her unromantic martyrdom, and I made a feeble effort to shake the dew-drops from my mane, and, so to speak, look myself in the face. I must give this life over, I thought; and I will give it over; an I do not, I am a villain.

After all, there are not two sides to this question; there is only one; and you may trust an overclean man to be an authority on the evil effects of bathing, upon mind, body, and estate; just as the grogbibber is our highest authority on headaches, fantods, and bankruptcy.

The Spartans (so ran my reflections) were as much addicted to dirt as the Sybarites to cleanliness; and just compare the two communities. The conquering races of later ages—Goths, Huns, Vandals, Longobards, &c.—were no less celebrated for one kind of grit than for the other. It is the Turkish bath that has made the once-formidable Ottoman Empire the sick man of Europe. *Latifundia perdidere Italian* (Large estates ruined Italy). Yes. Blame it on the large estates. Would a large estate ruin you? Bathing did the business for Italy, as it does the business for all its victims. If Rome had left to the soft Capuan his baths and his perfumes, she would have pulled-through. But think of the polished Roman debating the question of survival with the superlatively dirty barbarian of the North! Polished is good, for, in the ruins of the fatal Roman baths, the innumerable *strigulæ*, used by the bathers to polish their skins, bear sad testimony to the suicidal cleanliness of that doomed race. And just compare your *strigula*-polished Roman, morally and physically, with his contemporary, the filth-encrusted anchorite of the Thebaid—the former flickering briefly in a puerile, semi-vital way, and going out with a sulphurous smell; the latter, on a ration of six dates per week, attaining an interminable longevity, and possessing the power of striking scoffers dead, or blind, or paralytic, at pleasure.

And, talking of hermits—do you think Peter of Picardy could have launched the muscular Christianity of Western Europe against the less muscular, because cleaner, Islamism of Western Asia, but for his well-advertised vow, never to change his clothes, nor wash himself, till his contract should be completed? Prouder in his rags than the Emperor in his purple! and justly too, for he achieved the very apotheosis of dirt—animate, no doubt, as well as inanimate. Or take the first Teutonic Emperor of Rome—conqueror, arbitrator, legislator, and what not. In those middle ages, you know, it was the custom to name monarchs from some peculiarity of person or habitude—and I put it to any reasonable soul; Was this mere Yarman Brince likely to have become the central figure of the 10th century, but for such rigid abstinence from external application of water as is implied in the significent name of Otto the Great?

Indeed, the most sweepingly appropriate bestowal of the title,

'Great,' is made when we refer to the adherents of the dirt-cult, collectively, as the Great Unwashed. Again, Dr. Johnson's biographies lovingly preserve the personal habits of most of the loftiest and sweetest poets that ever trod English soil; and think what a large percentage of those Muse-invokers, according to their historian, carried a fair quantity of that soil perennially on their hides. And speaking of the Diogenes of Fleet Street himself, we know, on good authority, that his antipathy to the Order of the Bath caused him to appeal to more senses than one. He was another Otto the Great. The original Diogenes, by the way, revelled in dirt, as well as in wisdom. And the mighty scholar, Porson, as you may remember, never needed to wash, because he never perspired.

Yet in spite of this cloud of witnesses, and in the face of our own experience, we *will* entice external leakage of such incipient greatness as we have—soaking ourselves in water, as if we were possums, and our virility a eucalyptus flavour that we sought to dissipate. Look at myself—now a king; now thus! Thunder-and-turf! have I fallen so low? And yet I was once like our Otto and Co.!

Before touching the forbidden thing, I felt as if I wanted to pursue an aspiring, if purposeless, journey up uncomfortable Alpine heights, with my Excelsior-banner in my hand, and a tear in my solitary bright blue eye; now, the maiden's invitation seems to be the only part of the enterprise that has any pith in it. Then, I gloried in the fiendish adage of, 'Two hours' sleep for a man, three for a woman, and four for a fool'; now, my liveliest ambition is to gaze my fill on yon calm deep, then, like an infant, sink asleep on this form, and so remain till dinner-time—lunch-time, I should say; belonging, as I do, to the better classes. Then, I was like Hotspur on his crop-eared roan; now, I merely wish the desert were my dwelling-place, with one fair Spirit for my minister. To confess the truth, I note a certain weak glimmer of self-righteousness investing the thought that I would be content with one fair Spirit. Go to, go to! By virtue, thou enforcest laughter.

"I wish I was as happy as you," murmured Ida, who had again silently approached. "Here 's two newspapers; they done with them in the house. O, Mr. Collins!"—and the girl's tears broke forth afresh, whilst ungovernable sobs shook her from head to foot—"I can't git it off o' my mind what Mrs. Bodyzart said."

"Ida! Ida!" I remonstrated; "you 're making your nose red." The information acted like a charm; her crying was over, though she still persisted in chewing her grievance.

"I can prove there ain't one word o' truth in it," she continued pertinaciously.

"What 's your idea of proof, Ida?"

"I can prove it on the Bible," she replied eagerly.

"That settles the matter beyond controversy—considering that you rightly belong to the Middle Ages."

"Indeed I don't!" she replied, with a flash of resentment. "I was twenty-seven last birthday; an' I don't care who knows it—on the third of July, it was—an' I would n't care tuppence if her lady-ship snoke roun' tellin' people I was forty. But to put a slur on me like that! I leave it to your own self, Mr. Collins—was it right?"

"Right?" I repeated wearily. "In heaven's name, girl, what does it signify to you whether it was right or otherwise? That 's Mrs. Beaudesart's own business, not yours. Why, if she charged me with stooping to folly, I would merely say, 'Sorry to undeceive you, ma'am; but I 've been too much given to letting "I dare not" wait upon "I would," like the poor bandicoot i' the adage.' But I certainly should n't concern myself with a question lying entirely between herself and Saint Peter."

"Ah! but you 're different," replied the girl sadly.

"Simply because I 'm a philosopher, Ida. I 've held communion with the Unfathomable, and watched the exfoliation of the Inscrutable; and, you know, these things are altogether beyond the orbit of the girl-mind. Now clear off, like a good fellow, and let me read the papers."

But I was too far gone to take any interest in either of the loathsome contemporaries; too much afflicted even to drift down to the swimming-hole again, much as I desired to do so. I also longed for the opinion of my mighty pipe on the dirt-question; but that faithful ally was packed among my things, forty feet away, and it might as well have been forty miles. So I just lay on the seat, clean, frail, and inert, as a recumbent statue, moulded in blanc-mange; whilst the ancient t'other-sider oscillated his frame-saw, and the pious Pawsome lightened his toil with selections from Sankey, and the perspiring Priestley hurried up his bullocks from the ration-paddock, and Sling Muck, the gardener, used his hoe among the callots and cabbagee, with the automatic stroke of a man brought up to one holiday per annum, and no Sunday. Meanwhile, the unreturning sands of Life dribbled through the unheeded isthmus of the Present Moment; and the fixed cone of the Past expanded; and the dimple deepened in the diminished and hurrying Future.

Nevertheless, I collected the wreckage of what had been very fair faculties, and attempted to grapple with an idea which Ida's conversation had suggested. Finding this impossible, I made a mental memo. of the inspiration—and by the same token, I neatly utilised it within the next few hours. Your attention will be drawn to the circumstance in due season.

At mid-day, the bell sounded from the hut. Pawsome and the tribesmen quitted their work, and went to dinner. Priestley had started an hour before, bound for Nalrooka, with the remaining half of his load.

All the Levites, except Moriarty, were out on the run, but Martin, the head boundary rider, had timed himself for lunch. This man's status was a vexed question. He certainly rated—but did he rate high enough for the barracks? As head boundary man, decidedly not; but as recent proprietor of a small station absorbed by Runnymede, he was not destitute of pretensions. Out in the open air, he was, of course, as good as any Levite, but——Well, though we rather resented his presence in the Inner Court, we yielded him the benefit of the doubt; and he took that benefit, just as if he had been born in the purple, like ourselves.

Martin was an Orangeman of rank. He had attained the Black Degree. It was whispered that he held all the loyal brethren of Riverina under the whip, by reason of his being the only man in the region beyond the Murrumbidgee who could confer the Purple Degree. For, owing to an inherent haziness in the theses and aims of Orangeism, there are Orders in the Society as hard to attain as those German university degrees which no man ever took and had his eyesight perfect afterwards; though, to be sure, there is a certain difference in the relative value of the two species of attainment.

Moriarty—whose front name was Felix—was, if anything, a Catholic; and, partly on this account, partly on account of his being a young fellow, and partly on account of Miss King, the governess, Martin set him. Now, there was just one man within a hundred miles who knew less of Irish History than Martin, and that man was Moriarty; consequently, the two jostled each other as they rushed into that branch of learning where scholars fear to tread— each repeatedly appealing to me for confirmation of his outlandish myths and clumsy fabrications. I listlessly confirmed anything and everything. Having lost all mental, as well as physical, energy where King John lost his regalia, namely, in the Wash, the line of least resistance was the line for me.

After a hearty lunch, I made my way back to the seat against the wall, while Moriarty lounged across to the store, and Martin went to speak to the High Priest at the door of the Sanctum Sanctorum. Then Martin mounted his horse, and rode away; and presently the tribesman, Jerry, brought a buggy and pair to the front door. Montgomery and Folkestone—the latter in knickerbockers—took their seats in the buggy, and whirled away down the horse-paddock fence. Then all was still, save for the faint pling-plong of a piano in the Holy of Holies.

Whom have we here? Moriarty to disturb me. Let him come. It is meat and drink to me to see a clown; by my faith, we that have good wits have much to answer for; we shall be flouting; we cannot hold.——

The young Levite, closing the door of the store behind him, advanced with the indescribably weary step of a station man when the day is warm and the boss absent, and seated himself by my side.

"Why ain't you in the barracks having one of your quiet palavers with Mrs. Beaudesart?" he asked.

"Prithee be silent, boy; I profit not by thy talk," I murmured.

"Something I wanted to ask you, Collins," he resumed; "but I 'm beggared if I can think what it is. Slipped away like a snake, while you 're looking round for a stick. Singular how a person can't remember a thing for the life of them, when once they forget it; and suddenly it crops up of its own accord when you 're not thinking of it."

"Parse that," said I, listlessly.

"Parse your granny!" he retorted. "I don't believe you could parse it yourself, as clever as you think you are. Beggar conceitedness; beggar everything. I wish I was about forty."

"And know as much as you do now?" I barely articulated.

"Yes—and know as much as I do now," he repeated doggedly. "In fact, I never met anyone that knows as much as I do; but people won't pay any attention to a young fellow, no matter if he was Solomon. That Martin wants a lift under the ear."

"Does he?" I asked faintly. "I did n't hear him express the desire."

"Gosh! you 've been on the turkey; you 'll be cutting yourself some of these times. I wish Toby was back with the mail. I hope he 'll forget to ask for your letters."

"Now the Lord lighten thee; thou art a great fool," I sighed. "What time does Toby generally get back?"

"Any time between two in the afternoon and sunrise next morning, according to the state of the mailman's horses. Beggar such a life as this. At it, early and late; working through accounts, and serving-out rations, and one thing or another; and no more chance of distinguishing myself than if I was in jail. I can't stand it much longer, and what 's more, I won't. I wish the mail was in. I 've got a presentiment of something good this time. If you don't speculate, you won't accumulate, as the saying is; and if a man can't make a rise by some sort of gambling, he may as well lie down and die, straight-off. But the first rise is the difficulty; and, of course, you 've got to take the risk."

"What do you do with the rise when you get it?" I asked, drowsily.

"Why, distinguish yourself, of course—what else? There 's a great future sticking out for a fellow, if he 's got his head screwed on right."

"So there is. Well, what shall it be? Mechanics? Fine opening for an inventive genius there—but you must be up and doing, as the poet says."

"You had all the chances when you were my age," replied Moriarty bitterly. "I 'm too late arriving. Everything 's invented now."

"True," I observed. "I had n't thought of that objection. Then why not take up some interesting study, and work it out from post to finish? Political Economy, for instance?"

"Anybody could do that," replied the young fellow contemptuously. "*I* want to distinguish myself."

"Then I 'll tell you what you 'll do, Moriarty. Take a narrow branch of some scientific study, and restrict yourself to that. Say you devote your life to some special divisoin of the *Formicæ*?"

"The what?"

"*Formicæ.* The name is plural. It embraces all the different species of ants."

"Why, there 's only about three species of ants altogether; and there 's nothing to learn about them except that they make different kinds of hills, and give different kinds of bites. That sort of study would about suit you. Fat lot of distinction a person could get out of ants."

"Still, every avenue to distinction is not closed," I urged. "We 're knocking at the gates of Futurity for the Australian pioneer of poetry—fiction—philosophy—what not? You 've got all the working plant ready in your office. There you are!"

"No use, Collins," he replied hopelessly. "I 've got the talent, right enough, but I have n't got the patience. In fact, I 'm too dash lazy."

"Charge it on the swimming-hole, brother," I sighed.

"No; I can't very well do that. I have n't been there for the last month. I 'd go to-night if I had a horse."

"Heavens above!" I murmured; "what would he be like if he was clean? He would distinguish himself in one direction. The material is there."

"Jealousy, jealousy," replied Moriarty disgustedly. "Never mind. "I 'll make things hum yet. Do you know—I stand to win twenty-four notes on the regatta, besides my chance of the station sweep on the big Flemington, let alone private bets. We 'll get news of both events to-day; and I have a presentiment of something good. Gosh! I wish Toby was here!"

"And how much do you stand to lose, if your mozzle is out?" I asked. "By-the-way, did n't I incidentally hear that you were playing cards all last Sunday?"

"I don't believe that has anything to do with it," replied Moriarty, in an altered tone. "But, to tell you the truth, I dare n't count up how much I 'll lose if things go crooked. I 've plunged too heavy —there 's no doubt about that—but I did it with the best intention. I made sure of scooping; and, for that matter, I make sure of it still. But whatever you do, don't begin to preach about the evils of gambling—not now, Collins; not till after we get news of these events. Does n't everybody gamble, from the Governor downward —bar you, and a couple or three more sanctimonious old hypocrites, with one foot in the grave, and the other in the devil's mouth? Why, Nosey Alf is the only fellow on this station that has no interest in the sweep, besides no end of private bets."

"Is n't that Toby?" I asked, indicating a horseman, half-a-mile away.

"Gosh, yes!" replied Moriarty nervously. "I wonder what brings him from that direction? Come, Collins—will you give me five to one he has letters for you? I 'll take it at that."

"Indeed you won't, sonny."

"Well, let 's have some wager before he gets any nearer," persisted Moriarty, with an unpleasant laugh. The suspense was beginning to tell upon a mind not originally cast in the Stoic mould. So much so, that I felt inclined to lose a trifle to him, even as a tee-

totaller would administer a nip to a man who was beginning to see
things. "Come!" he continued recklessly; "I 'll give you two to one
he has letters for you; twenty to one he has letters for the station"
——And so he gabbled on, whilst, drifting into my Hamlet-mood, I
charted the poor fellow's mind for my own edification.

"Hold on, Moriarty," I interrupted, recalling myself. "Let 's hear
that fifty-to-one offer again. Am I to understand that if Toby has
letters for the station and none for me, you win; if he has letters for
me and none for the station, *I* win; and, failing the fulfilment of
either double, the wager is off?"

"That 's it. Are you on?"

"Make it a hundred to one."

"Done! at a hundred to one—in what?"

"Half-sovereigns," I replied, feeling for the purse which, vulgar
as it is, bushmen even of aristocratic lineage are compelled to carry.
I placed the little coin—about one-tenth of my total wealth—in
Moriarty's hand. He shrank from the touch.

"What do you mean?" he asked petulantly. "I might n't win it,
after all. Don't be more disagreeable than you can help."

"You intend to get it without giving an equivalent—don't you?
You know it 's yours. Are n't you betting on a certainty? Lay it on
the window-sill, if you like, and pick it up when you can read your
title clear. If you don't speculate, you won't accumulate; and I suppose you 've no objection to looking into the morality of your speculation"——

I had cleared my throat for a disquisition which would have been
intolerable to the unprincipled reader, when a very curious thing
arrested the attention both of Moriarty and myself—the strangest
coincidence, perhaps, within the personal experience of either of us
—a conjuncture, in fact, which for a moment threw us both staggering back on the theology of childhood. At the present time, I feel
too meek to attempt any unravelment, and too haughty to offer any
apology other than that such is life.

The half-caste had cantered up to the horse-paddock gate, had
dismounted, had divested his horse of the saddle and bridle, and had
given the animal a slap with the latter. Now he was depositing those
equipments in the shed. Now he approached us, taking two letters
and a newspaper from the tail-pocket of what had once been an
expensive dress-coat of Montgomery's.

"Yours, Collins," said he. "Don't say I never gave you nothing.
Nix for you, Mr. (adj.) Moriarty."

"You 're very laconic," observed the storekeeper in a hollow voice, yet eyeing the prince sternly; "very laconic, indeed, I must say. If I was you, I would n't be quite so laconic. How the (sheol) comes it that you did n't fetch the mail?"

"Need n't look in that paper for the Flemington, Collins," said the heir-apparent; "she 's a day too soon. I took a squint at her, comin' along."

"I was asking how the (adj. sheol) you managed to come without the mail?" repeated Moriarty, with dignity.

"I heard you, right enough. I ain't deaf. Well, I come on a moke. Think I padded it? Fact was, Moriarty, I met Magomery at Bailey's Tank, an' he told me go like blazes to Scandalous Sandy's hut, on Nalrooka, an' tell him a lot o' his sheep was boxed with ours in the Boree Paddick. 'I 'll fetch the mail home myself,' says he. There now."

"And why did n't you go to Scandalous Sandy's?" nagged Moriarty.

"Well, considerin' you 're boss o' this station, an' my bit o' filthy lucre comes out o' your pocket, I got great pleasure informin' you I met ole Gladstone, comin' to tell us the same yarn. Anything else you want to know?"

"Did you hear which crew won the regatta?" asked Moriarty, almost civilly.

"Sydney," replied the prince. "Think you Port Phillipers could lick *us*?"

"That 's a lie!" exclaimed Moriarty, catching his breath.

"Right. It 's a lie, if you like. I got no stuff on it. See what Collins's paper says. An' now I feel like as if I could do a bit o' dinner—unless you got any objections?"

He stalked away toward the hut, whilst I opened what turned out to be a love-letter—evidently intended for some other member of our diffusive clan, for I could make neither head nor tail of it; nothing, indeed, but heart, and such heart as it has never been my luck to capture. Meanwhile, Moriarty had cut the string of the newspaper, and was running his eye over its columns.

"My mozzle is out, Collins," said he, with an effort. "I 'll never clear myself—never in the creation of cats. It 's all up!"

"Yes; you suffer by comparison with the sanctimonious old hypocrites now," I replied, in a fatherly tone, as I took the half-sovereign from the window-sill. "Feel something like an overproof idiot—don't you? We 'll talk about that presently. But see what I 've got here."

My second letter ran:—

K3769
No. 256473

Central Office of Unconsidered Trifles,
Sydney, February 1, 1884.

Mr. T. Collins.

Sir,—I am directed to inform you that the Deputy-Commissioner purposes visiting Nyngan on the 17th prox. You are required to attend the Office of the Department in that township at 11 a.m. on the day above mentioned, to furnish any information which he may require.

I am, Sir,
Ynnnnnnnnnnnly
MMMnnynnlnny
pro Assistant-Under-Secretary.

"Not a whisper about the M form," I remarked. "Perhaps it 's in your mail. No odds. Montgomery can complete it, and send it on, just as well as if I had n't been near the place at all. But here 's something like two hundred and thirty miles to be done in seven days—and the country in such a state. This is the balsam that the usuring senate pours into captains' wounds. Never mind. The time is only too near, when I 'll sit in my sumptuous office, retaliating all this on some future Deputy-Assistant-Sub-Inspector. And, in the meantime, this long dusty ride will make a man of me once more. I must start at once; and I could do with some money. Moriarty, you 're owing me fifty notes."

"I know I am," replied the storekeeper, in a quivering voice. He was as punctiliously honourable in some ways as he was perfidious in others—being amiably asinine in each extreme.

"Now, including your little liability to me, how much are you out, even if the Flemington gamble goes in your favour?" I asked.

"Only sixty-eight notes," he faltered. "I 'll clear it, right enough, if I 'm not rushed, and if I don't get the sack off the station."

"But, by every rule of analogy, you 're also badly left on the Flemington," I continued serenely. "How much does that leave you out?"

"Ninety-seven notes, and my rifle," he replied, steadying his voice by an effort. "Mad—mad—mad! I wish I were dead!"

"Will you swear off gambling altogether till my claim is discharged? On that condition, I can extend the time—say to the Greek Kalends."

"If you think I could raise the money by that time," replied the poor fellow dubiously. "Anyway, I give you my solemn promise.

But, I say," he continued, with seeming irrelevance—"when do you
expect promotion?"

"At any moment. My presentiments, being based on the deepest
inductions of science, and the subtlest intuitions of the higher
philosophy, are a trifle more trustworthy than yours; and I have a
presentiment that the thing is impending. But you need n't congratulate me yet. Think about yourself."

"That 's just what I 'm doing. If you tell her about this wager,
I 'll suicide, or clear."

"Well, upon my word! Do you think I'd condescend to under-
mine you, you storekeeper? Look out for Martin; never mind me."

"I don't mean her," mumbled the young fool; "I mean Mrs.
Beaudesart. You 're going to marry her when you get your promotion—ain't you?"

There was such evident sincerity in his tone that I maintained a
stern and stony silence, whilst his eyes met mine with a doubtful,
deprecating look; then he remarked doggedly,

"Well, that 's what she told Mrs. Montgomery, last Sunday; and
she said it seriously. Miss King was present at the time; and she
told Butler, and Mooney, and me, across the gate of the flower-
garden, the same evening. Mrs. Beaudesart takes it for granted,
and so does everybody else. She says she accepted you some time
ago."

"You lying dog!" I remarked wearily.

"I hope I may never stir alive off this seat if I 'm not telling
you the exact truth. Ask Mooney or Butler."

"If I do sleep, would all my wealth would wake me," I murmured, half-unconsciously.

"You don't want to marry her, then, after all?"

"How long do you suppose I would last?"

"Well, *don't* marry her."

"Does it occur to you," I asked, with some bitterness, "that there
are some things a person can do, and some things he can't do? If
the head of my Department orders me to Nyngan, I can reply by
letter, telling him to mind his own business, and not concern himself about me; but if Mrs. Beaudesart assumes—if she merely takes
for granted—that I 'm going to marry her, I must do it, to keep
her in countenance. How, in the fiend's name, can I slink out of it,
now that I 'm accepted? Can I tell her I 've examined my heart,
and I find I can only love her as a sister? Now, would n't that
sound well? No, no; I 'm a done man. Of course, she had no
business to accept me unawares; but as she has done so, I must help

her to keep up the grisly fraud of feminine reluctance; for, as the abbot sings, so must the sacristan respond. It is kismet. This is how all these unaccountable marriages are brought about; though, to be sure, I have the dubious satisfaction of knowing that the enterprise brings me a good many days' march nearer home."

The expression of heavenly beatitude on Moriarty's face goaded my mind to activity. Sweeping, with one glance, the whole horizon of expediency and possibility, I caught sight of the idea glanced at in a former page, and suggested, you will remember, by my dialogue with Ida.

"By the way, Moriarty," said I; "respecting that trifling debt of honour—there 's another condition that I did n't think of. As a sort of payment on account, you must privately and insidiously circulate a very grave scandal for me."

"Well, I won't!" exclaimed the young fellow, after a moment's pause. "I don't mind telling a lie when I 'm driven to it; but a woman's a woman. Do your own dirty work!"

"Then, by Jove, I 'll post you!"

If anyone had used this threat to me, I would have asked how the posting was usually done, and what results might be expected to follow; but Moriarty's lip quivered under the threat.

"Do your worst," said he, swallowing the lump in his throat.

"You may depend on that," I replied quietly. "However, the scandal was only about myself."

"I don't understand."

"I 'll enlighten you. I was going to ask you to take Nelson, or Mooney, or both of them, into your confidence. Then you would arrange that Mrs. Beaudesart should overhear you discussing some horrible scandal in connection with me. And mind, she would have to believe it, or you would be a ruined man for the rest of your life—you would be a defaulting gambler, a byword, a hissing, an astonishment, with the curse of Cain upon your brow. Then she would spurn me with contumely, and I would be my own man again. I would be in sanctuary, so to speak; inviolable by reason of my disgrace. Metaphorically, you could lay the blast, and fire it at your leisure, in my absence. I would leave all details to your own judgment, only holding you responsible for quality of fuse, and quantity of powder. I 'd stand the explosion."

"I 'm on!" exclaimed Moriarty, brightening up. "Gosh! I 'll give you a character to rights! Mind, it 'll make you look small."

"The smaller the better. I have a small aperture to crawl through, and no other means of escape. Of course, being innocent all the time, the scandal won't even fizz on my inner consciousness. In fact, I 'll feel myself taking a rise out of everyone that believes the yarn; and I 'll live it down in good time. Now lay your plans carefully, Moriarty, and make a clean job of it, for your own sake."

This being definitely settled, I soon demonstrated to the young fellow that his case, as regarded other liabilities, was by no means desperate; and his elastic temperament asserted itself at once. I may add, in passing, that he has never broken his anti-gambling pledge; also, that my £50 remains unpaid to this day.

"Now I must go and catch my horses," said I. "Can you come?"

"Hold on," replied Moriarty; "here comes Toby; we 'll send him."

As the half-caste lounged out of the front door of the hut, the cook went out by the back door, and gathered an armful of firewood. Toby turned, and glided back into the hut, and, a moment later, the cook also re-entered, at the opposite side. Then the prince bounded out through the front door, with a triumphant grin on his brown face, and an enormous cockroach of black sugar in his hand. The next moment, a piece of firewood whizzed through the open door, smote H.R.H. full on Love of Approbation, ricochetted from his gun-metal skull, and banged against the weatherboard wall of an out-house.

"Will yo ever go home, I dunno?" laughed the prince, picking up his hat, while the baffled cook recovered his stick, and returned to the hut.

"Now what 's the use of arguing that a blackfellow belongs to the human race?" queried Moriarty—the last ripple of trouble having vanished from the serene shallowness of his mind. "That welt would have laid one of us out. And did you ever notice that a blackfellow or a half-caste can always clear himself when his horse comes down? The first thing a whitefellow thinks about, when he feels his horse gone, is to get out of the way of what 's coming; but it 's an even wager that he 's pinned. Never so with the inferior race. Now, last Boxing Day, when we had races here, we could see that the main event rested between Admiral Rodney—a big chestnut, belonging to a cove on a visit to the boss—with Toby in the saddle; and that grey of M'Murdo's, Admiral Crichton, with"——

"Repeat that last name, please?"

"Admiral Cry-ton. That slews you! Did n't I tell you you 'd be cutting yourself? It 's M'Murdo's own pronunciation; and if he does n't know the proper twang, I 'm dash well sure you don't; for he owns the horse. But was n't it a curious coincidence of name—

considering that neither the owners nor the horses had ever met before? Well, Young Jack was to ride Admiral Crichton; and I had such faith in the horse, with Jack up, that I plunged thundering heavy on him. So did Nelson. But, by jingo, the more we saw of Admiral Rodney, the more frightened we got—in fact, we could see there was nothing for it but to stiffen Toby. Toby was to get a note if he won the big event, and nothing if he lost; but it paid us to give him two notes to run cronk"——

"One moment," I interrupted—"just oblige me with the name and address of that horse's owner?"

"Shut-up. It 's blown over now. But as I was telling you, the chestnut had been a few times round the course, under the owner's eye, and he knew the road; and to make matters better, you might break the reins, but you could n't get a give out of his mouth; and he could travel like a rifle-bullet; so when Toby tried to get him inside the posts, he pulled and reefed like fury, and bolted altogether; and came flying into the straight, a dozen lengths to the good. Of course, losing the race made a difference of a note to Toby; so he caught the horse's shoulder with his spur, and turned him upside down, going at that bat. Then, to keep himself out of a row, he gammoned dead till we poured a pint of beer down his throat; and he lay groaning for two solid hours, winking now and then at Nelson and me. But that 'll just tell you the difference. Neither you nor I would be game to do a thing like that; we could n't be trained to it; simply because we belong to a superior race. I say, Toby!"—for the half-caste had seated himself near Pawsome's bench, and was there enjoying his cockroach—"off you go, like a good chap, and fetch Collins's horses."

"Impidence ain't worth a d—n, if it ain't properly carried out," replied the inferior creation. "Think you git a note a week jist for eatin' your (adj.) tucker an' orderin' people about? I done my day's work. Fork over that plug o' tobacker you 're owin' me about the lenth o' that snake. Otherways, shut up. We ain't on equal terms while that stick o' tobacker 's between us."

"I 'll straighten you some of these times," replied Moriarty darkly. "It 's coming, Toby!"

"No catchee, no havee, ole son!" laughed the prince. "The divil resave ye, Paddy! Macushla, mavourneen, tare-an'-ouns! whirroo! Bloody ind to the Pope!"

"Toby," said Moriarty, with a calmness intended to seem ominous; "if I had a gun in my hand, I 'd shoot you like a wild-dog. But I suppose I 'd get into trouble for it," he continued scornfully.

"Jist the same 's for layin' out a whitefeller," assented the prince, still rasping at his cockroach, like Ugolini at the living skull of Ruggieri, in Dante's airy conception of the place where wrongs are rectified. (That unhappy mannerism again, you see.)

"Permit me to suggest," said Moriarty, after a pause, "that if you contemplated your own origin and antecedents, it would assist you to approximate your relative position on this station. Don't you think a trifle of subordination would be appropriate to"——

"A servile and halting imitation of Mrs. B.; and imitation is the sincerest flattery," I commented. "I 'll tell Miss K."

"Manners, please!—Appropriate, I was saying, to a blasted varmin like you? Permit me to remind you that Mrs. Montgomery, senior, gave a blanket for you when you were little."

"I know she did," replied the prince, with just a suspicion of vain-glory. "Nobody would be fool enough to give a blanket for you when you was little. Soolim!"

"Come on, Moriarty," said I, rising; "I must take a bit off the near end of my journey to-night."

"Howld your howlt, chaps," interposed the good-natured half-caste. "I 'll run up your horses for you. I was on'y takin' a rise out o' Mr. Mori-(adj.)-arty, Esquire; jist to learn him not to be quite so suddent." And in another minute, he was striding down the paddock, with his bridle and stockwhip.

Half an hour later, my horses were equipped; and, all the Levites being absent, four or five tribesmen slowly collected under Pawsome's shed, waiting to see what would happen. Cleopatra was not without reputation.

"Tell you what you better do," said Moriarty to me—"better hang your socks on Nosey Alf's crook to-night. His place is fifteen mile from here, and very little out of your way. Ill-natured, cranky beggar, Alf is—been on the pea—but there 's no end of grass in his paddock. And I say—get him to give you a tune or two on his fiddle. Something splendid, I believe. He 's always getting music by post from Sydney. Montgomery had heard him sing and play, some time or other; and when old Mooney was here, just before last shearing, he sent Toby to tell Alf to come to the house in the evening, and bring his fiddle; and Alf came, very much against his grain. Young Mooney was asked into the house, on account of his dad being there; and he swears he never heard anything like Alf's style; though the stubborn devil would n't sing a word; nothing but play. And he was just as good on the piano as on the fiddle, though his hand must have been badly out. Mooney thinks he jibbed on singing because the women were there. Alf 's a mis—mis—mis—dash it"——

"Mischief-maker?" I suggested.

"No.—Mis—mis"——

"Mysterious character?"

"No, no.—Mis—mis"——

"Try a synonym."

"Is that is? I think it is. Well Alf 's a misasynonym—woman-hater—among other things. When he comes to the station, he dodges the women like a criminal. And the unsociable dog begged of Montgomery not to ask him to perform again. One night, Nelson was going past his place, and heard a concert going on, so he left his horse, and sneaked up to the wall; but the music suddenly stopped, and before Nelson knew, Nosey's dog had the seat out of his pants. Nosey came out and apologised for the dog, and brought Nelson in to have some supper; and Nelson stayed till about twelve; but devil a squeak of the fiddle, or a line of a song, could he get out of Alf. But, as the boss says, Alf 's only mad enough to know the difference between an eagle-hawk and a saw—foolish expression, it seems to me. Best boundary man on the station, Alf is. Been in the Round Swamp Paddock five years now; and he 's likely a fixture for life. Boundary riding for some years in the Bland country before he came here. Now I 'll show you how you 'll fetch his place"—Moriarty began drawing a diagram on the ground with a stick—"You go through the Red Gate—we 'll call this the gate. The track branches there; and you follow this branch. It 's the Nalrooka track; and it takes you along here—mind, you 're going due east now"——

"Wait, Moriarty," I interrupted—"don't you see that you 're reversing everything? A man would have to stand on his head to understand that map. There is the north, and here is the south."

"Don't matter a beggar which is the real north and south. I 'm showing you the way you 've got to go. We 'll start afresh to please you. Through here—along here—and follow the same line from end to end of the pine-ridge, with the fence on your right all the way"——

"Hold on, hold on," I again interrupted—"you 're at right angles now. Don't you see that your line 's north and south?—and did you ever see a pine-ridge running north and south? Begin again. Say the Red Gate is here; and I turn along here. Now go ahead."

"No, I 'm dashed if I do! I 'm no hand at directing; but, by gosh, you 're all there at understanding."

"Jack," said I, turning to the primeval t'other-sider—"can you direct me to Nosey Alf's?"

"I 'll try," replied the veteran; and he slowly drew a diagram, true to the points of the compass. " 'Ere 's the Red Gate—mind you shet it—then along 'ere, arf a mile. Through this gate—an' mind 'ow you leave 'er, f'r the wire hinclines to slip hover. Then straight along 'ere, through the pine-ridge, f'm hend to hend. You 're hon the Nalrookar track, mind, t' wot time you see a gate hin the fence as you 're a-kerryin' hon yer right shoulder. Gate 's sebm mile f'm 'ere. Nalrookar track goes through that gate; b't neb' you mind; you keep straight ahead pas' the gate, hon a pad you 'll 'ar'ly see; han jist hat the fur hend o' the pine-ridge you 'll strike hanuther gate; an' you mus' be very p'tic'lar shettin' 'er. Then take a hangle o' fo'ty-five, with the pine-ridge hon yer back; an' hin fo' mile you 'll strike yer las' gate—'ere, hin the co'ner. Take this fence hon yer right shoulder, an' run 'er down. B't you 'll spot Half's place, fur ahead, w'en you git to the gate, ef it ain't night."

"Thank you, Jack," I replied, and then imprudently continued— "It would suit some of these young pups to take a lesson from you."

"You hain't fur wrong," replied the good old chronicle, that had so long walked hand in hand with Time. "Las' year, hit war hall the cry, 'Ole hon t' we gits a holt o' Cunnigam's mongreals!'— 'Ole hon t' we gits a holt o' Thompson's mongreals!'—'We 'll make hit 'ot f'r 'em!' Han wot war the hupshot? 'Stiddy!' ses Hi— 'w'e 's y' proofs?' 'Proof be dam!' ses they—'don't we know?' They know a 'ell of a lot! Has the sayin' his:—'Onct boys was boys, an' men was men; but now boys his men, an' men 's"—— (I did n't catch the rest of the sentence). "Han what were the hup-shot? W'y, fact was Cunnigam an' Thompson 'ad bin workin' hon hour ram-paddick wun night; an' six Wogger steers got away, an' a stag amongst 'em; makin' f'r home; an' they left a whaler mindin' the wagons; an' the two o' them hover'auled the steers way down hin hour Sedan Paddick. Well, heverybody—Muster Magomery his self, no less—heverybody ses, 'Ole hon t' we gits a holt of 'em fellers' mongreals!—bin leavin' three o' hour gates hopen; an' the yowes an' weaners is boxed; an' puttin a file through Nosey Half's 'oss-paddick, an' workin' hon it with 'er steers!' 'Stiddy!' ses Hi— 'w'e 's y'r proofs?' Way it war, Collings; 'ere come a dose o' rain jis' harter, an' yer could n't track. Well, wot war the hupshot? W'y, Warrigal Half war hunloadin' hat Boottara; an' a yaller bullick 'e 'd got, Pilot by name"——

"Yes," I gently interposed. "Well, I 'll have to be"——

" 'Is Pilot starts by night f'm Boottara ration-paddick, an' does 'is thirty mile to hour 'oss-paddick; an' the hull menagerie tailin' harter. 'Shove 'em in 'e yaad, Toby,' ses Muster Magomery. Presinkly, up comes Half, an' 'is 'oss hall of a lather. 'Take yer dem mongreals,' ses Muster Magomery; 'an' don' hoversleep y'self agin.' Think Half war goin' ter flog 'is hanimals thirty mile back? Not 'im"——

"It would hardly be right," I agreed. "Well, I must be jogging"——

"Not 'im," pursued Jack. " 'E turns horf o' the main track t' other side the ram-paddick; through the Patagoniar; leaves hall gates hopen; fetches Nosey's place harter dark; houts file, an' hin with 'is mob, an' gives 'm a g—tful. Course, 'e clears befo' mo'nin'; an' through hour Sedan Paddick, an' back to Boottara that road. 'Ow do Hi know hall this?—ses you?"

"Ah!" said I wisely. "Well, I must be"——

"No; you 're in for it," chuckled Moriarty.

"Tole me 'is hown self, not three weeks agone. Camped hat hour ram-paddick, shiftin' Stewart's things to Queensland. An' wot war the hupshot? 'Stiddy, now,' ses Hi—'w'e 's y' proofs?' 'Some o' these young pups horter take a lessing horf o' you, Jack,' ses you, jist now. You 're right, Collings. Did n' Hi say, las' lambin'— did n' Hi say we war a-gwain ter hev sich anuther year as sixtyhate? Mostly kettle wot we hed then, afore the wool rose; an' wild dogs bein' plentiful them times; an' we 'd a sort o' 'ead stockkeeper, name o' Bob Selkirk; an' this feller 'e started f'm 'ere with hate 'underd an' fo'ty sebm 'ead"——

"And he would have his work cut out for him," I remarked, in cordial assent. "You 've seen some changes on this station, Jack. Well, I must be going."

Leaving the old fellow talking, I threw the reins over Cleopatra's head, and drew the near one a little the tightest. He stood motionless as a statue, and beautiful as a poet's dream.

"Would n't think that horse had a devil in him as big as a bulldog," observed the horse-driver. "Shake the soul-bolt out of a man, s'posen you *do* stick to him."

"And yet Collins can't ride worth a cuss," contributed Moriarty confidentially. "He 's just dropped to this fellow's style. Boss wanted to see him on our Satan, but Collins knew a thundering sight better." ·

A slight, loose-built lad, with a spur trailing at his right heel, advanced from the group.

"Would you mind lettin' me take the feather-edge off o' this feller?" he asked modestly. "If he slings me, you can git on-to him while he 's warm, an' no harm done. I 'd like to try that saddle," he added, by way of excuse. "Minds me o' one I got shook, five months ago, with a red-headed galoot I 'd bin treatin' like a brother, on account of him bein' fly-blowed, an' the both of us travellin' the same road. Best shape saddle I ever had a leg over, that was. Will I have a try?"

"Not worth while, Jack," I replied. "He might prop a little, certainly; but it 's only playfulness." So I swung into the deep seat of the stolen saddle, and lightly touched the lotus-loving Memphian with both spurs.

First, a reeling, dancing, uncertain panorama of buildings, fences, and spectators; then a mechanical response to the surging, jerking, concussive saddle, and a guarded strain on the dragging reins. Also a tranquil cognisance of favourable comment, exchanged by competent judges—no excitement, no admiration, remember; not a trace of new-chum interest, but a certain dignified and judicious approbation, honourable alike to critic and artist. Fools admire, but men of wit approve.

"You see, it 's—only playfulness—" I remarked indifferently; the words being punctuated by necessity, rather than by choice. "Magnificent, but—not war. There 's not a—shadow of vice in his com—position. As the poet says:—

> This is mere—madness,
> And thus awhile the—fit will work—on him.
> Anon as patient as the female—dove,
> When that her—golden couplets have dis—closed,
> His silence will—sit drooping.

There you are!" And Cleopatra stood still; slightly panting, it is true, but with lamb-like guilelessness in his madonna face.

Then, as the toilers of the station slowly dispersed to see about getting up an appetite for supper, Moriarty advanced, and laid both hands on Cleopatra's mane.

"Collins!" he exclaimed; "I 'm better pleased than if I had won ten bob. What do you think?—that verse you quoted from Shakespear brought the question to my mind like a shot of a gun; the very question I wanted to ask you a couple of hours ago. I know

it 's been asked before; in fact, I met with it in an English magazine, where the writer uses the very words you quoted just now.
I thought perhaps you had never met with the question, and it
might interest you—Was Hamlet mad?"

Of some few amiable qualities with which it has pleased heaven
to endow me beyond the majority of my fellows, a Marlborough-
temper is by no means the least in importance. I looked down in
the ingenuous face of the searcher after wisdom, quenching, like
Malvolio, my familiar smile with an austere regard to control.

"*Semper felix*," I observed hopelessly. "You 're right in saying
that the question has been asked before. It has been asked. But
daylight in the morning is the right time to enter on that inquiry.
For the present, we must leave the world-wearied prince to rest in
his ancestral vault, where he was laid by the pious hands of Horatio
and Fortinbras—where, each in his narrow cell for ever laid, the
rude forefathers of The Hamlet sleep."

"Quotation—ain't it?" suggested Moriarty critically.

"No," I sighed.

"Well then, I 'm beggared if I can see anything in that sort of
an answer," remarked the young fellow resentfully.

"Dear boy," I replied; "I never imagined that you could. I
would you had but the wit; 'twere better than your dukedom. By-
the-way—what is Jack's other name?"

"Which Jack? Old Jack, or Young Jack, or Jack the Shellback,
or Fog-a-bolla Jack?"

"Young Jack; the chap that offered to ride Cleopatra."

"Jack Frost."

"Right. Good-bye. And remember our arrangement."

"Good-bye, ole man. Depend your life on my straightness."

Then I whistled to Pup, noticed that Bunyip had n't got on the
wrong side of the fence, and turned Cleopatra's head toward the
Bogan.

G. P. R. James rightly remarks that nothing is more promotive
of thought than the walking pace of a horse. We may add that
nothing on earth can soothe and purify like the canter; nothing
strengthen and exhilarate like the gallop. The trot is passed over
with such contempt as it deserves. So, for the first mile I was
soothed and purified; for the next half-mile I busied myself on a
metaphysical problem; and so on for about five miles.

The metaphysical difficulty (if you care about knowing) arose in
connection with the singular issue of that preposterous wager.
Whence came such an elaborate dispensation? If from above, it

was plainly addressed to Moriarty, as a salutary check on his growing propensity; if from beneath, it must have been a last desperate attempt to decoy into evil ways one who was, perhaps, better worth enlisting than the average fat-head. To which of these sources would you trace the movement? Mind you, our grandfathers—to come no closer—would have piously taken the event on its face value of £50, as a blessing to the Prodistan, and a chastisement to the Papish. But we move. And, by my faith, we have need.

Presently I entered on the narrow pine-ridge; and now, carrying a line of fence on my right shoulder, I followed the pleasant track, winding through pine, wilga, needle-bush, quondong, and so forth. Two miles of this; then on my right appeared the white gate, through which ran the Nalrooka track. Up to this time, I had been following the route which a harsh usage of the country had interdicted to Priestley.

Montgomery and Folkestone, returning from their drive, had just come through this gate; the buggy, turned toward home, was on the track in front of me, and Montgomery was resuming his seat, after shutting the gate. The station mail-bag, loosely tied, was lying on the foot-board.

I had just done explaining where I was bound for, and on what business, and where I intended staying that night, when I nearly tumbled off my horse with a sort of white horror.

For straight behind the buggy, and less than eighty yards away, Priestley's fourteen-bullock team came crawling along the fence, with the evident purpose of catching the Nalrooka track at the gate. Priestley had chanced it. Knowing every gate on the run, he had merely gone round the ration-paddock, and had already made a seven-mile stage in ten miles' travelling—that is, losing three miles in the detour. Once through this gate, the track would be lovely; the wagon would chase the bullocks; evening would soon be on; he would fetch feed and water at the Faugh-a-ballagh Tank, in the quiet moonlight; moreover, if he met a boundary man, he could easily say he had permission from the boss; in any case, it would soon be not worth while to order him back; and he would be off the run some time to-morrow forenoon. I could read his thoughts as I looked at him across Montgomery's shoulder. Concealed from distant observation by the timber of the pine-ridge, he had dismissed all apprehension, and allowed his mind to drift to a bend of the Murrumbidgee, a couple of miles above Hay. There were his young barbarians all at play; there was their dacent mother; he, their sire, looking blissfully forward to superhuman work, and plenty of it.

Straight into the lion's mouth! Heaven help—but does heaven help the Scotch-navigator. I question it. Half an hour's loafing, at any time during the day, would have timed his arrival so as not only to obviate the present danger, but to spare him the disquieting consciousness of narrow escape. And heaven helps those who help themselves.

He knew the gate was near; and, with the automatic restlessness of an impatient dog tied under a travelling dray, he walked back and forward, backward and forward beside his weary team; often looking back to see the wagon clear the trees, but never, by any chance, looking forward against the blaze of the declining sun intently enough to notice the back of the buggy, partly concealed, as it was, by an umbrageous wilga. As I watched him, I wished, with Balaam, that there were a sword in mine hand, that I might slay the ass.

I dare n't ride past the buggy, for fear of Montgomery looking round to say something. I half-heard him tell me that the Sydney crew had won the regatta, and that Jupiter was starting a hot favourite for the Flemington. And all this time, the unconscious son of perdition was crawling nearer; not a jolt nor a click-clock came from his wagon as it pressed the yielding soil; and the faint creaking of the tackle was drowned in the rustle of a hot wind through the foliage.

"I 'm sorry to see you starting so late in the day, and Saturday too," continued the squatter courteously. "The barracks will be lively to-night over these sporting events."

I bowed. I would have licked the dust to see him stand not upon the order of his going, but go at once. "Well, I must be moving," I mumbled hastily, glancing behind me at the sun, and backing Cleopatra into the scrub, to let the buggy pass—noting also that Priestley was n't forty yards away.

"Now, confess the truth, Collins—you 've been having a tiff with Mrs. Beaudesart?" continued Montgomery. "Lovers' quarrel? That 's nothing. I did n't think you were so pettish as to run away like this."

"Indeed, Mr. Montgomery," said I earnestly; "I assure you I 'm only going at the call of duty. I 'll show"——here it struck me that the production of my letter would delay things worse, and——

"By the way, there 's a parcel for Alf Jones in the mail-bag," continued the squatter, with hideous dilatoriness. "I see it 's a roll of music. Better take it. And his newspaper. Get him to give you a tune on his violin, if you can. It will be something to remember."

"Thank you for the suggestion, sir," I continued slavishly, whilst backing Cleopatra a little further into the scrub, and clearing my throat with a sharp, penetrating sound, as if I had swallowed a fly.

Just then, the bullocks stopped of their own accord, within ten yards of the buggy; and Priestley, pre-occupied in laying out fresh work for himself, was roused by my loud r-r-rehm! and took in the situation.

Montgomery seemed amused at my tribulation. "Why, your manner betrays you, Collins! Never mind. You 'll grow out of that in good time. When is it coming off?" He crossed his knees, and held the reins jammed between them, whilst deliberately filling and lighting his pipe. Meanwhile, Priestley, in silent communion with his Maker, stood by his team as if waiting to be photographed. The buggy was in a cool, pleasant shade; and Montgomery would maintain this flagitious procrastination of his managerial duties while I remained a butt for his ill-timed chaff. Critical is no name for the state of affairs.

But an angel seemed to whisper me soul to soul. I responded to the inspiration.

"Well, I 'll show you the letter, Mr. Montgomery," said I, with a petulance tempered by sycophancy. I first felt, then slapped, my pockets—"By japers! I 've left my pocket-book on the seat in front of the barracks!" I continued hurriedly, as I turned Cleopatra back toward the station, and bounded off at a canter. I had n't gone five strides, when, flick! went the buggy-whip; the vehicle started after me; and Priestley was saved. But there is no such thing as permanent safety in this world. The first rattle of the wheels was followed by a loud, pompous, bank-director cough from one of the bullocks.

"Hullo! what the (sheol) have we here?" It was Montgomery's voice, no longer jocular. I turned and rode back, as he swung his buggy round on the lock, skilfully threading the trees and scrub, till he resumed his old position, but now facing the bullock team. "And what, in the devil's name, brings you round this quarter?" he demanded sternly. "This is a bad job!"

"You 're right, Mr. Magomery," assented the bullock driver, with emphasis; "it *is* a bad job; it 's a (adj.) bad job. Way it comes: you see, I got a bit o' loadin' for Nalrookar"——

"Two-ton-five. I know all about that, though I 'm not interested in the transaction," retorted Montgomery. "I asked you what the (sheol) brings you here?"

"Well, that's just what I was goin' to explain when you took the word out o' my mouth. You see, Mr. Magomery, the proper road for me would 'a' been back along the main track to the Cane-grass Swamp, an' from there along the reg'lar Nalrookar track; but I was frightened o' the Convincer, so I thought I'd just cut across"——

"Great God! You thought you'd just cut across! Do you own this run?"

"Well, no, Mr. Magomery, I don't; *that's* (adj.) certain. But if I'd 'a' thought you'd any objection, I'd 'a' ast leaf."

"That's what you should have done. You've acted like a d—d fool."

"You'd 'a' give me leaf?" suggested the bullock driver, in a tone full of unspoken entreaty.

"I'd have seen you in (sheol) first. I decline to make a thoroughfare of the run. But by condescending to ask me, you'd have saved yourself some travelling. The nearest way to the main road is past the station. Here! rouse up your d—d mongrels, and make a start along this track. I'll see that you're escorted. If you loose-out before you reach the main road, I shall certainly prosecute you. Once there, I'll take care you don't trespass again during this trip. Come! move yourself!"

Priestley had never been taught to order himself lowly and reverently to all his betters; yet there was deeper pathos in the rude dignity of his reply than could have attended servility.

"It's this way, Mr. Magomery—I don't deny I got here in a sneakin' way. I feel it, Mr. Magomery; by (sheol) I do. Still, I'm here now. Well, if I tackle this track out to the main road, there's three o' them bullocks'll drop in yoke before I fetch the station. Would you like to see the bones layin' aside this track, every time you drive past? I bet you what you like, you'd be sorry when your temper is over. Then we'll say I'm out on the main road— how'm I goin' to fetch Nalrooka? Not possible, the way I'm fixed. I wouldn't do it to you, Mr. Magomery."

I had ridden to the side of the buggy. "Mr. Montgomery," said I; "I wish to heaven that you were under one-tenth of the obligation to me that I am under to you, so that I might venture to speak in this case. But the remembrance of so much consideration at your hands in the past, encourages me. There's a great deal in what Priestley says; my own experience in bullock driving brings it home to me; and I sympathise with him, rather than with you. Of course the matter rests entirely in your hands; but to me it appears in the light of a responsibility. It is noble to have a squatter's strength, but tyrannous to use it like a squatter."

Something like a smile struggled to Montgomery's sunburnt face; and I could see that the battle was over.

But another was impending. It was now half-an-hour since I had met the buggy. Folkestone had calmly ignored me from the first. When the trouble supervened, his haughty immobility had still sustained him at such an altitude as to render Priestley, as well as myself, invisible even to bird's-eye view. But the small soul, rattling about loose in the large, well-fed body, could n't let it pass at that. On my interposing, he placed a gold-mounted glass in his eye, and, with a degree of rudeness which I have never seen equalled in a navvies' camp, stared straight in my face till I had done speaking. Then the lens dropped from his eye, and he turned to his companion.

"Who is this person, Montgomery?" he asked.

The squatter looked plainly displeased. He was as proud as his guest, but in a different way. Folkestone, being a gentleman *per se*, was distinguished from the ordinary image of God by caste and culture; and to these he added a fatal self-consciousness. Don't take me as saying that caste and culture could possibly have made him a boor; take me as saying that these had been powerless to avert the misfortune. He was a gentleman by the grace of God and the flunkeyism of man. Montgomery was also a gentleman, but only by virtue of his position. So that, for instance, Priestley's personal fac-simile, appearing as a well-to-do squatter, would have been received on equal terms by Montgomery; whereas, Folkestone's disdain would have been scarcely lessened. The relative manliness of the two types of 'gentleman' is a question which each student will judge according to his own fallen nature.

"Pardon me for saying that you Australians have queer ways of maintaining authority," continued the European, lazily raising his eyebrows, and speaking with the accent—or rather, absence of accent—which, in an Englishman, denotes first-class education. "A vagrant, by appearance, and probably not overburdened with honesty, is found trespassing on your property; then this individual —by Gad, I feel curious to know who our learned brother for the defence is—bandies words with you on the other fellow's behalf. I confess I rather like his style. I expected to hear him address you as 'old boy,' or 'my dear fellow,' or by some such affectionate title.

Pardon my warmth, I say, Montgomery! but this phase of colonial life is new to me. Placed in your position (if my opinion, as a landlord, be worth anything), I should make an example of the trespassing scoundrel; partly as a tonic to himself, and partly as a lesson to this cad. If I rightly understand, you have the power to punish, by fine or imprisonment, any trespass on your sheep-walks. You don't exercise your prerogative, you say? By Gad, you 'll have to exercise it, or, let me assure you, you will be sowing thorns for your children to reap. Here, I should imagine, is an excellent opportunity for vindication of your rights as a land owner."

This reasoning would n't have affected Montgomery's foregone decision to suspend his own rights in the current case, had not Priestley been too industrious to notice the opening avenue of escape. But to the bullock driver's troubled mind it appeared that he had managed to wander inside the wings of the stockyard of Fate, and that Folkestone was lending a willing hand to hurroo him into the crush. Moreover, the rough magnanimity of the man's nature was outraged by some supposed insult sustained by me on his behalf.

Just three words of comment here. Built into the moral structure of each earthly probationer is a thermometer, graduated independently; and it is never safe to heat the individual to the boiling-point of his register. You never know how far up the scale this point is, unless you are very familiar with the particular thermometer under experiment. Romeo, for instance, pacific by nature, and self-schooled to forbearance by the second-strongest of inspirations, meets deadly public insult by the softest of answers—'calm, dishonourable, vile submission,' his friend calls it. But the slaying of that friend touches Romeo's 212° Fahrenheit—then! 'Away to heaven, respective lenity, and fire-eyed fury be my conduct now!' Whereupon, Tybalt, the tamperer, is scalded to death. In Ida, as we have seen, the insinuated aspersion of unchastity touched 100° Centigrade; and the experimentalist was glad to retreat, with damaged dignity, from the escaping steam. So, in Priestley, the wanton hostility of Folkestone touched 80° Reaumur; and the billy boiled over, wasting the water, and smothering the owner with ashes.

One moment more, please. Nations, kindreds, and peoples are individuals in mass; and here the existence of an overlooked boiling-point is the one thing that makes history interesting. Cowper puts on paper a fine breezy English contempt for the submissiveness and ultra-royalism of the pre-Revolutionary French—and lives to wonder at the course of events. Macaulay's diction rolls like the swelling of Jordan, as he expatiates on the absolute subserviency, the settled incapacity for resistance, of the Bengalee—till presently the Mutiny (a near thing, in two widely different senses, and confined to the Bengalee troops) shakes his credit. So it has ever been, and ever shall be. But for that ingrained endowment of resilience, Man would long ago have ceased to inhabit this planet.

When Priestley came to the boil, all considerations of expediency, all natural love of peace and fear of the wrath to come, all solicitude for wife and children, vanished from his mind, leaving him fit for treasons, stratagems, and spoils. I must suppress about half the language in which he clothed his one remaining thought.

"An' who are you?" he thundered, advancing toward the buggy. "A loafer!—no better!—an' you must shove in your lip! I don't blame Magomery for bein' nasty; he 's got a right to blaggard me, the way things is; an' I give him credit. But you! Cr-r-ripes! if I had you a couple o' hundred mile furder back, I 'd learn you manners! I 'd make you spring off o' your tail!"

Folkestone, his head canted to a listening angle, noted with a half-amused, half-tired smile the outlaw's tirade. Then he rose, drew off his light coat, and laid it across the back of the buggy seat.

"I will thump this fellow, Montgomery," said he, and he certainly meant it. Priestley was a man of nine stone.

By your favour, once more, and only once. The Englishman proper is the pugilist of the world. The Australian or American maxima may be as brutal, or even more so, but the average efficiency in smiting with the fist of wickedness is, beyond all question, on the English side. 'English fair-play' is a fine expression. It justifies the bashing of the puny draper's assistant by the big, hairy blacksmith; and this to the perfect satisfaction of both parties, if they are worthy the name of Englishmen. Also, the English gentleman may take off his coat to the potsherd of the earth; and so excellent is his discrimination that the combat will surely end even as your novelist describes; simply because no worshipper can make headway against his god, when the divinity hits back. At the same time, no insubordinate Englishman, named Crooked-nosed Yorkey, and made in proportion, ever did, or ever will, suffer manual mauling at the hands of an English gentleman—or any other gentleman, for that matter. What a fool the gentleman would be! No; Crooked-nosed Yorkey is always given in charge; and it takes three policeman to run him in.

English fair-play! Varnhagen von Ense tells us how Continental gentlemen envied the social usage which permitted Lord Castlereagh, in 1815, to show off his bruising ability at the expense of a Viennese cabman—probably some consumptive feather-weight, and certainly a man who had never seen a scrapping-match in his life. But English fair-play does n't stand transplantation to Australia, except in patches of suitable soil. For instance, when bar-loafer meets pimp, at £1 a side, then comes the raw-meat business. The back-country man, though saturnine, is very rarely quarrelsome, and almost never a pugilist; nevertheless, his foot on his native salt-bush, it is not advisable to assault him with any feebler weapon than rifle-and-bayonet. There is a radical difference, without a verbal distinction, between his and the Englishman's notions of fair-play. Each is willing to content himself with the weapons provided by nature; but the Southern barbarian prefers a natural product about three feet long, and the thickness of your wrist at the butt—his conception of fair-play being qualified by a fixed resolution to prove himself the better counterfeit.

So Priestley, with a sinister glitter in his patient eyes, had reversed his whipstick, pliant end downward, and bent along the ground. He knew the nature of seasoned pine. A sharp jerk, and the whipstick would snap, supplying a nilla-nilla which would make him an over-match for a dozen Folkestones in rotation. My hand was on Cleopatra's mane, and my off-foot clear of the stirrup; it would be a Christian act to save Folkestone from the father of a batin', and Priestley from that sterner father, namely, old father antic, the law. But imminent as the collision seemed, it did n't come-off.

"Sit down, Folkestone," said Montgomery, holding his companion's sleeve with a firm grip, whilst gazing steadily northward through the narrow fringe of timber. Following his eye, I saw a horseman, a mile and a half distant, heading for the homestead at a walk.

"Is that Arblaster, Collins?" demanded the squatter.

I brought my binocular to bear on the horseman. "Nelson," I replied.

"Better still. Signal him."

I galloped out into the plain, wheeled broadside on, and waved my hat. The equestrian profile changed to a narrow line, and I returned to the buggy, followed, at a decent interval, by Nelson. I was glad to see Priestley in the act of driving through the gate.

"Come here, Priestley," said Montgomery quietly. "You have my permission to follow this track to the Nalrooka boundary"——

"I hope I 'll git some slant to do as much"——

"Silence!—But if you trespass on my feed or water, by God I 'll prosecute you. Another thing. Never in future load anything for me, or come to this station expecting wool. And I may as well warn you that every boundary man in my employ will be on the look-out for you from this time forward. Nelson; you ride behind his wagon to the boundary, and see that he keeps the track."— A frown gathered on the young fellow's face, reinforced by a burning blush as Montgomery went on—"Perhaps you scarcely expected me to concur in your opinion, that one ought to spring a bit in a season like this; yet I have no intention of crushing a poor, decent, hard-working devil—that is, if he can add nine miles more to to-day's stage, without unyoking. I have already given him a thorough good blackguarding for calculating upon crossing the run. If he trespasses on feed or water—if he does n't go straight on with his team, wagon or no wagon—you and I may quarrel." Who was the spy? Ah! who is the ubiquitous station spy?

"Good-bye, Mr. Montgomery," said I abjectly.

"Are n't you coming back to the station for your pocket-book?" he asked, with a glance out of the corner of his eye.

"I find I 've got it here all the time—wonder how I came to overlook it."

"Thinking too much about Mrs. Beaudesart," suggested the squatter. "She won't be at all displeased to hear of it. Good-bye, Collins. Safe journey."

I raised my wideawake to Folkestone, who again placed his glass in his eye, and stared at me wonderingly till we tore ourselves apart.

Another mile, and I cleared the pine-ridge. Looking back to the right, I could see Priestley and his guard of honour crawling toward the Faugh-a-ballagh Sand-hills, which lay two miles from the gate where we had parted. They would reach the tank as twilight merged into moonlight. Then Nelson would say, 'I 'm going to have a drink of tea at Jack's hut. I 'll be back in three or four hours. Pity you 're not allowed to loose-out, for there's a grand bit of crow's-foot round that pine tree in the hollow. Don't kindle a fire, unless you want to get lagged.' And Priestley would get to the boundary by ten o'clock on the morrow, without the loss of a beast; thanking heaven that he had n't been escorted by Arblaster or Butler, and racking his invention to provide for the coming night.

Also, Montgomery would, within a week, know all the details of the trip (station spy again), but, being a white man, he would silently condone Nelson's disobedience.

One more little incident enlivened the monotony of my journey to Alf's hut. Whilst giving my horses a half-mile walk, I took out the newspaper Toby had brought. I did n't look for any marginal marks, having recognised Jeff Rigby's handwriting in the address. Rigby is a man who never writes except on his own account. His way of acknowledging a letter is to pick up a newspaper, of perhaps a month old, tie a string round it, stamp and address it, and drop it in the nearest letter-box. This paper, however, happened to be the latest available issue of a Melbourne daily, and contained a copious account of the regatta, followed by the coarsely-executed portrait of a young man, with the neck and shoulders—and, by one of Nature's sad, yet just, compensations, also the face and head—of the average athlete. Rude as the engraving was, the subject of it at once suggested what the Life-Assurance canvassers call an 'excellent risk'; and underneath ran the title: MR. RUDOLPH WINTERBOTTOM—STROKE OF THE WINNING CREW. An ensuing paragraph briefly sketched the hero's history, habits, and physical excellencies. He was twenty-two years of age; had a good position in the N.S.W. Civil Service; and was now on leave of absence. He was a non-smoker, a life-abstainer, and in a word, was distinguished in almost every branch of those gambol faculties which show a weak mind and an able body. It gave me quite a turn. *Sic transit,* thought I, with a sigh. Such is life.

The cranky boundary rider's little weatherboard hut, standing just inside his horse-paddock fence, was neater than the average. The moonlight showed that a radius of five or six yards from the door had been swept with a broom; while some kerosene-tins, containing garden-flowers, occupied the angle formed by the chimney and the wall. The galvanised bucket and basin on the bench by the door were conspicuously clean; and the lamp-light showed through a green blind on the window.

A black-and-tan collie gave a few perfunctory barks as I drew near, whereupon Alf, with sleeves rolled up, and hands freshly blooded to the wrists, appeared at the door, and drew back on seeing me. I brought my horses through the gate, and he met me outside the hut; his hands washed, and his shirt-sleeves buttoned. He stood by, scarcely speaking, whilst I introduced myself, gave him his parcel and newspaper, and unsaddled my horses. Then I followed him into the hut, and he cleared away from the table the anatomy

of a fine turkey, shot during the day. Sullenly he replenished the
kettle, and put the fire together; then washed the table, and laid it
for one.

But the newspaper revelation, in giving me a turn, had turned
me philosophic-side-upward; and I cared little for Alf's sullenness,
provided he listened with attention to my discourse on the mut-
ability of things. By the time he had poured out my tea, he was a
vanquished man. He filled a cup for himself, to keep me company,
and guardedly commented on the news I brought from the station
and the Pine-ridge Gate. Still I was touched to observe that he
kept his disfigured face averted as much as possible.

Did you ever reflect upon how much you have to be thankful for
in the matter of noses? Your nose, in all probability, is your dram
of eale—your club foot—your Mordecai sitting at the king's gate
—but you would look very queer without it.   In your morbid
hypercriticalness, you may wish this indocile, undisguisable, and
most unsheltered feature had been made a little longer, or a little
shorter, or a little wider, or not quite so wide. Or perhaps you
wish the isthmus between your eyes a little higher, or the ridge of
the peninsula a little straighter, or the south cape a little more, or
less, obtuse. Or possibly you wish that the front elevation (elevation is good) did not admit, through the natural grottoes above
your moustache, so clear a perspective of the interior of Ambition's
airy hall—forcing upon you the conviction that your own early disregard of your mother's repeated admonitions against wiping
upward, had come home to you at last, and had come to stay.
Check that rebellious spirit, I charge you.   Your nose is good
enough; better, probably, than you deserve; be thankful that you
have one of any design at all.

This poor boundary man had none to speak of. And it seemed
such a pity. More beautiful, otherwise, than a man's face is justified
in being, it was (apart from sex) as if Pygmalion's masterpiece
had fallen heavily, face downward, and then sprung into life, minus
the feature which will least bear tampering with. The upper half
of his nose was represented by an irregular scar, running off toward
the left eye, which was dull and opaque; the other was splendid,
soft, and luminous. And as he sat in the full light of the lamp,
with his elbow on the table, in order to shade with his hand the
middle part of his face, the combination of fine frontal development with exquisite and vigorous contour of mouth and chin was
so striking that I involuntarily glanced round the hut for the book-
shelf.

His lithe, graceful movements had at first led me to mark him down as a mere lad; but now the lamp-light showed a maze of incipient wrinkles on the sunburnt neck, and a few silver threads in the thick, strong, coal-black hair. Moreover, owing to inadvertence or ignorance on the part of people who should have known better, he had been christened in immediate succession to a girl. It is well and widely known that this oversight, small as it looks, will free a man for life from any rude inquiry as to when he is going to burn off the scrub. Alf had no scrub to burn off, except a faint moustache, unnoticeable but for its dark colour. For the rest, he was slightly above medium height, and by no means a good stamp of a man—tapering the wrong way, if I might so put it without shocking the double-refined reader. And, from stiff serge jumper to German-silver spur, he (Alf, of course) was unbecomingly clean for Saturday. The somewhat wearisome minuteness of this description is owing to his being, at least in my estimation, the most interesting character within the scope of these scrappy memoirs.

I looked round for the book-shelf. It was a book-case this time; a flat packing-case, nailed to the wall, fitted with shelves, and curtained on the front. I rose and inspected the collection: fifty or sixty volumes altogether—poetry, drama, popular theology, reference, and a few miscellaneous works; history meagrely represented, science and yellow-back fiction not at all.

"You don't find many people of my name in the country?" remarked the boundary man trivially, after a pause.

"Not many," I replied, wondering whether he referred to his nickname or to the inexpensive, but lasting, gift of his godfathers and godmothers, at the time of their annoying mistake.

"I suppose you hardly know one," he persisted.

"Not that I can think of," I replied. "Have you any swapping-books?"

"Yes; you 'll find *Elsie Venner* lying on top of the upper shelf."

"I 've read it years ago, but we 'll change," I replied. "When I first got my swapping-book, it was by Hannah More; now it 's by Zola, and smutty enough at that; it has undergone about twenty intermediate metamorphoses, and it 's still going remarkably strong —in both senses of the word. Therefore I can recommend it."

"I don't think it does a person any good to read Zola," remarked the boundary man gravely.

"Not the slightest, Alf—that is, in the works by which he is represented amongst us. But do you think it does a person any good to read Holmes? Zola has several phases; one of them, I admit, blue as heaven's own tinct; but Holmes has only one phase, namely, pharisaism. Zola, even as we know him here in Riverina, has this advantage, that he gives you no rest for the sole of your foot—or rather, for the foot of your soul; whilst Holmes serenely seduces you to his own pinchbeck standard. Zola is honest; he never calls evil, good; whilst Holmes is spurious all through. Mind you, each has a genuine literary merit of his own."

"But don't you like Holmes's poetry?" asked Alf.

"Well, his poems fill a little volume that the world would be sorry to lose; but why did n't he write one verse—just one—for the Abolitionists to quote?"

"Because it 's not in his nature to denounce things," objected Alf.

"Neither was it in Longfellow's nature; yet Longfellow's poems on Slavery are judged worthy to form a separate section of his works. But Holmes can denounce most valiantly. He denounces witch-burning and Inquisition-persecution, like the chivalrous soul that he is. He has achieved the distinction of being the only American poet of note who blandly ignores Slavery, and takes part with the aristocrat, as against the lowly. The same spirit runs through all his writings. He has a range of about three notes; a flunkeyish koo-tooing to soap-bubble eminence; a tawdry sympathy with aristocratic woe; and a drivelling contempt for angular Poor Relations, in bombazine gowns. Bombazine, by-the-way, is a cheap, carpetty-looking fabric, built of shoddy, and generally used for home-made quilts"——

"No, it 's not!" broke in Alf, with a rippling laugh; "it 's a very good dress-material; silk one way, and wool the other; and it 's mostly black, or maroon, or"——he stopped with a gasp. "Why don't you sit down?" he continued, in an altered tone. "And that reminds me, my day's work 's not done yet."

He cleared the table, and placed upon it his half-dissected turkey, in a milk-dish. I had the conversation to myself till he finished his work and took the turkey outside to hang it on the meat-pole. This was a sapling of fifteen or twenty feet high, with a fork at the top, through which ran a piece of clothes-line. I followed him to the door, discoursing on literature, whilst he attached one end of the clothes-line to the turkey's legs, hauled it up to the fork, and hitched the fall of the rope to the pole. But just as the turkey reached its place, he had dropped his head with a movement of pain; and, after securing the rope, he groped his way into the hut, holding his hand over his right eye.

"Bit of bark, or something, dropped right into my eye," he muttered. "It does n't suit me to have anything wrong with the one I have left."

By the bright lamp-light, I soon relieved him of what proved to be a small ant; then he went out to the washing-bench, and I heard the dabbling of water.

"I got a grass-seed in my eye the New Year's Day before last," he remarked, in a sort of sullen self-commiseration, after we had sat in silence for a minute. "I could n't see to catch a horse; and it took me about six hours to grope my way along the fences to Dick Templeton's hut. I thought I 'd have gone mad."

"Ah!" said I sympathetically, "that reminds me of an incident that came under my own notice on the very day you speak of. I 'll tell you how it happened." By this time, Alf had lit a meek and lowly meerschaum, whilst a large grey cat had jumped on his knees, and settled itself for repose. "You asked me awhile ago whether I knew anyone of your name in this part of the country. I forgot at the moment that one of my most profitable studies is a namesake of yours—Warrigal Alf, a carrier on these roads."

"What 's his other name?" asked the boundary man, in a suppressed voice.

"Morris."

"Why don't you call him so, then? I hate nicknames."

Poor fellow, thought I, and I continued, "I was coming down from Cobar, with a single horse; and on the New Year's Day before last, I reached the Yellow Tank—about forty miles from here, is n't it? I left my saddle and things at the tank, and was taking my horse out to a place where there 's always a bit of grass, when I noticed a wagon in the scrub, and identified it as Alf's"——

"Did you know him before?" murmured the boundary man.

"Certainly."

"Is he a married man?"

"Widower."

"Widower?" repeated Alf, almost in a whisper. "Did you know his wife?"

"Personally, no; inductively, yes. She was one of those indefinably dangerous women who sing men to destruction—one of those tawny-haired tigresses, with slumbrous dark eyes—name, Iolanthe."

"What?"

"Iolanthe de Vavasour," I replied good-humouredly. "More appropriate than Molly—is n't it?"

The boundary man, after picking up his pipe, which had fallen on the slumbering cat, fixed his Zitska eye on my face with a puzzled, shrinking, defiant look, whilst drawing his seat a little further away. Ah! years of solitary life, with the haunting consciousness of frightful disfigurement, had told on his mind. Moriarty was right. And I remembered that the moon was approaching the full.

"Alf was sitting under a hop-bush," I continued, "with his hand across his eyes.

" 'What 's the matter, Alf?' says I.

" 'Is that you, Collins?' says he, trying to look up. 'You 're just in time to do more for me than I would care about doing for you. I 've met with an accident. I was lying on my back under the wagon this morning, tightening some nuts, when a bit of rust, or something, fell straight into my eye. Frightful pain; and it 's affecting the other eye already; giving me a foretaste of hell. No doubt it 's a good thing; but I don't want a monopoly of it; I wish I could pass it round.' This was Alf's style of philosophy. Our friend, Iolanthe, is largely, though perhaps indirectly, responsible for it."

"Yes—go on," said the boundary man nervously.

"Well, as I was telling you, it was after sunset, and there was no time to lose, so I whittled a bit of wood to a point, and essayed the task in which I claim a certain eminence, namely, the extraction of a mote from my brother's eye.

" 'You 're right, Alf,' says I; 'it 's a flake of rust, about the size of a fish's scale, lodged on the coloured part, which we term the iris—or, strictly speaking, on that part of the cornea which covers the iris. But I can't shift it with this appliance. Must get something sharper.'

"So I took a pin out of my coat, and grubbed the mote as well as I could by the deficient light. I don't know what Alf thought of it at the time, but I considered it a lovely operation. When it was over, Alf signified to me that I was n't wanted any longer, so I went about my business.

"Next morning, as I was going toward my horse-bell, I gave my patient a purely professional call, and found his eye worse than ever. I subjected him to another examination; and, this time having the advantage of full daylight, I discovered that the cause of his trouble was n't a flake of rust, after all; but a small, barbed speck of clean iron, embedded in the white of the eye. I discovered something else. Alf's eyes are as blue as those of Zola's *Nana*; and in the iris of the affected one there is, or rather, was, a brown spot. I had often noticed this before; but, in the defective light, and the hurry of the operation, I had never thought of the thing, and had wasted time and skill on it, as I tell you. I have often laughed to remember"——

"You were badly off for something to laugh at!" Again I recalled Moriarty's remark; for the boundary man's voice trembled as he spoke, and his splendid eye blazed with sudden resentment. But the fit passed away instantly, and he asked, in his usual subdued tone, "When did you see this—this Alf Morris last?"

"About two months ago," I replied. "He was camped at that time in the Dead Man's Bend, at the junction of Avondale and Mondunbarra."

"When are you likely to see him again?" asked the boundary man. "But, of course, you can't tell. It 's a foolish question. I don't know what 's come over me to-night."

Ignorance is bliss, in that instance, poor fellow! thought I, glancing out at the weirdly beautiful moonlight; and I replied, "Most likely I 'll never see him again. These wool-tracks, that knew him so well, will know him no more again for ever. He's gone to a warmer climate."

"That decides it!" muttered the lunatic, swaying on his seat, whilst he clutched the edge of the table.

"Alf! Alf!" I remonstrated, laying my hand on his shoulder. He shrank from the touch, and immediately recovered himself. "Let me explain," I continued soothingly. "He has gone four or five months' journey due north, in charge of three teams loaded with lares and penates, and tools, and cooking utensils, and rations, and other things too numerous to particularise, belonging once to Kooltopa, but now to a new station in South-western Queensland. Hence I say he 's gone to a warmer climate. Not much of a joke, I admit."

"And what 's—what 's become of Kooltopa?" asked the boundary man, panting under his effort at self-control.

"Old times are changed, old manners gone; a stranger fills the Stewart's throne," I replied, with real sadness. "Kooltopa 's sold to a Melbourne company, and is going to be worked for all it 's worth. And I 'm thinking of the carrier, coming down with the survivors of a severe trip, and the penniless pedestrian, striking the station at the eleventh hour. These people will miss Stewart badly.

For the guest flies the hall, and the vassal from labour,
Since his turban was cleft by the infidel's sabre."

"Whose turban?" asked Alf, with a puzzled look.

"Stewart's. I spake but by a metaphor. As with Antony, 'tis one of those odd tricks that sorrow shoots out of the mind."

There was a few minutes' silence. I was thinking of the Christian squatter, and so, no doubt, was many another wanderer at the same moment.

"But he 'll come back to Riverina when he delivers the loading?" suggested the boundary man.

"Who?"

"This—Alf Morris."

"I don't think so. I know he does n't intend it."

Another pause. Glancing at my companion, as he sat with his elbows on the table, and one hand, as usual, across the middle of his face, I noticed his chest heaving unnaturally, and his shapely lips losing their deep colour.

"Are you sick, Alf?"

"Yes—a little," he whispered.

I filled a cup at the water-bag, and set it before him. He drank part of it.

"Quakers' meeting!" he remarked at length, with a slight laugh. "Why don't you say something? I 'm not much of a talker myself, but I 'm a good listener. Tell us some yarn to pass the time. Anything you like. Tell us all about that camp on the Lachlan, and what passed between you and your friend, Morris."

Upon this hint I spake. I recounted consecutively the incidents which form the subject of an earlier chapter, whilst an occasional inquiry, or an appreciative nod, proved my eccentric auditor in touch with me from first to last.

"Three or four weeks afterward," I continued, "I met this Bob Stirling in Mossgiel. He had a bit of a head on him at the time, having just got through five notes—three from Stewart, and two from Alf. I got a bob's worth of brandy to straighten him up; and we had a drink of tea together, while my horses went through a small feed of bad chaff at sixpence a pound.

"His account was, that Stewart, after parting from me, drove straight to Alf's camp, and deposited him there to look after things. Stewart himself only stayed a few minutes, and then drove to Avondale, to see Mr. Wentworth St. John Ffrench, Terrible Tommy's boss. Next morning, a wagonette came from Avondale, with a few parcels of eatables, and a few bottles of drinkables, and other sinful lusts of the flesh. Four days after that, again, Stewart drove round on his way back to Kooltopa. By this time, Alf was able to crawl about, trying his best to be civil to Bob, and succeeding fairly well for a non-smoker.

"However, when Stewart called, he got into a yarn with Alf, and had a drink of tea while Bob held the horses. Presently, according to Bob's account, the conversation grew closer; and, after an hour or so, Stewart told Bob to unharness the horses, and hobble them out where they could get a bite of grass. Altogether, Stewart stayed about half a day. In a few days more, Alf was able to yoke and unyoke a few quiet bullocks; then he and Bob started for Kooltopa together. Arrived at their destination, Stewart and Alf each paid Bob, as already hinted; and Bob, having urgent business in Moss-giel, hurried away to transact it. He had just completed the deal when I met him."

Here I paused to light my pipe.

"And what makes you think he has left Riverina for good?" asked the boundary man absently.

"Catch him leaving Riverina. He knows he has a good character as a quiet, decent, inoffensive sundowner—nobody's enemy but his own—and experience has taught him that any kind of toler-able reputation is better than no reputation at all."

"I don't mean him," said the boundary man constrainedly.

"Of course not. I beg your pardon. Well, I heard it from him-self. I met him about three weeks ago—that would be about three weeks after my interview with Bob Stirling. He 's fairly in love with what he saw of Queensland, before last shearing; and, between bad seasons and selectors—not to mention his own presentiment of a rabbit-plague—he 's full-up of Riverina. But that reminds me that I have n't brought Alf Morris's story to a proper conclusion. I heard the rest of it from Stewart, on the occasion I speak of. Stewart has bought his plant, and engaged him permanently. His first business is to take Stewart's teams to their destination—no easy matter at this time of the year, and such a year as this; but if any man can do it, that man is Alf. He started some weeks ago, a little shaky after his sickness, but recovering fast. Entirely changed in disposition, Stewart tells me; and those who know him will agree that a change would n't be out of place. But Stewart speaks of him as one of the noblest-minded men he ever knew. He says he just wants a man like Alf, and he does n't intend to part with him. I fancy our love of paradox makes us prone to associate noble-mind-edness with cantankerousness—at all events, nobody ever called me noble-minded. But such is life."

"Then this new situation is a permanent thing for him?" suggested the boundary man.

"For Alf? No; I 'm sorry to say, it 's not."

"Why?"

"Because Stewart's about sixty, and Alf 's somewhere in the neighbourhood of thirty-seven. The Carlisle-tables would give Stewart an actuarial expectation of ten or fifteen years, and Alf one of twenty-five or thirty. And there will be old-man changes in the personnel of the station staff when the grand old Christian sleeps with his fathers, and his dirty-flash son reigns in his stead. Such, again, is life. But this won't affect Alf's interests to any ruinous extent. He has a stockingful of his own. It 's a well-known fact that few carriers of Riverina cleared as much money as he did, and probably not one spent less. Stewart gave him £200 for his plant, and he never broke the cheque; posted it whole; Stewart himself took charge of it, as he told me in his gossiping way. Let Alf alone. He knows how to come in out of the wet; in fact, the rainy day is his strong point. Such, for the third and last time, is life."

Whilst I spoke, my unfortunate companion was persistently trying to light his empty pipe, his hands trembling, and his breath quickening. The Maroo fly was at him again. I tried to divert his attention.

"By the way," said I; "did n't you blame Thompson and Cunningham for duffing in your horse-paddock, ten or twelve months ago?"

"I did n't make any song about it," replied the boundary rider half-resentfully.

"Of course not. Still you owe them an apology—which I shall be happy to convey, if you wish it. Alf Morris was the depredator. He was hovering about your hut that night like a guardian angel, while his twenty bullocks had their knife-bars going double-speed on your grass, and you slept the sleep of the unsuspecting. Ask old Jack; he 'll give you chapter and verse, without much pressing. He told me about it this afternoon."

But the fit came on, after all. The boundary man stared at me with a wild, shrinking look, and the same paling of the lips I had noticed before; then he drank the remaining water out of the cup, and, rising from his seat, walked slowly to his bed, and lay down with his face toward the wall.

Far gone, i' faith, thought I. Presently I went to the door, and, shoring up one of the posts with my shoulder, looked out upon the cool, white moonlight, flooding the level landscape.

Strange phenomena follow the footsteps of Night. It has long been observed that avalanches and landslips occur most frequently about midnight, and especially on moonless midnights, when the sun and moon are in conjunction at the nadir. This is the time when mines cave in; when loose bark falls from trees; when limbs crash down from old, dead timber; when snow-laden branches break; when all ponderable bodies, of relatively slight restraint, are most apt to lose their hold. This may be definitely and satisfactorily accounted for by the mere operation of Newton's Law. At the time, and under the conditions, specified, the conjoined attraction of sun and moon—an attraction sufficient to sway millions of tons of water, in the spring tides—is superadded to the centric gravity of the earth, the triple force, at the moment of midnight, tending toward the nadir, or downward. So that, when these midnight phenomena are most observable at one point of the globe, they will be least likely to make mid-day manifestation at the antipodes to that point.

And, though changes of the moon—as copiously proved by meteorological statistics—have no relation whatever to rainfall, the illuminated moon, on rising, will rarely fail to clear a clouded sky. This singular influence is exercised solely by the cold light of that dead satellite producing an effect which the sunlight, though two hundred times as intense, is altogether powerless to rival in kind. When we can explain the nature of this force adherent to moonlight, and to no other light, we may inquire why, in all ages and in all lands, the verdict of experience points to moonlight as a factor in the production and aggravation of lunacy. An empirical hypothesis, of course; but in the better sense, as well as in the worse. For the perturbing influence of moonlight, if it be a myth, is about the most tenacious one on earth. This anomalous form of Force may or may not be observable in asylums, where the patients are not directly subjected to it; but anyone who has lived in the back country, camping out with all sorts and conditions of oddities, need not be accounted credulous if he holds the word 'lunatic' to rest on a sounder derivation than 'ill-starred,' or 'disastrous.'

But the sub-tropical moonlight—strong, chaste, and beautiful as its ideal queen—soothes and elevates the well-balanced mind. I took from my pack-saddle the double-tongued jews-harp I always carry; and, sitting on the floor with my back against the door-post, unbound the instrument from its square stick, and began to play.

It is not the highest class of music, I am well aware; and this paragraph is dictated by no shallow impulse of self-glorification. But I never had opportunity to master any more complicated instrument; and even if I had, it would n't be much use, for I know only about three tunes, and these by no means perfectly.

So I played softly and voluptuously, till my scanty repertory was exhausted, and then drifted into a tender *capriccio*. I noticed Alf move uneasily on his bed; but, knowing the effect of music on my own mind, and remembering Moriarty's and Montgomery's independent panegyrics on the boundary man's skill, I felt put on my mettle, and performed with a power and feeling which surprised myself.

"Do you like music?" asked Alf, at length.

"Like it!" I repeated. "I would give one-fourth of the residue of my life to be a good singer and musician. As it is, I 'm not much of a player, and still less of a vocalist; but I 'll give you a song if you like. How sweetly everything sounds to-night." Bee-o-buoy-bee-o-buoy-bee-o-buoy——

"Do you like jews-harp music?" interrupted Alf, sitting up on the bed.

"Not if I could play any better instrument—such as the violin, or the concertina; though I should in any case avoid the piano, for fear of flattening the ends of my fingers. Still, the jews-harp is a jews-harp; and this is the very best I could find in the market. Humble as it looks, and humble as it undeniably is, it has sounded in every nook and corner of Riverina. Last time I took it out, it was to give a poor, consumptive old blackfellow a treat; and now, you see, I tune, to please a peasant's ear, the harp a king had loved to hear." Bee-o-buoy-bee-o-buoy-bee-o-bee-o-bee-o-buoy——

"I 'll give you a tune on the violin, if you like," exclaimed my companion, rising to his feet.

"Thank-you, Alf."

I carefully re-packed my simple instrument, while the boundary man took from its case a dusky, dark-brown violin. Then he turned down the lamp till a mere bead of flame showed above the burner, resumed his seat by the table, and, after some preliminary screwing and testing, began to play.

Query: If the relation of moonlight to insanity is a thing to be derided, what shall we say of the influence of music on the normal mind? Is it not equally unaccountable in operation, however indisputable in effect? Contemplate music from a scientific standpoint —that is, merely as a succession of sound-waves, conveyed from the instrument to the ear by pulsations of the atmosphere, or of some other intervening medium. Music is thus reduced to a series of definite vibrations, a certain number of which constitute a note. Each separate note has three distinct properties, or attributes. First, its intensity, or loudness, which is governed by the height, depth, amplitude—for these amount to the same thing—of the waves produced in the medium. Second, the timbre, or quality, which is regulated by the shape, or outline, of these waves. Third, the pitch, high or low, which is controlled by the distance from crest to crest of the sound-waves—or, as we say, from node to node of the vibrations.

To the most sensitive human ear, the highest limit of audibleness is reached by sound-waves estimated at twenty-eight-hundredths of an inch from node to node—equal to 48,000 vibrations per second. The extreme of lowness to which our sense of hearing is susceptible, has been placed at 75 feet from node to node—or 15 vibrations per second. This total range of audibleness covers 12 octaves; running, of course, far above and far below the domain of music. The extreme highness and lowness of sounds which convey musical impression are represented, respectively, by 2,000 and by 30 vibrations per second—or by sound-waves, in the former case, of $6\frac{1}{2}$ inches, and in the latter, of $37\frac{1}{2}$ feet.

Therefore, there are not only sounds which by reason of highness or lowness are unmusical, but, beyond these, others to which the tympanum of the human ear is insensible. Nature is alive with such sounds, each carrying its three distinct properties of intensity, timbre and pitch; but whilst this muddy vesture of decay doth grossly close us in, we can no more hear them than we can hear the 'music of the spheres'—apt term for that celestial harmony of motion which guides the myriad orbs of the Universe in their career through Space. But, to take an illustration from the visual faculty: any sound beyond the highest limit of audibleness would resemble a surface lined so minutely and closely as to appear perfectly plain; whilst a sound too low in pitch to be heard would be represented by superficial undulations of land or water so vast in extent that the idea of unevenness would not occur. We have fairly trustworthy evidence that whales communicate with each other by notes so low in pitch—by sound-vibrations so long in range, so few per second—that no human ear can detect them. Bats, on the other hand, utter calls so high—producing such rapid pulsations—as to be equally inaudible to us.

Unison of musical notes is attained when the respective numbers of pulsations per second admit a low common-divisor. For instance, the note produced by 60 vibrations per second will chord with one produced by 120—each node of the former coinciding with each alternate node of the latter. 60 and 90 will also chord; 60 and 70 will produce discord; 60 and 65, worse discord. And so on. The science of musical composition lies in the management of sound-pulsation, and is governed by certain rigid mathematical laws—which laws the composer need not understand.

Air-movement may, of course, take place without sound-vibration, for air is only incidentally a sound-conductor. Earth, metal, water, and especially wood (along the grain), are better media than the atmosphere, for transmission of sound. But sound may be transmitted without vibration of intervening sound-media. The electric current, passing along the telephone wire, picks up the sound waves at one end, and instantaneously deposits them, in good order and condition, at the other end—say, a couple of hundred miles away.

So that the brilliant pianist of the concert hall; the cornet-player of the 'Army' ring; the blind fiddler at the corner; the mother, singing her angel-donation to sleep; Clancy, thundering forth something concerning his broken heart, whilst tailing up the stringing cattle; the canary in its cage; the magpie on the fence—are each setting in motion the complex machinery of music, and with about equal scientific knowledge of what they are doing. To the philosophic mind, however, they are not playing or singing; they are producing and controlling sound-vibrations, arbitrarily varied in duration and quality; a series of such pulsations constituting a note; a series of notes constituting an air. These vibrations are diffused from the instrument or the lips, at a speed varying with temperature, media, and other conditions; they ripple, spread, percolate, everywhere; they penetrate and saturate all solids and gases, yet are palpable corporeally only to the tympanum of the ear, and mechanically (as yet) only to the diaphragm of the phonograph.

Such, however, is the scientific analysis of music. Spoken language appeals by the same process, but with very different effect. No one can understand a language which he has not previously learned, word by word; and the verbal appeal, however imaginative or spiritual, comes in concrete form—that is, in the nature of information. Spoken words inform the emotional side of our nature, through the intellectual; whereas music, operating outwardly in the same manner, speaks over the head of intellect to an inborn sense which ceases not to receive as a little child. And herein lies its mystery.

For the music thus impassively anatomised by Science is a voice from the Unseen, pregnant with meaning beyond translation. A mere ripple of sound-vibration, called into existence by human touch; a creation, vanishing from its birth, elusive, irreclaimable as a departing soul, yet strong to sway heart and hand as the tornado sways the pliant pine. It is a language peculiar to no period, race, or caste. Ageless and universal, it raises to highest daring, or suffuses with tenderness, to-day and here, as once on Argo's deck, or in the halls of Persepolis. Purely material in origin and analysis, easily explicable in mere physical operation, its influence is one of the things that are not dreamt of in the philosophy of Science. Why should a certain psychological effect ensue upon certain untranslatable sounds being placed in a given relation to each other, and not when the same sounds are placed in another relation?—and why should that effect be always upward? Why should the composer be perforce a prophet of the sphere above earth's murky horizon—the musician his interpreter—charged with embassy of peace, and fortitude, and new-born ardour, to the troubled, and weary, and heavy-laden? Has ingenuity never distilled from music any spirit of evil?

None. Euterpe alone of the Muses defies seduction. Harmony is intrinsically chaste. There is no secular music; all music is sacred. Whatever the song the Sirens sang, its music was pure; and no less pure were the notes which breathed from Nero's lute, whilst the blaze of ten thousand homes glutted his Imperial lust for spectacle. Divorce the unworthy song, stay the voluptuous dance, and the music suffers no clinging defilement; the redeemed melodies, stainless as fresh-fallen snow, may be wedded to songs of gallant aspiration or angelic sympathy, which shall raise the soul awhile above earth's sordid infection, disclosing the inextinguishable affinity of the divine part of man's dual nature with the dream-like possibility of Eden-purity, and fearless faith, and love unspeakable.

The story of the Thracian lyre soothing the horrors of the underworld, and melting to relentment its gloomy king—the story of the shepherd-minstrel's harp chasing the shapeless penumbra of looming insanity from the first Hebrew brow crowned in Jehovah's despite—the story of the mighty prophet Elisha, fettered to earth by wrath and scorn till, at his own command, the music swelled, and his enfranchised spirit rose on its viewless wings to behold the veiled Future already woven from the tangled skein of the troubled Present—the thousand-fold story of music's magic and mystery, stretches back into the forgotten Past, and onward into the imagined Future.

Onward into the fathomless eternity; for though 'the heaven of each is but what each desires'—though the Aryan heaven be a place of gradation and precedence, a realm to reign in—though the heaven of the Jewish apostle-seer burn with the gold and sparkle with the gems dear to his race—though the paradise of the sun-scorched Arab be dark with shade of evergreen trees, and cool with ripple of never-failing streams—yet is the universal art so inter-twined with ideal bliss that no heaven of conscious enjoyment has been pictured by belated humanity but music rings for ever there. For alas! what else of mundane achievement can fancy conceive as reproduced in regions of eternal perfection, or transplanted thither? Science is of the earth; ever bearing sad penalty, in toil of mind and body—and what art, save music, has man dedicated to Deity-worship, without disappointment and loss? Doubtfully, Architec-ture; and for such consecration we have found no more expressive name than 'frozen music.'

This unknown anchorite's playing was both a mystery and a revelation. I had never before heard anything to compare with it, nor do I expect ever to hear the like again. Talent, taste, feeling, were there, all in superlative degree, and disclosed with the unas-suming confidence of power; whilst long and loving practice in solitude had averted a certain artificiality which, in the judgment of the uninitiated, generally accompanies musical skill. His was no triumphant mastery of a complicated and perplexing score; he was a sympathetic interpreter, a life-breathing, magic-lending exponent of his composer's revelations, now his own. Solitary practice, with no one but himself to please, would unavoidably give a distinct character to his performance, and this character was evident from the first; it was melancholy—a weary, wistful melancholy, beyond repining or tears, beyond impatience or passion; it was the involun-tary record of a gentle heart breaking slowly under discipline untempered by one ray of earthly hope.

My own incompetence to identify by name a tune which I spiritually recognise is, perhaps, the most disgraceful manifestation of my neglected musical education—at all events, it is the one which causes me most uneasiness. Experience has warned me never to ask a player for the *Marseillaise*, or *Croppies Lie Down*, or what not; for he is pretty sure to say, 'Why, that 's just what I 've been giving you,' or words to similar effect. Alf at last grew tired of my non-committal remarks and replies, and, with a tact which impressed me more afterward than at the time, named each tune before and after playing it. For instance, the yearning tenderness of an exquisitely rendered air would seem to bring back some lost consciousness of an earlier and happier existence, suffusing my whole being with a pensive sadness not to be exchanged for any joy. I would feel the notes familiar, but whether of five years or five million years before, or whether in the body or out of the body, I could n't tell. Alf, on concluding, would simply murmur, *"Home, Sweet Home,"* and all would be explained. Then, perhaps, he would say, *"The Last Rose of Summer"*; and I would be able to follow him intelligently right through.

But he did n't confine himself to the comfortable vulgarity of popular airs. He played selections from Handel, Mozart, Wagner, and I don't know whom; while the time passed unnoticed by both of us. At length he laid the violin across his knees, and, after a pause, his voice rose in one of the sweetest songs ever woven from words. And such a voice!—rich, soft, transcendent, yet suggesting ungauged resources of enchantment unconsciously held in reserve. I sat entranced as verse after verse flowed slowly on, every syllable clear and distinct as in speech; the subtle tyranny of vocal harmony admitting no intruding thought beyond a regretful sense that the song must end.

> But sorrow 's sel' wears past, Jean,
> And joy 's a-comin' fast, Jean,
> The joy that 's aye to last,
> I' the land o' the leal.
>
> A' our freens are gane, Jean,
> We 've lang been left alane, Jean.
> We 'll a' meet again
> I' the land o' the leal.

"How happy Jean Armour must have been to be with poor Burns, while this cold world seemed to slip away from his feet, and leave him to rest with his forgiving Saviour," murmured the boundary man, laying his violin on the table, whilst he gazed absently into the expiring fire. "That song was composed by Burns, on his death-bed. Is n't it beautiful?"

"It is one of the most beautiful songs in the language," I replied; "but Burns is not the author. The song was composed by a woman —Baroness Nairne. It is not for men to write in that strain. As for Jean Armour—well, she had a good deal to forgive, too."

"Ah! do you think a woman loves less because she has much to forgive?" returned Alf sadly, and then added, with sudden interest,

"But what difference do you notice between the poetry of men and women? What is the mark of women's work?"

"Sincerity," I replied. "Notwithstanding Mrs. Hemans, and others, you will find that, as a rule, men's poetry is superior to women's, not only in vigour, but in grace. This is not strange, for grace is, after all, a display of force, an aspect of strength. But in the quality of sincerity, woman is a good first. Take an illustration, while I think of it: Compare the verses of my ancestor, Collins, *On the Grave of Thompson*, with Eliza Cook's verses, *On the Grave of Hood*"——

"But Collins was never married," interposed Alf.

"True," I replied pleasantly. "But our family is aristocratic, and a baton-sinister only sets us off. However, in the two poems I was speaking of, the subject matter is similar; the pieces are about the same length; and the writers have adopted the same iambic octo-syllable, with alternate rhymes. Now, my ancestor's poem is not excelled in grace by anything within the range of our literature; but there 's nothing else in it whatever. Eliza Cook's versification is, in a measure, forced and imperfect, her language occasionally homely and rugged, but the strong beating of a sincere, sympathetic heart is audible in every line."

"But your ancestor is the most artificial writer of an artificial school, and Eliza Cook is the most spontaneous writer of a spontaneous school," replied Alf, with the contradictive impulse which amusingly accompanied his teachableness. "Of course," he added deprecatingly, "I would n't presume to criticise such a poet as Collins; but you said, yourself"——

"Oh, that 's all right," said I generously. "However, though your argument blunts the force of my illustration, it does n't weaken my contention. You 'll find the distinction I 've pointed-out hold good in a greater or less degree throughout literature; you 'll find examples by the thousand, and of course, exceptions by the dozen. But sing again, Alf, please. Every minute you 're silent, is a minute wasted. Sing anything you like—only sing."

"I wanted to have a talk," remonstrated Alf. "You were speaking of the difference between men and women in their literary work. I believe you 're right, though it never struck me before. Now there 's another question that might be worth comparing notes upon. Your remark just brought it into my mind. Here it is"—he hesitated a moment, then went on, with a certain constraint in his voice; the constraint we are apt to feel when forced to plump out the word 'love,' in its narrower sense—"When women love, they don't know why they love; they just love because they do—so they say, and we 're bound to believe them. But when we love women, why do we love them? Being more logical, we ought to know. Do we love a woman for her beauty?—or for her virtues?—or for her accomplishments?—or for what? I fancy, if we understood ourselves, we should be able to say we loved her for some particular quality; and the others are—as you might say—Oh, *you* know! What quality is it, then, that we love a woman for? There 's a problem for you!"

"I can solve it with mathematical certainty, Alf—that is to say, in such a manner as to convey the impossibility of the solution being otherwise than according to my finding. When I 'm allowed to work-out these things in my own circuitous way—which is seldom the case—there are few questions in moral or psychological philosophy which the commission of my years and art can to no issue of true honour bring. But you have to sing six songs first. I 'll leave the choice of them to yourself."

"Very well," replied Alf readily. "I 'll sing the songs as they come to my mind. Remember your promise, now."

Then, rich, soft, and sweet, rose that exquisite voice in easy volume, flooding with new and vivid meaning old familiar verses. Here was my opportunity. I was interested in this boundary man, and resolved to know his history. Rejecting Alf Jones as an assumed name, Nomenology would be at fault here; yet knowing already, by a kind of incommunicable intuition, that he was a Sydney-sider, and had been in some way connected with the drapery-business, I expected to have my knowledge so supplemented by the character of his songs, that—counting reasonably on a little further information, to be gathered before my departure—I should be able to work-out his biography at least as correctly as biographies are generally worked-out.

For the esoteric side of his history, I counted much on his spontaneous choice of songs. Man is but a lyre (in both senses of the phonetically-taken word, unfortunately) ; and some salient experience, some fire-graven thought, some clinging hope, is the plectrum which strikes the passive chords. An old truism will bear expansion here, till it embraces the rule that, whatever else a man may sing, he always sings himself. But you must know how to interpret.

I have said that melancholy was the key-note of Alf's playing. Fused with this, and deeply coloured by it, the tendency of his songs was toward love, and love alone—chaste, supersensuous, but purely human and exclusive love. No suggestion of national inspir-

ation; no broad human sympathies; no echo of the oppressed ones'
cry; no stern challenge of wrong; only a hopeless, undying love,
and an unspeakable self-pity. He was n't even a lyre; he was a
pipe for Fortune's finger to sound what stop she pleased; and,
judging from the tone of his playing, and the selection of his songs,
it had pleased that irresponsible goddess to attune the chords of
his being to a love, pure as heaven, sad as earth, and hopeless as
the other place.

Who is she? thought I.

Silence again sank on the faint yellow lamplight of the hut, as
the last syllables of the sixth song died mournfully away—*She is
far from the Land where Her Young Hero Sleeps*. Then the boundary rider lit his pipe, and slightly moved his seat, placing himself
in an easy listening attitude, with his elbow on the table, and his
hand across his face.

"Alf," said I impressively; "you 'll certainly find yourself shot
into outer darkness, if you don't alter your hand. You 're recklessly transgressing the lesson set forth in the parable of the Talents.
Don't you know it 's wrong to bury yourself here, eating your own
life away with melancholia, seeing that you 're gifted as you are?
Maestros, and high-class critics, and other unwholesomely cultured
people, might possibly sit on you, or damn you with faint praise;
but you could afford to take chance of that, for beyond all doubt,
the million would idolise you. I 'm not looking at the business
aspect of the thing; I 'm thinking of the humanising influence you
would exercise, and the happiness you would confer, and, altogether, of the unmixed good that would lie to your credit, if you
made the intended use of your Lord's money. And here you are,
burying it in the earth."

"O, I would n't be here, I suppose, only for the disfigurement of
my face," he replied, swallowing a sob.

"That 's nothing," I interjected, deeply pained by his allusion.
and inwardly soliciting forgiveness without repentance whilst I
spoke. "Did the British think less of Nelson—Did Lady Hamilton
think less of him, if it comes to that—for the loss of his arm and
his eye? Why, even the conceited German students value scars on
the face more than academic honours. Believe me, Alf, while a
man merely conducts himself as a man, his scars need n't cost him
a thought; but if he 's an artist, as you are, what might otherwise
be a disfigurement becomes the highest claim to respect and sympathy. It 's pure effeminacy to brood over such things, for that 's
just where we have the advantage of women. 'A woman's first

duty,' says the proverb, 'is to be beautiful.' If Lady Hamilton had
been minus an eye and an arm, she would scarcely have attained
her unfortunate celebrity."

The boundary man laid down his pipe, rested his forehead on
his arm upon the table, and for a minute or two sobbed like a
child. It was dreadful to see him. He was worse than Ida, in an
argument with Mrs. Beaudesart; he was as bad as an Australian
judge, passing mitigated sentence on some well-connected criminal.

Presently he rose, and walked unsteadily to the other end of the
hut; his dog, with a low, pathetic whine, following him. Perceiving
that he was off again, I turned up the flame of the lamp, with a
view to neutralising the effect of the moonlight.

"Are you not well, Alf?"

No answer. He was lying on his back on the bed, one arm across
his face, and the other hanging down; whilst his dog, crouched at
the bedside, was silently licking the brown fingers. Then my eye
happened to fall on the American clock over the fire-place. Not
that time, surely! But my watch had beaten the clock by ten
minutes.

"I say, Alf; I don't know how to apologise for keeping you up
till this time. It 's half-past eleven."

Still no answer. I brought in my possum-rug, and began to
spread it on the floor. Alf had risen, and rolled his blankets back
off the bed. He now took out the mattress of dried grass, and laid
it on the floor, then re-arranged his blankets.

"But I certainly won't rob you of your tick," said I. "One characteristic of childhood I still retain is the ability to sleep anywhere, like a dog."

"You must take it, if you sleep in this hut," he replied curtly.
"Take that too." He handed me his feather pillow.

"Do you shut your door at nights?" I asked. "Because, if you
do, I 'll chain Pup to the fence. He likes to go in and out at his
own pleasure; and, if he found himself shut-out, he might get lost."

"It can stay open to-night," replied Alf.

"Right," said I; and I began to disrobe, as I always do when
circumstances permit. Sleeping with your clothes on is slovenly;
sleeping with your spurs on is, in addition, ruinously destructive to
even the strongest bed-clothes.

"By-the-way, Alf," I remarked, as I pulled off my socks; "I was
forgetting your problem. The solution is clear enough to me, but
the inquiry opens out no end of side-issues, each of which must be
followed out to its re-intersection with the main line of argument.

if we wish to leave our conclusion unassailable at any point. The question, then, is: Do we love a woman for her beauty, for her virtues, or for her accomplishments? Now let us make sure of our terminology." I paused, but Alf maintained silence.

"In the first place," I continued, kicking off the garment which it is unlawful even to name, "we must inquire what the personal beauty of woman is, and wherein it consists. It consists in approximation to a given ideal; and this ideal is not absolute; it is elastic in respect of races and civilisations, though each type may be regarded as more or less rigid within its own domain. Passing over such racial ideals as the Hottentot Venus, and waiving comparison between the Riverine ideal of fifty years ago and that of to-day, we have the typical Eve of Flanders as one ideal, and the typical Eve of Italy as another." Again I paused, but Alf remained silent.

"Moreover," I continued, settling myself down into the comfortable mattress—"if no specimen of classic art had survived the dark ages, I question whether we would implicitly accept as our present ideal the chiselled profile, in which physiognomists fail to find any special indications of moral or intellectual excellence. But when we based our modern civilisation on the relics of classic Greece—directly, or through Rome—we naturally accepted the ideal of beauty then and there current. Attila or Abderrahman might have deflected the European standard of beauty into a widely different ideal, but it was not to be. And we 're too prone to accept our classic ideal as being identified with civilisation and refinement. We should remember that the flat features of the Coptic ideal looked out on high attainments in art and science when our Hellenic archetypes, in spite of their chiselled profiles, were drifting across from the Hindo-Koosh, in the blanket-and-tomahawk stage of civilisation. Also, the slant-eyed ideal of China has a decent record. Further still, the German is facially coarser, and mentally higher, than the Circassian." Again I paused.

"Are n't you sleepy?" asked Alf, gently but significantly.

"I ought to be," I replied, humouring his present caprice, though grieved to withhold the solution which he had so earnestly desired an hour before. "Just as the secondary use of the bee is to make honey, and his primary one to teach us habits of industry, so the secondary use of the hen is to lay eggs, and her primary one to teach us proper hours. But, unfortunately, we don't avail ourselves of the lessons written for us in the Book of Nature; we simply eat the honey and the eggs, allowing our capability and god-like reason to fust in us, unused. Such is life, Alf." And in thirty seconds I was asleep.

On awaking, as usual, to listen for bells, I became conscious of something between a sigh and a groan, outside the hut. This was repeated again and again, until, actuated by compassion rather than curiosity, I crept to the door, and looked out. Six or eight yards away, Alf was kneeling at the fence, his arms on one of the wires, and the poor, disfigured face, wet with tears, turned westward to the pitiless moon, now just setting.

Thou art in a parlous state, shepherd, thought I; and it then occurred to me that my own acute, philosophic temperament was one of the things I ought to be thankful for. But I could n't feel thankful; I could only feel powerless and half-resentful in the presence of a distress which seemed proof against palliative, let alone antidote. At length the moon disappeared; then the boundary man's forehead sank on his arms, a calm came over him, and I knew that his shapeless vagaries had taken form in prayer. So I withdrew to my possum-rug, speculating on the mysterious effect of a ray of lunar light on grey matter protected by various plies of apparently well-arranged natural armour.

When I woke again, the early sunlight was streaming through the open door, and Alf, with a short veil of crape concealing the middle of his face, was frying chops at the fire. The fit had passed away, and he was perfectly sane and cheerful.

My first solicitude was for Pup, but I soon saw that he was more than merely safe. He was lying at the foot of the meat-pole, gorged like a boa-constrictor, while a pair of half-chewed feet, still attached to the loosened rope, were all that remained of the turkey. Probably he had stood on his hind-feet, scratching at the rope, till the hitch, hurriedly secured in the first place, had come undone. I was too well accustomed to such things to feel any embarrassment; and as for Alf, I could n't help thinking that the loss of his turkey enhanced the cordiality of his manner.

"Grandest dog I 've seen for years," he remarked, as he set the table. "Do you get many kangaroos with him?"

"Oh, no," I replied; "I never get one, and don't intend to. I never let him go after anything. It 's quite enough, and sometimes more than enough, for him to do his regular travelling. The hot weather comes very severe on him; in fact, some days I have to give him a drink every hour, or oftener. Then he has the hard ground to contend with; and when the rain comes, the dirt sticks between his toes, and annoys him. Windy weather is bad for him, too; and frost puts a set on him altogether. Then he 's always swarming with fleas, and in addition to that, the flies have a particular fancy for him. And, seeing that one half of the population is always plotting to steal him, and the other half trying to poison him, while, for his own part, he has a confirmed habit of getting lost, you may be sure we have plenty to occupy our minds, without thinking about kangaroos. He 's considerably more trouble to me than all my money, but he 's worth it. As you say, he 's a fine dog. I don't know what I should do without him."

"I don't know what I should do without my dog, either," replied Alf. And he related some marvellous stories of the animal's sagacity; to which, of course, I could n't respond on Pup's behalf.

Then, whilst we saddled-up and rode off together at a walk, the conversation naturally drifted to horses, until about ten o'clock, when we stopped at a little wicket-gate in the north-east corner of Alf's ten-by-five paddock.

"You 're in the Patagonia Paddock now," said he, as I passed through the gate. "You 'll strike the track in six miles. Can I do anything for you at the station?" he added, after a pause. "Any message, or anything?"

"By-the-way, yes, Alf, if you 'll be so good. When will you be going across?"

"To-day," he replied. "I 'm not going round the paddock."

I drew my writing-case from Bunyip's pack; and this was the note I pencilled:—

Wallaby Track, 10/2/'84.

Dear Jack,

When you remarked, yesterday, that the saddle on my horse was very like one that a red-headed galoot had stolen from you, you displayed a creditable acuteness, combined with a still more creditable unsuspicious-ness. It was your saddle once, but it is yours no longer. It is mine.

> Demand not how the prize I hold;
> It was not given, nor lent, nor sold.
>
> *Rokeby.*

You will find three one-pound notes in this letter. Please accept the same as compensation for loss of the article in question. This is all you are likely to get; for though the saddle is honestly worth about twice that amount, my conscience now acquits me in the matter; moreover, my official salary is so judiciously proportioned to my frugal requirements that I can afford no more. If you duly receive this money, and at the same time feel hopelessly mystified concerning the saddle, a double pur-pose will be fulfilled.

Yours, in a manner of speaking,
THOMAS COLLINS.

"I 'll put this into Jack's hand, if I live," said the boundary man, with amusing solemnity, as he buttoned his jumper-pocket over the letter.

"Thank you, Alf. And now," I continued, retaining for a moment the hand he extended in farewell—"take my advice, and, while you 're at the station, give Montgomery notice. Let some more capable boundary man take your place. You 're not worth your damper at this work; for no man's ability is comprehensive enough to cover musical proficiency such as yours, and leave the narrowest flap available for anything else. I can see through you like glass. I could write your biography. And, believe me, you 're no more fitted for this life than you are to preside over a school of Stoic Philosophy. You 're a reed, shaken by the wind. Be a man, Alf. Turn your face eastward or southward, and challenge Fortune with your violin and your voice."

He made no reply, but below the edge of the crape mask I saw his lips move, as he bent his head in unconscious acquiescence.

A quarter of an hour afterward, I looked back to see him and his history a shapeless speck, far away along the diminishing perspective of the line of fence. There was something impressive in the recollection that, during the whole of our companionship, he had never uttered one objectionable or uncharitable word, nor attempted any witticism respecting Mrs. Beaudesart.

CHAPTER VII

THE reader, however unruly under weaker management, is by this time made aware of a power, beyond his own likes and dislikes, controlling the selection and treatment of these informal annals. That power, in the nature of things, resides napoleonically with myself, and has, I trust, been exercised toward the information and edification of the few who fall under its jurisdiction—suggesting, as it does, Tom Hood's idea of perfect rule: An angel from heaven, and a despotism.

Encouraged by this assurance, and prompted, as usual, by a refinement which some might construe into fastidiousness, I shall once more avail myself of the prerogative hitherto so profitably sustained. The routine record of March 9 is not a desirable text. It would merely call forth from fitting oblivion the lambing-down of two stalwart fencers by a pimply old shanty-keeper; and you know this sort of thing has been described ad sickenum by other pens, less proper than mine—described, in fact, till you would think that, in the back-country, drinking took the place of Conduct, as three-fourths of life; whilst the remaining fourth consisted of fighting. Whereas, outside the shearing season, you might travel a hundred miles, calling at five shanties, without seeing a man the worse for drink; and you would be still more likely to go a thousand miles, calling at fifty shanties, without seeing any indication of a fight. Of course, there are some queer tragedies, and many melancholy farces, enacted at the shanties; but speaking in a broad, statistical way, the shanty-keeper gets such a miserably small percentage of the money earned out-back that he usually lives in saint-like indigence, and dies in the odour of very inferior liquor. Here and there, the exceptional case of a shanty-keeper retiring on his Congealed Ability goes to show the fatuity of the curse-hypothesis, rounding us up on the one unassailable bit of standing-ground, namely, that such is life.

It would do you no good to hear how the old Major (he was an ex-officer of the Imperial army) fawned on my officialship, and threw himself in rapport with my gentlemanship—how his haggard, handsome wife leered at me over his shoulder—how the open-hearted asses of fencers, in weary alternation, confidentially told me fragmentary and idiotic yarns—how they shook hands with me till I was tired, and wept over me till I was disgusted—how they irrelevantly and profusely apologised for anything they might have said, and abjectly besought me, if I felt anyway nasty, to take it out of their (adj.) hides—I say, it would do you no good.

So, for this and two other reasons, I shall take as my text the entry of March 28, and a portion of the following verse. This arbitrary departure in dates will give you another glimpse of Alf Jones. Also, the peculiar scythe-sweep of my style of narrative will take in a rencontre with another person, to whom, in your helpless state as a reader, you have already been introduced. And if you take it not patiently, the more is your mettle.

FRI. MARCH 28. Wilcannia shower. Jack the Shellback.

SAT. MARCH 29. To Runnymede. Tom Armstrong and mate.

I had spent the night of the 27th at Burke's camp, on Boottara; my horses faring decently for the season. Burke, the regular station-contractor, had been off work for a month, keeping his twenty horses and twenty-four bullocks in the Abbotsford Paddock, and watering them daily at Granger's Tank. The Abbotsford Paddock, having gone dry in the spring, had fair grass in it, but, of course, no station stock.

In spite of all the loafing I could do, the season was telling on my horses. Their hoofs were worn to the similitude of quoits; you could count their ribs a quarter of a mile off; and they had acquired that crease down the hip pathetically known as 'the poor man's stripe.' Cleopatra's bucking had become feeble and mechanical, and so transparently stagey that I used to be ashamed of it. Still, my aversion to lending the horse, or having him duffed, compelled me to keep his performance up to the highest standard compatible with justice to himself.

Runnymede homestead—to which that strange fatality was again driving me—was thirty miles from Burke's camp; but, by losing a few miles in a slight detour, I could make a twenty-mile stage to Alf Jones's, and, next day, a fifteen-mile stage to the station. This rate of travelling, with frequent holidays, was fast enough for a man without official hopes, or corresponding fear of the sack. If Alf was gone, so much the better for himself; if he was still in the old spot, so much the better for me. That was the way I looked at it.

In view of the soul-destroying ignorance which saturates society, it may be well to repeat that this central point of the universe, Riverina Proper, consists of a wide promontory of open and level plain, coming in from the south-west; broken, of course, by many pine-ridges, clumps of red box, patches of scrub or timber, and the inevitable red gum flats which fringe the rivers. Eastward, the plain runs out irregularly into open forests of white box, pine, and other timber. Northward—something over a couple of hundred miles from the Murray—the tortuous frontier of boundless scrub meets the plain with the abruptness of a wall. Boottara is half plain and half scrub; Runnymede is practically all plain.

When I left Burke's camp, heading south-west for Alf's paddock, there was a strong, dry, and—as it seemed to me then—useless, north-west wind tearing through the tops of the trees. I thought it might lull before I left the shelter of the scrub, but it only increased. The willowy foliage of the scattered myalls on the plain stood out horizontally to leeward; and an endless supply of lightly-bounding roley-poleys were chasing each other across the level ground. I lashed my hat on with a handkerchief, one side of the brim being turned down to keep some of the sand and dust out of my weather-ear. The horses, with ears flattened backward and muzzles slanted out to leeward, caught the storm on their polls, and, leaning side-ways against the still-increasing pressure, pushed on gallantly. They remembered Alf's grass as well as I remembered his music.

About mid-day—having crossed the main track diagonally, with-out seeing it—I came upon the portable engine and centrifugal pump belonging to Runnymede, set up for work at Patagonia Tank.

On a well-managed station, like Runnymede, a tank is, whenever possible, excavated on the margin of a swamp. The clay extracted is formed into a strong wall, or enclosing embankment, a couple of yards back from the edge of the excavation; and under this wall, an iron pipe connects the swamp with the tank. The swamp being full, and the water in the tank having reached the same level, the outer end of the pipe is closed, and the portable pumping plant sent out to fill the space inside the wall, thus doubling the capacity of the tank.

Three days before the time I speak of, a thunderstorm of a few miles' area had filled the Patagonia Swamp; and Montgomery, dreading a rainless winter, had seized the opportunity to secure a supply of water. The pumping plant had been set-up on the evening before, but not started; and now the wind had swept all the water to the other end of the swamp. The engine-driver and his mate had struck their tent to prevent its being blown away, and were lying in the lee of the tank wall, trying to get a smoke.

Young Mooney had come early from the station, to see how the pump started, and had been drawn into a controversy with his half-broken colt; the point in dispute being whether it was safe to go within forty yards of the engine. Mooney had maintained the affirmative, and the colt, the negative. The Pure Logic which the colt had opposed to Mooney's Applied Logic had ultimately prevailed, and the narangy had withdrawn from the argument on his ear, whilst the colt had disappeared through the rising dust-storm. Now Mooney was sitting in the lee of the embankment, cursing the day he elected to be a squatter rather than a clergyman.

I watered my horses and Pup at the tank, condoled with Mooney, joined the two other chaps in severe criticism on the weather, replenished my water-bag, and passed on. I may add that the pump was n't started on that occasion at all; the water being blown clean out of the swamp, and scattered, fine as dust, through the thirsty atmosphere.

The steady intensity of the shower augmented as I went on. It got under my hat, and the next moment that product of German industry was flying across the wilderness, for the good of trade. At last I had to give-in. The increasing broadside pressure, with the sand and dust, was becoming too much for the horses; and, in any case, I should have had to stop on Pup's account. I turned Cleopatra's head to leeward, and began carefully to dismount. But the wind ballooned the back of my coat and the right branch of my other garment, and I went three yards through the air, like a bird shot on the wing. Recovering foothold, I fought my way to Bunyip, and relieved him of his pack. Then, with Cleopatra's rein over my arm, I sat down on the ground to see it out. At this low elevation, the air was thick with skipping crumbs of hard dirt, which rattled on my skull like hail; in fact, everything not anchored to the ground was at racing speed, and all in the same direction.

But this strong, thirsty wind, coming from the north-western deserts with a clear fetch of a thousand miles, was not going to last many hours; meantime, I set myself to work out scientifically its genesis, operation, and hidden purpose. The first and second considerations were merely matters of research and calculation; the third was largely speculative, admitting of no more definite conclusion than that the time had come when hygienic necessities required a thorough rousing and ridding-out of microbes, bacteria, and other pests too minute to be worth particularising. But I was better enlightened before another day had gone over my head.

Whilst engaged in these not unpleasing studies, I caught a momentary glimpse of something, ten yards away to the left, which seemed to be moving slowly against the wind. The volume of flying dust was, of course, far from uniform in density; and presently I caught sight of the object again. It was a man, creeping slowly and painfully across the stubbly knobs of cotton-bush on his hands and knees. I hailed him in a voice that took the skin off my throat, but another glimpse showed him still travelling; his head bent almost to the ground. I rose carefully to my feet, facing the shower, but only to be hurled down on top of the faithful Pup, and savagely snapped at. Then I went like a quadruped till I reached the wayfarer, and caught him by the ankle. He looked round; I beckoned, and crept back to my former seat, whilst he followed close behind. Then a bearded, haggard, resolute face, framed by an old hat tied down over the ears, confronted me.

"You look like some worn and weary brother, pulling hard against the stream," I shouted.

The dry, cracked lips moved without speech, and the bloodshot eyes left my face to scan the pack-saddle beside me.

"Water?" I suggested.

He nodded. Cleopatra was close behind me, propped against the wind. I drew myself up by the near stirrup, till I could unbuckle the water-bag from the cantle. Though filled with half a gallon of water not two hours before, it was now half-empty. I drew the cork; my visitor clasped the cool, damp canvas between his trembling hands, and, with fine self-control, barely wetted his lips again and again. At last he took a moderate drink.

"Making for Patagonia Tank," he hoarsely remarked.

"You were going past it. It 's about a mile and a half straight across there. I 've just come from it."

"Disappointed of water last night," he continued. "It was dark when I struck the little tank I was making for, and I found her dry; and my throat like a lime-kiln. Too dog-tired to go any further, so I rested till morning, and then struck for the Patagonia, with a devil of a headache to help me along. I knew of another tank nearer, but I would n't trust myself to find her in the dust. I helped to sink the Patagonia. Fine tank—ain't she?"

"First-class. Have you no swag?"

"I had a very good one a few hours ago, but Lord knows where she is now. I left her behind when the wind put me on all-fours. Kept pretty well in the same quarter, I think?"

"About the same."

"That 'll be a bit of a guide. You 'll be staying here till she slackens-down?"

"There 's nothing else I can do."

"Well, I 'll stay with you. If you shoot me straight for the swamp, I 'll be right. I 'll spell to-night at the tank, and then have a try for my swag."

"You 'll find two very decent coves camped at the tank, with the engine and pump. They 'll put you on your feet."

"Good again."

"Which way are you travelling?" I asked.

"Any way. Work 's scarce; contractors camped for want of water; too late for burr-cutting; nothing doing. I wish to God the rabbits would come something worth while."

And so the profitless conversation (conversation is generally profitless) went on by fits and starts, till the sand and dirt-pellets ceased to drift. Half-an-hour later, it was an almost perfect calm, though the air was still charged with dust.

By this time, I had re-packed, and was ready to start. My guest was now on his feet, but shaky enough. With Bligh-like impartiality, I meted out half a pint of water to him, the same quantity to Pup, and the remaining quarter-pint to myself.

"Got a bit of tobacco to spare?" he asked. "Mine 's all in my swag."

"Certainly," I replied. "Are you hard-up? Because I can lend you five bob till we meet again."

"No, thank-you. I've got a couple or three notes left; and even if I had n't, I 'd think twice before I touched your money. Money 's a peculiar thing."

"Especially in the sense of being peculiar to certain sections of society," I replied. "Now strike straight across there, and you 'll fetch the tank in a mile and a half."

"What 's your name?" he demanded, as I placed my foot in the stirrup.

"Collins."

"Well, so-long!"

"So-long."

My horses went off freely. I struck the wicket-gate with accuracy, and bowled on toward the declining sun, which showed dull and coppery through suspended dust; till, just at that hour which calls the faithful Mussulman to prayer, and the no less faithful sun-downer to the station store, I reached my destination.

One glance was enough. Two strange horses were in the pad-dock; the kerosene-tins still stood in the sheltered angle by the chimney, but the flowers were dead; the smooth-trodden radius round the door was no longer swept except by the winds of heaven, and was becoming a midden whence antiquaries of future ages might sift out priceless relics with unpronounceable names. A strange dog came to the door-step, gave a single bark, and re-en-tered; then Jack the Shellback appeared, and, recognising me, got a larger quantity of profanity and indecency into his cordial wel-come than you might think possible. Scarce as water was, he cursed me into washing the sand out of my hair with two conse-cutive goes of the precious liquid, whilst he swore the saddles off my horses, and obscene-languaged some supper for me. Even before the shower, the whole area of my mortal shrine, back from high-water mark round neck and wrists, had been pistol-proof with a thousand samples of dust, patiently collected over the same num-ber of miles; but that did n't trouble me. I could get rid of it— along with much moral and mental virtue, unfortunately—possibly at the Runnymede swimming-hole, or failing that, at the place where the Lachlan had been.

"Stiff little breeze we had," I remarked, as I sat down to supper. "Well, no," replied Jack, in reluctant and compassionate nega-tive; and this was the only part of his long reply fit to place before the sanctimonious reader. He went on to tell me, in the vulgar tongue, that if I had ever been at sea, I would think nothing of a whiff like that. He told me of storms he had weathered—parti-cularly, one off Christiana Cooner, a solitary island in the south Atlantic—and the effect of his discourse is that I have ever since been careful, in the company of sailors, to avoid speaking of the winds I have encountered.

"I 'll fix you up for a hat," he continued, in language of match-less force and piquancy. "Bend *her*; she 'll about fit you. I dropped across her one day I was in the road-paddock."

'She' was a drab belltopper, in perfect preservation, with a crown nothing less than a foot and a half high, and a narrow, wavy brim. She proved a perfect fit when I 'bent' her. I wore her afterward for many a week, till one night she rolled away from my camp, and I saw her no more, though I sought her diligently. Take her for all in all, I shall not look upon her like again.

"Now, if you 'd a pair o' skylights athort your cutwater, you 'd be set up for a professor of phrenology, or doxology, or any other ology," suggested Jack, with one oath, two unseemly expletives, and two obscenities.

"How is that for high?" I asked, putting on a pair of large, round, clouded lenses, which my experience of ophthalmia has warned me to carry continually. Then, without interrupting my good host's torrent of unrepeatable congratulation, I turned aside and unstrapped a portion of Bunyip's pack. Presently I advanced and resumed my seat, with the ancestor of all pipes pendent from my mouth. The hat, glasses, and pipe chorded (if I may use that expression) so perfectly that Jack's merriment died-away in a reverent petition to be struck dead.

The pipe has already been referred-to in these annals. It was probably the most artistic, the most opulent-looking, the most scholarly, the most imposing, and, from a Darwinian point of view, the most highly specialised, meerschaum ever seen on earth. It was a pipe such as no smoker parts with during life, but bequeaths to his best-beloved son—a pipe such as would make any man wish to have a Benjamin, but for the fear that the heir-presumptive might be exposed to unfair temptation, and the old man himself to grave peril.

This nonpareil lies before me now, on an old, cracked dinner-plate, with my knife and tobacco. Its head, ideally perfect as that goddess who rose from similar material, carries, in spite of its vast size, no suggestion of the colossal, but rather of the majestic. Its aspect would be overpowering but for the soothing and reassuring effect of colour—as where, at point of contact, the opaque snow of the upper half, with cirrhus-like edge, overlies rather than meets the indescribable wealth of lucent and fathomless umber, which soul-satisfying colour intensifies toward the rounded heel, softening to a paler tint in its serene re-ascent, till the meerschaum terminates in a heavy, semi-cylindrical collar, of almost audacious simplicity. Then a thick, flexible, silk-chequered stem takes up the wondrous tale, in its turn extending, with a most magnanimous restraint, barely four inches ere transferring its glories to the worthy keeping of such a piece of Baltic amber as you shall not match in any democratic community. The slight silver mounting hints a princely concession to the great pipe family; and the two little red crackers, depending from the junction of mouthpiece and stem, whilst giving no encouragement to presumptuous rivalry, soften the austere, unapproachable, super-Phidian perfection of the whole ongsomble.

Here it occurs to the subtle critic that this is something like what a novelist would write. A novelist is always able to bring forth out of his imagination the very thing required by the exigencies of his story—just as he unmasks the villain at the critical moment, and, for the young hero's benefit, gently shifts the amiable old potterer to a better land in the very nick of time. Such is not life. And to avoid any shadow of the imputation in which that incident-begging novelist wallows, I must now turn aside for one moment to tell how I came into possession of such a pipe as no other Australian bush-man ever owned. As for the digression—well, I suppose even the most insubordinate reader is by this time educated up to my style.

Shortly before the previous wool-season, I had found myself, on a rather chilly night, drawing toward the western boundary of Gun-bah, on the track from Hillston to Hay. A spark of red fire, miles ahead, told of someone camped at a clump on Illilliwa, just about the spot I had marked out as my own destination—there being grass anywhere inside the boundary of Illilliwa, and none in the road-paddocks of Gunbah. As I drew nearer, the impotent tinkle of one of those hemispherical horse-bells indicated a new-chum's camp.

I casually noticed a man sitting before the fire, though he van-ished before I arrived, leaving an empty camp-stool. As I unsaddled my horses, he reappeared out of the darkness—a large, blonde, heavily-moustached young fellow, with a light rifle in the hollow of his arm. Being too hungry for conversation, I merely tendered about three words of civil remark whilst raking out some coals for my quart-pot; and he resumed his seat in silence, watching me across the fire.

But during my ample repast—the second one of the day—I intro-duced myself more fully, and partly won my way through the suspicious reserve of the strong man armed. By the time my supper-service was re-packed, and I was stretched in Aboriginal contentment beside the fire, I had noticed, by the uncertain light, an eight-by-six tent, which seemed to contain two camp-bedsteads, on one of which lay a sleeping man. Some yards behind the tent stood a spring-cart.

My new acquaintance, becoming quite frank and cordial, sup-ported his end of the conversation in rather laboured English, with a slight foreign accent. Gold-mining was the topic which had risen to the surface; and, as an hour—two hours—passed, I was fairly abashed by the extent and accuracy of his information. He talked so confidently, so scientifically, and, as far as my knowledge went, so veraciously, not only of the principal Australian gold-fields, but

of the different notable claims, that curiosity broke through ceremony, and I asked him how long he had been out.

Just three weeks, he told me. His name, he added, with an inimitable bow, was Franz von Swammerbrunck, very much at my service.
His friend, Schloss, and himself, fellow-students, had left Frank-
fort only three months before.

"Frankfort-on-the-Main, or Frankfort-on-the-Oder?" I asked,
veiling a mild and inoffensive pedantry under the guise of friendly
interest.

His courteous reply tailed-off naturally into such a volume of
condensed information as re-impressed on my mind a fact which
we are, perhaps, too prone to lose sight of—namely, the existence
of a civilisation north of Torres Straits. Desiring, of course, to
avail myself of some few rays of this boreal light, I tried to steer
the conversation in the direction of bainting and boetry (for such
subjects go well at camp-fires), but Franz hung so persistently on
one rein that I had to give him his head, and he edged back to gold-
mining. Turn the discourse whatever way I would, that wearisome
topic was adroitly made to occur as if of its own accord.

"But don't let me be keeping you out of bed," I remarked, at
length.

"Tear Mr. Tongcollin, you haf dot impertinence perpetrate
nefer," replied my companion earnestly. "Dis schall pe mine
period mit der sentry-vatch. Dot molestation to youzelluf solitary
vill pe, unt von apology ver despicable iss to me reqvire ass der
conseqvence. Bot you magnificent-superb garrulity mos peen to der
strange-alien-isolate in dot platty dilemma mit Schloss unt mine-
zelluf, invaluable unt moch velcome. Dot goot-define kevartz reef,
by instance, vich you loquacious-delineate, mit der visible golt
destitute—by tam! he schall mine eyes from der skleep fly-away
mit der enchantment-glitter! Ach Gott! Nefer py vhite man vit-
ness, you schall say, pefore fife unt seex yare pass-gone, unt by
pushmen diminutive nomber unt platty few altogedder. Bot der
localisation-topography unt der route you schall py der map mit
you gross magnanimity indicate, unt Gott pless! Tousand pig
tank you, Mr. Tongcollin! For von trifle-moment, you ver munificent reprieve"——

He entered the tent, and spoke to the sleeper, with suppressed
eagerness in his voice. The watch below attired himself and came
forth; then followed a formal introduction; and in another couple
of hours—such was the clearness and receptivity of these young
men's minds—I had made them acquainted with all I knew of the

geology of Upper Riverina. And not less remarkable than their
infatuation for non-auriferous reefs was their vivid interest in bushrangers and blackfellows; but whereas they received my crude geo-
logical information with the attention which its frankness certainly
merited, it was plain that their idea of prospecting the back-blocks
with the pick in one hand and the rifle in the other, remained
unshaken by my repeated assurances of peace and safety. That was
all right. The topography of the wilderness was the thing they
wanted; they would manage the peace and safety for themselves.
Schloss, in particular, was almost as eager for the inevitable brush
with outlaw or savage as he was for the no less inevitable golden
reef.

In due time, the stars paled to indistinctness, then to invisibility,
and the landscape came into view in the fresh, chilly dawn, showing a strong grey horse feeding with Fancy and Bunyip, two hundred yards away. I was in no hurry to start, but my friends were
like greyhounds in the leash. Therefore, whilst I dozed off to sleep,
they packed up their elaborate camp, and harnessed their horse in
the spring-cart. They would stop for breakfast after a few hours'
travelling; meantime, they had a cup of coffee. I roused myself to
reiterate the directions I had already given respecting the locality
of half a dozen reefs in the back-blocks; then my friends stowed
away their maps and diagrams, and shook hands with me so affec-
tionately—so Germanly, in fact—that I called up a certain sardonic
expression of face, as the best safeguard against possible kissing.
Finally, when they were seated side by side under the tilt of the
spring-cart, Swammerbrunck said, whilst his blue eyes twinkled
with merriment,

"Vit Mr. Spreenfeldt shall you peen von acquaintance?"

Yes; I was slightly acquainted with Mr. Springfield. He was the
landlord of a hotel in Hay.

"Vill you said, mit you proximate-ensuing interview, dot der two
Yarman moreprogues schall peen ass pig fools ass efer!"

I promised to deliver the message, whereupon the wise men of
the north laughed heartily. Then the three of us raised our hats
with aristocratic gravity; and the vehicle moved away toward the
land of Disillusionment. As I lay down again, I heard the poor
fellows burst into unintelligible song; and, after the spring-cart
had jogged a quarter of a mile, one of the adventurers looked past
the edge of the tilt toward me, and waved his handkerchief. Not
having any similar article on me at the time, I half-rose and
returned the farewell with my hat.

As big fools as ever! Between asleep and awake, I pondered on the quantity and quality of Australian-novel lore which had found utterance there. The outlawed bushrangers; the lurking black-fellows; the squatter's lovely Diana-daughter, awaiting the well-bred greenhorn (for even she had cropped-up in conversation)— how these things recalled my reading! And yet they were quite as reasonable as the discovery of the rich reef by the soft-handed, fastidious young gentleman-digger.

I had only wasted time in asseverating that barren reefs are twice as plentiful as half-tucker reefs; ten times as plentiful as wages reefs; and a hundred times as plentiful as pile reefs. Both mar-graves had listened with polite toleration when I compassionately added that the pile reef is always discovered by an ungrammatical person, named Old Brummy, or Sydney Bob, or Squinty-eyed Pete, or something to the same general effect; and this because few 'gentlemen' can stoop low enough, and long enough, and doggedly enough, to conquer; whereas Brummy &c., does n't require to stoop at all—and *his* show is little better than Buckley's.

Also, the barons had derived keen enjoyment from my honest suggestion, that the 'gentleman's' best show is to discover the dis-coverer, and prevail upon the latter, per medium of fire-water and blarney, to affix his illegible signature to some expropriating docu-ment. And yet those visionaries were highly informed men—at least, as far as schools, lecture-rooms, laboratories, museums, and the whole admirable machinery of modern academic and technical training could take them. This, let me add, is the record of an actual occurrence. It will just show you how much the novelist has to answer for; following, as he does, the devices and desires of his own heart; telling the lies he ought not to have told, and leaving untold the lies that he ought to have told.

I am not forgetting the pipe. Leaving the camp at about ten in the forenoon, I noticed, lying among the tussocks where the spring-cart had stood, something which, at the first glance, I took for the sumptuous holster of an overgrown navy revolver. I need say no more. It may have been the landgraves' pipe-case, or, on the other hand, it may not. At all events, regarding the article as treasure-trove, within the meaning of the Act, I formally took possession under 6 Hen. III., c. 17, sec. 34; holding myself prepared at any time to surrender the property to anyone clever enough to sneak it, and cunning enough to keep it; though a sense of delicacy might prevent me chasing the Kronprinzes round the country, as if they had stolen something. When the pipe had eaten its magnificent head off in tobacco, then, of course, I sold it to pay expenses, and bought it in myself. So I have it still. And if the censorious reader has detected here and there in these pages a tendency toward the Higher Criticism, or a leaning to State Socialism, or any passage that seemed to indicate a familiarity with cuneiform inscriptions, or with the history and habits of Pre-Adamite Man, he may be assured that, at the time of writing such passage, I had been smoking the mighty pipe—or rather, the mighty pipe had been smoking me—and the unlawful erudition had effervesced per motion of my scholastic ally.

"I can better that yet," remarked Jack unprintably. "I 'll swap you coats. Yours ain't a bad one, but your arms goes a foot too fur through the sleeves, an' she 's ridiculous short in the tail. She 'll jist about fit my soul-case; an't I got an alpacar one here, made a-purpose for some clipper built (individual) like you. I would n't 'a' speculated in her, on'y she was the last the hawker had left. She 's never bin bent." He produced a slate-coloured alpaca coat, which, when I tried it on, extended down to my knuckles and knees, trailing clouds of glory where there was none before. "You 'll do a bit o' killin' at the station, in that rig-out," continued my host, with a lewd reference to some person who shall be nameless.

"By-the-way, what 's come of Alf Jones?" I asked, as we resumed our seats.

"Gone to (sheol)," replied his successor tersely. Alf, it appeared, had left the station six or eight weeks before, bound for no one knew where. Jack's opinion was that in so doing he had made a slippery-hitch. I spoke of Alf's singing; and Jack told me how the fellows at the station had persuaded him to give them a couple or three songs before he left.

"Was n't he something wonderful?" I remarked.

"Well, no," Jack replied, deferentially but positively; "nothing like what you 'd hear in a fo'c'sle."

In fact, according to Jack's account, he used to be reputed a middling singer himself. And he straightway rendered a mawkishly sentimental song, and a couple of extremely unchaste ones, in a voice which made the tea-embrowned pannikins on the table rattle in sympathy.

I remembered Alf's minstrelsy, and the contrast was painful. Jack noticed a depression creeping over me, and, with the intuition of true hospitality, exerted his conversational powers for my entertainment. His discourse ran exclusively on a topic which, sad to say, furnishes, in all grades of masculine society, the motif of nearly every joke worth telling. In this line, Jack was a discriminating anthologist, and, moreover, a judicious adapter—all his gestes being related in the first-person-singular. His autobiographical record was a staggerer; but I happened to recognise amongst his *affaires de cœur* several very old acquaintances, and made allowance accordingly. If he had been a truthful man, the floor of the hut would have opened that night and swallowed him alive; but his vain-glorious emulation of St. Paul's chief-of-sinners hyperbole covered as with a mantle his multitude of *bonâ-fide* transgressions, and preserved him for better things.

Yes; better things. For, mind you, beyond this rollicking black-guard there stood a second Jack, a soft-hearted, self-sacrificing other-phase, chivalrous to quixotism, yet provokingly reticent touching any act or sentiment which reflected real credit on himself. Not that every blackguard is a Bayard, any more than every wife-beater is a coward; but almost all moral and immoral qualities are in reality independent of each other. And Jack, for one thing, was eminently religious—as indeed were those greater geniuses and equally hard cases, Dick Steele and Henry Fielding. Says the First Lord (neither of the Admiralty nor the Treasury), 'The web of our life is of a mingled yarn, good and ill together; our virtues would be proud if our faults whipped them not; and our crimes would despair if they were not cherished by our virtues.'

"I always make a bit of a prayer before turnin'-in," remarked Jack, in appendix to a story which Chaucer or Boccaccio would have rejected with horror; then the poor fellow laid his pipe on the table, and, kneeling by his bedside, repeated in a firm, reverent voice an almost unrecognisable version of the Lord's Prayer, and an unconscious parody on Ken's Evening Hymn:—*Glory to Thee, my God, this night.*

"See, it 's this way with me," he continued, rising from his knees and re-lighting his pipe—"las' time I seen my pore mother—widow-woman, she was, for my ole man he 'd shipped bo'sun o' the Rag-lan, las' time she weighed—'Jack,' says the old woman to me, an' the tears rollin' down her face—it 'll be goin' on five year ago now —'Jack,' says she; 'promise me you 'll always make a bit of a prayer before turnin'-in; for the Lord says anybody that 's ashamed o' Him, He 'll be ashamed o' him at the day o' judgment.' Awful— ain't it? Course, I promised; but it went in o' one ear, an' out o' the other, till about two year after, when I got word she was dead. I was on Runnymede then—for I come straight here when I bolted from the ship—an' I begun to bethink myself that she could see

how I was keepin' my promise; so I braced-up, an' laid a bit closer.
Lord knows, I gev her worry enough while she was alive, without
follerin' her up any furder." I have taken some trouble in weeding
the language of Jack's confession, so as not to destroy its consecu-
tiveness.

And, co-existing in the worthy fellow's mind with this childlike
simplicity, was a really fine store of the best kind of knowledge,
namely, that acquired from observation and experience. It is surprising how much a landsman, however well-informed, may gather
from a sailor when he listens like a three-years' child, and the
mariner hath his will. I only wish I was as well posted up in devil-
fish, stingarees, krakens, and other marine commonplaces, as I am
—thanks to Jack's information—in the man-o'-war hawk and the
penguin. It came about in this way:

The door was left open for ventilation when we retired to rest,
Jack in his bunk, and I on the floor. We were both asleep, when
I became aware of an icy touch on my face, accompanied by a
breath strongly suggesting to my scientific nose the hydro-car-
buretted oxy-chloro-phosphate of dead bullock. Drowsily opening
one eye, I saw Pup standing by my side. He had thought I was
dead; but, finding his mistake, he walked away through the gloom
with an injured and dissatisfied air, and began trying to root the
lid off Jack's camp-oven with his pointed nose. One peculiarity of
the kangaroo-dog is, that though he has no faculty of scent at the
service of his master, he can smell food through half-inch boiler-
plate; and he rivals Trenck or Monte Cristo in making way through
any obstacle which may stand between him and the object of his
desires.

The clattering of the oven-lid roused Jack. He looked up, and
then left his bed.

"Pore creature 's hungry," is near enough what he said. He
opened a sort of safe, and took out all the cooked mutton, which
he divided into two unequal portions, then gave the smaller share
to his own dog, and the larger to Pup. "Bit evener on your keel
after you 've stowed that in your hold," he soliloquised profanely.

"Thank-you, Jack!" said I. "Would you just see that everything 's safe from him before you turn-in again. There 's always a
siege of Jerusalem going on in his inside. The kangaroo-dog 's the
hungriest subject in the animal kingdom."

"Well, no," replied Jack forbearingly, as he returned to his bed;
"he ain't in it with the man-o'-war hawk. That 's the hungriest
subject goin'; though, strictly speakin', he don't belong to no king-

dom in particular; he belongs to the high seas. If you 'd 'a' had a chance to study man-o'-war hawks, like I 've had, you 'd never think a kangaroo-dog was half hungry. Why, he dunno what proper hunger is."

Then he gave me such a description of this afflicted bird as, in the interests of science, I have great pleasure in laying before the intelligent public. I must, however, use my own language. Jack's rhetoric, though lucid and forcible, would look so bad on paper that the police might interfere with its publication.

The man-o'-war hawk, it appears, utters a thrilling squeal of hunger the moment his beak emerges from the shell; and this hunger dogs him—kangaroo-dogs him, you might say—through life. At adult age, he consists chiefly of wings; but, in addition to these, he has a pair of eager, sleepless eyes, endowed with a power of something like 200 diameters; and he has also a perennially empty stomach—the sort of vacuum, by the way, which Nature particularly abhors. He can eat nothing but fish; and, since he suffers under the disadvantage of being unable to dive, wade, or swim, some one else must catch the fish for him. The penguin does this, and does it with a listless ease which would excite the envy of the man-o'-war hawk if the unceasing anguish of hunger allowed the latter any respite for thought.

The penguin also lives on fish, but there the resemblance happily ends. In every other respect he presents a pointed antithesis to the man-o'-war hawk; and that is the only pointed thing about him, for he consists wholly of a comfortable body, a blunt neb, and a pair of small, sleepy eyes. He has no neck, for he never requires to look round; no wings, for he never requires to fly; no feet, for he stands firmly on one end, like a 50lb. bag of flour, which, indeed, he closely resembles. His life is unadventurous; some might call it monotonous. He takes his position on a smooth rock; protected from cold by the beautiful padded surtout which clothes him from neb to base, and from heat by the cool, limpid wave, softly lap-lapping against the impenetrable feathers. He feels like a stove in the winter, and like a water-bag in the summer. When, from a sort of drowsy, felicitous wantonness—for he never requires to act either on reason or impulse—he desires to visit an adjacent island, he simply allows the tide to encircle him to about two-thirds his total altitude; then, by the floatative property of his peerless physique, and by the mere volition of will, he transports himself whither he lists.

He has few wants, and no ambition. Dreaming the happy hours

away—that is his idea. He knows barely enough to be aware that
with much wisdom cometh much sorrow; therefore, no Pierian
spring, no tree of knowledge, thank you all the same. He is right
enough as he is; the perpetual sabbath of absolute negation is good
enough for him. His motto is, 'Happy the bird that has no history.'
Once a day, he experiences a crisp, triumphant appetite, which
differs from hunger as melody differs from discord; then he slowly
half-unveils his currant-like eyes, and selects from the finny multitudes swimming around him, such a fish as for size, flavour, and
general applicability, will best administer to his bodily requirements, and gratify his epicurean taste.

Whilst he is in the act of dipping his neb in the water to help
himself to the fish, a man-o'-war hawk espies him from a distance
of, say, five miles. Emitting a quivering shriek of hunger, the
strong-winged sufferer cleaves the intervening air with the speed
of a telegram, and has seized and swallowed the fish before his own
belated shriek arrives.

The penguin, living in total ignorance of the man-o'-war hawk's
existence, vaguely and half-amusedly apprehends his deprivation.
In this way. You have heard the boarding-house girl rap at your
bedroom door, and tell you that breakfast is on the table. You
have thought to yourself: Now I 'm turning out; now I 'm putting
on my——; now, my socks; now—Why, I 'm in bed still, and no
nearer breakfast than at first! Here we have a reproduction of the
penguin's train of thought, plus the slight shock of surprise which
marks your own relatively imperfect organisation. The whole thing
does n't amount to a crumpled rose-leaf beneath the penguin's base;
so he apathetically depresses his dreamy eyes in casual quest of
another fish.

Now if the feathered martyr could only wait one minute, he
might obtain the second morsel on the same terms as the first; but
Nature has so constructed him that, in his estimation, the most
important of all economies is the economy of time; and his Dollond
eye has descried another penguin, seven miles distant, in the very
act of dipping for a fish. Can he make the return trip? He must
chance it. He negotiates with lightning speed the interspace
between his tortured stomach and the second penguin's provender,
whilst his own steam-siren screech of famine comes feebly halting
after, and blends with the desolate plop of his prey into the
abysmal emptiness of his ever-yearning epigastrium. Then, wheel-
ing madly round—his Connemara complaint freshly whetted by
what he has taken—he sees the first penguin dropping asleep as the

fish he has just caught slides down head-foremost, to be assimilated by the simple clockwork of his interior.

Too late, by full fifteen seconds! and the wild despair of lost opportunity lends a horrid eeriness to the banshee utterance with which the man-o'-war hawk greets this crushing discovery, barbed, as it is, by the prior knowledge that every penguin within twenty miles is in Nirvana for the present. Now he must wait—ah! heavens, wait!—while one with moderate haste might tell a hundred. By that time, the bird beside him will have caught another fish; and though it be only—By my faith, he must wait longer; for the penguin, concluding that his own appetite will be more finely matured by another half-hour's sleep, is just dozing off. Woe for the man-o'-war hawk! he must decide on something without delay, and he must do that something quickly—quickly—quickly— for there will be loafing enough in the grave, as the great American moralist says.

But, five hundred miles away across the restless, hungry waste of waters is another rock, where penguins steep themselves in sinless voluptuousness; and, with one prolonged, ear-splitting yell, wrung from him by the still-increasing torment of his fell disease, the unhappy bird expands his Paradise-Lost pinions, and, with the speed of a comet passing its perihelion, sweeps away to that rock; for, like Louis XVI, he knows geography.

After listening with much interest to the description here loosely paraphrased, I fell asleep with the half-formed longing to be a penguin, and the liveliest gratitude that I was not a man-o'-war hawk.

Next morning, whilst I caught and equipped my horses, Jack tailed his own two into the catching-yard. Every Runnymede boundary man was expected to find himself in horses; and Jack, on being rated, had purchased the two quietest and most shapeless mokes on the station—or, indeed, off it. 'Mokes' is good in this connection. But in a week or two, lazy as the mokes were, Jack could n't grapple either of them, stabbard or port, in the open paddock, they had learned to await, and even approach him, starn-on. So he had to pelt them into the little yard, where an ingeniously devised adjustable crush, formed by one barbed wire, kept them broadside-on till he caught the one he wanted for the day. Let Jack alone.

Having caught one of his mokes, he caparisoned the—(I forget his own designation) with what, in dearth of adequate superlative, I shall simply call a second-hand English saddle, of more than ordinary capacity. The barrow-load of firewood which had once formed the tree was all in splinters, so that you could fold the saddle in any direction; and the panel had from time to time been subjected to so much amateur repairing that, when Jack mounted, he looked like a hen in a nest, so surrounded he was with exuding tufts of wool, raw horse-hair, emus' feathers, and the frayed edges of half a dozen plies of old blanket, of various colours. But when he said it was the softest saddle on the station, though it would be nothing the worse for a bit of an overhaul, I was bound to admit that the statement and the reservation were equally reasonable.

We journeyed together as far as the western gate of Jack's paddock; and, the conversation turning on saddles, he expressed himself in actionably misdemeanant language on the folly of riding horses like Cleopatra and Satan without a specially-rigged purchase. His idea of such a purchase was simple enough—merely the ordinary saddle, with two standing bulkheads of, say, thirty inches in height by eighteen in width, rigged thortships, one forrid of the rider, and one aft, and each padded on the inside surface. A couple or three rope-yarns, rove fore-and-aft on each side, would prevent the rider listing to stabbard or port, while the vertical pitch would be provided for by a lashing rove across each shoulder. If the horse reared and fell back, you would just draw your head in, like a turtle, and let the bulkheads carry the strain. With such a tackle (*pr.* tayckle), Jack would undertake to ride the Evil One himself, let alone his namesake at the station; whereas, there was Young Jack at work on the (horse) for the last week, while the (horse) aforesaid, knowing the purchase he had on his rider, would be a fool to give in. But these young Colonials had nothing in them; and Jack's spirit was moved within him by reason of their degeneracy.

After parting from this secret of England's greatness, I detected a certain spontaneous self-complacency creeping over my soul, and slightly swelling my head; a certain placid cockiness not to be fully accounted for by the consciousness of birth, which naturally broadened as I approached Runnymede. I thereupon resolved myself into a committee of inquiry, and, applying the analytical system befitting these introspective investigations, discovered, in the first place, furtively underlying my philosophy, a latent ambition to be regarded as a final authority on things in general. Hitherto this aspiration had fallen short, partly owing to the clinging sediment of my congenital ignorance, but more especially because I lacked, and knew I lacked, what is known as a 'presence.' Now, however, the high, drab belltopper and long alpaca coat, happily seconded by large, round glasses and a vast and scholarly pipe, seemed to get over the latter and greater difficulty; and, for perhaps the first time in my life, I enjoyed that experience so dear to some of my fellow-pilgrims—the consciousness of being well-dressed. This would naturally come as a revelation to one who had always been satisfied with any attire which kept him out of the hands of the police. There was something in presenting an academic-cum-capitalistic appearance even to the sordid sheep, as they looked up from nibbling their cotton-bush stumps, and to the frivolous galahs, sweeping in a changeably-tinted cloud over the plain, or studding the trees of the pine-ridge like large pink and silver-grey blossoms, set off by the rich green of the foliage. But outside all possible research or divination lay the occult reason why my bosom's lord sat so lightly on his throne. This will be explained in its proper place.

In the last sheep-paddock, just after clearing the pine-ridge, I met Young Jack on Satan. Satan was an ornament to the station; a magnificently beautiful cream-coloured horse, with silver mane and tail; but unfortunately spoiled, a couple of years before, in the breaking-in.

Now the shallow, inattentive reader may not grasp all that is implied in the remark that a specialist, unconscious of his own peculiar and circumscribed greatness, and cheaply replaceable in case of extinction, was exercising a seasoned colt, thoroughly spoiled beforehand. Your novelist, availing himself of his prerogative, fancifully assigns this office to the well-educated, well-nurtured, and, above all, well-born, colonial-experiencer, fresh from the English rectory. But I am a mere annalist, and a blunt, stolid, unimaginative one at that; therefore not entirely lost to all sense of the fitness of things.

Listen, then: When, after an assiduous and inglorious apprenticeship, you can wheel a galloping horse round in his own length, without paraboling over his head, or turning him upside down—when you can take him safely across any leap he is able to clear—when you can send him at his uttermost, with perfect safety, through forest or scrub—you are scarcely one step nearer to the successful riding of an equine artist that has sworn to get you off, or perish. Scarcely one step nearer than you were at first, unless you constitutionally possess certain qualifications, and are at the same time distinguished by a plentiful lack of other gifts and acquirements, for which, notwithstanding, you are fain to take credit. This rather obscure apostrophe is written expressly for the benefit of such imaginative litterateurs and conversational liars as it may concern.

For it should be known that the perfect rider *nascitur, non fit*, to begin with; that his training must begin in early boyhood, and be followed up *sans* intermission; that his system of horse-breaking must be the Young-Australian, which is, beyond doubt, the most trying in the world; that his skill is won by grassers innumerable; that, in short, there is no royal road to the riding of a proper out-law—a horse that, not with any view of showing-off before girls, but with the confirmed intention of flattening out his antagonist, plays such fantastic jigs before high heaven as make the angels peep.

And yet, to be an ideal rider, man wants but little here below, nor is it at all likely he will want that little long. He wants—or rather, needs—a skull of best spring steel; a spinal column of standard Lowmoor; limbs of gutta-percha; a hide of vulcanised india-rubber; and the less brains he has, the better. Figuratively speaking, he should have no brains at all; his thinking faculties should be so placed as to be in direct touch with the only thing that concerns him, namely, the saddle. Yet his heart must not be there; he must by no means be what the schoolboys call a 'frightened beggar.'

Perfect horsemanship is usually the special accomplishment of the man who is not otherwise worth his salt, by reason of being too lazy for manual labour, and too slenderly upholstered on the mental side for anything else. Sir Francis Head, one of the five exceptions to this rule—Gordon being the second, 'Banjo' the third, 'Glenrowan' the fourth, and the demurring reader the fifth—says the greatest art in riding is knowing how to fall. And here we touch the very root of the matter. It is the moral effect of that generally-fulfilled apprehension which makes one salient difference between the cultivated, or spurious rider, and the ignorant, or true rider. In this case, Ignorance is not only bliss, but usurps the place of Knowledge, as power.

Edward M. Curr knew as much of the Australian horse and his rider as any writer ever did; and this is what he says of the back-country natives:—

'They are taciturn, shy, ignorant, and incurious; undemonstrative, but orderly; hospitable, courageous, cool, and sensible. These men ride like centaurs,' etc., etc.

Yes, yes—but why? Looking back along that string of well-selected adjectives, does n't your own inductive faculty at once place its finger on Ignorance as the key to the enigma? Notice, too, how Curr, being a bit of a sticker himself, is thereby disqualified from knowing that the centaurs were better constructed for firing other people over their heads than for straddling their own backs.

Your true rider must audibly and sanguineously challenge every unfamiliar scientific fact stated in conversation, and be prepared to stake his rudimentary soul on the truth of anything read aloud from a book. He must believe, with the ecclesiastics of yesterday, that the earth is flat and square; like them, he must be a violent supporter of the geocentric theory; unlike them, his æschatological hypothesis must be that the fire we wot of is only a man's own conscience—the wish, in his case, being father to the thought. Above all, he must have no idea how fearfully and wonderfully he is made. He must think upon himself as a good strong framework of bones, cushioned and buffered with meat, and partly tubular for the reception and retention of food; he must further regard it as a rather grave oversight in his own architectural design that the calf of his leg is not in front. Just consider what advantages such a man enjoys in cultivating the art of knowing how to fall. Why, a spill that perils neck or limb, a simple buster is to him, and it is nothing more.

But it is a great deal more to one who has been nourishing a youth sublime with the curious facts of Science and the thousand-and-one items of general information necessary to any person who, like the fantastical duke of dark corners, above all other strifes contends especially to know himself; and that physically, as well as morally. To him it is a nasty scrunch of the two hundred and twenty-six bones forming his own admirably designed osseous structure; a dull, sickening wallop of his exquisitely composed cellular, muscular, and nervous tissues; a general squash of his beautifully mapped vascular system; a pitiless stoush of membranes, ligaments, cartilages, and what not; a beastly squelch of gastric and pancreatic juices and secretions of all imaginable descriptions—biliary, glandular, and so forth. And all for what? Why, for the sake of emulating the Jack Frosts of real life in their own line!

My contention simply is, that the Hamlet-man is only too well seized of the important fact that his bones cost too much in the breeding to play at heels-over-tip with them. And I further maintain that, for reasons above specified, the man of large discourse, looking before and after (ah! that is where the mischief lies!) never, in spite of his severest self-scrutiny, knows what a frightened beggar he is till he finds himself placing his foot in the stirrup, preparatory to mounting a recognised performer.

Just take yourself as an example. You remember the time you were passing the old cattle-yards in the flat, and saw four fellows of your acquaintance putting the bridle on a black colt in the crush? You remember how the chaps inspected your saddle, and, the concurrence of opinion being that it was the best on the ground, how they asked the loan of it for an hour? You lent it with pleasure, you will remember, and assisted them to girth it on. You liked to be at the second backing of a colt—not as the central figure, of course, but in the capacity of critic and adviser. There was the probability of some decent riding; also the probability of a catastrophe. You may, perhaps, further remember that whilst the ceremony of saddling was in progress, you casually related one of your most ornate and unassailable anecdotes—how, with that very saddle, you had once backed a roan filly that on the preceding day had broken a circus man's collar-bone? For reasons of your own, you located the performance a hundred miles away; and for proof, you pointed to the saddle itself. Yes; I see you remember it all like yesterday.

The colt, with a handkerchief across his eyes, was led out of the yard to some nice level ground; then a dead-lock supervened. The chap who had backed him on the previous evening for a couple of hours, and was to have ridden him again, did n't like the set of your saddle, now that he saw it girthed-on. The owner of the colt, speaking for himself, frankly admitted that he never pretended to be a sticker. The third fellow, whilst modestly glancing at his own unrivalled record, regretted he was sworn with a book-oath against backing colts for the current year. The fourth was also out of it. Owing to a boil, which kept him standing in the stirrups even on his own old crock, he was compelled to forgo the one transcendant joy of his life. But you——

Well, to begin with, there was your own saddle on the colt; secondly, your conversation had not been that of a man who did n't pretend to be a sticker; thirdly, the book-oath expedient was simply out of the question; and fourthly, it was too late in the day to allege a boil. What was the use of your remarking that the first backing of a colt is nothing—that, in this case, it is the second step that costs? The four fellows knew as well as you did—everyone except the tenderfoot novelist knows—that in nearly every instance, a freshly backed colt is like a fish out of water; stupid, puzzled, half-sulky, half-docile. It is at the second backing that he is ready to contest the question of fitness for survival; he has had time to think the matter over, and to note the one-sidedness of the alliance. Again, there is a large difference between riding a colt upon a warm evening, and doing the same thing on a cold, dry, gusty morning, when his hair inclines to stand on end. But there was your own reminiscence of the roan filly staring you in the face.

One of the fellows holds the blindfolded colt, whilst another rubs the saddle all over with a wet handkerchief. The colt stands still and composed, with one ear warily cocked, the other indifferently slouched; with his back slightly arched, and—ah! the saints preserve us!—with his tail jammed hard down. Carelessly humming a little tune, you hang your coat on the fence; and in the saying of two credos (note the appositeness of Cervantes's expression here), you are in the saddle—the same saddle, by the way, with which you took the flashness out of the roan filly that had broken the circus man's collar-bone. What! have I pinch'd you, signior Gremio?

The chap should have let the colt go at once, for, in situations like yours, a person keeps breaking-up as the moments pass. But no——

"Ready, Tom?"

"Yes."

"You 're sure you 're ready?"

"Yes."

"I think he 'll buck middlin' hard."

Is there no pity sitting in the clouds, that looks into the bottom of your woe? We 'll see presently. Meantime, console yourself with the recollection of the roan filly that had broken the circus man's collar-bone.

"You 've got the off stirrup all right, Tom?"

"Yes."

"I 'm goin' to let the beggar rip."

"Go ahead."

"Look out now"——

"Right." But your voice is not what it ought to be, and the soles of your boots are rattling on the flat part of the stirrup-irons.

The chap draws the handkerchief from the colt's eyes, and walks backward. The colt catches sight of your left foot, and skips three yards to the right. In doing so, he catches sight of the other foot, and skips to the left. Then everything disappears from in front of the saddle—the wicked ears, now laid level backward—the black, tangled mane—the shining neck, with the sweeping curve of a circular saw—the clean, oblique shoulders—they have all disappeared, and there is nothing in front of the saddle but a precipice. There is something underneath it, though.

How distinctly you note the grunting of the colt, the thumping of his feet on the ground, and the gratuitous counsel addressed to you in four calmly critical voices:—

"Lean back a bit more, Tom, and give with him."

"Don't ride so loose if you can help it, Tom."

"Hold yourself well down with the reins, and stick to him, Tom."

"Stick to him, Tom, whatever you do."

Ay! stick to him! Stick to the lever of a steam hammer, when the ram kicks the safety-trigger! Stick to the two-man tug-of-war rope, when an Irish quarryman, named Barney, has hold of the other end! Stick to him, quotha! Easier said than done—is it not? And yet you 've been riding all manner of horses, on and off (mark the significance of that expression) since you were a mere kiddie. However, you have stuck to him for a good solid sixty seconds; now, one of your knees has slipped over the pad, and your stirrup is swinging loose. Good night, sweet prince.

And away circles the colt, slapping at the bit with his front feet, whilst your historic saddle shines in the sun, and the stirrup-irons occasionally meet high in the air. And away in chase go two of the chaps on their bits of stuff. Meanwhile, you explain to the other two that the spill serves you right for riding so carelessly; and that, though your soul lusts to have it out with the colt, a stringent appointment in the township will force you to clear as soon as you can get your saddle. Such is life.

Satan approached, carrying his negatively gifted rider, at a free, flying canter; his gregarious instinct prompting him to join my horses. His tawny skin was streaked with foam, and his off flank slightly stained from the repeated puncture of Jack's spur. Ten yards from where I had pulled-up, he suddenly sulked, and stood.

"Good morning, Jack."

"Well, I be dash! Did n't know you from a crow! Reckoned some member o' Parliament, or bishop, or somebody, had bin swappin' horses with you. You are comin' out! Oh, I say! Nosey give me the letter, with the three notes in it; but I could n't make head or tail of it about the saddle. No more could n't Moriarty."

"I 'll explain all that to you some time. How are you getting on with Satan?"

"Bad," replied Jack humbly. "You can easy enough steady him down, but then, the swine, he wants a spell; an' when he gits a spell, you jist got to steady him down agen. Always got some new idear in his head. There!"—hastily rooting the horse's side with his spur—"he 's goin' to lay-down, an' make chips o' the saddle. Up! you swine"—and, lying backward, he reached down to grip the sensitive membrane connecting the swine's hind-leg with his body. The maddened beast shot past me like a yellow streak for another ten yards; then, with a flaring bound and a snort that was between a whistle and a shriek, spun half-round in the air, and alighted rigidly on his front feet, his ears between his knees, and his neck and back describing a vertical semicircle, with the saddle and Jack on the centre of its forward curve.

"Jist his style," continued Jack dejectedly. "Never be worth a dash for general"——I lost the next word or two, for the young fellow's face was buried in the mass of silver mane, as the horse reared rampant to the balancing point; and the next word, again, was dislocated by a blow from the crupper buckle, just below the speaker's shoulder-blade. "An' Magomery wants a person to make a lady's hack out o' sich an outlawr as him!" he continued, in hopeless protest, whilst the 'outlawr' exerted his iron muscles to the utmost, and the saddle creaked like a basket. "Nummin' good horse, too; on'y spoiled with—Jist look at that!" Satan had suddenly gathered his lithe, powerful limbs, and was tearing across toward the adjacent pine-ridge, spinning round, every thirty yards, in two or three terrific bucks. "I don't want to sawr his mouth," shouted Jack over his shoulder, in polite apology—"I 'll see you agen by-'n'-by"——

"Away on the evergreen shore, probably," I soliloquised, resuming my journey. But, turning in the saddle, and pushing up my glasses out of the way, I watched the receding contest. I saw Jack wrench the horse aside from the timber; whereupon the animal reared rather too rashly, and just saved himself from falling backward by dropping on his quarters and flapping down on one side. When his broadside touched ground, Jack was standing beside him; and when he leaped to his feet, Jack was in the saddle. *Exeunt* fighting.

Toby, with his bare feet and brown, good-humoured face, was the only person visible on the station premises as I rode up.

"Gosh, I did n't know you till I seen you side-on, when you was shuttin' the Red Gate," he remarked. (The Red Gate was about a mile and a half distant.) "I thought you was somebody comin' to buy the station. Magomery, he 's buzznackin' roun' the run as usual," he continued, helping me to unsaddle. "Butler, he 's laid up with the bung blight in both eyes. All the other fellers is out.

Mrs. Bodysark"—and his grin deepened—"she 's all right. Moriarty, of course, he 's loafin' in the store; lis'n him now, laughin' fit to break his neck at some of his own gosh foolishness. I 'll shove your horses in the paddick. I say! ain't they fell-away awful?"

"Yes; the season 's telling on them. Now will you look after Pup, like a good chap? Here 's his chain. I want to keep him fresh for travelling."

"Right. I don't wish you no harm, Collins; but I would n't mind if you was in heaven, s'posen you left me that dog."

I went across to the store, and looked in. Moriarty's laughing suddenly ceased, as his eye fell on me; and he respectfully rose to his feet.

"Wherefore that crackling of thorns under a pot?" I asked sternly, as I removed my belltopper and placed it on the counter. "Don't you see the spirits of the wise sitting in the clouds and mocking you?"

"Well, I 'll be dashed!" he exclaimed admiringly. "You are coming out in blossom. Now you only want the upper half of your head shaved, and you could start a Loan and Discount bank, with a capital of half a million."

"Thanks, worthy peer," I replied, with dignity. "But, talking of finance, I trust you have n't forgotten the trifle that there is between us, and the terms of our agreement?"

"I 'm not likely to forget. Take that chair. I 've got such fun here." He had sliced some corks into flat discs; into the centre of each disc he had stuck a slender piece of pine, about two inches in height, and spatulated at the upper end, like a paddle. Then to the flat part of each upright he had attached a blow-fly, by means of a touch of gum on the insect's back, and had placed in the grasp of each fly a piece of pine an inch long, cut into the shape of a rifle. The walking motion of the fly's feet twirled and balanced the stick in rather droll burlesque of musketry drill; and a dozen of these insects-at-arms, disposed in open order on the counter, were ministering to the young fool's mirth.

"Just you notice the gravity of the beggars," he laughed. "Not a smile on them. Solemn as Presbyterians. 'Tention! Present! Recover! Not a lazy bone in their bodies. I say, Collins: a person could make a perpetual motion, with a fly on a sort of a treadmill? Ah! but then it would n't pass muster unless it went of its own accord—would it? Perpetual motion 's a thing I 've been giving my attention to lately. You remember you advised me to study mechanics? Well, I 've been thinking of arranging a clock so as to wind itself up as it went on. That 's one idea. Another is a little more complicated. It 's a water-wheel, driving a pump that throws a stream into the race that feeds the water-wheel, so that you use the same water over and over again, and the whole concern 's self-acting. The idea came into my head like an inspiration. Mind, I 'm telling you in confidence, for there 's a thousand notes hanging on to it."

"Moriarty," said I sadly; "you 're worse than ever. Try something else. You 're not a born mechanician."

"If I 'm not, I 'd like to know who the devil is?" replied the young fellow hotly. "Possibly, your own self? Was n't my father a foreman in one of the largest machine-shops in Victoria, in his day? I know what 's the matter with you. Jealousy."

"It must be so. Plato, thou reasonest well," said I hopelessly. "But supposing you are a born mechanician, you have neither the theoretical nor the practical training. Do you know for instance, the use of the brass slide you often see on a carpenter's rule?"

"Of course I do! Why I could calculate with that slide before I was ten years old."

One to Moriarty. I should have remembered that his abnormal breadth across the temples qualified him to do a sum in his head, in ten seconds, that I could n't do on a slate in ten hours, nor for that matter, in ten years. No accounts in Riverina were better kept than those of Runnymede.

"Good, so far," I replied benevolently. "But how much do you know of prismoidal formulæ, or logarithmic secants?—not to speak of segmental ordinates, or the cycloidal calculus; or even of adiabatic expansion, or torsional resistance, or the hydrostatic paradox, or the coefficient of friction? Now, these things are the very A B C of mechanics, as you 'll find to your utter confusion."

Moriarty's countenance fell; but happening to glance at the performing flies, he laughed himself weak and empty. "Just look at the beggars," he murmured, wiping his eyes.

"Business first," said I. "How about my scandal?"

"It 's going grand!" replied Moriarty, beaming with new pleasure. "I carried out your suggestions to the letter. First, I took Mooney and Nelson into my confidence; and we arranged to meet accidentally, one evening after dusk, under that willow beside her bed-room. At last we sat down, with our backs against the weatherboard wall, and talked about"——

"Day, chaps," said a stranger, appearing at the door of the store. "Got any pickles in stock, Moriarty?"

"Lots. Half-a-crown a bottle."

"Say three bottles," replied the stranger, seating himself on the counter. "And—let's see—a pound of tobacco; a dozen of matches; a tin of baking-powder; and a couple of hobble-chains. I 'll make that do till I get as far as Hay. My chaps are squealing for pickles," he continued, turning to me. "I did n't know you at the first glance. Your name 's Collins—is n't it? You might remember me passing by you last spring, a few miles back along the track here, where you 'd been helping Steve Thompson and a big, gipsy-looking fellow to load up some wool on a Sydney-pattern wagon? So that chestnut was a stolen horse, after all. Smart bit of work. Another devil of a season—is n't it? I 've been trying to shift 900 head of forward stores from Mamarool to Vic.; but I advised the owner to give it best, though it was money out of my pocket, when I had none in it to begin with. Managed to arrange for them on Wooloomburra till the winter comes on."

While speaking, he had opened his knife and removed the capsule and cork from one of the bottles of pickles; then, after drinking some of the vinegar out of the way, he began harpooning the contents of the bottle, and eating them with a relish that was pleasant to see.

I made a suitable reply, whilst Moriarty, having made up his order, noted the items and price on the paper which contained the tobacco.

"I see Alf Jones is gone, Moriarty," I remarked, after a pause— the stranger being occupied with his pickles. "Wisest thing he could do."

"Foolishest thing he could do," replied the storekeeper. "Nosey was a fixture on Runnymede; he was one of Montgomery's pets; and if he thinks he can better that in Australia, he 's got a lot to learn. And what a hurry he was in, to get out of the best billet he 'll ever have, poor beggar! with his shyness and his disfigurement. But he 's been on the pea, like a good many more. Let 's see—it was just the day after you went away that he came to Montgomery, and said he must go. That 'll be six or eight weeks ago now. Montgomery went a lot out of his way to persuade him to stop, but it was no use; he was like a hen on a hot griddle till he got away. Decent chap, too; and, by gosh! can't he sing and play! We found afterward that he had given his books to the station library, with the message that we were to think kindly of him when he was gone. I felt sort of melancholy to see him drifting away to beggary, with his fiddle-case across the front of his saddle, and his spare horse in his hand. He knew no more where he was going than the man in the moon."

"Don't you believe it," I replied. "These cranky fellows have always sane spots in their heads; and Alf is particularly lucky in that respect. There 's not above two—or, at the most, three—lobes of that fellow's brain in bad working order. Just you watch the weekly papers, and you 'll get news of him in his proper sphere. He 's gone to Sydney, or perhaps Melbourne, to do something better than boundary riding."

"No; he 's gone to Western Queensland," remarked the stranger, who had been watching Moriarty's flies, without the trace of a smile on his saturnine face. "I met him sixty or eighty mile beyond the Darling, on the Thargomindah track, three weeks ago."

"Not the same fellow, surely?" I suggested.

"Well," replied the stranger tolerantly, "the young chap I 'm speaking of had some disfigurement of the face, so far as I could distinguish through a short crape veil; and he was carrying a box that he evidently would n't trust on his pack-horse, but whether it was a violin-case or a child's coffin, I was n't rude enough to ask. Old-fashioned Manton single-barrel slung on his back. Good-looking black-and-tan dog. Brown saddle-horse; small star; WD conjoined, near shoulder; C or G, near flank. Bay mare, packed; J S, off shoulder; white hind-foot. Horses in rattling condition; and he was taking his time. He 'd been boundary riding in the Bland country before coming here. Peculiar habit of giving his head a little toss sometimes when he spoke."

"That 's him, right enough," said Moriarty. "Had you a yarn with him?"

"Not much of a yarn certainly," replied the stranger, holding his bottle up to the light while he speared a gherkin with his knife. "It was coming on evening when I met him; and, says he, 'I 'm making for the Old-man Gilgie—have n't you come past it?' So I told him if he wanted to camp on water, he 'd have to turn back five mile, and come with me to where I knew of a brackish dam. I 'd just been disappointed of water, myself, at the Old-man Gilgie. It had been half-full a few days before, but a dozen of Elder's camels had called there, carrying tucker to Mount Brown; and each of them had scoffed the full of a 400-gallon tank. Talk about camels doing without water!"—Just here, though the stranger's ordinary language was singularly quotable in character, he digressed into a searching and comprehensive curse, extending, inclusively, from Sir Thomas Elder away back along the vanishing vista of Time to the first man who had conceived the idea of utilising the camel as a beast of burthen.

"So we camped late at night," he resumed, in a relieved tone; "and this friend of yours cleared-off early in the morning. He was n't interested in anything but the Diamantina track, and I was nasty over the gilgie, so we did n't yarn much. However, that chap 's no more off his head than I am. Bit odd, I daresay; but that 's nothing. I often find myself a bit odd—negligent, and forgetful, and sort of imbecile—but that 's a very different thing from being off your head. Why, just now, I saw your two horses in the paddock as I came up; and, if I was to be lagged for it, I could n't think where I had seen them before—in fact, not till I recognised you. Want of sleep, I blame it on. Well, if I don't shift, there won't be many pickles left for my chaps. They were to boil the billy at the Balahs. Better give us another bottle." He handed Moriarty the money for the goods, and stowed them in a small flour-bag. "So-long, boys—see you again some day." And the imbecile stranger trailed his four-inch spurs from our presence.

"Do you know him, Moriarty?" I asked.

"I can't say I do," replied the storekeeper. "One day, last winter, I happened to be out at the main road when he passed with 400 head of fats; and somehow I knew that his name was Spooner. Never saw him again till now. But how about Nosey Alf—was n't I right for once?—and were n't you wrong for once?"

"So it appears," I replied. "But you have n't told me how you worked the scandal. You were sitting with your backs against the wall—Go on"——

"Sitting with our backs against the wall," repeated my agent complacently. "Well, we began to talk about the jealousy there was amongst the station chaps on account of Jack the Shellback being picked to take Nosey's place; and from that we got round to gossip about you stopping with Nosey the evening you left here, and wondering how you got on together, being queer in different ways. Then the conversation settled down on you; and we even quoted a remark Mrs. Beaudesart had made about you, only a couple of hours before. She had said that, though you were such a wonderful talker, you were surprisingly reticent respecting your own former life, and your family connections, and the place you came from. We commented on this remark, and laughed a bit, not at you, but at her. Clever engineering—was n't it?"

"Not unless she was in her room, with her ear against the wall."

"Trust her," replied my ambassador confidently. "She saw us sitting-down as she went across the yard; and we counted on her. We knew her meanness in the matter of listening."

"Don't say 'meanness,'" I remonstrated. "I must take her part there. You can't judge even a high-minded woman by the standard of a moderately mean man, in this particular phase of character. Our deepest student of human nature makes his favourite Beatrice, on receiving a hint, run down the garden like a lapwing, to do a bit of deliberate eavesdropping; whilst her masculine counterpart, Benedick, has to hear his share of the disclosure inadvertently and reluctantly. Similarly, in *Love's Labour Lost*, when the mis-delivered letter is handed to Lord Boyet to read, he says:—

> This letter is mistook; it importeth none here;
> It is writ to Jaquenetta.

That, of course, settles the matter in his mind; but the Princess, true to her sex, says eagerly, and with a perfectly clear conscience:—

> We will read it, I swear;
> Break the neck of the wax, and let every one give ear.

Don't let us judge women by our standard here, for we can't afford to be judged by their standard in some other"——

"Hear, hear; loud applause; much laughter," interrupted the delegate flippantly. "Well, we were yarning and laughing over Mrs. Beaudesart's simplicity; and it came out that Nelson and Mooney knew there was some reason why you dare n't go back to where you were known; but they had never heard the story; so I put them on their honour, and told them the whole affair."

"How did the story run?" I asked.

My vicar repeated it. (Which is more than I can do.)

"Well, *that* ought to drum me out of her esteem," I remarked, with the feeling of a man respited on the scaffold. "And it hangs together fairly well for a fabrication. But I 'm honestly sorry to have been forced to put such an office on you, Moriarty. Indeed, I wonder how you could have the nerve to tell such a yarn in a woman's hearing."

"Friendship, old man," replied my factor warmly. "But it ain't a fabrication. I found I could n't invent anything with the proper ring of truth about it; so, the evening before the disclosure, when Jack the Shellback was in the store getting some things to take out

with him, I asked him what was the most blackguardly prank he
ever got off with; and that was the yarn he told me. Of course, I
altered it a bit to suit you."

"And Mrs. Beaudesart believes it?" I queried hopefully.

"I don't see what else she can do, considering the way the thing
came-off. She would have to be like one of the ancient prophets."

"And you think it has the proper effect?"

"No effect at all," replied the nuncio decidedly. "Her manner's
just the same when she hears you talked about promiscuously; and
she does n't take it any way ill to overhear a quiet joke about the
thing that 's supposed to be coming-off some time soon. It 's a
failure so far as that goes. Certain as life."

"Well, Moriarty, if dishonour has no effect, we must try disgrace."

"Why, they 're the same. You better go back to school, Collins."

"They 're entirely independent of each other—if you insist on
bringing me back to school, to waste my time over one barren
pupil. Poverty, for instance, is disgrace without dishonour;
Michael-and-Georgeship is dishonour without disgrace. In cases
like mine, the dishonour lies in the fact, and the disgrace in the
publicity. You must set the whole station commenting on your
scandal."

"That 's just what the whole station is doing at the present time,"
replied my legate unctuously. "Surprising how these things spread
of themselves, when they 're once fairly started. And everybody
believes the yarn; bar Mooney, and Nelson, and myself; and you
can depend your life on us to keep it jigging. No, I 'm wrong;
Montgomery 's got the inside crook on us."

"Montgomery?" said I inquiringly.

"Yes. I got a fright over that," explained the diplomatist. "The
other morning, I was at some correspondence here, and I heard a
quick step, and when I looked up, who should I see but Montgomery, as black as thunder.

" 'Moriarty!' says he, in a voice that made me jump; 'what is
this story I hear of Collins? Now, no shuffling,' says he; 'I 've
traced it home to you, and I want your authority. I always looked
upon Collins as a decent sort of oddity,' says he; 'and I 'm determined to sift this matter thoroughly.' Frightened me out of a year's
growth." Moriarty paused, and drew a long breath.

"Well?" said I, hazily; wondering whether this piteous wreckage of plot was owing to some defect in my own strategy, or to bad
lieutenantry in the working out.

"So I had to make a clean breast of it," continued the pleni-
potentiary, in a reluctant and apologetic tone. "No use talking.
It was impossible to stand to the yarn, when Montgomery's eye was
on me—let alone being taken by surprise. It was dragged from me
by a sort of hypodermic influence; and all the fun seemed to have
died out of it, till it sounded mean and small and unmanly. Yes;
I had to tell him the fix you were in, and the commission you had
given me, and everything from first to last; bar that infernal wager.
Well, you know, Montgomery never laughs; but I saw his face
twitching, once or twice; and before I had done, he wheeled round
and stood looking out of the door, as if I was n't worth listening
to. Then he went away, coughing fit to break his neck."

"I may thank him for being tree'd, in the first place; and he
knows it," I remarked, with a sourness which appears pardonable
even at this distance of time.

"What had he got to do with it?" asked Moriarty.

"How the *tempus* does *fugit*!" I replied. For the mid-day bell
was ringing at the hut.

"Best sound since breakfast-time," said Moriarty, rising. "Come
on to lunch."

As we left the store, half-a-dozen representatives of the lower
classes were stringing-in from different directions toward the hut,
to attend to the most ancient and eminent of human institutions—
the institution which predicates and affirms the brotherhood of our
race as positively, and, to the philosophic mind, as touchingly, as
death itself; being recognised and remembered by the aristocrat
who forgets his own personal dirt-origin and dirt-destination; by
the woman who forgets the date of her birth; by the friend who
forgets the insulting language he used to you when he was under
the influence; and by the boy who forgets his catechism. The meal-
signal is the real Ducdame, ducdame, ducdame; the Greek invoca-
tion which calls fools into a circle as surely as wise men; for neither
folly nor wisdom is proof against its spell.

Just then, two swagmen on foot came into the yard, and approached Moriarty and me. I fixed my belltopper, adjusted my
specs, and assumed my stately pipe, whilst my soul went forth in
psalms of thanksgiving. Here was the true key to the Wilcannia
shower; here was the under-side of my imagined precaution against
ophthalmia; here was the hidden purpose of that repetitional picking and sorting of the hawker's stock which had left Jack the Shellback his Hobson's choice in coats; here was a Wesleyan converging
of the whole vast order of the universe toward the happiest issue.

For here was Tom Armstrong at last; and I stood prepared to force a temporary renewal—albeit for double the original amount—of the bill, drawn by me on the Royal Inevitable, and now about to be presented by the legitimate holder.

"Is the bose at hame?" asked the holder briskly, turning first to Moriarty and then to me. "Losh! it 's no Tam M'Callum!"—he swung his swag to the ground, and extended his hand—"Mony 's the thocht A had o' ye, mun. Ma certie, A kent weel we wad forgather ir lang. An' hoo 're ye farin' syne?"

"Excellent, i' faith—of the chameleon's dish," I replied, with winning politeness, and a hearty hand-grip, though I felt like a man in the act of parrying a rifle bullet. "I have a wretched memory for faces, yet yours seems familiar; and I 'm certain I 've heard your voice before. Pardon me if I ask your name?"

"Tam Airmstrang," replied my creditor, in an altered tone.

"Now, where have we met before?" I pondered. "Armstrong? I know several of the name in Riverina, and several in Victoria. Wait a moment—Did we meet at the Caledonian Sports, in Echuca, two years ago, past? No! Well, perhaps—yes—did n't we have a drink together, at Ivanhoe, three or four months ago?"

"Od sink 't," muttered the honest fellow, in vexation; "A thocht ye was yin Tam M'Callum, frae Selkirksheer."

"I 'm a Victorian myself, and my people are Irish," I remarked gently. "But my name 's Collins," I continued, brightening up; "and Collins sounds something like M'Callum."

"Ye 'se no be the mon A thocht ye was," replied Tam decidedly —and the unconscious double-meaning of his words sank into my heart—"Bit hae ye onything tae dae wi' Rinnymede?"

"No; I 'm only a caller, like yourself. Moriarty, here, is the storekeeper."

"D' ye want ony han's?" continued Tam, addressing Moriarty.

"I think we do," replied the young fellow, moving toward the barracks. "The boss was saying there was a few burrs that would have to be looked after at once. Call again in the evening, and see him."

"Yon wad fit mysen like auld breeks," persisted Tam; "bit A 'm takkin' thocht o' Andraw here. Puir body's sicht 's nae fit fir sic wark; an' A mauna pairt wi' him the noo. An ye henna onythin' firbye birr-kittin', we maun gang fairther ava."

He resumed his swag. I made a sign, perceptible only to Moriarty, and the latter hesitated a moment.

By virtue of a fine tradition, or unwritten law, handed down from the time of Montgomery's father, a subaltern officer of Runnymede had power to send any decent-looking swagman—or a couple of them, for that matter—to the hut for a feed. Certain conditions, however, had formulated themselves around this prerogative: first, the stranger must of necessity be a decent-looking man; second, he must be within the precincts of the homestead at the ringing of the bell; third, the officer must walk down to the hut with him, as a testimony; fourth, no particular sub must make a trade of it. The prerogative was something like one enjoyed by abbots, and other ecclesiastical dignitaries, in the ages of faith; namely, the right to extend the jurisdiction and protection of the Church over any secular prisoner accidentally met on his way to execution—a prerogative, the existence of which depended on its not being abused. And though Moriarty was only on the Commissariat, and was therefore unmercifully sat-on by the vulgar whenever he presumed to give orders, he held this right through a series of forerunners extending back to the time when Montgomery I. had been his own storekeeper. Don't you believe the yarns your enthusiast tells of the squatter's free-and-easy hospitality toward the swagman. Such things were, and are; but I would n't advise you to count upon the institution as a neat and easy escape from the Adamic penalty. You might fall-in. Hence Moriarty's personal reluctance in the matter was perfectly natural. The meal at the hut, and the pannikin of dust at the store, are two widely different things. But a faithful and exhaustive inquiry into the ethics of station hospitality would fill many pages, for the question has more than one aspect.

"Go down to the hut, and have some dinner," said Moriarty, turning back; and we preceded the two men on their way. "Can you make room for these chaps, Matt?" he asked, looking into the hut.

The cook growled assent; and the two strangers took their places at the table.

"Scotty thought he knew you," observed Moriarty, with characteristic profundity, as we turned again toward the barracks. The remark broke a spell that was coming over me.

"And I thought I knew his mate, though I can't manage to locate him," I replied. "But, as I was telling Scotty, I have the worst memory in the world for faces."

"Ay, that poor wreck would n't fetch much in the yard," remarked Moriarty, referring to Tam's mate. "When a fellow comes to his state, he ought to be turned out for the summer in a swamp paddock, with the leeches on his legs; then you ought to sell him to Cobb and Co., to get the last kick out of him. Or else poll-axe the beggar."

"Very good system, Moriarty. Apply it to yourself also. You 're not dead yet."

"But I 'll never come to that state of affairs."

"Assuredly you will, sonny—just for the remark you 've made. But I 'd like to see that fellow again. Go on to the barracks; I 'll be after you in two minutes."

Confused identity seemed to be in the air. Had I seen that weary-looking figure, and that weather-worn face, before? I could n't determine; and I can't determine now—but the question has nothing to do with this record. At all events, impelled partly by a desire to have another look at the man, and partly, perhaps, by a morbid longing to flaunt myself before Tam, I grandly dipped my lofty belltopper under the doorway of the hut, and, without removing it, helped myself to a pannikin of tea from the bucket by the hearth, and sat down opposite the silent swagman. Farther along the table, Tam was already breast-deep in the stream of conversation. In answer to some question, he was replying that he had been only twelve months in the colonies.

"And what part of the Land o' Cakes are you from?" I asked, wantonly, but civilly.

"A 'm frae Dumfriessheer—frae a spote they ca' Ecchelfechan," he replied complacently. "Bit, de'il tak 't, wha' gar 'd ye jalouse A was a Scoatsman?"

"What the (sheol) was the name o' that (adj.) place you come from?" asked the station bullock driver, with interest.

"Ecchelfechan."

"Nobody 's got any business to come from a place with sich a (adj.) name."

"An' wha' fir no?" demanded Tam sternly. "Haud tae ye 'se hae ony siccan a historic name in yir ain domd kintra. D' ye ken wha, firbye mysen, was boarn in Ecchelfechan syne? Dinna fash yirsel' aboot"——

"I say, Scotty," interposed Toby; "Egglefeggan's the place where they eat brose—ain't it?"

"A 'll haud nae deeskission wi' the produc' o' hauf-a-dizzen generations o' slavery," replied Tam haughtily. "A dinna attreebute ony blame tae yir ain sel', laddie; bit ye canna owrecam the kirse o' Canaan."

"Cripes! do you take *me* for a (adj.) mulatter?" growled the descendant of a thousand kings. "Why, properly speaking, I own this here (adj.) country, as fur as the eye can reach."

"Od, ye puir, glaikit, misleart remlet o' a perishin' race," retorted Tam—"air ye no the mair unsicker? Air ye no feart ye 'se aiblins see yon day gin ye 'se thole waur fare nir a wamefu' o' gude brose? Heh!"

"Oh, speak English, you (adj.) bawbee-hunter!" muttered H.R.H. "Why, they 're a cut above brose in China—ain't they, Sling?"

"Eatee lice in China," replied the gardener, with national pride. "Plenty lice—good cookee—welly ni'."

"By gummies! Hi seed the time Hi 'd 'a' stopped yer jorrin', Dave!" said a quavering voice, dominating some argument at the other end of the table. "Hi seed me fightin' in a sawr-pit f'r tew hewrs an' sebmteen minits, by the watch; an' fetched 'ome in a barrer. Now wot 's the hupshot? Did 'n' Hi say, 'Look hout! we 'll git hit to rights'?"

"But you (adv.) well thought we 'd get rain," persisted the old man's antagonist—an open-mouthed, fresh-faced rouseabout, who was just undergoing that colonising process so much dreaded by mothers and deplored by the clergy.

" 'Ow the (fourfold expletive) do you hundertake to know wot Hi thort? But wot war the hupshot? 'Look hout!' ses Hi; 'we 'll git hit to rights!' An' did we, hor did we not? Straight, now, Dave?"

"You 're like Cassandra, Jack," I observed, to fill up the pause which marked Dave's discomfiture.

"That bloke as spoke las', 'e 's got more hunder 'is 'at nor a six-'underd-an'-fo'ty-hacre paddick full o' sich soojee speciments as you fellers," said the old man impressively. "Wich o' you knows hanythink about Cassandra? Hin 'twenty-six hit war, an' hit seems like las' week. Hi druv ole Major Learm'th to them races, Hi did; an' wen the 'osses comes hin, 'e looks roun' an' ses to 'is labour, a-stannin' aside the kerridge, 'Cassandra fust,' ses 'e, 'an' the rest nowheers,' ses 'e. Now what 's the hupshot? Collings 'll see the day. Them 's ole Jack Goldsmith's words, an' jis' you mark 'em. Collings 'll see the day! Yes, Dave," continued the heart of the old man to the Psalmist; "Hi won ten bob on Cassandra that day; an' ten bob war ten bob them times," &c., &c.

All this while, I had been observing the silent swagman, who seemed to grow uneasy under my notice.

"I was remarking to a friend just now that I fancied I had seen you before," I explained.

"Well, they ain't actilly sore, so much as sort o' dazzly and dim," replied the man, in evident relief. "I been tryin' mostly everything this last four year, but I got better hopes now nor ever I had before. A boundary man he give me a little bottle o' stuff the other day; an' it seems to be about the correct thing. Jist feels like a spoonful o' red-hot ashes in your eye; an' if a drop falls outside, it turns your skin black. That ought to cut away the sort o' glassy phlegm off o' the optic nerve?"

"No; you want none of these burning quack remedies; you want three months' careful treatment"——

"I ain't denyin' it," interrupted the man, sadly and sullenly. "An' I don't thank Tom for bein' so fast," he continued, raising his voice in attempted anger. "He ain't the man I took him for—an' I 'm sayin' it to his face."

The general conversation dropped, and Tam, pannikin in hand, rose and advanced to his mate's side.

"An' wha' is 't ye 're sayin' till ma face, Andraw?" he asked loudly, but with gentleness and commiseration. "Puir body 's haird o' hearin'," he explained to the company.

"I 'm sayin' you 'd no right to go blurtin' out about a man gittin' a stretch for a thing o' that sort. Seems like as if there was a job for one of us on this station, an' you was takin' a mean advantage to collar it. It ain't like you"——

"Od, whisht! ye puir thrawart body!" interrupted Tam hastily.

"You might 'a' went about it a bit more manly," continued the other, with the querulousness of a sick child. "I don't deny I done three months; but so help"——

"Whisht! ye daft"——

"So help me God, I never deserved it. I knowed no more about it nor the babe unborn, till I got it off o' the bobby that nabbed me."

"But how could you (adj.) well get three months for a thing you (adj.) well knew nothing about?" asked the catechumen rouse-about. (Henceforth, the reader will have to supply from his own imagination the clumsy and misplaced expletive which preceded each verb used by this young fellow.)

"Ye moight foine it dang aisy yeerself, Dave," observed a middle-aged diner significantly.

"I been a misfortunate man, there 's no denyin'," continued the swagman; "but I never done a injury to nobody in my life, so fur as I 'm aware about."

"What did he get the three months for?" asked Dave, turning to Tam.

"Gin ye speer onythin' frae me," replied Carlyle 's townie, after slowly surveying his questioner from head to foot, "A maun inform ye A ken naethin' bit gude o' Andraw; an' A hae warkit wi' him mair nir fowr minth. 'Deed, the puir body taks owre muckle thocht fir ithers, an' disna' spare himsel' ava. A ken naethin' aboot yon three minth; yon 's atween Andraw an 's Makker; an' A 'll nae jidge onybody, sin we maun a' be judgit by Ane wha jidgeth iprightly. Bit as lang 's A hae a pickle siller, Andrew 'll no want." And Tam returned to his seat.

"What would *I* want of burnin' a stack?" remonstrated Andrew, blinking defiantly round the table. "Tell you how it come. Hold on a minute"—he went to the bucket, and refilled his pannikin—"It was this way: I was jist startin' to thatch a new haystack for two ole bosses o' mine, on the Vic. side o' the Murray, when up comes a trooper.

" 'What 's your name?' says he.

" 'Andrew Glover,' says I.

" 'Well, Andrew Glover, you 're my prisoner—charged with burnin' a stack,' says he. 'I must fetch you along,' says he. So he gives me the usual warnin', an' walks me off to the logs."

"And how did it go?" shouted Dave, who had shifted his pannikin and plate to Andrew's side.

"Well, the Court day it come roun'; an' when my case was called, the prosecutor he steps down off the bench, an' gives evidence; an' I foun' him sayin' somethin' about not wantin' to press the charge; an' there was a bit of a confab; an' then I foun' the Bench askin' me if I 'd sooner be dealt with summary, or be kep' for the Sessions; an' I said summary by all means; so they give me three months."

"What was the prosecutor's name?" shouted Dave.

"Waterman."

"So called because he opens the carriage-doors," I remarked involuntarily.

"Do you know him, Collins?" persisted Dave.

"I neither know him nor do I feel any aching void in consequence," I replied, pointedly interpolating, in two places, the quid-nunc's flowers of speech.

"How did the evidence go, mate?" asked the young fellow greedily.

"Eh?"

"How did the evidence go?"

"Oh yes! Well, I 'm a bit hard o' hearin'—I dunno if you notice it on me, but I am—an' sometimes I 'm worse nor other times; so I did n't ketch most o' what went on; an' the prosecutor he was a good bit off o' me; an' there was a sort o' echo. But I foun' one o' the magistrates sayin', 'Quite so, Mr. Waterman—quite so, Mr. Waterman,' every now an' agen; an' I was on'y too glad to git off with three months. I 'd 'a' got twelve, if I 'd bin remanded for a proper trial. The jailer told me after—he told me this Waterman come out real manly. Seems, he got the charge altered to Careless Use o' Fire. So I can't help giving him credit, in a manner o' speakin'. But, so help me God, I never burned no stack."

"Did you know this Waterman?" interrogated Dave. "Was you ever on his place?"

"Well, yes; I was on his place, askin' him for work, as it might be this mornin'; an' he give me rats for campin' so near his place, as it might be las' night. Seems, it was nex' mornin' his stack was burnt, jist after sunrise. But, so help me God, I never done it."

"(Adj.) shaky sort o' yarn," commented the bullock driver, in grave pity. "Let it drop, Dave."

"Divil a shaky," interposed the hon. member for Tipperary. "Arrah, fwy wud the chap call on the Daity? Fishper—did ye iver foine justice in a coort? Be me sowl, Oi 'd take the man's wurrd agin all the coorts in Austhrillia. An' more betoken—divil blasht the blame Oi 'd blame him fur sthrekin a match, whin dhruv to that same."

"Shoosteece iss (adj.) goot, *mais* revahnsh iss (adj.) bat," remarked another foreigner—a contractor's cook, who had come to the homestead for a supply of rations. "Vhere iss de (adj.) von? —vhere is de (adj.) *autre*? All mix—eh? De cohnseerashohn iss —I not know vat you vill call him ohn Angleesh, *mais* ve vill call him ohn Frahnsh, (adj.) cohnplecat."

"Much the same in English, Theophile," I observed.

"You vill barn de (adj.) snack," continued Theophile, turning politely to me; "you vill call him shoosteece; mineself, I vill call him revahnsh. Mineself, I vill not barn de (adj.) snack; I vill be too (adj.) flash. I vill go to (sheol)."

"Not for your principles, Theophile," I replied, with a courteous inclination of my belltopper.

"Course, it 's all in a man's lifetime," pursued Andrew resign-edly. "Same time, it seems sort a' hard lines when a man 's shoved in the logs for the best three months in the year for a thing he never done. 'Sides, I was on for a good long job with two as decent a fellers as you 'd meet in a day's walk. I 'd met one o' them ten mile up the river, as it might be this afternoon; an' the fire it took place as it might be to-morrow mornin'."

"But where was you when the fire broke-out?—that 's the ques-tion," demanded Dave, with a pleasant side-glance round the table.

"Eh?"

"You 'll be bumpin' up agen a snag some o' these times, young feller," muttered the bullock driver.

"I was only askin' him where he was when the fire broke out," protested Somebody's Darling; then in a louder voice he repeated his question.

"Dunno. Somewhere close handy," replied the swagman hope-lessly. "Anyhow, I never done it. Well, then, I 'd jist got well started to work on Monday mornin', when up comes the bobby, an' grabs me. 'S'pose you 'll have to go,' says the missus—for the bosses was both away at another place they got. 'S'pose so,' says I. 'Better take my swag with me anyhow.' Course, by the time my three months was up, things was at the slackest; an' I could n't go straight back to a decent place, an' me fresh out o' chokey. Fact, I can't go back to that district no more. But as luck would have it, I runs butt agen the very man I 'd ratherest meet of anybody in the country." The swagman paused, and slowly turned toward me, in evident trouble of mind—"He did n't tell you two blokes I was logged for stack-burnin'?" And the poor fellow's flickering eyes sought my face appealingly.

"Indeed he did n't, mate."

"Why, you let the cat out of the bag yourself!" exclaimed Dave triumphantly. Then the conversation took a more general turn.

By this time, I had provisionally accounted for my vaguely-fancied recognition of the man. With the circumspection of a seasoned speculatist, I had bracketed two independent hypotheses, either of which would supply a satisfactory solution. One of these simply attributed the whole matter to unconscious cerebration. But here a question arose: If one half of my brain had been more alert than its duplicate when the object first presented itself—so that the observation of the vigilant half instantaneously appeared as an intangible memory to the judgment of the apathetic half—it still remained to be determined which of the halves might be said to be in a normal condition. Was one half unduly and wastefully excited?—or was the other half unhealthily dormant? The thing would have to be seen into, at some fitting time.

But this hypothesis of unconscious cerebration seemed scarcely as satisfactory as the other—namely, that, having at a former time heard Terrible Tommy mention the name of Andrew Glover, my educated instinct of Nomenology, rising to the very acme of efficiency, had accurately, though unconsciously, snap-shotted a corresponding apparition on the retina of my mind's eye.

Then there were lessons to be gathered from Tom Armstrong's prompt acceptance of such *alibi* evidence, touching myself, as would have merely tended to unfathomable speculations on metempsychosis in an ether-poised Hamlet-mind. Tom, though crushing for a couple of ounces, was one of your practical, decided, cocksure men; guided by unweighed, unanalysed phenomena, and governed by conviction alone—the latter being based simply, though solidly, upon itself. These men are deaf to the symphony of the Silences; blind to the horizonless areas of the Unknown; unresponsive to the touch of the Impalpable; oblivious to the machinery of the Moral Universe—in a word, indifferent to the mysterious Motive of Nature's all-pervading Soul. In such mental organisms, opinion, once deflected tangentially from the central Truth, acquires an independent and stubborn orbit of its own. But the Absolute Truth is so large, and human opinion so small, that the latter cannot get away altogether, however eccentric its course may be; indeed, the more elongated the orbit of Error, the greater chance of its being swallowed up by the scorching Truth, on its return trip. In the present instance, my own ready co-operation with a marvellously conducive Providential legislation had been sufficient unto the deflection of Tom's opinion; and I was content to let the still-impending collision take thought for itself, particularly as Mrs. Beaudesart's conjunction was just about falling due. Then I rose to go.

"Here, mate," said I, fearlessly removing my clouded glasses, and handing them, with their case, to Andrew; "you 'll find the advantage of these."

There was no trace of recognition in Tom's look of gratitude as his eyes rested on my face. But I sighed to reflect that he was still looking out for the tracks of that miserable impostor from the braes o' Yarra.

Now I had to enact the Cynic philosopher to Moriarty and Butler, and the aristocratic man with a 'past' to Mrs. Beaudesart; with the satisfaction of knowing that each of these was acting a part to me. Such is life, my fellow-mummers—just like a poor player, that bluffs and feints his hour upon the stage, and then cheapens down to mere nonentity. But let me not hear any small witticism to the further effect that its story is a tale told by a vulgarian, full of slang and blanky, signifying—nothing.

THE END.